# KILLJOY

*Also by Julie Garwood*
*in Large Print:*

Come the Spring
Heartbreaker
Mercy
Ransom

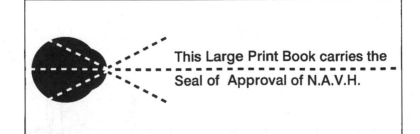

This Large Print Book carries the
Seal of Approval of N.A.V.H.

# KILLJOY

# JULIE GARWOOD

**Thorndike Press • Waterville, Maine**

Published in 2002 by arrangement with The Ballantine Publishing Group, a division of Random House, Inc.

Thorndike Press Large Print Core Series.

The tree indicium is a trademark of Thorndike Press.

The text of this Large Print edition is unabridged.
Other aspects of the book may vary from the original edition.

Set in 16 pt. Plantin by Christina S. Huff.

Printed in the United States on permanent paper.

**Library of Congress Cataloging-in-Publication Data**

Garwood, Julie.
    Killjoy / Julie Garwood.
        p. cm.
    ISBN 0-7862-4366-X (lg. print : hc : alk. paper)
    1. Government investigators — Fiction.    2. Women detectives —
Fiction.    3. Murder for hire — Fiction.    4. Kidnapping —
Fiction.    5. Colorado — Fiction.    6. Aunts — Fiction.    7. Large
type books.    I. Title.
PS3557.A8427 K55 2002
    813'.54—dc21                                          2002073235

*For Mary K. Wahlstedt Murphy,
my sister and my friend.*

*With your steady strength, your quiet grace,
and your wonderful sense of humor,
you make the world a better place.*

# PROLOGUE

Avery Elizabeth Delaney's mother was a frickin' maniac.

Fortunately her mother, Jilly, left for parts unknown just three days after Avery was born.

Avery was raised by her grandmother Lola and her aunt Carrie. The three generations of females lived quietly and modestly in a two-story frame house on Barnett Street just two blocks from the city square in Sheldon Beach, Florida. The atmosphere on Barnett Street was vastly different after Jilly left home. The household, which had once been in a constant uproar, was now peaceful. Carrie even learned to laugh again, and for five wonderful years, life was very nearly idyllic.

The previous years with Jilly had taken their toll on Grandma Lola, however. She hadn't become a mother until she was almost old enough to begin the change of life, and she was an old, tired woman now. The day Avery turned five, Lola began having chest pains. She could barely get the icing on the child's birthday cake without having to sit down and rest a spell.

Lola didn't tell anyone about her problem, and she didn't see her regular doctor in Sheldon Beach because she didn't trust him to keep quiet about his findings. He might just take it upon himself to tell Carrie about her illness. She made an appointment with a cardiologist in Savannah and drove all the way there to see him. After giving her a complete physical, his diagnosis was grim. He prescribed medication that would ease the pain and help her heart, told her she had to slow down, and also, as gently as he could, suggested that she get her affairs in order.

Lola disregarded his advice. What did that quack of a doctor know about anything? She may have one foot in the grave, but by God, she was going to keep the other firmly planted on the ground. She had a granddaughter to raise, and she wasn't going anywhere until she got the job done.

Lola was an expert at pretending everything was fine. She'd perfected the art during the turbulent years trying to control Jilly. By the time she got home from Savannah, she had convinced herself that she was as healthy as an ox.

And that was that.

Grandma Lola refused to talk about Jilly, but Avery wanted to know everything she could about the woman. Whenever she asked a question about her mother, her grandmother would pucker her lips and always answer the same way.

"We wish her well. We wish her well away."
Then, before Avery could try again, her grandmother would change the subject. And that, of course, wasn't a satisfactory answer, especially for a curious five-year-old.

The only way Avery could find out anything about her mother was to ask her aunt. Carrie loved to talk about Jilly, and she never forgot a single one of the bad things her sister had ever done, which, as it turned out, added up to a considerable number.

Avery idolized her aunt. She thought she was the most beautiful woman in the whole world, and she wished more than anything that she looked like her instead of her no-good mama. Carrie had hair the exact color of Grandma's homemade peach jam and eyes more gray than blue, like the furry white cat Avery had seen colored pictures of in one of her storybooks. Carrie was constantly on a diet to lose twenty pounds, but Avery thought she was perfect just the way she was. At five feet six inches, Carrie was tall and glamorous, and when she put on one of her glittery barrettes to keep her hair out of her eyes while she was studying or working around the house, she looked just like a princess. Avery loved the way her aunt smelled, too, like gardenias. Carrie told Avery it was her signature fragrance, which Avery knew had to be special. When Carrie was away from home and Avery was feeling lonely, she would sneak into her bedroom and squirt some of the special perfume on her arms and legs and pretend her aunt was there in the next room.

What Avery loved most about Carrie, though, was that she talked to her like she was a big person. She didn't treat her like a baby the way Grandma Lola did. When Carrie spoke about Avery's no-good mama, Jilly, she always began by saying in her no-nonsense tone of voice, "I'm not going to sugarcoat the truth just because you're little. You've got a right to know."

One week before Carrie moved to California, Avery went into her bedroom to help her pack. She kept getting in the way, and when Carrie had had enough, she sat her niece down at her vanity table and placed a shoe box filled with cheap costume jewelry in front of her. She'd collected the baubles at neighborhood garage sales as a present to give to Avery before she left. The little girl was thrilled with the sparkling treasures and immediately began to primp in front of the oval mirror.

"How come you got to go all the way to California, Carrie? You're supposed to stay home with Grandma and me."

Carrie laughed. "I'm 'supposed to'?"

"That's what Peyton says her mama says. Peyton says her mama says you already went to college and now you're supposed to stay home and help take care of me 'cause I'm a handful."

Peyton was Avery's best friend, and because she was a year older, Avery believed everything she said. In Carrie's opinion, Peyton's mother,

Harriet, was a busybody, but she was nice to Avery, and so Carrie put up with her occasionally butting into family business.

After folding her favorite, baby blue, angora sweater and placing it inside the suitcase, Carrie once again tried to explain why she was leaving.

"I've gotten that grant, remember? I'm going to get my master's, and I know I already explained at least five times why the extra schooling is important. I have to go, Avery. It's a wonderful opportunity for me, and after I've started my own company and I've become rich and famous, then you and Grandma will come and live with me. We'll have a big house in Beverly Hills with servants and a swimming pool."

"But then I can't take my piano lessons, and Mrs. Burns says I have to 'cause I've got ears."

Since her niece sounded so serious, Carrie didn't dare laugh. "She said you've got the ear, and that means that if you practice, you could be good, but you can take piano lessons in California. You could take karate lessons there too."

"But I like taking karate here. Sammy says I'm getting stronger with my kicking, but you know what, Carrie? I heard Grandma tell Peyton's mama she doesn't like me taking karate. She says it isn't ladylike."

"Too bad," Carrie said. "I'm paying for the lessons, and I want you to grow up knowing how to defend yourself."

"But how come?" Avery asked. "Peyton's mama asked Grandma how come too."

"Because I don't want anyone to be able to push you around the way Jilly used to push me," she said. "You're not going to grow up being afraid. And I'm sure there are wonderful self-defense schools in California with teachers just as nice as Sammy."

"Peyton's mama says that Grandma said Jilly went away to be a movie star. Do you want to be a movie star too, Carrie?"

"No, I want to build a company and make tons of money. I'll make other people stars."

Avery turned back to the mirror and clipped on a pair of fat green rhinestone earrings. Then she untangled the matching necklace and put it around her neck. "You know what else Peyton said?" She didn't wait for a reply. "She says her mama says when Jilly had me, she was old enough to know better."

"That's right," Carrie answered. She pulled out her sock drawer, dumped the contents on the bed, and began to match the pairs. "Jilly was eighteen."

"But what did Peyton's mama mean? How come she should know better?"

"She meant that Jilly should have taken precautions."

The drawer fell on the floor. Carrie picked it up and slid it into the dresser, then went back to the chore of sorting through the pile of socks.

"But what does that mean?" Avery asked. She was making faces at herself in the mirror as she put on the second necklace.

Carrie ignored the question. She didn't want to get into a long-winded discussion about sex and birth control. Avery was too young to hear about all that now. Hoping to turn her niece's attention, she said, "You know, you're very lucky."

" 'Cause I have you and Grandma to look after me 'cause I'm a handful?"

"That's right," she agreed. "But you're also lucky because Jilly wasn't drinking like a fish or taking feel-good pills by the fistful when she was carrying you. If she had put all that garbage inside her, you would have been born with serious problems."

"Peyton says her mama says I'm lucky I got borned at all."

Exasperated, Carrie said, "Peyton's mother sure likes to talk about Jilly, doesn't she?"

"Uh-huh," she said. "Are 'feel-good pills' bad?"

"Yes, they are," Carrie said. "They'll kill you."

"Then how come people take them?"

"Because they're stupid. Put that jewelry away and come sit on this suitcase so I can get it closed."

Avery carefully put the earrings and the necklaces back in the shoe box. She climbed up on the canopy bed.

"Can I have this?" she asked as she picked up a small book with a blue vinyl cover.

"No, you can't. That's my diary," Carrie answered. She snatched the book from Avery's hand and tucked it into one of the side pockets. She closed the suitcase and Avery scooted on

13

top. Leaning on it with all her weight, Carrie finally got the latches to lock.

She was helping Avery off the bed when her niece asked, "How come you're packing now and not next week? Grandma says you're doing it backwards."

"Packing before I paint the room for you isn't backwards. This way, my things will be out of the way, and we can get you all set up in your new room before I leave. Tomorrow, you and I will go to the paint store and pick out the color."

"I know. You already told me I could pick the color. Carrie?"

"Yes?" she asked as she set the suitcase by the door.

"Did my no-good mama hate me when she saw me?"

Carrie turned around, saw the worry in Avery's eyes, and was instantly furious. Even though Jilly wasn't there, she was still causing pain. Would it never end?

Carrie remembered, as though it had happened yesterday, the night she found out her sister was going to have a baby.

Jilly had graduated from high school on a balmy Friday evening in May. She then came home and ruined the celebration by announcing that she was almost six months pregnant. She was just barely showing.

Reeling from the shock, Lola at first thought about the embarrassment and shame the family would have to endure, then came to her senses.

"We're a family," she said. "We'll work this out. We'll figure a way to get through this. Isn't that right, Carrie?"

Standing at the dining room table, Carrie picked up the knife and cut herself a piece of the sheet cake Lola had spent all morning decorating. "In this day and age you've got to be really dumb to get pregnant. Haven't you ever heard of birth control, Jilly, or are you a complete moron?"

Jilly was leaning against the wall, her arms folded, glaring at Carrie. Lola, hoping to avoid a screaming match between the two daughters, hastily interjected, "There isn't any need to be snide, Carrie. We don't want to get Jilly upset."

"You mean *you* don't want to get her upset," Carrie corrected.

"Carrie, you will not take that tone with me."

Contrite, she bowed her head and scooped the piece of cake onto a plate. "Yes, ma'am."

"I did think about birth control," Jilly snapped. "I went to the doctor over in Jacksonville to get rid of it, but he refused to do it because he said I was too far along."

Lola slumped into a chair and covered her face with one hand. "You went to a doctor . . ."

Jilly had already lost interest in the subject. She went into the living room, plopped down on the sofa, grabbed the channel changer, and turned on the television.

"She causes the trauma and then she walks

away," Carrie muttered. "Leaving us to clean up the mess. How typical."

"Don't start, Carrie," Lola pleaded. She rubbed her brow as though to ease a headache and then said, "Jilly just doesn't always take the time to think things through."

"Why should she? She has you to clean up her mistakes. You've let her get away with everything but murder just because you can't stand her fits. I think you're afraid of her."

"That's ridiculous," Lola blustered. She got up from the table and went into the kitchen to do the dishes. "We're a family and we're going to get through this," she called out. "And you're going to help, Carrie. Your sister needs our moral support."

Carrie clenched her fists in frustration. What was it going to take to get her mother to open her eyes and see the selfish bitch she'd raised? Why wouldn't she see the truth?

The rest of that summer was an awful memory. Jilly was her usual demanding nightmare, and their mother was run ragged waiting on her hand and foot. Fortunately, Carrie had a summer job at Sammy's Bar and Grille, and she did her best to get as much overtime as possible so she wouldn't have to go home.

Jilly went into labor the end of August. After she gave birth in the county hospital, she took one look at the squirming, blotchy-faced infant who had caused her so much pain and decided that she didn't want to be a mother. Not now, not ever. If the doctors had agreed, she would have had her uterus yanked out or her tubes tied that very day.

Lola dragged Carrie to the hospital to see her sister. They hadn't even walked into the room before Jilly announced that she was too young and pretty to be saddled with a baby. There was a big world outside of Sheldon Beach, Florida, just waiting to pay her some attention, but no man with any money would ever notice her if she was lugging a baby around on her hip. No, motherhood wasn't for her. Besides, she had her heart set on becoming a famous movie star. She would get her start by being crowned Miss America. She had it all figured out, she told them. Boasting that she was much prettier than those cows she had seen on television last year marching around the stage in their swimsuits, she was positive that, as soon as the judges got a good look at her, they would give her the crown.

"God, you're ignorant," Carrie muttered. "They don't give the crown to girls who have had babies."

"You're the ignorant one, Carrie."

"Hush, you two," Lola ordered. "Do you want the nurses to hear you?"

"I don't care if they hear me or not," Jilly said.

"I told you to hush," Lola snapped. "Use your head, Jilly. You're a mother now."

"I don't want to be a mother. I want to be a star," Jilly screamed.

Mortified, Lola pulled Carrie into the room and told her to shut the door. Gripping the potted plant she'd brought Jilly in one hand, Lola held on to Carrie's arm with the other so she wouldn't bolt.

Carrie was annoyed that she was being forced to be supportive. She leaned against the door and glared at her sister.

"Now, Jilly, I don't care what you want," Lola said in a low, furious whisper.

Her mother didn't usually use that tone with Jilly. Carrie perked up and began to pay attention to the conversation.

"You're going to be responsible," Lola said. Her voice turned earnest as she moved toward the bed. "You will be a good mother, and Carrie and I will help you raise the baby. It will all work out. You'll see. I do think you should call the baby's father —" Jilly's laugh stopped her. "What's so funny?"

"You," Jilly replied. "You've got my life all mapped out, don't you? Always trying to make me behave and act the way you think I should act. Really, mother. I'm a grown-up now. I'm eighteen," she reminded her. "And I'll do whatever I want to do."

"But, Jilly, the father has a right to know he has a daughter."

Fluffing her pillow behind her head, Jilly yawned loudly. "I don't know who the father is. It could be the college boy from Savannah, but I can't be sure."

Lola let go of Carrie. "What do you mean, you can't be sure? You told me —"

"I lied. You want me to tell you the truth? Fine, I will. The father could have been a dozen other men."

Lola shook her head. She refused to believe her daughter. "Stop talking like that. Tell me the truth."

Carrie's head came up. "Oh, my God, Jilly."

Jilly loved shocking people and being the center of attention. "I am telling the truth. I really have lost count of the men I've been with. I couldn't possibly know who the father might be." She saw the disgust in her mother's face. "Have I upset you?" Jilly asked, inordinately pleased by the possibility. "Men love me," she boasted. "They'll do anything I want just to please me. They give me expensive gifts and cash too, which I've had to hide from you and Carrie so you wouldn't get jealous and act like you are now, so holier than everybody else. You would have taken the money and the jewelry away from me, wouldn't you? Only, I wouldn't give you the chance. I'm smarter than you think, Mother."

Lola closed her eyes, battling the waves of nausea. "How many men have there been?"

"How would I know? Weren't you listening? I just told you I lost count. All I had to do was let them use my body for a little while. They adore me and I let them. I'm much more beautiful than all the actresses in Hollywood put together, and I'm going to be more famous. You

19

just wait and see. Besides, I like sex. It feels good when they do it just right. You just don't understand the modern woman. You're old, Mother, and all dried up inside. You probably don't remember what sex is."

"Taking money for sex? Do you know what that makes you?"

"Liberated," Jilly snarled.

Carrie stepped away from the door. "No, it doesn't. It makes you a dirty little whore, Jilly. That's all you'll ever be."

"You don't know what you're talking about," Jilly shouted. "Men don't want you the way they want me. I can drive them crazy, and they don't give you the time of day. I am liberated and you're just jealous."

"Come on, Mother. Let's leave." Carrie touched her mother's shoulder.

Turning her head into the pillow, Jilly muttered, "Yes, leave. I'm sleepy now. Go away and let me rest."

Carrie had to help Lola to the car. She had never seen her mother so distraught, and it scared her.

As they drove away from the hospital, Lola stared blankly out the window. "You've always known what she was like, and you tried to tell me, but I wouldn't listen to you. I've been living in a fog, haven't I?"

Carrie nodded. "Something's wrong with Jilly. The mean streak inside of her goes beyond . . . it isn't normal."

"Did I do that to her?" Lola asked, sounding bewildered. "Your father spoiled her, and after he left us, I spoiled her too so she wouldn't feel abandoned. Did I make her the monster she's become?"

"I don't know."

Neither one of them said another word until they reached home. Carrie pulled the car into the driveway, parked it in front of the garage, and turned the motor off. She was opening the door when Lola grabbed her arm.

"I'm so sorry for the way I've treated you." She began to weep then. "You're such a good girl, and I've taken you for granted all these years. Our lives have revolved around Jilly, haven't they? It seems I've spent the better part of her eighteen years keeping her calm . . . happy. I just want you to know that I'm proud of you. I've never told you so, have I? I guess it took this nightmare to make me realize what a treasure you are. I love you, Carrie."

Carrie didn't know how to respond. She couldn't remember if or when her mother had ever told her she loved her before. She felt as though she'd just won some kind of a contest, but by default. The golden child was tarnished, and because she was the only one left, she got the prize.

It wasn't enough. "What are you going to do about Jilly?" she asked.

"I'm going to make her do the right thing, of course."

21

Carrie pulled away. "You still don't get it. She won't do the right thing. Maybe she can't. I don't know. She's sick, Mother."

Lola shook her head. "She's spoiled, but I can work on —"

Carrie stopped her. "You're still living in dreamland," she muttered. She slammed the door when she got out of the car and went into the house.

Lola followed her into the kitchen, took an apron from the wooden peg on the wall, and tied it around her waist.

"Do you remember what happened on my eighth birthday?" Carrie asked as she pulled a chair from the kitchen table and dropped into it.

Hoping to avoid the unpleasant remembrance, Lola didn't turn around. "Not now, dear. Why don't you set the table and I'll start dinner."

"You gave me that Barbie doll I wanted."

"Carrie, I don't want to talk about this now."

"Sit down. We need to discuss this."

"It happened a long time ago. Why do you need to go over it again?"

Carrie wasn't going to back down this time. "I came into your bedroom that night."

"Carrie, I don't —"

"Sit down, damn it. You can't keep living this way. You have to face the facts. Sit, Mother." She wanted to grab her by the shoulders and shake some sense into her.

Lola gave in. She took the chair across from

her daughter, and primly folded her hands in her lap. "I remember your father was very upset by your accusations," she said. "And Jilly was crying. You woke the whole household that night carrying on."

"She wanted my doll," Carrie said. "When I wouldn't give it to her, she told me she was going to cut my eyes out with scissors. I woke up around midnight and she was standing over me with your shears in her hand. She had this sick smile on her face. She was opening and closing the scissors making this horrible clicking sound. Then she held up my new Barbie doll and I saw what she'd done to it. She'd stabbed the eyes out, Mother, and that smile on her face . . . it was so awful. As I was about to scream, she leaned down and whispered, 'Now it's your turn.' "

"You were too young to remember exactly what happened. You've blown this little incident way out of proportion."

"Oh, no, I haven't," she said. "That's exactly how it happened. You didn't see the look in her eyes, but I'm telling you she wanted to kill me. If I had been alone in the house with her, she would have done exactly what she wanted to do."

"No, no, she was just trying to scare you," Lola insisted. "She never would have hurt you. Jilly loves you."

"If you and Dad hadn't been there, she would have hurt me. She's crazy, Mother. I don't care what happens to her, but there's an innocent baby now." She took a deep breath, and then blurted out, "I think we should encourage Jilly to give the baby up for adoption."

Lola was outraged by the suggestion. "Absolutely not," she said, and slammed her hand down on the table. "That baby is your niece and my granddaughter, and I'm not going to let strangers raise her."

"It's her only hope for a decent future," Carrie argued. "She's already got one huge strike against her with Jilly as her mother. I only hope whatever is broken inside of Jilly isn't genetic."

"Oh, for heaven's sake. The only thing wrong with Jilly is that she's used to getting her way. Lots of young women are fooling around with men these days. It's wrong," she hastily added, "but I understand why Jilly wanted men to love her. Her father left her, and she's been trying to —"

"Will you listen to yourself?" Carrie shouted. "For a little while, I thought you were finally seeing what Jilly was, but I guess I was wrong. You're never going to open your eyes. You asked me if you had made her the monster she's become, remember?"

"I meant to say that her behavior was monstrous, but Jilly's a mother now. When I go back to the hospital to bring her and the baby home, you'll see. She'll be all right."

It was like talking to a brick wall. "You think

the maternal instincts are going to kick in?"

"Yes, I do," Lola said. "You'll see," she repeated. "Jilly will want to do the right thing."

Carrie gave up. Sickened, she went to her room and stayed there the rest of the night. When she came down the following morning, there was a note on the kitchen table. Her mother had gone to Sears to purchase a crib, baby clothes, and an infant car seat.

"Dreamland," Carrie muttered.

On Monday morning, Lola went to the hospital to bring Jilly and the still unnamed baby home. Carrie refused to go with her mother. She told her she had to work an early shift at Sammy's and left the house before Lola could question her.

Jilly was waiting for her mother. She was dressed and standing in front of the bathroom mirror brushing her hair. She waved her hand toward the screaming infant she'd dropped in the middle of the unmade bed seconds after the nurse had left the room and told Lola she could either keep her, sell her, or give her away — she didn't much care what she did with her. She then picked up her overnight bag and walked out of the hospital with the money she'd stolen from her sister's college fund tucked into her bra.

The withdrawal didn't appear on the bank statement until two weeks later. Carrie was outraged. She'd worked hard to save the money, and she was determined to get it back. She tried to report the theft to the police, but Lola wouldn't let her.

"Family business stays in the family," she decreed.

Carrie graduated from high school the following spring and worked two jobs that summer. Lola used some of her savings to help with Carrie's college tuition, and Carrie found part-time work on campus to help with expenses. When she came home for Christmas break, she could barely look at Jilly's baby.

However, Avery wasn't the kind of child who put up with being ignored. It only took a couple of drooling smiles, and Carrie was smiling back. Each time she returned home, the bond grew stronger. The child adored her, and the feeling, though never openly stated, was reciprocated.

Avery was the sweetest, most intelligent little girl, and Carrie in every way possible had become her substitute mother. She certainly had all the protective instincts of a mother. She would do anything to keep Avery safe.

Yet here they were, five years later, and Jilly was still able to cause the family pain.

"Did she, Carrie? Did she hate me?"

Carrie forced herself to concentrate on the child's question. Planting her hands on her hips, she took a deep breath and then asked, "What do you care what Jilly thought about you?"

Avery lifted her shoulders. "I don't know."

"Now, you listen to me. Your no-good mama

probably did hate you, but not because of who you are or what you looked like when you were born. You were a perfect baby. Jilly just didn't want responsibility." She pointed to the chair adjacent to the bed. "I'm going to tell you something important, and I want you to pay attention, so sit down."

Avery hurried to do as she was told.

"You're probably too young to hear this, but I'm going to tell you anyway. Your mother's a frickin' maniac."

Avery was disappointed. She thought she was going to hear something new. "You already told me that, Carrie. Lots of times."

"That was just another reminder," she said. "Jilly has never been normal. Fact is, she should have been locked up in a loony bin a long time ago."

Avery was intrigued by the thought of her mother being locked away. "What's a loony bin?"

"It's a place where sick people go."

"Is Jilly sick?"

"Yes," she answered. "But not the kind of sick where we feel sorry for her. She's mean and hateful and just plain crazy. She'd have to be crazy to walk away from someone as wonderful as you," Carrie added. Leaning forward, she brushed the hair out of Avery's eyes. "Your mother grew up with something important miss- ing from inside her head. She might not be a pure sociopath, but she's damn close."

27

Avery's eyes widened. In a hushed voice she said, "Carrie, you just said *'damn.'*"

"I know what I said, and I know what I'm talking about."

Avery got out of her chair and went to sit beside Carrie on the bed. She latched on to her hand and said, "But *I* don't know what you're talking about."

"I'm going to explain. A sociopath is a person who doesn't have a conscience, and before you ask, I'll tell you what a conscience is. That's what's inside your head that tells you when you've done something wrong. Your conscience makes you feel . . . bad."

"Like when I told Grandma I already practiced on the piano, but I didn't, and then she told me I was a good girl, but I wasn't 'cause I lied, and then I felt bad?"

"Yes, just like that," she said. "Your mother doesn't have any heart or soul, and that's the truth."

"Like the song you like to sing? Is it that kind of heart and soul?"

"Yes, just like the song," Carrie assured her. "Jilly doesn't have room in her heart to feel any emotion that doesn't directly involve or benefit her."

Avery was leaning into her side, looking up at her with those wonderful violet blue eyes that were so much more beautiful than her mother's. Carrie could almost see the purity and goodness behind them. "Jilly's too busy loving herself to love anyone else, but you can't waste your time feeling bad about that. None of it is your fault. You believe me, don't you?"

Avery solemnly nodded. "It's my no-good mama's fault, all right."

Carrie smiled. "That's right."

"Do I have a soul?"

"Yes, you do. Everyone but your no-good mama has a soul."

"Before Jilly hurt Whiskers and made him die, did he have a soul?"

"Maybe," she allowed, thinking of the kitten Jilly had cruelly taken from her.

"Where is it?"

"Your soul?" Carrie had to think about the question for a few seconds before answering. "It's inside you, wrapped around your heart. Your soul is as pure as an angel's, and I mean to help you keep it that way. You're nothing like Jilly, Avery."

"But I look like her. You said so."

"It's not what you look like that's important. It's what's inside you that matters."

"Does Jilly love you and Grandma and just not me?"

Carrie was exasperated. "I thought you understood what I was telling you. Jilly doesn't love anyone but herself. She doesn't love Grandma, she doesn't love me, and she doesn't love you. Now do you understand?"

Avery nodded. "Can I play with the jewelry now, Carrie?"

Carrie smiled. The child, it seemed, had moved on to more important matters. She watched her sit at the vanity and begin to dig through the box again. "You know what's the best thing that ever happened to you?"

Avery didn't look around when she answered. "Having you for my Aunt Carrie."

"Is that what you think is the best thing?" she asked, surprised and pleased. "How come?"

" 'Cause that's what you told me is the best thing."

Carrie laughed. "Yeah, well, there's something even better."

"What?"

"You aren't growing up afraid all the time the way I was. Jilly's never going to come back. You won't ever have to see her . . . not ever. That's definitely the best thing."

A shiver ran down Carrie's back the second the words were out of her mouth. Was she tempting fate by making such a boast? Could one summon up a demon simply by proclaiming that it didn't exist? The chill felt like a premonition. But of course it wasn't. She was just a worrier, that was all. Shaking off her grim feeling, she went back to work.

The following week was busy. Avery chose pink for her walls, and Carrie added white trim. She thought the bedroom looked like an explosion of Pepto-Bismol, but Avery loved it. She was all settled in the big front bedroom by Sunday afternoon. Carrie's suitcases had been packed in the trunk of the car. Carrie was going to sleep in Avery's old bedroom on the grossly uncomfortable daybed her last night.

They had all of Carrie's favorite foods for dinner that night — forbidden food on her perpetual diet — fried chicken, mashed potatoes and gravy, and green beans simmering in bacon fat. Lola had made a fresh salad, using the vegetables she'd grown in her backyard, but Carrie barely touched it. Since she'd already decided to take a day off from her diet — one wonderful, guilt-free day — she ate two helpings of everything else with unbridled gusto.

After Grandma Lola had read Avery a story and tucked her into bed, Carrie went in to kiss her good night. She turned on the nightlight, shut the bedroom door, and then went back downstairs to put some last-minute paperwork in her carry-on.

One task led to another, and she didn't get back upstairs until after eleven. Lola was already asleep in her room at the back of the house. Carrie checked on Avery — oh, how she was going to miss the pip-squeak — and she almost burst into laughter when she spotted her niece in the big bed. The child was wearing at least five necklaces and four bracelets. The tarnished tiara with most of its glass diamonds missing was tangled in strands of her hair and tilted to the side of her head. She was sleeping on her back clutching a worn-out teddy bear in her arm. Carrie sat down on the bed and tried not to disturb her

31

niece as she gently removed the jewelry.

After she put the trinkets back in the box, she walked quietly to the door. She was pulling it closed when Avery whispered, "Good night, Carrie."

She'd already closed her eyes by the time Carrie turned around to look at her. In the soft glow from the streetlight the little girl looked like a cherub. Carrie didn't think she could love her any more than if she were her very own child. The instinct to protect was overwhelming. She hated the thought of going away, felt as though she were abandoning her.

She had to leave, she reminded herself. Avery's future depended on her. When she was financially secure, she would be able to support her mother and her niece in the style she felt they both deserved. Guilt was a powerful deterrent, but Carrie wasn't about to let it interfere with her plans. She had her goals and her dreams, and Avery and Lola were tied to both.

"I'm doing the right thing," she whispered as she walked down the hall to the bathroom. She was still trying to convince herself when she stepped into the shower.

Carrie had just turned on the water full blast when the slamming of the car doors awakened Avery. She heard a deep laugh and got out of bed to see who was making the noise. She saw a man and a woman. They were standing by the side of an old, beat-up car, their heads together, laughing and talking.

The woman had golden hair. The man was as dark as she was fair. He had something in his hand. Avery peeked around the side of the window so they wouldn't see her and maybe shout at her to stop being nosy. The man raised a bottle and took a big drink. Then he offered the bottle to the woman, and she tilted her head back and took a drink too.

What were they doing in front of Grandma's house? Avery got down on her knees and hid behind the lace curtains. She ducked when the woman turned and started up the sidewalk. The mean-looking man didn't follow her. He leaned against the fender of the car, one ankle crossed over the other. He took another drink, then threw the empty bottle into the street. The sound of the glass shattering was almost as loud as Avery's gasp. It was bad to litter. Grandma Lola told her so.

The man wasn't looking at the house. He was watching the street, so Avery thought it was safe to straighten up and get a better look. She saw something sticking out of his back pocket when he turned toward the car. What was it? Maybe another bottle?

The mean-looking man wearing the dirty T-shirt must be awful thirsty 'cause he reached behind and pulled the bottle out. Only it wasn't a bottle after all. She gasped again. The bad man was holding a shiny black gun. Just like the kind she'd seen on television.

She was too excited to be scared. Just wait

until she told Peyton what she was seeing. Should she wake up Grandma and Carrie and tell them about the gun? Maybe they'd call Officer Friendly at the police station, and then he would come and take the bad man away.

Avery jumped when the banging started at the front door. It was the lady, she thought, calling on Grandma in the middle of the night.

The lady was shouting terrible bad words. Avery ran back to bed and hid under the covers in case her grandmother checked on her before she went downstairs to tell the lady to stop making so much noise. She knew what her grandma would say to the woman. "Are you trying to wake the dead?" That's what she'd say, all right. It was the same thing she always said to Carrie when she had the television or the stereo up too loud. But if Grandma looked in and saw that Avery was out of bed before she went downstairs, then Avery would never know what was going on.

Sometimes you had to do bad things to find out anything important. Peyton had told her that it wasn't awful bad to listen to other people talking as long as you didn't ever tell anyone what you heard.

The banging turned into pounding as the lady demanded that Grandma let her in.

Grandma opened the door, and Avery heard the lady shouting some more. She understood every word she said. Avery suddenly wasn't curious any longer. She was terrified. Throwing

34

the sheet off and jumping to the floor, she dropped to her belly and crawled underneath the bed. She scooted up to the headboard and rolled into a ball with her knees tucked under her chin. She was a big girl, too big to cry. The tears streaming down her cheeks were just there because she was squeezing her eyes shut so tight. She cupped her hands over her ears to block out the terrible yelling.

Avery knew who the bad lady was. She was her no-good mama, Jilly, and she had come back to take her away.

# CHAPTER 1

The wait was making Avery crazy. She sat in her little square cubicle, her back against the wall, one leg crossed over the other, drumming her fingertips against the desktop with one hand and holding an icepack against her wounded knee with the other. What was taking so long? Why hadn't Andrews called? She stared hard at the phone, willing it to ring. Nothing. Not a sound. Turning in her swivel chair, she checked the digital clock for the hundredth time. It was now 10:05, same as it was ten seconds ago. For Pete's sake, she should have heard something by now.

Mel Gibson stood up and leaned over the partition separating his workspace from Avery's and gave her a sympathetic look. That was his honest-to-goodness, real name, but Mel thought it was holding him back because no one in the law enforcement agency would ever take him seriously. Yet, he refused to have it legally changed to "Brad Pitt," as his supportive coworkers had suggested.

"Hi, Brad," Avery said. She and the others were still trying out the new name to see if it fit. Last week it was "George Clooney," and that name got about the same reaction "Brad" was getting now, a glare and a reminder that his name wasn't "George," it wasn't "Brad," and it wasn't "Mel." It was "Melvin."

"You probably should have heard by now," he said.

She refused to let him rile her. Tall, geeky-looking, with an extremely prominent Adam's apple, Mel had the annoying habit of using his third finger to push his thick wire-rimmed glasses back up on his ski nose. Margo, another coworker, told Avery that Mel did it on purpose. It was his way of letting the other three know how superior he felt he was.

Avery disagreed. Mel wouldn't do anything improper. He lived by a code of ethics he believed personified the FBI. He was dedicated, responsible, hardworking, ambitious, and he dressed for the job he wanted . . . with one little glitch. Although he was only twenty-seven years old, his clothing resembled the attire agents wore back in the fifties. Black suits, white long-sleeved shirts with button-down collars, skinny black ties, black wingtip shoes with a perfect shine, and a crew cut she knew he got trimmed once every two weeks.

For all of his strange habits — he could quote any line from *The FBI Story*, starring Jimmy Stewart — he had an incredibly sharp mind and was the ultimate team player. He just needed to lighten up a bit. That was all.

"I mean, don't you think you should have heard by now?" He sounded as worried as she felt.

"It's still early." Then, less than five seconds later, she said, "You're right. We should have heard by now."

"No," he corrected. "I said that *you* should have heard. Lou and Margo and I didn't have anything to do with your decision to call in the SWAT team."

Oh, God, what had she been thinking? "In other words, you don't want to take the flak if I'm wrong?"

"Not flak," he said. "The fall. I need this job. It's the closest I'm going to get to being an agent. With my eyesight . . ."

"I know, Mel."

"Melvin," he automatically corrected. "And the benefits are great."

Margo stood so she could join the conversation. "The pay sucks, though."

Mel shrugged. "So does the work environment," he said. "But still . . . it's the FBI."

"What's wrong with our work environment?" Lou asked as he too stood. His workstation was on Avery's left. Mel's was directly in front of hers, and Margo's cubicle was adjacent to Lou's. The pen — as they lovingly called their hellhole office space — was located behind the mechanical room with its noisy water heaters and compressors. "I mean, really, what's wrong with it?" he asked again, sounding bewildered.

Lou was as clueless as ever, but also endearing, Avery thought. Whenever she looked at him, she was reminded of Pig-Pen in the old *Peanuts* cartoon. Lou always looked disheveled. He was absolutely brilliant, yet he couldn't seem to find his mouth when he was eating, and his short-sleeved shirt usually had at least one stain. This morning there were two. One was jelly from the raspberry-filled doughnuts Margo had brought in. The big red spot was just above the black ink stain from the cartridge pen in his white shirt pocket.

Lou tucked in his shirttail for the third time that morning and said, "I like being down here. It's cozy."

"We work in the corner of the basement without any windows," Margo pointed out.

"So what?" Lou asked. "Where we work doesn't make us any less important. We're all part of a team."

"I'd like to be a part of the team that has windows," Margo said.

"Can't have everything. Say, Avery, how's the knee?" he asked, suddenly changing subjects.

She gingerly lifted the icepack and surveyed the damage. "The swelling's gone down."

"How'd it happen?" Mel asked. He was the only one who hadn't heard the grizzly details.

Margo ran her fingers through her short dark curls and said, "An old lady nearly killed her."

"With her Cadillac," Lou said. "It happened

in her parking garage. The woman obviously didn't see her. There really ought to be an age restriction on renewing a driver's license."

"Did she hit you?" Mel asked.

"No," Avery answered. "I dove to get out of her way when she came roaring around the corner. I ended up flying across the hood of a Mercedes and whacked my knee on the hood ornament. I recognized the Cadillac. It belongs to Mrs. Speigel, who lives in my building. I think she's about ninety. She's not supposed to drive anymore, but every once in a while I'll see her taking the car out to do errands."

"Did she stop?" Mel asked.

She shook her head. "I don't think she had a clue I was there. She was accelerating so fast I was just glad there weren't any other people in her way."

"You're right, Lou," Margo said. She disappeared behind her cubicle wall, bent down to push the box of copy paper into the corner, and then stood on top of it. She was suddenly as tall as Mel. "There should be an age limit on keeping a license. Avery told us the woman was so little she couldn't see her head over the back of the seat. Just a puff of gray hair."

"Our bodies shrink as we age," Mel said. "Just think, Margo. When you're ninety, no one will be able to see you."

Margo, a petite five feet two inches, wasn't offended. "I'll just wear higher heels."

The phone rang, interrupting the conversation. Avery jumped at the sound, then checked the time. It was 10:14.

"This is it," she whispered as it rang a second time.

"Answer it," Margo anxiously demanded.

Avery picked up the phone on the third ring. "Avery Delaney."

"Mr. Carter would like to see you in his office at ten-thirty, Miss Delaney."

She recognized the voice. Carter's secretary had a distinct Maine accent. "I'll be there."

Three pairs of eyes watched her as she hung up the phone. "Oh, boy," she whispered.

"What?" Margo, the most impatient of the group, demanded.

"Carter wants to see me."

"Uh-oh. That can't be good." Mel made the remark, and then, as if he realized he'd said something he shouldn't have, added, "You want us to go with you?"

"You'd do that?" Avery asked, surprised by the offer.

"I don't want to, but I would."

"It's okay. I'll take the bullet alone."

"I think we should all go," Margo said. "A mass firing. I mean, we're all in this together, right?"

"Yes," Avery agreed. "But you three tried to talk me out of going to Andrews. Remember? I'm the only one who screwed up." She stood, put the icepack on top of the file cabinet, and reached for her jacket.

"This can't be good," Mel repeated. "They're breaking the chain of command. It must be really bad to get the boss's boss involved. Carter was just promoted to head of in-house operations."

"Which means he's now the boss's boss's boss," Margo pointed out.

"I wonder if all the bosses will be there," Lou said.

"Right," Avery muttered. "Maybe all three of them want to take a turn firing me." She buttoned her suit jacket and then said, "How do I look?"

"Like someone tried to run over you," Mel said.

"Your hose are shredded," Margo told her.

"I know. I thought I had another pair in my drawer, but I didn't."

"I've got an extra pair."

"Thanks, Margo, but you're a petite, and I'm not. Mel, Lou, turn around or sit down."

As soon as they turned their backs, she reached up under her skirt and pulled off her panty hose. Then she put her heels back on.

She was sorry now she'd worn the suit. She usually wore pants and a blouse, but she was going to a luncheon today and so she'd pulled out all the stops and put on the Armani suit her Aunt Carrie had sent as a present two years ago. The color was a wonderful taupe gray and had a matching sleeveless V-neck shell. At one time there had been an obscene slit up the side, but

Avery had sewn it together. It was a great-looking suit. Now it would be remembered as the suit she wore the day she got fired.

"Catch," Margo said as she threw the new package of panty hose at Avery. "These are the one-size-fits-all kind. They'll work just fine. You have to wear hose. You know the dress code."

Avery read the label. It did say the hose would fit every size. "Thanks," she said as she sat down again. Her legs were long, and she was afraid of tearing the hose when she pulled them up over her hips, but they seemed to fit.

"You're going to be late," Mel told her when she stood up again and adjusted her skirt. Why hadn't she noticed how short it was? The hem barely touched the top of her knees.

"I've got four minutes left." After she'd put on some lip gloss and clipped her hair back behind her neck with a barrette, she slipped the heels back on. Only then did she notice how loose the right heel was. She must have broken it when she slammed into the hood of the car.

Can't do anything about it now, she thought. She took a deep breath, straightened her shoulders, and limped toward the aisle. With every step, her left knee throbbed.

"Wish me luck."

"Avery," Mel shouted. He waited until she turned around, then hurled her clip-on ID. "You should probably wear this."

"Yeah, right. They'll want to take it from me

before they escort me out of the building."

Margo called after her. "Hey, Avery, think of it this way — if you get fired, you won't have to worry about all the work piling up while you and your aunt chill out at that fancy spa."

"I haven't decided if I'm going to meet my aunt or not. She still thinks I'm chaperoning those kids around D.C."

"But now that that got canceled, you ought to go get pampered," Margo argued.

"That's right, you should go," Lou said. "You could stay at Utopia a whole month and work on your résumé."

"Not helping, guys," Avery said without looking back.

Carter's office was four flights up. On any other day she would have taken the stairs as aerobic exercise, but her left knee ached too much, and the heel on her right shoe was too wobbly. She was exhausted by the time she reached the elevator. While she waited for it, she rehearsed what she would say when Carter asked what in God's name she thought she was doing.

The doors parted. She took a step forward and felt something snap. Glancing down, she spotted the heel of her shoe lodged in the seam between the elevator and the floor. Since she was alone, she hiked her skirt up and bent down on her good knee to pry the heel loose. It was then that the elevator doors closed on her head.

Muttering an expletive, Avery fell back. The

car began to move and she grabbed the railing. She clutched the broken heel in her hand and pulled herself to her feet just as the doors opened on the first floor. By the time she reached the fourth floor, the elevator was full of passengers, and she was squeezed to the back of the car. Feeling like an idiot, she excused her way to the front and limped off.

Unfortunately, Carter's office was located at the end of a long corridor. The glass doors were so far away she couldn't even read the name etched above the brass handle.

Suck it up, she thought as she started walking. She was halfway there when she stopped to check the time and give her leg a rest. She had one minute. She could make it, she thought as she started walking again. Her barrette slipped out of her hair, but she caught it before it fell to the floor. She clipped it back in place and continued on. She was beginning to wish Mrs. Speigel's car had actually struck her. Then she wouldn't have to come up with any excuses, and Carter could call her at the hospital and fire her over the phone.

Suck it up, she repeated. Could it get any worse?

Of course it could. At precisely the second she was pulling the door open, her panty hose began to slip. By the time she'd limped over to the receptionist, the waistband was down around her hips.

The stately brunette woman wearing a knock-off Chanel suit looked a bit startled as she watched Avery approach.

"Miss Delaney?"

"Yes," she answered.

The woman smiled. "You're right on time. Mr. Carter will appreciate that. He keeps a tight schedule."

Avery leaned forward as the woman picked up the phone to announce her. "Is there a ladies' room close by?"

"It's down the hall, past the bank of elevators, on your left."

Avery glanced behind her and considered her options. She could be late for the appointment, try to run like hell down the mile-long hallway and rip off the damn panty hose, or she could —

The receptionist interrupted her frantic thoughts. "Mr. Carter will see you now."

She didn't move.

"You may go inside," she said.

"The thing is . . ."

"Yes?"

Avery slowly straightened. The panty hose stayed put. Smiling, she said, "I'll go on in then."

She pivoted and held her smile as she grabbed the edge of the desk, and then tried to walk as though her shoe still had a heel. With any luck, Carter wouldn't even notice her condition.

Who was she kidding? The man was trained to be observant.

Tall, distinguished-looking, with a thick head

of silver-tipped hair and a square chin, Tom Carter stood when she entered. She hobbled forward. When she reached the chair in front of his desk, she wanted to throw herself into it, but waited for him to give her permission.

Carter reached across the desk to shake her hand, and it was then, as she was stretching forward, that her panty hose gave up the fight. The crotch was now down around her knees. In a panic, she grabbed his hand and shook it vigorously. Too late she realized she was clutching the heel of her shoe in her right hand. She hadn't sweated this much since she took the graduate record exam.

"It's a pleasure to meet you, sir. An honor, really. You wanted to see me? My, it's warm in here. Would you mind if I removed my jacket?"

She was rambling but couldn't seem to stop. The remark about the temperature had gotten his attention, though. Thank God, the rumors were right. Carter did have his own thermostat and liked to keep his office just below freezing. It was like an Alaskan tomb. Avery was surprised she couldn't see her breath when she exhaled. That's when she realized she wasn't breathing.

Calm down, she told herself. Take a deep breath.

Carter enthusiastically nodded. He didn't mention the heel that had dropped on top of a stack of files on his desk. "I thought it was warm, but my assistant keeps telling me it's cold in here.

Let me just turn down the thermostat a notch."

She didn't wait for him to give her permission to sit. The second he turned his back, she snatched the heel off the files — which she noticed were labeled with her name and the names of the other members of the pen — and then fell into the chair. Her panty hose were in a wad around her knees. She frantically unbuttoned her jacket, removed it, and draped it over her lap.

Her arms and shoulders were covered in goose bumps seconds later.

Suck it up, she thought. It was going to be okay. Once he sat down behind his desk, she could slowly work the hose down her legs and get rid of them. Carter would never be the wiser.

It was a great plan, and it would have worked if Carter had cooperated, but he didn't return to his chair. He walked over to her side, then leaned back to sit on the edge of his desk. She wasn't short by Margo's standards, but she still had to tilt her head back in order to look into his eyes. There seemed to be a twinkle, which she thought was quite odd, unless, of course, he enjoyed firing people. God, maybe that rumor was true too.

"I noticed you were limping. How did you hurt your knee?" he asked. He bent down to pick up the barrette that had fallen to the floor.

"An accident," she said, taking the barrette and dropping it in her lap.

She could tell from the quizzical look in his eyes she hadn't given him a satisfactory answer.

"An elderly lady . . . quite elderly, as a matter of fact, driving a rather large vehicle, didn't see me when I was walking toward my car in my parking garage. I had to jump out of the way so she wouldn't hit me. I ended up on top of a Mercedes, and I think that's when I broke my heel and bruised my knee." Then, before he could make a comment about the unfortunate incident, she plunged on. "Actually, I only loosened the heel then. It broke off in the elevator as the doors were closing on my head." He was staring at her as though she had just turned into a babbling fool. "Sir, it hasn't been a good morning."

"Then I'd brace myself if I were you," he said, his voice suddenly grim. "It's going to get worse."

Her shoulders slumped. Carter finally went behind his desk and sat down. She seized the opportunity. Slipping her hands under her jacket and skirt, she worked the panty hose down her legs. It was awkward but doable, and, other than appearing to be squirming in the hot seat, she managed the feat. While he opened her file and began to read the notes he or someone else had compiled against her, she grabbed the hose and wadded them into a ball. She had her shoes back on by the time he looked up at her again.

"I received a call from Mike Andrews," he began. There it was again, that grim, you're-gonna-get-your-ass-fired tone of voice.

Her stomach felt as though it had just dropped to her ankles. "Yes, sir?"

"I believe you know him?"

"Yes, sir. Not well," she hastened to add. "I found his number and called him before I left the office."

"And during that phone call you convinced him to deploy a SWAT team to First National Bank on . . ." He looked down again, searching the file for the location.

She rattled off the address, adding, "The branch is near the state line."

He leaned back, crossed his arms, and said, "Tell me what you know about these robberies."

She took a deep breath and tried to relax. She was on safe ground now, in control. Since she had typed all the agents' reports into the computer and looked at the bank tapes, she'd learned, and pretty much memorized, every little detail.

"The robbers call themselves the Politicians," she said. "There are three of them."

"Continue," he urged.

"There have been three robberies in the past three months. The men, all wearing white clothes, entered the first bank, First National Bank and Trust on Twelfth Street, on March fifteenth, exactly three minutes after the bank had opened for business. The men used guns to subdue the personnel and one customer, but they didn't fire those weapons. The man shouting the orders held a knife against the security guard's neck. When the other two were running toward the door, the leader stabbed the guard, dropped the knife, and then left. The guard had done nothing to provoke the man. There was absolutely no reason to kill him."

"No, there wasn't," Carter agreed.

"The second robbery took place on April thirteenth at the Bank of America in Maryland. A bank manager, a woman, was killed during that robbery. The leader was on his way out the door. He suddenly turned around and fired point-blank. Once again, there didn't seem to be a reason, because the personnel had been desperately trying to cooperate."

"And the third robbery?"

"That one took place on May fifteenth at Goldman's Bank and Trust in Maryland," she said. "As you know, the violence escalated. Two people were killed, and a third was left for dead but has miraculously recovered."

"Okay, you've got your facts down," he said. "Now, tell me. What made you think a little branch of the First National Bank in Virginia would be the next target?"

His stare was unnerving. She glanced down at her lap while she gathered her thoughts and then looked up again. She knew how she had arrived at the conclusion, but explaining it to the head of in-house operations was going to be difficult.

"I guess you could say it's all in how I look at things. It was all there . . . most of it anyway, in the file."

"No one else saw it in the file," he pointed out. "They hit different banks with the three robberies, but you convinced Andrews that they were going to hit another branch of First National again."

"Yes, sir, I did."

"It's . . . remarkable how you talked him into it."

"Not really," she said, hoping Andrews hadn't told Carter every word she'd said.

"You used my name."

She inwardly cringed. "Yes, sir. I did."

"You told Andrews the order came from me. Is that correct, Delaney?"

Here it comes, she thought. The you're-getting-your-ass-fired part. "Yes, sir."

"Let's get back to the facts, shall we? Here's what I want to know. The Politicians had struck on March fifteenth, April thirteenth, then May fifteenth. We didn't know why they were hitting on those specific days, but you did, didn't you? That's what you told Andrews," he reminded her. "But you didn't go into an explanation."

"There wasn't time."

"There's time now. How did you arrive at your conclusion?"

"Shakespeare, sir," she answered.

"Shakespeare?"

"Yes, sir. The robberies all followed the same pattern, almost like a ritual of some kind. I got a printout of the first bank's records for the week prior to the robbery. I did the same with the other two banks. I thought something might show up that would link them," she said.

She paused to shake her head. "I had reams and reams of printouts all over the office, and I did find something a little curious. Fortunately, I had the discs from the banks, and I was able to cross-check with the computer."

Carter rubbed his jaw, distracting her. She could see a hint of impatience in his eyes. "Sir, bear with me another minute. Now, the first bank was robbed on March fifteenth. Does that date trigger anything in your mind?"

Before he could answer, she plunged ahead. "The ides of March? Julius Caesar?"

He nodded.

"That must have been in the back of my mind last night while I was reading all the printouts, and I noticed an ATM withdrawal was made by a man named Nate Cassius. I still hadn't quite put it together," she admitted. "But I realized, if I was right, and I was hoping to heaven I was, that the leader of the Politicians was leaving us clues. Maybe he was playing some twisted game. Maybe he was waiting to see how long it would take us to catch on."

She had his full attention now. "Continue," he said.

"As I mentioned before, the dates frustrated me until I did my research. I looked up the Roman calendar and found that when the Romans were calculating the length of the months, they also figured the date of the ides. We know from Shakespeare's play, *Julius Caesar*, that the ides of March falls on the fifteenth. But not all the months. Some fall on the thirteenth. So, using that logic, I went back over the ATM withdrawals the week prior to the second and third robberies, and guess what I found?"

"Did Nate Cassius make a withdrawal from those banks?"

"No, sir," she answered. "But a William Brutus did in one bank, and Mario Casca did in the other . . . and the withdrawals happened just two days before the robberies. I think they were sizing up the layout of the banks."

"Go on," he said, leaning forward now.

"I didn't put it together until the last minute. I had to pull up the transaction records for all of the banks in the tri-state area from the eleventh on."

"Because the other two withdrawals were made exactly two days before the actual robberies."

"Yes," she said. "I spent most of the night cross-checking with the data I had in the computer for the eleventh, and by gosh, there it was. Mr. John Ligarius had made a withdrawal from that little branch of The First National Bank at three-forty-five in the morning. All of these names — Cassius, Brutus, Casca, Ligarius — they were conspirators against Caesar. I didn't have time to run a check on the people who owned these cards, but I did find out that the cards were issued from banks in Arlington. It added up. Ligarius made a withdrawal from The First National Bank. So, The First National Bank was the next target.

"I thought that time was critical, and my superior, Mr. Douglas, wasn't available. He had already left to catch a four-hour flight, and it wasn't possible for me to talk to him. I used initiative," she stressed. "And I would rather have been wrong and lose my job than keep silent and find out after the fact that I was right. Sir, my conclusions and subsequent actions will be in the report I'm typing up, and when you read it, you will note that I take full responsibility for my actions. My coworkers had nothing to do with my decision to call Andrews. But in my defense," she hastened to add, "I, like the others in my department, have a master's degree, and we're all very good at what we do. We aren't simply typists transferring agents' notes into the database. We analyze the information we're given."

"So does the computer program."

"Yes, but the computer doesn't have heart or instincts. We do. And, sir, now that we're on the subject of job descriptions, I would like to mention that the minimum wage has gone up, but our salaries have not."

He blinked. "Are you hitting me up for a raise?"

She winced. Maybe she had said too much, but at least if she was going to lose her job, Lou and Mel and Margo might benefit. She felt a sudden burst of anger because she and her co-workers were so undervalued. She folded her arms and looked directly into his eyes. "As I've reviewed the facts for you, I've become more convinced than ever that I was right. I had no other choice than to notify Andrews, and he wouldn't move until I used your name. I know I overstepped my authority, but there simply was no time and I had to —"

"They got them, Avery."

She stopped short and then said, "Excuse me, sir?"

"I said Andrews and his men got them."

She didn't know why she was so shocked by the news, but she was. "All of them?" she asked.

He nodded. "Andrews and his team were waiting, and at precisely three minutes after ten, the three men stormed the bank."

"Was anyone hurt?"

"No."

She sighed. "Thank heavens."

Carter nodded. "They were wearing white. Did you figure out the significance of the color?"

"Sure. The Roman senators wore white robes."

"The three men are being interrogated now, but I imagine you have already figured out what their game was."

"They probably consider themselves anarchists trying to bring down the government. They'll tell you they're trying to kill Caesar and probably even hail themselves as martyrs for the cause, but you know what? When you cut through all the phony baloney, it's the same old same old. Greed was the real motivator. They were trying to be clever about it. That's all."

She was smiling, feeling quite pleased with herself, when a sudden thought occurred to her. "Sir, you said my morning was going to get worse," she reminded him. "What did you mean?"

"There's going to be a press conference in . . ." He paused to glance at the clock. ". . . ten minutes, and you're the star attraction. I understand you have an aversion to being in the spotlight. I don't like press conferences either, but we do what we have to do."

Avery could feel the panic building. "Mike Andrews and his team should do the press conference. They apprehended the suspects. I was simply doing my job."

"Are you being modest, or —"

She leaned forward as she interrupted him. "Sir, I'd rather have a root canal."

He caught himself before he smiled, but the twinkle had returned to his eyes. "So this aversion is deep-rooted then?"

"Yes, sir. It is." She appreciated his attempt to lighten the mood, but she couldn't get rid of her growing apprehension. "May I ask you a question?"

"Yes?"

"Why is my file on your desk? I did follow procedure . . . as best I could," she pointed out. "And if you didn't plan to fire me . . ."

"I wanted to familiarize myself with your department," he said as he picked up the file.

"May I ask why?"

"You're getting a new superior."

She didn't like hearing that. She and the others got along well with Douglas, and change was difficult.

"Is Mr. Douglas retiring, then? He's been talking about it for as long as I've been here."

"Yes," Carter answered.

Bummer, she thought. "May I ask who my new boss is?"

He glanced up from the folder in his hand. "Me," he answered. He let her absorb the information before continuing. "The four of you will be moved into my department."

She perked up. "We're getting new office space?"

Her excitement was quickly squelched. "No, you'll stay where you are, but starting Monday morning, you'll report directly to me."

She tried to look happy. "So, we'll be running up and down four flights of stairs every time we need to talk to you?" She knew she sounded like a whiner, but it was too late to take the words back.

"We do have elevators, and most of our employees are able to ride them without getting their heads caught between the doors."

The sarcasm didn't faze her. "Yes, sir. May I ask if we'll be getting raises? We're all way past due for our evaluations."

"Your evaluation is taking place right now."

"Oh." She wished he'd mentioned that fact starting out. "How am I doing?"

"This is the interview portion of the evaluation, and during an interview I ask the questions, and you answer them. That's pretty much how it works."

He opened her file and began to read. He started with the personal statement she'd written when she'd applied, then scanned her background information.

"You lived with your grandmother, Lola Delaney, until the age of eleven."

"That's correct."

She watched him flip through the pages, obviously checking facts and dates. She wanted to ask him why he felt the need to go over her history, but she knew that if she did, she'd sound defensive and maybe even antagonistic, and so she gripped her hands together and kept quiet. Carter was her new superior, and she wanted to start off on the right foot.

"Lola Delaney was murdered on the night of . . ."

"February fourteenth," she said without emotion. "Valentine's Day."

He glanced up. "You saw it happen."

"Yes."

He began to peruse the notes once again. "Dale Skarrett, the man who killed your grandmother, was already a wanted man. There was a warrant for his arrest in connection with a jewelry heist where the storeowner was murdered, and over four million in uncut stones were stolen. The diamonds weren't recovered, and Skarrett was never formally charged."

Avery nodded. "The evidence against him was circumstantial, and it's doubtful they would have gotten a conviction."

"True," Carter agreed. "Jill Delaney was also wanted for questioning in connection with the robbery."

"Yes."

"She wasn't at the house the night your grandmother was murdered."

"No, but I'm sure she sent Skarrett to kidnap me."

"But you didn't cooperate."

Her stomach began to tighten. "No, I didn't."

"No one knew what had happened until the next morning, and by the time the police arrived, Skarrett was long gone and you were in critical condition."

"He thought I was dead," she interjected.

"You were airlifted to Children's Hospital in Jacksonville. One month later, when you had recovered from your injuries — a remarkable feat given the extent of the damage — your Aunt Carolyn took you to her home in Bel Air, California." He leaned back in his chair. "That's where Skarrett came after you again, didn't he?"

She could feel the tension building inside her. "Yes," she said. "I was the only eyewitness who could put him away for life. Fortunately, I had a guardian angel. The FBI was protecting me without my knowing it. Skarrett showed up at school just as it was letting out."

"He was unarmed and later told the authorities he only wanted to talk to you. Skarrett was arrested and charged with second degree murder," he said. "He was convicted and is currently serving his sentence in Florida. He was up for parole a couple of years ago and was denied. His next hearing should be coming up sometime this year."

"Yes, sir," she said. "I regularly check with the prosecutor's office, and I will be sent notification once the date for the hearing is set."

"You'll need to go."

"I wouldn't miss it, sir."

"What about the new trial?" he asked. He tapped the papers with his knuckles and said, "I was curious to know why his attorney thinks he has grounds."

"I'm afraid he does have grounds," she said. "The brief that was filed accused the prosecutor of withholding vital information. My grandmother had a heart condition, and the physician who treated her came forward after he read about her death. That information wasn't handed over to Skarrett's attorney."

"But you haven't heard yet if, in fact, there will be a new trial?"

"No, sir, I haven't."

"Now let's get back to you," he said.

She couldn't be cooperative a second longer.

"Sir, may I ask why you're so interested in my background?"

"You're being evaluated," he reminded her. "Two weeks after Skarrett was convicted, Jill Delaney was killed in an automobile accident."

"Yes."

Avery had forgotten much of her childhood, but she remembered that phone call clearly. She had just celebrated Carrie's birthday, a belated event since Avery had been in the hospital on the actual date, and was helping the housekeeper put the vegetables on the table before they all sat down to dinner. Avery had placed the mashed potatoes next to Uncle Tony's plate when Aunt Carrie answered the phone. A funeral director was calling to tell her that Jilly had been cremated in a fiery car crash, but there were enough of her remains left to put in an urn. He wanted to know what Carrie wanted done with the ashes and the personal effects, which included a charred driver's license. Avery was standing in front of the bay window staring out at some frantic hummingbirds when she overheard Carrie tell the man to throw them in the nearest Dumpster. She could recall every second of that moment.

Carter drew her attention back to their discussion when he suddenly switched subjects.

"You did your undergraduate work at Santa Clara University, graduated with honors with a major in psychology and a minor in political science and another minor in history. You then

62

went to Stanford and received a master's in criminal justice." Having said that, he closed her file. "In your personal statement you said you made up your mind to become an FBI agent when you were twelve years old. Why?"

She knew he'd already read her answer. It was there in the personal statement she'd made when she'd applied to the Bureau. "An FBI agent named John Cross saved my life. If he hadn't been watching out for me . . . if Skarrett had taken me from school, my life would have been over."

Carter nodded. "And you believed you could make a difference working for the Bureau."

"Yes."

"Then why didn't you become a field agent?"

"Bureaucracy," she said. "I ended up in my current position. I was going to put in another six months and then request a transfer."

His assistant interrupted. "Mr. Carter, they're waiting for you."

The panic grabbed her again. "Sir, Mike Andrews really should handle the press conference. Any credit should go to him and his team."

"Look, none of us likes doing this," he snapped. "But this was such a high profile case, and frankly, most people would appreciate receiving some recognition."

"My coworkers and I would rather have raises . . . and windows, sir. We'd like windows too. Are you aware that our offices are located behind the mechanical room?"

"Space is at a premium," he said. "And when

did you get the idea we were negotiating?"

Her back stiffened. "Sir, in an evaluation —"

He cut her off. "You told me you acted alone when you called Andrews."

"Yes, that's correct, but the others were . . . integral. Yes, sir, they were integral in helping me go through those files for names."

One eyelid dropped. "You do realize that lying won't get you a raise, don't you?"

"Sir, Mel and Lou and Margo and I are a team. They did help. They just weren't as convinced as I was . . ."

The buzzer sounded on his intercom. Carter impatiently hit the button and said, "I'll be right there."

Then he reached for his suit jacket and put it on, frowning at her all the while.

"Relax, Delaney," he finally said. "You're off the hook. I'm not going to make you do the press conference."

Her relief made her weak. "Thank you, sir."

She stood when he walked around the desk, the wadded panty hose hidden under the jacket draped over her arm. Carter stopped at the door and then turned back with the frown still creasing his brow.

"Don't ever use my name again without my permission, Delaney."

"Yes, sir."

"One more thing," he said.

"Yes, sir?"

"Good work."

# CHAPTER 2

*Marriage isn't for the squeamish. Both husband and wife must be willing to let their inner children play dirty if they want their marriage to survive and flourish. They must let their inner children roll around in the mud. Mistakes will be inevitable, of course, but a shower of love and forgiveness will cleanse the union, and the healing will then begin.*

What a crock. Carolyn Delaney Salvetti sat in wide-eyed disbelief as she listened to the garbage the marriage counselor pontificated from his self-help, self-published manual, aptly and ludicrously titled *Let Your Inner Child Get Dirty.* Was the moron talking about marriage or mud wrestling? Carrie didn't know, and at the moment she didn't particularly care.

Without being too obvious about it, she pushed the sleeve of her silk blouse up over her wrist and glanced down at her Cartier watch. Ten minutes to go. God, could she last that long?

She took a deep breath, let go of her sleeve, and leaned back in the plush chair, nodding ever so sagely so her husband and the moron would think she was paying attention.

Marriage isn't for the squeamish, he repeated in his slow, nasal, baritone drawl. His voice was like a loofah made of steel wool, irritating every nerve in her body.

The counselor was a pompous, fat, flatulent fraud who insisted on being called Dr. Pierce because he felt his full name, Dr. Pierce Ebricht, was too formal for such an intimate discussion. After all, he was supposed to be helping them bare their guts. After the first session, Carrie had dubbed him Dr. Prick. Her husband, Tony, had chosen him because he was "in" at the moment. The counselor, with his drive-through-window degree, was the newest guru whom everyone who was anyone flocked to for marriage rejuvenation. Dr. Pierce was the Dr. Phil for the rich and famous, but unlike Dr. Phil, the prick was a complete buffoon.

But then, so was Tony. He sat beside Carrie, his sweaty palms held together as though in prayer, looking so earnest and engaged, like a wooden Howdy Doody the counselor manually manipulated, nodding in quick agreement whenever Dr. Prick paused from reading his bible to look up expectantly.

Chewing on her lip was the only way she could keep from laughing . . . or screaming. Oh, how she wanted to scream. She didn't dare, though. She had made a bargain with her faithless sleazebag of a husband, and if she didn't behave and pretend that she was really trying to save their *Titanic* marriage, she would be paying alimony for the rest of her life. It was a chilling possibility.

The odds were against her. Tony came from a long line of centenarians. His uncle Enzo was still chugging wine out on his postage-stamp piece of land on the good side of Napa at the ripe old age of eighty-six and didn't seem to be slowing down at all. His only concession to living healthy was, at the age of eighty-five, to quit smoking his unfiltered Camels — a three-pack-a-day habit — and increase the amount of garlic he put on everything he ate, including his morning wheat toast. If Tony turned out to be as healthy and fit as Enzo was, by the time Carrie croaked, she would be drained dry financially, and there would be nothing left in the coffers to leave to the only person she had ever loved, her niece, Avery. If, on the other hand, she cooperated with Tony and attended all ten sessions with Dr. Prick, and the marriage still ended — a foregone conclusion, in her opinion — then, Tony promised, he would give up his interest in the business and not ask for a dime in alimony.

Carrie wasn't a fool. Cynical to the bone, she wasn't about to accept the word of a man she considered a habitual liar and a thief. There was a hundred and twenty-three thousand dollars missing from one of their business accounts. She couldn't prove that Tony had helped himself to the money, but she knew he had taken it, most likely to buy expensive trinkets for his mistress. The bastard. And so, to insure he couldn't change his mind and come after her for alimony, she had made him put his promise in writing, then had called in her assistant to witness her husband signing the document. The paper was now safely locked away in her safe-deposit box at First Commerce Bank.

How had they come to this? she wondered. Tony used to be a loving and thoughtful man.

Carrie remembered the night she'd awakened in excruciating pain. She was sure her agony was due to food poisoning — they had eaten dinner at a new Thai restaurant all of her friends had been raving about. She refused to go to the hospital, and Tony was beside himself with worry. He finally picked her up, carried her to the car, and drove her to the hospital. He saved her life that night. After treatment in the emergency room, she was admitted, and Tony sat in a chair the rest of the night watching over her. He charmed the hospital staff into putting up with her complaints and demands, and filled the room with gerbera daisies, her favorite flowers.

Tony was so charismatic then. He still was, damn it, which was probably why all the young wanna-be starlets flocked around him. Was the temptation too much to resist? After all, she was getting older, and the years were beginning to show. Was that the reason he'd decided to be unfaithful?

Surreptitiously checking her watch again, she suppressed a heartfelt sigh. In just five minutes the last session would be over and she wouldn't have to pretend to be nice to Dr. Prick. Then, like it or not, she was going away for a little rejuvenation of her own. Her Prada workout clothes were stuffed into her Gucci bags, along with her state-of-the-art laptop computer, three battery packs, and two cell phones with chargers. The luggage waited in the trunk of the limo that would take her from Dr. Prick's office to the airport.

The forced vacation was the first time she would be away from her company, Star Catcher, in over eight years, and she was filled with trepidation. She had a good staff, and she knew they could handle any problems that came up while she was away, but she was admittedly a control freak and couldn't stand the idea of letting anyone else make decisions, if only for fourteen days. According to Avery, Carrie was a Type A personality. She couldn't abide being idle or bored. She hadn't even taken time off for a honeymoon when she'd married Tony. The short weekend in Baja had felt like a year away from her fledgling company, which was damned ironic considering she had allegedly been in the throes of love at the time.

The gold embossed reservation from the posh Utopia Spa had arrived three weeks ago — just after their second session with Dr. Prick, and Carrie, after taking one look at the invitation, had been certain that Tony was behind the scheme to get her out of L.A. Her husband had feigned surprise, but she hadn't been fooled. He'd been urging her to take some time off for months now and use the hiatus to work on their struggling marriage.

No matter how she nagged him to admit it, Tony wouldn't 'fess up. He insisted he hadn't made the reservation or paid the outrageous fee, and because he was even more stubborn than she was, she finally gave up trying to pry the truth out of him.

The reservation was accompanied by an elaborate brochure displaying the luxurious facility and outlining the treatments available at Utopia. There was also a letter attached with a list of testimonials from famous men and women who were regular clients.

She had heard of the spa — everyone in Hollywood knew about it — but she hadn't known how obviously popular it was with the rich and famous. Because the cost was so exorbitant, she hadn't ever considered it.

Carrie was torn. How important was it for her to go? Where one was seated at the "in at the moment" restaurants in L.A. was of paramount importance because one was seen and noticed, but a spa? It was so elegantly quiet and hush-hush, who would ever know besides the people attending that she had been there? Would the owner ask her to give a testimonial? God, wouldn't that be wonderful? If her name went on the list of the rich and famous, what an incredible boost that would be for her company. In her line of work, the only reason for doing anything these days was with the singular goal of impressing others and making them squirm with envy. Only the high rollers who didn't need to work got work in Hollywood.

What guarantee did she have that her name would go on that list, though? Carrie did the math, figured out to the penny how much each day would cost, and decided to stay home. She wasn't about to let Tony spend so much of her money. She would call the spa in the morning and request a refund. No way in hell was she going to fork over that much. She must have shouted those very words to Tony at least five times before he began to read aloud the names of those who regularly attended the rejuvenation spa and sang Utopia's praises. She stopped shouting when she heard the name Barbara Rolands. Everyone referred to the aging actress with three Oscars under her belt as the best face-lift on the coast. Barbara had disappeared for three weeks just last year, and when she next made a public appearance at a trendy fund-raiser, she looked incredible. Had she had the work done at the spa?

Carrie snatched the papers out of Tony's hands. She read the names of the personnel on call to attend to the client's every need. Two world-renowned plastic surgeons topped the list.

Would she be getting evaluated by the same

physicians who had worked on some of the most influential men and women of the century? God only knew she could use some freshening up. Not a face-lift — she wasn't even forty-five yet — but the bags under her eyes were getting more and more pronounced, and she really did need to do something about that. Lack of sleep, long hours of work, and twenty cups of strong coffee every day without ever taking time to work out had definitely taken their toll.

According to the letter, she would fly from L.A. to Denver, then go by smaller plane to Aspen. Utopia was located in the mountains, fifteen minutes away from the closest ski resort. She would arrive in the shank of the evening, and the following morning she would be evaluated by the physicians there. Liposuction, she noticed, was offered as one of the choices available. The procedure was listed just below full body massage.

How could she refuse? How could she, indeed, especially after Tony mentioned that the anonymous gift was nonrefundable. She just knew he'd used company money to pay for the trip. The man couldn't keep a dime in savings. Since they had merged their two companies and she had brought in their first multimillion-dollar account, he had been living high off the hog. He had absolutely no business sense.

Tony said it didn't matter where it came from and suggested she take the vacation as an early birthday present. He firmly believed one should never look a gift horse in the mouth. He told her he hoped she would use the time to reflect on all the wonderful words of wisdom Dr. Prick had spoken about the sanctity of marriage. She knew Tony was hoping that, once she slowed down, as one was wont to do on a vacation, she would realize how she had wronged him with her accusations and she would know in her heart that she still loved him.

Carrie had her own agenda. While she was being "redone," she would work on coming up with a killer commercial that would land her company another Clio. It had been too long since she'd received the last award, almost four years now, and she was becoming more and more anxious. Advertising was a cutthroat business, and her competition, based mostly in Manhattan, was fierce. The twenty-year-old set was taking over. Some executives wouldn't even speak to a man or woman over the age of thirty, which was why Carrie had added three young, with-it, business majors to her staff. She called the Nintendo fanatics her babies.

It was imperative that Carrie stay in the moment, every moment. In her work, it didn't matter how many past achievements there had been. With all the new movers and shakers pushing their way into her circle of influence, Star Catcher had to be out there as much as possible. Hollywood was a fickle town. Those with the power were only interested in who was creating the buzz that day. If Carrie didn't keep pushing her staff to grab bigger and bigger accounts, she would find herself in the has-been category overnight.

She owed her first Clio to her niece. She'd begged Avery to step in when the temperamental teen actress she'd hired threw a tantrum and demanded double her fee at the last moment. The silly girl thought she had Star Catcher by the balls because of the time crunch, and if Avery hadn't come to the set with Carrie that day, Carrie would have had to pay the little bitch. Avery had been mortified by what Carrie wanted her to do, but she had a good voice and a great body, and that was all that was required. The soap commercial was a resounding success, and Carrie, acting as Avery's agent, could have gotten her at least a year's work. Avery wasn't interested, though. As soon as spring break was over, she went back to finish high school and then went on to college.

Her niece did continue to work with Carrie every summer, but she hated leaving the office to meet with company executives. Carrie couldn't understand her reserve. Avery didn't seem to know — or if she did know, she didn't particularly care — that she was, as Tony often remarked, a knockout.

The problem with her niece was that she wasn't the least bit superficial. She was sweet and wholesome and had a firm grasp on what was important in life, and what wasn't. But what could Carrie expect? After all, she'd raised her to sort out such things. Ironic, Carrie thought, that she herself should end up working in a field consumed with the superficial. What a hypocrite she had turned out to be. When would she learn to practice what she had constantly preached to Avery? Maybe after she made another couple of million?

Carrie had eventually become excited about the spa. Once she had made the decision to go, she called Avery and begged her niece to join her at Utopia for one week. She knew Avery was using part of her vacation to chaperone teenagers around D.C., and Carrie tried to guilt-trip her into giving her family equal time. Carrie was feeling confident that Avery would come for at least a few days, but knew she would have heart failure if she ever found out how much the stay would cost her aunt. Carrie didn't have any qualms about paying the fee for Avery. She would do anything for her, anything at all. Probably because Avery never asked her for anything. Carrie didn't know how her niece could live on the tiny salary she made, and though she offered her money every time she talked to her, Avery always declined. She was doing just fine, or so she said.

Avery kept her grounded, and in the back of her mind, she knew that her niece wouldn't let her get swept up in the moment at Utopia and sign up for every treatment available.

Avery was going to pitch a fit when she found out that Carrie was thinking about booking an appointment for liposuction. She smiled as she thought about the argument her niece would give. Avery would shake her head when she saw her workout clothes too. Everything matched and had designer labels. Oh, yes, Avery would roll her eyes, no doubt, and then launch into her favorite lecture about getting fit and healthy.

God, how she missed the brat.

"What are you smiling about, honey?" Tony asked.

Jarred back to the present, she realized both her husband and their marriage counselor were staring at her. She shrugged to cover her embarrassment. "I was thinking about all the things I need to think about." That nonsense was the best she could come up with on the spur of the moment.

Dr. Prick looked pleased enough to roll around in the mud with his inner child. He nodded agreement and then stood, indicating the session was finally over.

Tony towered over her as he walked by her side to the waiting limo.

"You sure you don't want me to ride to the airport with you?"

"I'm sure."

"Did you remember to bring the reservation?"

"Yes." She pulled away from her husband when the driver opened the back door for her. "I still haven't heard from Avery, and I've left three messages for her. I was hoping to talk to her before I left L.A."

"You know how busy she is at work. She probably just hasn't had time to call you."

"But what if there's an emergency while I'm away?"

"Then she'll call me or try to get you on your cell phone."

"I don't like the idea of her working with children. It's too hard for her. She —"

"She wouldn't do it if she didn't love it," he pointed out. "You've got to stop worrying. Avery's a big girl now."

"Check my e-mails when you get home," she said then. "Maybe she sent me a message."

"Yes, I'll check and call you."

"The parole hearing is the sixteenth. I wonder if Avery was notified yet. I just got my —"

"Of course she knows. Why are you worrying about that now?"

"I can't miss," she snapped. "I always go with Avery. Both of us speak before the board decides . . ."

"Honey, you aren't going to miss the hearing, and neither will Avery. It's a month away, for Pete's sake. You didn't miss the last one, and you won't miss this one. Now try to relax. I want you to enjoy yourself."

She nodded. "Yes, okay."

She hadn't sounded sincere. Frowning he said, "You're tense because you haven't had any time off in such a long time. It's just last-minute jitters."

She nodded again, then tried to get into the

car, but Tony grabbed her by the shoulders and kissed her. "I love you," he whispered. "I've always loved you. From the moment we met. I want this marriage to work again."

"Yes, I know," she answered, her tone dismissive.

The second the car pulled away from the curb, Carrie reached for her laptop. She had just turned it on when her cell phone rang. Assuming that it was Tony calling to once again nag her about their marriage, she answered curtly.

"What is it now?"

"Guess what?" Avery said.

"Hi, sweetie. I thought you were Tony. Are you enjoying your vacation?"

"Not yet," she answered. "I'm finishing up some last-minute details at the office. I had a big meeting with my new boss a couple of days ago, and I can't wait to tell you about the case I helped solve. How about sharing a late dinner in Aspen?"

Carrie screeched. "You're going to join me? All my nagging and browbeating worked?"

"If I say yes, then you'll just get worse. Guilt worked this time, Carrie, but don't think —"

"What happened to the kids you were going to drag around Washington?"

"The trip got rescheduled."

"Ah. So I win by default."

"Do you want me to come or not?"

"Of course I want you to come. I'll call Utopia

right away. Have you got your flight yet?"

"I'm looking at the computer screen right now. I can get a connecting flight in Denver, but I won't get in until late," she warned.

"Now I'm excited. We're going to have such fun. Let me know your arrival time. As soon as you've booked it, call me back. See you soon, Avery. Love you."

Carrie's frame of mind vastly improved. She disconnected; then she called Utopia. After that, she went to work. She made notes until the limo pulled up to the airport. The lines through security moved at a snail's pace. Carrie, shifting the strap of her carry-on from one shoulder to the other, took a palm recorder from her purse and dictated instructions for her office staff. When the plane had taken off and she was comfortably seated in business class with a chilled glass of Chardonnay, she opened her laptop and went to work again.

Her thoughts kept going back to Avery. She could call her now, she decided, and find out what time her flight was. She reached for the phone hooked into the armrest, then changed her mind. Better to wait. If she used the plane phone, she'd have to shout to be heard over the drum of the engines and the static, and then the other passengers around her would hear every word.

As soon as she got off the plane in Aspen, she moved out of the main traffic stream and sat down to dig through her carry-on for her cell phone. She'd pulled everything out before she remembered she'd stuck the phone in her purse. It wasn't like her to be so disorganized, she thought as she closed the carry-on. She happened to glance up and see the man holding a sign with her name on it. Another limo driver, she assumed, dressed in a dark navy business suit. He was quite distinguished-looking and handsome, a younger version of Sean Connery. She quickly stood as she tucked the phone in the pocket of her blazer. Adjusting the collar of her blouse, she called out, "I'm Carolyn Salvetti."

His smile was dazzling. "Good afternoon, Mrs. Salvetti." He had a charming British accent. The name tag pinned to his lapel read "Mr. M. Edwards."

"Are you with Utopia? . . . the spa?" she asked.

"Yes, I am," he said. "Do you have your reservation with you?"

She reached for her travel bag. "It's right here."

"Oh, I don't need to see it, Mrs. Salvetti. I was to make certain you had the papers with you. Shall we go get your luggage?"

She felt ridiculous, all but running in her Manolo Blahnik slingbacks, trying to keep pace with her long-legged escort. She slipped once, and if he hadn't grabbed her arm to steady her, she would have fallen on her face. She'd meant to change her shoes before she got on the plane, but then she'd gotten caught up in work and had forgotten about it.

They passed a phone bank that reminded her she still needed to know Avery's flight itinerary. Damn it, she'd told her to call as soon as she'd booked her flight. Carrie knew what had happened. Avery had gotten waylaid with work and then had to run to get everything done.

It was probably too late to catch her at work or at home. She was probably already at the airport or perhaps on the plane now. Still, Carrie wanted to try. Maybe Avery would check her phone messages when she got to Denver. Yes, she would call as soon as they reached the baggage claim area.

"Will any other guests be going with us to the spa?" she asked.

"Yes," he said. "There are two other guests. They're waiting in the lounge. As soon as I pick up your luggage, we'll head out."

"Do you have anyone scheduled for pickup this afternoon or this evening?"

"No, this is my last trip. Why do you ask?"

"My niece, Avery Delaney, is joining me at the spa."

Her comment so surprised him he stopped in the middle of the corridor. "You were expecting Miss Delaney to join you?"

Hadn't she said so? "Yes," she said. "But she's flying out of D.C. If you aren't scheduled to come back and pick her up, the spa must be sending another escort."

They continued walking. "Yes, that must be so," he said, sounding somewhat preoccupied.

"I don't have Avery's flight information, but she might have called the spa to tell them so someone would pick her up. Could you call Utopia and find out? It would be lovely if we could wait for her. I do know she's coming through Denver," she thought to add.

"I'll be happy to call the spa," he said. Glancing around, he nodded toward a line of empty chairs in front of a deserted gate. "Why don't you have a seat."

He was placing her carry-on at her feet when she asked, "What does the 'M' stand for?"

"Pardon me?"

"Your name. 'Mr. M. Edwards.' What does the 'M' stand for?"

He saw no reason to lie. "Monk. The 'M' stands for Monk."

"How delightfully different."

"I prefer that all clients call me Mr. Edwards."

What a stiff-neck, she thought. "Yes, of course."

"If you'll excuse me . . ." He moved to the window as he pulled out his cell phone. Carrie grabbed her bag and went after him. She wanted to ask him to find out if there were any messages waiting for her at the spa.

His back was to her as she approached. She tapped him on the shoulder. "Mr. Edwards."

Startled, he whirled around. "Hold on," he said into the phone. Then, "Yes?"

"Would you ask the receptionist if I have any messages?"

He repeated the question, waited a moment,

and then shook his head. Carrie felt foolish standing there and so she went back to the chair and sat down.

He wasn't on the phone long, and when he returned to her side, he picked up her bag and apologized for the delay.

"There is another escort assigned to Miss Delaney."

"Couldn't we just wait?"

"I'm sorry. Did you say something?" he asked.

His preoccupation was irritating. "I asked if we could wait for my niece."

"I'm afraid not," he replied. "The other two clients have been waiting for you. I couldn't ask them to wait even longer. I hope you understand."

"Yes, of course."

"Thank you," he said. "The others will, no doubt, appreciate your cooperation."

"Who are they?" she bluntly asked.

"I'm sorry?"

"I was asking, Mr. Edwards, who the other clients are."

"Mrs. Trapp is from Cleveland, and Judge Collins's plane arrived from Miami."

Carrie hadn't heard either name before and wondered if they were famous. She certainly hoped so. She could use as many influential connections as she could get. Maybe the judge was one of those celebrities on television. Wouldn't that be something?

They finally reached the baggage claim area

and joined the hordes of passengers pushing their way to the front. "How long will the drive to the spa take?"

"Not long," he answered. "You won't be going directly to Utopia this evening, however," he added. "There was a problem with the water main, but it will be repaired by midnight. So that you won't be inconvenienced, the director has made arrangements for you and Mrs. Trapp and Judge Collins to spend the night at a private retreat."

Carrie was about to protest that, yes, it was an inconvenience. She would have to unpack and then pack again, but then Mr. Edwards said in a casual, off-handed way, "I believe Mr. Cruise and a companion were the last guests."

Her eyes widened. "Tom Cruise?"

"That's right. Then tomorrow morning," he continued smoothly, "you'll be taken to the spa."

"Will my niece be staying at the retreat too?"

"I'm not certain. If the problem has been solved by the time her flight arrives, then she'll be taken directly to the spa."

"Is the retreat near Aspen?"

"Just outside, high up in the mountains in an area called Land Between the Lakes. It's quite beautiful there. Cold nights and warm, mostly sunny days this time of year. Great climate for hiking and camping."

"I'm not the outdoor type, but you certainly look like you are," she said, noticing the thickness in his shoulders and the bulging muscles straining the fabric of his obviously custom-made suit. What were they paying chauffeurs these days?

They must have stood side by side for a good ten minutes before the bags began to roll along the conveyor belt.

"That one's mine," she said, pointing to an overstuffed, black Gucci bag moving along the conveyor. "Be careful," she warned. "It's heavy."

"Is this the only one?"

Surely he was joking. "No, there are three more."

"How long are you going to be at the spa?" he asked.

"Two weeks. How long have you worked there?" she asked, making idle chitchat to pass the time while she waited for the rest of the luggage. If they lost any of her bags, she was up a creek because her extra batteries for her laptop and her other cell phone were packed inside.

"A year," he answered.

"That's nice," she remarked, not really interested. Where the hell were her other suitcases? She could feel herself getting anxious and took a deep breath. Relax, she told herself. You're on vacation.

She glanced around the luggage area, spotted a ladies' room and said, "Before we leave, I'd like to splash some cold water on my face."

"If you could wait until we get to —"

"Actually, I can't wait," she interrupted. She handed him her carry-on but kept her purse.

"Don't let go of that bag. It's got my laptop and my cell phone inside."

Then she hurried into the rest room. As she was washing her hands, she remembered she'd put the other cell phone in her pocket and decided to call Avery right then.

Carrie went into the last stall so she would have some privacy, prayed the signal wouldn't get blocked, then hit speed dial. She called Avery's apartment first, listened to the answering machine, and told her to call her as soon as she got this message. Then, thinking she might have left for the airport, Carrie hit speed dial again. The number was a direct line to Avery's desk. Her voice mail picked up on the second ring.

"Damn it, Avery, you were supposed to call me back with your flight information, but you forgot, didn't you? I hope to heaven you're on the plane now and will check your messages from Denver. I think I'm obsessing because I don't want you to bail on me. I know how that job of yours sucks you in. If I find out you've missed your plane because you got stuck in one of those horrid meetings, I'll pitch such a fit your ears will be ringing for a month. Honestly, Avery, when I think about all the things you could be doing and all the money you could be making, and here you are, stuck in that windowless dungeon analyzing God only knows what. It's a waste of your talents. Surely you realize that. I wish you'd let me help you change careers."

Carrie realized what she was doing and

laughed. "Listen to me going on and on. You've heard it all before, haven't you? Anyway, I called to tell you I'm in Aspen now. I wanted to wait until you landed so we could ride to the spa together, but there are other guests here, and it would be too much of an inconvenience to make them sit and wait. I won't be going to the spa tonight. They had some kind of plumbing problem, which my escort tells me should be fixed by the time you get there. I'll be sound asleep by then. The other two women and I will be spending a luxurious night at a posh mountain retreat. I've already forgotten the other women's names, but one of them is a judge. I'll bet she's famous. Then tomorrow," she continued, "I'll check in at Utopia and find you."

Carrie felt another burst of excitement. "The retreat is called The Land Between the Lakes. How quaint is that? Tom Cruise was their last guest, so you know it has to be incredibly beautiful. I mean, he's on top of the A list, and they wouldn't put him in anything shabby. I better hang up now before my escort comes looking for me in the ladies' room. I can't wait to see you. We're going to have such fun. Oops, I hear my escort calling my name. The spa sent a real hunk to carry my luggage. He's kind of stiff and formal, and he has the faintest British accent. And, oh, is he sexy. His name's Monk Edwards, but trust me, he doesn't look like any monk I've ever seen. Maybe they'll send another hunk to pick you up. Bye, brat. See you soon."

# CHAPTER 3

The trail led to Utopia. John Paul Renard had been tracking the professional killer for over a year now, but he hadn't had much success. The last known hit had taken place on the Riviera, an execution of a wanted man named John Russell, but since then, the killer calling himself Monk seemed to have vanished off the face of the earth. There had been a hint of his work in Paris and in Cannes, but nothing substantial enough to be considered a real lead.

Until now.

When John Paul had been in the Marines and then, for a short time, had worked for the Agency, he'd learned patience. He figured that eventually the killer would return to the United States. It had been a hunch, nothing more, but lo and behold, he'd been right. Just three weeks ago, Monk had finally resurfaced. He'd actually messed up too. He'd used one of his old credit cards. It was such a sloppy thing to do and so out of character for a man who, up until now, had been pretty damned flawless in his executions. John Paul wondered if Monk had thrown the card away and someone else had found it and used it.

It was worth checking out. A charge had been made at a spa in Colorado called Utopia for a woman named Carolyn Salvetti. John Paul ran a credit check on her and discovered that she had more than enough money tucked away in her IRAs and her pension plans to buy a couple of spas. Was there a connection to Monk here? Had she hired him to kill someone? Or was she his next victim?

John Paul also ran her name through the government database. He used his old code to get access, knowing full well that as soon as he logged on, the men who had run him would immediately know it and would leap to the incorrect assumption that he was ready to come back. For that reason he didn't stay on the computer long. In less than two minutes he found out what he needed to know. Salvetti was clean as a whistle. No warrants outstanding, no parking tickets, no illegal activities of any kind. Her husband was also clean. Carolyn Salvetti was president of a company called Star Catcher. Tony Salvetti was vice president.

The database hadn't given him any answers. If Carolyn Salvetti was Monk's next target, then who had hired him? Who wanted the woman dead?

John Paul was determined to find out. Since his brother, Remy, lived in Colorado Springs, he decided to drive there to see him. Known in his hometown, Bowen, Louisiana, as a surly recluse, John Paul shocked his family and few friends when he purchased an old Ford SUV. He made a few alterations, souped up the engine, packed it with a couple of kitchen chairs he'd made for Remy, and headed out.

He spent two days with his brother, but on June sixteenth, the day Salvetti was scheduled to arrive at the spa, John Paul was there waiting for her. His hope was that Monk was right behind her, and he could nail the bastard.

Carolyn Salvetti didn't show. The desk clerk, an uptight, exceedingly nervous young man with weird, oversized, capped teeth, told John Paul that Mrs. Salvetti had canceled her reservation at the last minute. "But it's noted right here, under her old reservation, that her niece, Avery Delaney, will be staying at the spa. Miss Delaney will only be here one week," he thought to add. "Is that at all helpful?"

Instead of answering the question, he asked to speak to the manager. The clerk tripped when he hastily pivoted, then went running to fetch his employer.

Tim Cannon showed up a minute later, with the clerk half hiding behind his back. Since John Paul had left the Agency, he didn't have any credentials to threaten the tight-lipped, sweaty little man, and so he used intimidation. As usual, it worked like a charm. For some reason he couldn't quite understand, people tended to be afraid of him. His sister, Michelle, told him it was because of his size and the fact that he rarely smiled. Though he thought it was peculiar that strangers backed away from him, he used their fear to his advantage. Cannon, operating under the false assumption that John Paul worked for the government — an assumption John Paul had hinted at but hadn't actually stated — and obviously embarrassed to admit that he was afraid of John Paul, didn't call security or ask to see identification. The fact was, the manager couldn't have been more helpful. He invited him into his office, offered him the use of his desk and phone, and then, stammering about an emergency errand he simply had to complete, he left his office and pulled the door closed behind him.

The second he was alone, John Paul turned on Cannon's computer, found the site, and typed in his access code. How he hated the technology, but it was the only way he could get the information he needed. He wanted to see if an alert had been posted regarding Monk and was pleasantly surprised that there hadn't been. The spa wasn't swarming with agents yet — in John Paul's estimation, they were as easy to spot as nuns in black habits — which could only mean that the Bureau didn't know that Monk was back in the States. John Paul wasn't inclined to tell them. The FBI would only screw it up. Monk would spot the agents, get spooked, and vanish into thin air again.

John Paul wasn't about to let that happen. He was one step in front of the Bureau, and that was all he needed. He had a personal reason for going after the killer, and he wasn't going to let anyone get in his way.

A little over a year ago, Monk had tried to kill John Paul's sister, Michelle, and had it not been for her husband and a friend, he would have succeeded. Monk got away, which, in John Paul's estimation, was unforgivable. He vowed he wouldn't rest until he had hunted the bastard down and sent him to Hell where he belonged.

Once he started doing the research, John Paul's need for vengeance intensified. One case in particular had really shaken him up. A father had hired Monk to kill his teenage daughter so that he could collect the insurance money and pay his gambling debts. The FBI knew Monk had murdered the girl because the killer always left behind a rose, and though the father had removed the evidence, a thorn was found in the girl's bedspread. There wasn't any other family to mourn or seek justice for the young girl. John Paul knew there were other victims the FBI didn't even know about yet. How many more innocents would die before the killer was stopped?

# CHAPTER 4

Monk kept the three women entertained while he drove them to their destination. Carrie thought he was charming and oh so terribly correct. He was her idea of the perfect English butler.

He had transferred their luggage into the back of a brand-new, fully equipped Land Rover, explaining that the SUV was suited for the mountain roads, and for that reason he hadn't driven one of the spa's limos. Anne Trapp sat in the front, and Carolyn sat next to Judge Sara Collins in the back. The seats were plush beige leather and very comfortable.

All of them were excited and nervous, but there was little conversation among them. Monk told them a brief history of the spa and then regaled them with several fascinating stories about some of the famous people who had stayed at the mountain house he was taking them to.

Carrie wasn't sure how long they had been driving. She hadn't checked the time when they'd left the airport, but it seemed that at least an hour had passed, maybe even more. Monk's stories so intrigued her she didn't mind the long drive or the slight case of car sickness. While Sara ooh'd and ah'd over the scenery as they climbed higher and higher up the mountain and Anne sat in stony silence, Carrie questioned Monk about the previous guests he'd served. She wasn't particularly interested in hearing about politicians. She wanted to hear all about the peculiarities of the movie stars.

"Russell Crowe was a guest? What was he like?"

Monk replied with an amusing tidbit about the Australian actor. "He was quite fond of the house," he added, "and wanted to purchase it."

"It must really be nice," Sara remarked.

Monk assured them that the house had all the amenities and that he would be acting as their butler until they checked into Utopia.

"I certainly hope there won't be any more screwups," Anne said irritably.

"Was there a screwup?" Sara asked her.

"There certainly was," Anne said. She turned in her seat so she could look at Sara while she explained. "No one from the spa was waiting for me at my gate to help me with my carry-on, and if I hadn't seen Mr. Edwards holding up the sign at your gate as I was walking toward the baggage claim area, I would have been left to fend for myself. I was quite weary," she added. "And the thought of carrying my luggage to a taxi stand was more than I could bear."

"There were skycaps around who could have assisted you," Carrie told her.

"That isn't the point," Anne snapped. "I shouldn't have been inconvenienced."

What a bitch, Carrie thought. The look on Anne's face was almost comical. She was pouting like an eight-year-old.

"I assure you, Mrs. Trapp, your every need will be taken care of by an excellent staff, and I once again apologize for the inconvenience."

"Will there be servants at the retreat?" she asked.

"Yes, of course."

"How many?"

"Four," he answered. "They'll be arriving from the spa shortly."

"I wish to have one of them assigned to me," Anne demanded. "Will you see to it?"

"Yes, of course."

Anne nodded. "Good," she said, and she sounded mollified.

Sara and Carrie exchanged a look that spoke volumes. Then Anne said, "I'm pleased to know we won't be alone tonight . . . in the event something should happen . . . or break. You just never know."

"The house is getting a new alarm system. The wires haven't been properly hidden yet, but it's workable," he promised. "Once it's turned on, you won't be able to open your windows or outside doors, of course, but it does get quite chilly up here at night, so I can't imagine you would want to keep any windows open."

Carrie studied her traveling companions. They both looked vaguely familiar to her, but she couldn't pinpoint where they might have met.

She stared at the back of Anne's head and then finally tapped her on her shoulder and asked. The blond woman with deep-set brown eyes half turned in her seat and smiled slightly.

"I don't believe we've ever met," she said. "Have you ever been to Cleveland?"

"No," Carrie answered.

Up close, she noticed how sallow the woman's complexion was. She didn't think Anne was at all well. Her eyes were dull and lifeless, and her skin was almost waxy, but that could have been due to the heavy makeup she was wearing. Perhaps Anne had paid her fee for some kind of miracle cure for her waiflike, nearly anorexic body. Carrie judged her to be around her own age, give or take a few.

Judge Sara Collins had just the opposite problem. She could have stood to lose a good sixty or seventy pounds. Perhaps she was going to have liposuction or stomach staples. She looked old, around seventy or so, and her face definitely showed her age. Maybe she was there to have a face-lift. Carrie was dying to ask but didn't dare.

Where could she have recognized her from? Maybe she'd seen her on television. Court shows were the rave now. Did Sara have her own program like Judge Judy?

She would have asked, but their chauffeur had turned into a tour guide and was keeping up a steady monologue about Colorado. One story led to another and another, but they were interesting tidbits, and Carrie thought it would be rude to interrupt. Still, he wasn't giving them time to get to know each other. She decided she'd ask Sara if she was a celebrity when they were settled in the house.

Then she began to wonder what the other women thought about her. She knew she looked older than her actual age. An old hag, she thought. Yes, that's what they probably thought.

They'd been on private roads now for quite awhile, and it was getting steeper. Winding around and around was making Carrie more carsick. Great, she thought. I'm going to throw up on our proper English butler. Wouldn't that be a wonderful way to impress the other houseguests?

"Does the company own all this land?" Sara asked Monk.

"Yes, madam," he answered.

"Is the house much farther?" Carrie asked.

"It's just around the next bend."

They were in the middle of nowhere. A wilderness, Carrie thought, and she began to feel uneasy . . . nervous. She suddenly realized she hadn't seen a house or even a cabin in quite a long time. Then it occurred to her that an alarm system wouldn't do any of them any good. If the alarm went off, who would hear it? Was it tied into the nearest police station, and if so, where in God's name was that? An hour away? Two hours? Or would the alarm sound at the spa?

Yes, that was surely how it worked. And that meant that the spa was close by. Having figured it out, Carrie leaned back in the leather seat and tried to relax.

The house suddenly came into view. It was incredible. Massive gables of natural cedar rose into the sky, and two-story panes of glass reflected the mountain peaks behind them, as if the magnificent structure were placed there with no other purpose than to pay tribute to the grandeur that surrounded it. A circle drive curved toward the wide porch that stretched across the front of the house. Waist-high stone walls were built as protective barriers from the sheer drop at the back.

Sara gasped. "Look at that wonderful porch and those lovely rocking chairs. I simply must try one of them out."

Monk parked the Land Rover in the center of the stone circle drive and rushed to open the doors for his passengers.

"If you stand on the porch and look in the window, you can see through the house to the vista beyond," he pointed out.

"Oh, it is lovely," Anne said. "It looks brand-new," she added as she walked to the wall on the side of the drive and looked down at the trees below.

"It was built four years ago."

"How in heaven's name did they get all the glass up these mountains?" Sara asked.

"Very carefully, I would imagine," Carrie replied.

"I believe you ladies will be very comfortable here," Monk said.

"Oh, yes, we will be." Sara was so enthusiastic that Carrie wouldn't have been surprised if she'd started clapping her hands.

Wasn't Sara used to such ambience? She was a judge, for heaven's sake. Surely she had money. And obviously so did Anne. Neither one of them would have been able to afford the spa if they weren't well-off.

"If you ladies would like to go inside, there's champagne chilling for you. I'll bring the luggage in."

Carrie opened the door and led the way inside. She noticed the thin wires up against the house and assumed they were part of the alarm system.

"Watch your step," she said. "Don't trip over the wires."

The floor plan was open, very spacious. To the left of the huge marble entry was a magnificent spiral staircase that reached up three stories. Light flooded the room, and when they raised their eyes higher, they could see the golden clouds through a long rectangular skylight.

"Isn't the staircase beautiful?" Sara said. "The wood . . . the steps, they're twice the length and depth of any I've ever seen. It must have cost a fortune to build it," she added. "Look at the railing. The craftsmanship is exceptional."

Carrie agreed. Then Anne called to them. "The mountains look like they're on fire with the sunset. Come see." Even Anne, a difficult woman to please, couldn't contain her enthusiasm.

Carrie stood in the foyer taking in the view. Colorful oriental rugs — high-quality rugs — were scattered across the living room's pale brown, marble floor. In harmony with the mountains, the furnishings were done in soft browns and beiges. The stone fireplace was at least sixteen feet high and similar, she thought, to the fireplace in the villain's house she'd admired when she'd watched one of her favorite movies, *North by Northwest*. The room was square like the living room in the movie too. No, this one was much better, the furniture updated and more exquisite.

Directly ahead, the sun was setting, and the burst from the fiery ball filled the room with a soft orange hue.

"I feel like I'm in heaven," Sara said.

"If you go to the top of that spiral staircase, you will be in heaven," Carrie joked.

Anne spotted the silver bucket with a bottle of champagne on the sideboard. There was a beautiful crystal vase with three long-stemmed, bloodred roses next to it. The petals were just beginning to open. "Shall we have a glass of champagne?"

"But of course," Sara answered.

The three women stood in front of the window overlooking the panorama as Anne struggled to get the bottle uncorked. She laughed nervously when the cork popped and the liquid bubbled over, then carefully filled each Waterford crystal flute.

"We should have a toast," Carrie said.

"Good idea," Sara agreed.

She and Anne lifted their glasses and waited for Carrie to do the honors.

"To us," she said. "May all our dreams come true."

"That's lovely," Anne said.

They sank down onto the plush, down-filled sofas and sipped their champagne, making idle chitchat, carefully avoiding any personal topics, while Monk carried their luggage upstairs to their suites. Carrie was still feeling a little nauseous, so she didn't drink more than one tiny sip.

Monk joined them ten minutes later with a tray of canapés. As he was placing the linen napkins next to the tray on the coffee table, Carrie heard a door close. She looked toward the hallway leading from the dining room and saw a woman wearing a black dress walk into the kitchen.

"Maids have arrived," she remarked to Sara.

"Do have one of these cucumber canapés," Anne suggested. She'd just finished eating the bite-size treat. "They're quite tasty."

Carrie didn't want to tell either woman she wasn't feeling well, and she certainly wasn't going to admit she'd gotten carsick.

"Yes, I will," she said. She popped the little sandwich into her mouth, barely chewing it before swallowing it down. "It is good," she said.

She couldn't make herself eat another and became even more queasy watching Anne eat two salmon puffs as well as the cucumber sandwiches, and Sara devour twice as many.

Within minutes they were all yawning. Monk noticed. "If you ladies will follow me, I'll show you to your rooms," he said as he leaned down to turn on one of the table lamps. Now that the sun was going down, the room was filled with shadows.

"I am so sleepy," Anne said.

"It must be the mountain air," Sara suggested. "I'm feeling lethargic myself."

They followed Monk to the spiral staircase. Carrie looked up and remarked, "Who would have thought stairs could be a work of art."

"I hate stairs," Anne said. "The next house I build will be a sprawling ranch."

Sara and Carrie ignored her comment. Monk drew their attention when he said, "I've unpacked your overnight bags. Mrs. Trapp, you and Judge Collins will be in suites on the second level on opposite ends of the floor. Mrs. Salvetti, you're one floor up. I hope you'll all find the accommodations satisfactory."

Anne followed Monk, then came Carrie, and

Sara, gripping the banister for support, was the last in line.

"I feel like I've been in this house before," Sara said. "Yet I've never seen a spiral staircase like this, so I don't know why I feel that way."

"I think it's the fireplace," Carrie said. She paused on a step to look down into the living room once again. "Did you ever see the movie *North by Northwest*? It starred Cary Grant and Eva Marie Saint, and in the climax, they had to climb out on the presidents' faces?"

"I do remember. The stone fireplace is very like the one in the movie. That must be why it seems so familiar to me."

"I never saw the movie," Anne said.

Carrie was floored. "You've got to be kidding. It was one of Hitchcock's best."

Anne shrugged. "I was busy running my business," she said. "I didn't have time to go to movies."

"But it's a classic. It's been on television at least a hundred times," Sara said.

"Oh, I never watch television."

Carrie didn't know how to relate to the woman. Anne sounded as though she were boasting about the fact that she didn't watch television. Carrie's life revolved around networks and sponsors. She looked up at Anne now as though she were an alien. Not watch television or go to the movies? Amazing. No wonder the woman was so dull.

She didn't feel at all guilty about her snap

judgment. Anne, unknowingly, had just insulted everything that Carrie worked for or believed in.

Monk showed Sara into her suite first.

"I think I'm going to call it a night," Sara said. "I'll see you in the morning."

"Good night," Carrie called as she followed Monk down the long hallway.

He opened Anne's door for her, and then turned to Carrie. "Your suite is directly above Judge Collins's," he said. He led her up the staircase to the next level.

"So there are four full suites?" Carrie asked.

"Yes," he answered.

They reached her door, and Monk stepped back to let her go inside. The large bedroom with an adjoining sitting room was a soothing amber color. Two overstuffed chairs flanked a fireplace, and the four-poster bed made of light, burled pine was covered with a thick down comforter.

She yawned loudly. Monk or one of the maids had laid out her robe and gown on the bed. She spotted her carry-on on the luggage rack. It was open and empty, and she was going to ask where her laptop was, but then a wave of nausea and dizziness struck, and she had to sit down. She took several deep breaths as she held on to the bedpost.

"Is everything all right, Mrs. Salvetti?"

She didn't want to be difficult or complain the way Anne did, and so she simply said that she was weary from the long day. "I'm usually a night owl, and I don't go to bed until two or three in the morning, but tonight I can barely keep my eyes open."

Monk's expression was sympathetic. "It takes awhile to get used to the mountain air, and the staff from the spa did suggest that all of you have an early night. Tomorrow promises to be quite busy."

"Yes, I'm sure it will be."

"I'll be the last to retire," he said as he walked to the door. "I'll set the alarm then. Please remember not to open any windows."

"What happens if the alarm goes off? Who will hear it?" she asked. "We're out in the middle of nowhere."

"The alarm is electronically connected to the spa. I thought I had mentioned that before. Should we need it, help will arrive in less than three minutes."

"The spa's that close?"

He nodded. "If it weren't for the trees, you'd be able to see the domes from your window. Would you like me to close the drapes?"

"No. I prefer them open." She turned away, gripping the bedpost now as the bile came rushing up into her throat. She was going to ask him where the servant quarters were located, but her throat burned too much to get the question out.

"Good night," she said. "Close the door behind you, please."

The second she heard the door click shut, she bolted from the bed and ran into the bathroom, one hand covering her mouth. She barely got the lid up in time before she threw up the canapé she'd eaten. The damn car sickness. She'd had the problem since she was a child. She should have spoken up and explained she couldn't sit in the backseat. Worried what the others would think of her, she hadn't said a word.

What the hell was the matter with her? What did she care what strangers thought about her? She would probably never see them again after breakfast.

Her stomach heaved at the thought of food. She hadn't felt this ill in years, not since that horrid case of food poisoning. Avery was fourteen at the time, and she'd stayed home from school to help take care of Carrie. Tony had been a real gem back then too. She remembered how he'd held her when the chills got so bad.

Carrie felt too weak to take a shower. She brushed her teeth, washed her face, and put on her nightgown. She stumbled back into the bedroom, heard the clinking of glasses, and assumed that Monk was cleaning up. Then she heard a woman's laughter. Was the maid flirting with him? Might as well, she thought. There wasn't anything else for them to do, since she and Anne and Sara were already going to bed. My heavens, it wasn't even nine o'clock yet, and she was so exhausted, she could barely focus.

The room kept spinning. God, she felt awful.

She fell into bed, struggled to get the covers up, and tried resting on her side. The nausea was still coming in waves. She slowly, carefully rolled onto her back. That was better, much better. She closed her eyes and fell asleep.

She didn't know how long she'd slept, but it was dark in the room when she heard someone faintly calling out to her. She couldn't respond. Then she heard a clicking sound over and over. No, the noise was snapping, like fingers coming together, or clinking, like knives being sharpened. Carrie couldn't understand why the noise wouldn't stop.

Someone nudged her shoulder, calling her name again.

She couldn't summon the strength to open her eyes. "Yes?" she whispered.

"Carrie."

"Yes?"

The noise made it difficult for her to concentrate. And, oh, she was so sleepy. She tried but couldn't even raise her hand to cover her eyes when a light went on.

"Go away," she said, her voice a croak.

"I heard your toast, Carrie. Do you remember what you said?"

"No . . ."

"May all your dreams come true. But what about your nightmares? Those come true too."

The words weren't making any sense. "What? Nightmares? No . . . no nightmares."

"Open your eyes, Carrie."

The sound was getting louder. "Come on. Look at me."

The voice floating above her became more demanding, more menacing. Carrie was finally able to open her eyes a little. She saw the scissors opening and closing in front of her face. They were shiny. That was the snapping noise, she realized. But why were there scissors?

And then the noise stopped, and the scissors vanished. A face appeared just inches above her own, and that smile, that hideous, gloating smile that was horrifically familiar.

She tried to scream. "No . . . no . . . no . . . oh, my God, help me . . . no . . . Jilly."

# CHAPTER 5

Avery lost track of the time. She was frantic to get as much work done as possible before she had to leave for the airport. Her desk had been clear when she'd left the night before. She'd gotten to the office at six-thirty that morning just so everything would be caught up.

She was so bleary-eyed now she could barely focus on her computer screen. And doing a slow burn. Someone, she didn't know who the culprit was, had dumped twenty-two files on her desk, and she was expected to transfer all the information into the database. She also had at least sixty e-mails to read and answer, and she hadn't remembered to check her private voice mail in over twenty-four hours.

Her cubicle still looked like a cyclone had hit. The files seemed to be multiplying, and how was that possible?

"Aren't you supposed to be on a plane?" Margo asked. She was juggling a stack of files, her empty water bottle, and a doughnut box.

"I've got a little time left," Avery answered as she typed a reply to one of her e-mails.

Lou stood and stretched his arms. "Margo, are there any Krispy Kremes left?"

"One," she answered. "Avery didn't eat hers."

"Help yourself," Avery said.

Lou grabbed the box out of Margo's arms and opened it. "When are you leaving?"

"Soon."

"Flying?"

"Of course she's flying," Margo said.

"I've got it all figured out down to the minute. If I leave at four-fifteen on the dot, I'll have time to drive home, change clothes, and pick up my luggage, then take the interstate to the airport, park in long-term, and make it to the gate in plenty of time."

Margo took her purse from her drawer and came back around the corner. "Hey, Avery, did you have time to call Mrs. Speigel's caretaker and tell her to do a better job of hiding those car keys?"

"No, I forgot."

"You want me to look up her phone number and call her? She's got to do something to protect the public from that woman."

"I'd appreciate it if you would call," Avery said. "But don't be bossy, Margo. Mrs. Speigel's a sweetheart. She knows she shouldn't be driving, but sometimes she gets confused."

"Avery, she almost killed you." Margo sighed then. "Okay, I won't be bossy."

Mel joined the conversation. "Everyone in D.C. will be on the interstate. There's bound to be a pileup. You ought to take the Jefferson Davis, then cut over to ninety-five. It'll save you a good twenty minutes."

Mel disagreed. "She's leaving in rush hour. The interstate is much faster."

Avery was only half listening. Her fingers were flying over the keyboard as she replied to inter-office inquiries. "I feel terrible leaving you guys with my mess," she said to no one in particular.

"Don't worry about it," Lou said.

"We'll all split the work," Margo said. "Lou, you've got some powdered sugar on your belt."

She reached over Avery's head, grabbed a tissue from the box on the shelf, and handed it to Lou. Then she turned back to Avery. "I'm planning to dump all my work on all of you when I go to San Diego next month for my cousin's wedding."

"I think I'd better type up that route you should take to the airport," Mel said. "I'll hand you the printout as you're leaving the office."

"As long as I'm out of here by four-fifteen."

"I'll make sure you are," Mel promised. "Shall we synchronize our watches?"

"That's a nerdy thing to do," Margo told him. "Now, Brad Pitt would never —"

Her phone rang, interrupting her thought. While she hurried to her cubicle, Lou picked up where she'd left off. "Face it, you guys. We are nerds."

"So what's wrong with that?" Mel asked. "I mean, think about it. Bill Gates is a nerd, and he's doing all right."

"Maybe, but we aren't making his billions, now are we? And we're thought of as nerds by everyone in the Bureau."

"I don't believe that," Mel argued. "We're all important members of the team."

Margo interrupted. "Agent Andrews is on his way down here," she called out. "Douglas's secretary heard him ask where the pen was."

"He's probably coming down to thank you, Avery, for letting him have the glory," Lou said.

"He's late," Margo said. "He should have thanked her the other day, after the press conference."

"Andrews is going to cut into your time," Mel said. "Maybe I better go ahead and print out that alternate route. You can decide which way to go once you're in the car. Just be sure to turn the radio on and listen to the traffic updates."

Avery tried not to smile. Mel did tend to obsess over the tiniest details. "Thanks, Mel."

"We'll let Andrews talk for what? Four? Five minutes?"

"That'd be good."

"Then you interrupt," Mel told Lou. "You're good at that."

Andrews ruined the schedule. Although Avery had never met the agent, she had him all figured out in less than a minute. He thought he was a charmer. It was an incorrect assumption on his part. He got the "thank you's" over with quickly but then perched on the edge of her desk and invited her to have dinner with him. His stare wasn't quite a leer, but it was damned close. Lou and Mel immediately tried to get rid of him.

"Avery's leaving on vacation," Mel said. "She's got a plane to catch."

When Andrews didn't take the hint, Lou decided to be more blunt. "You better leave. She's on a tight schedule, and you're messing it up."

Andrews's response was to fold his arms and widen his goofy smile.

It didn't take investigative skill to know what was happening. Andrews was suffering from LAFS, "lust at first sight," but that didn't make him unusual. Most of the men who got close to Avery became temporarily afflicted by the debilitating condition. Mel theorized that the syndrome was brought on by her big, baby blue eyes. When she looked at a man and gave him her full attention, his brain simply shut down. Lou didn't agree with Mel's assessment. Blue eyes might have had a little to do with catching a guy's interest, but it was Avery's killer body and long, silky blond hair that turned him into a blithering idiot.

Andrews was blithering now. It was sad, really, to watch a skilled professional sink so quickly into the quagmire.

Mel, the more protective of Avery, hoped Andrews would hurry up and compliment her.

They all did, sooner or later, and then Avery would send him on his way. Mel checked the time as he silently willed Andrews to tell Avery how pretty she was. If he didn't hit on her soon, Avery would miss her plane.

Come on, come on, Mel silently urged. Go for it. Tell her what a knockout she is.

"I've got to ask you something," Andrews said.

"Yes?" Avery asked.

"How come such a beautiful woman like you is stuck down here in the basement?" The agent all but crooned the question like a country singer. "With your looks —" It was as far as he got. Poor guy never knew what hit him.

Avery's voice sizzled as she curtly responded, "Agent Andrews, I had nothing to do with the way I look. Now, if you'll excuse me, I have work to do, and I assume you do too. Get off my desk and go away."

That having been said, she swiveled in her chair and began typing again. Andrews had that *what'd-I-say?* look of bewilderment on his face as he stood and slowly walked away, blushing like a girl.

Mel didn't start laughing until he was out of earshot. "So I guess you won't be going to dinner with Andrews when you get back from vacation?"

"I'm trying to work here."

Lou put his hand out, and Mel, frowning as he pulled his wallet from his back pocket, extracted a dollar bill and handed it to his friend. The two men had a standing bet as to the nature of the compliments given Avery. Since Andrews hadn't said anything about her legs, Lou won the dollar. Her legs were pretty amazing, and most men noticed them right away, but Andrews apparently wasn't a leg man.

"How come that never happens to me?" Margo asked. "I'm cute, aren't I?"

"Yeah, sure you are," Lou said.

"And I want to get married one day and have a family," she continued as though Lou hadn't answered. "Whereas Avery has made it perfectly clear on countless occasions that she's never going to get married. It's just not fair. I'd be perfect for Andrews. I really would. But he never even glanced my way."

"What makes you think you'd be perfect for him?" Lou asked.

"Because he's a hottie," she answered. "And no one appreciates a full-fledged hottie more than I. We'd be perfect for each other," she said over her shoulder as she went back to her workstation.

Mel shoved his wallet back into his pocket and went to work. At four-fifteen, he stood up and called, "It's time to leave, Avery."

"Just give me another ten minutes . . ."

The ten turned into forty-five, and she didn't get out of the office until after five. Fortunately, her knee was much better today, and she was able to run. Nevertheless, she still missed her flight. There was an accident on the interstate, blocking two lanes, and by the time she finally arrived at the airport and sprinted to the terminal, the plane was in the air.

Avery toyed with the idea of going back home and crashing in her own bed. She hadn't averaged more than four hours' sleep a night in over a week, and she was exhausted. She didn't dare give in to the urge, though. Carrie would kill her if she were a full day late.

Utopia wasn't her idea of a great vacation. She was going only to please her aunt. When she went someplace new, she wanted to see the sights, soak in the local color. She didn't relish the idea of being stuck in a spa for six days, but Avery had given her word, so she couldn't back out.

The next flight through Denver into Aspen was full, and she was forced to take a convoluted route from D.C. She ended up in Grand Junction, Colorado. She would have to wait until morning to board yet another flight. After she collected her luggage and checked into the hotel adjacent to the airport, she called Carrie on her cell phone. She got her voice mail on the first ring. She assumed her aunt was recharging her phone and had already gone to bed — it was midnight Aspen time. She left a message that she would arrive at the spa around noon tomorrow.

Then she called the spa to let them know she was delayed. Since she'd left a message on

Carrie's cell phone, she didn't ask the receptionist to connect her to her aunt's suite.

That night Avery slept like the dead. The following morning, while she ate her continental breakfast of toast, juice, and milk, she called her office voice mail. There were over twenty messages in her mailbox, but fortunately none of them was urgent. She made notes as she listened and then erased each one. Carrie's message made her smile. She sounded so excited about staying in a mountain house where Tom Cruise had allegedly been a guest. How like her aunt to get stars in her eyes over such a silly little thing. Avery erased that message and continued on until she was finally finished.

She was downstairs and checking out by eight-fifteen. While the receptionist printed her bill, Avery looked over a map of Colorado. Aspen wasn't all that far from Grand Junction, just two and a half hours away by car. Then she heard an elderly couple talking about the lovely sights in the area, and on the spur of the moment, she decided to rent a car and drive to the spa. She took the shuttle back to the airport, rented a sedan, and headed out.

Avery was wearing her weekend uniform, a pair of old jeans, a plain white T-shirt, and a pair of scuffed tennis shoes. Carrie wouldn't approve of the outfit, but Avery opted for comfort over fashion.

Once she was on I-70 heading east toward Aspen, she felt as if she was really on vacation. It was a beautiful, crisp, summer morning. The sun was shining, and the sky was such a brilliant shade of blue it looked almost artificial. She rolled the window down and took a deep breath. It was wonderful. The air was so clean and light, as though she were breathing pure oxygen. It was a refreshing change after the smog of the big, overcrowded city.

She stopped at a McDonald's for a bottle of water and a Diet Coke. After she paid for her order, she sat down in one of the booths to look over the map. There might be an interesting side trip she could take on her way to the spa, maybe see something historical. She knew that once she checked in, Carrie wouldn't let her leave, and she did want to see a little of Colorado. What she'd already seen on her drive was beautiful, but she felt she was only glimpsing a tip of what the state had to offer. Besides, Carrie was going to be irritated anyway because Avery was late. What difference did it make if she was another hour or two behind schedule?

She spread the map on the table in front of her and, first of all, tried to find the spot where Carrie had told her she'd spent the night. What was it? Land of the Lakes? No, that wasn't it.

"Are you lost, darlin'?"

The deep baritone voice jarred her. Annoyed her too. She simply wasn't in the mood to get hit on. Suppressing a sigh, she frowned as she looked up, ready to tell whoever was trying to bother her to go away, but then she saw the gentleman standing before her and she smiled. He was at least eighty years old. Immaculately dressed in a freshly pressed denim shirt with a turquoise bolo tie, and Levi's tucked into tan cowboy boots with scrollwork around the tops, he held a tan Stetson in one hand and a cup of steaming coffee in the other. His face was full of character, from his sparkling golden brown eyes and his leathered complexion to the handlebar mustache that was perfectly waxed and groomed. Both his mustache and his hair were pure white.

"Excuse me?"

"I asked you if you were lost," he repeated. "I saw you looking over that map, and I figured I might be able to help you get where you're wanting to go since I know just about every little nook and cranny in Colorado. I've lived here all my eighty-four years, come September."

"I was just looking over places of interest," she said. "Actually, I could use your help. Would you care to join me?"

"I'd be delighted," he said. He put his coffee down, then scooted into the booth across from her and carefully placed his Stetson on the seat next to him. "Can't stay but a couple of minutes. My granddaughter will be swinging by to pick me up. She's got a nice little Western store, and I help her with the customers two days a week. That's why I'm duded up," he explained. "Now, where are you headed?"

"Aspen."

"You couldn't be lost then. There are signs all around you. Aspen's just a few miles away."

"Yes, I know," she said. "But I was trying to locate an area called Land of the Lakes or Around the Lakes. Have you ever heard of such a place?"

"If you're talking about Land Between the Lakes, then, yes, I sure have heard of it. My name's Walt Gentry, by the way."

"Avery Delaney," she said as she offered her hand to shake his.

"It's a pleasure to meet you," he said. He moved his coffee so he wouldn't knock it when he stacked his hands on the table and said, "You won't find the place on that map, so you might as well stop looking. Most folks outside of Colorado wouldn't even know about it. You see, people come in here from California and Washington and buy a couple of acres of land. Then they build themselves a big house, and they think they ought to name the place, like it was the Ponderosa or something. Now, a fella named Parnell, Dennis Parnell, purchased about forty acres of prime land up high above Aspen some time back. He shouldn't have been able to buy it, but he did," he added with a shrug. "Then, about six years ago, he decided to build his dream home up there. It took more than two and a half years to finish it, and Parnell made those environmentalists crazy tearing up that beautiful, untamed land the way he did. Big old semis going up and down the mountain, tearing out trees to make

120

room for a road. It was a crying shame what he did, but Parnell got away with it because money talks, and he got every kind of permit he needed. Don't think that could happen today," he added. "In the last couple of years, we got stronger laws passed protecting our land. Anyway," he continued, "when Parnell's house was all finished, he put up a big fence all the way around it. I heard the house came in at eight million, but that was a few years ago, so I'm sure the price has more than doubled. It was rumored that Parnell paid cash and owns the house and the land free and clear. I didn't believe that gossip, but folks around here did, and then, of course, they had to speculate as to where he could have gotten his hands on so much money."

Avery was caught up in the story. "How did he?"

"Folks thought it must be drug money, but turns out Parnell owned a little computer company out in Silicon Valley. One of his engineers designed a new computer chip that revolutionized the business. Don't understand any of it," he admitted. "But since that engineer worked for Parnell, he got the patent. He made his fortune, sold the company before it went belly-up, and moved here."

"He doesn't still own the place, does he?" she asked, thinking that Parnell must have sold it to the owner of Utopia to use as a retreat for important visitors.

"He does and he doesn't," Walt replied. "This

is where the story takes a sordid turn. Parnell got married at the church about a mile from here. It was quite an event too, and cost a fortune. Five hundred people were invited to the reception," he said. "I heard it took a year to plan the big party. They even had flowers flown in from Europe. I guess the flowers in the United States weren't good enough. Anyway, the planning of the marriage lasted longer than the union. Parnell was only married eighteen months when he filed for divorce."

He paused to shake his head. Then he got sidetracked. "I sure don't understand this modern world. Me and my wife, Ona May, have been married forty-seven years, and sure, there have been times when I wanted to leave and never come back. I imagine she felt the same way every now and again, but we stayed together because we said our vows and we meant them. Now I read in the papers about this new trend called 'starter marriages.' Have you ever heard of them?"

She smiled. "I've heard the term."

"I don't understand it," he said. "Those couples ought to just live together and leave the vows out of it. I think Parnell thought he was in a starter marriage, the way he filed so quick. It's been a real nasty divorce with lots of mudslinging, which of course hits the papers. People gobble that trash right up. He filed over a year ago, and it's still dragging on. Everyone's waiting to hear who's gonna end up owning that house. The soon-to-be-ex-wife swears he promised it to her, and she thinks she ought to be able to keep it. The judge is deciding now which one of them is going to get it. Pamela Parnell says she'll die before she lets him have it, and he says that's fine with him. They're both acting like five-year-olds, if you ask me. Just last week Parnell gave another interview and was quoted as saying that no matter what the judge ruled, he was never gonna let his ex have that house. Those two are quite a pair," he added. "But the folks around and in Aspen are just as bad. Do you know they got a lottery going?"

"You mean they're betting over which one gets the house?"

"That's right. The odds are ninety to ten in favor of Pamela Parnell getting it because of the shady way Dennis got himself those permits. There's talk he'll be indicted. And the judge who's deciding which one of those sorry characters will get the house is a real dedicated environmentalist. Time will tell, I suppose."

He leaned forward, tapped the map with his forefinger. "Right there," he said. "That's Land Between the Lakes. It was so named, you see, because it sits between two big, clear-water lakes. Have you got a pen on you? I could circle it for you."

Avery dug through her backpack, found a ballpoint pen, and handed it to Walt. His fingers were crippled with arthritis. He had trouble holding the pen as he made the circle.

"From where we're sitting, it's about a two-hour drive away. There are some other fancy homes up there, but you won't get near any of them because all the roads are privately owned and gated."

"I thought my aunt was staying at a retreat called Land Between the Lakes, but I must have been mistaken. Maybe I didn't hear her correctly. There was a lot of static on the line."

"Could she have said Twin Lakes?" he asked. "Now, Land Between the Lakes is up north, but Twin Lakes is south of here, and it is marked on the map."

He pointed to the location. Avery nodded, then folded the map and put it in her backpack. She shook his hand again as she stood. "Thank you for helping me," she said.

"It was my pleasure," he replied. "You be sure to buckle up, darlin'. There are some crazy drivers out there, taking those winding roads at seventy miles an hour. They're begging for death. Don't you let them take you with them."

She got back in the car and started out again. Guilt prevented her from taking any side trips. Besides, she had soaked up a little local color when she'd visited with Walt. He was a genteel old man, and she'd thoroughly enjoyed listening to him.

Maybe she could talk Carrie into doing a little hiking. That thought was so absurd, she laughed. Avery had heard that her aunt actually had been quite a jock in high school. She'd played volleyball, basketball, and just about every other sport that was offered. Avery remembered playing with Carrie's tennis trophies. Did her aunt still have them, or had she thrown them away? Oh, well, no matter. Carrie definitely wasn't an outdoors girl now. She detested exercise.

Carrie's goal for her stay at Utopia was to be pampered, not whipped into shape. Avery sighed loudly. She hoped to heaven Carrie didn't make her do all that girly stuff with her, like mud baths and seaweed wraps. It wasn't that she had anything against being pampered, but she didn't have all that much time to have fun, and she would rather get muddy exploring the countryside.

Avery drove through Aspen and continued on. An hour later she was certain she was lost. She was about to pull over and check the map again when she spotted the sign for Utopia. The road curved sharply, then climbed and narrowed to a gravel driveway. Then the gate came into view. She stopped to give her name to the guard on duty.

"Your name isn't on the list for today's check-ins."

"I have a reservation," she insisted. "My name should be there."

He moved closer to the car and smiled. "I'm sure it's just a mix-up. You can straighten it out at the front desk."

"Thanks," she called out as she drove through.

They certainly were friendly at the spa if the

guard was an indicator. She glanced in her rear-view mirror and saw him standing in the middle of the road watching her drive away.

His salt-and-pepper hair reminded her of her Uncle Tony. Oh, Lord, she forgot to call him last night. As soon as she checked into her room, she'd do just that. Tony was such a worrier. Avery knew that he and Carrie were having problems, but she hoped that they would be able to work them out. Carrie was probably the reason they weren't getting along. Although Avery loved her aunt with all her heart, she wasn't blind to her faults. Carrie could be a real pain sometimes. Marrying Tony was the best thing she had ever done, and maybe, while she was relaxing at the spa, she would take the time to think about her priorities. She had always taken Tony for granted, and no marriage could survive long that way. Fortunately, her uncle had the patience of a saint. He'd hung in there longer than any other man would have.

She went around another sharp curve. For Pete's sake, where was the spa? Since passing through the gate, she had to have driven halfway up the mountain, and she was completely surrounded by wilderness. Then, when she was sure she must have taken a service road by mistake at the last fork, Utopia came into view.

It was aptly named. "My goodness," she whispered. The place was gorgeous and seemed to radiate tranquility. The buff-colored stucco buildings were nestled in the lush landscape of towering evergreens. The main structure looked as though it were part of the sloping mountain. Small bungalows dotted the hillside with stone paths winding in and around the thick pines. There were wildflowers everywhere. She could hear the sound of rushing water. She turned and saw a fountain of steps built into the side of the lower hill. The bubbling water rolled down the slate and splashed over a golden sphere suspended in a circular pool.

A maintenance truck pulled out in front of Avery's car from a service road. She braked and waited as the crew quickly unloaded some barrels, her gaze taking in the beauty and serenity of her surroundings. A young couple, obviously in love, caught her attention. They were holding hands as they strolled down the path parallel to the fountain. They stopped halfway, turned to each another, and kissed passionately.

Avery felt a pang of envy and forced herself to look away. And then she couldn't stop herself from glancing back at the couple and noticing the way they looked into each other's eyes. They were probably newlyweds, she thought.

The truck moved out of her path, and with a sigh, she drove up the steep incline. At the crest was a cobblestone circle drive. Huge clay pots overflowing with ivy and pink and yellow flowers were placed liked sentinels in front of the marble steps leading up to the entrance.

People were coming and going, all at a sedate pace. Like the lovey-dovey couple on the hillside, the guests were dressed in identical navy blue jogging suits. On the jacket, above the breast pocket, was a little logo of a sphere with the name of the spa printed in gold thread.

Avery put the car in park as the doorman rushed forward. He opened her door, put his hand out to assist her, and said, "Welcome to Utopia."

# CHAPTER 6

Monk was in love. Though he hadn't believed such a miracle could happen, he had met the woman of his dreams, and since then he had been acting like a crazy, ridiculous fool. Jilly was his soul mate. No doubt about it. They were absolutely perfect for each other, for they shared the same dreams, the same fantasies, the same goals, and most important of all, the same sense of unfair play.

She had hypnotized him from the moment they'd met in that dirty nameless little bar and grill on the outskirts of Savannah. His breath had caught in his throat when she walked in, a vision in a silky red dress and red stiletto heels. She was simply . . . magnificent. As he had instructed over the phone, he was waiting in the corner booth with a blue folder in his hands. When she saw him, she smiled, and in that instant, he knew he was lost.

The bloom of first love hadn't worn off. He still ached with his love for her. Even when he was supposed to be working, he couldn't stop smiling. These days his mind only had room for thoughts of her. While he was doing the necessary drudge work of surveillance, one of his favorite ways to pass the time was to recall, to the most intimate detail, the first time they had made love. It had happened exactly three hours after they had met. Jilly had taken him back to her hotel room, stripped him of his clothes and his inhibitions, and had made passionate love to him. He closed his eyes in bliss as the memory flooded his senses. The sweet taste of her in his mouth, the musky scent of her perfume, the heat of her silky body pressed against his, the deep, almost animal sounds she made when he touched her just so. She had been wild, forceful, and rough — just the way he liked it — and yet, at the same time, she had been exquisitely vulnerable.

Monk marveled over his lack of discipline when it came to Jilly. Never in his wildest imagination would he have believed he was capable of silly romantic behavior, or that he would ever marry. Yet, two months ago he had proposed — down on one knee, no less — and she had thrilled him with her acceptance. He told her he would do anything for her, anything at all, and then set about proving it. Desperate to please her, he knew he was putty in her hands, yet he couldn't seem to mind.

Jilly was the first person in the world whom he completely trusted to keep his secrets. He knew all of hers too. They had been living together for four months when, late one night, after they had made love and were cuddling together on the sofa in their silk robes and sipping chilled champagne, he opened up to her and told her all about his bleak life on the dried-up patch of farmland in Nebraska with his dried-up, stern, joyless parents. His father hadn't believed in sparing the rod, and his mother, a weakling who was afraid of her own shadow and who never went anywhere or did anything outside of the home except church on Sunday mornings, would stand with her hands folded behind her back and watch as her husband tried to whip the wanderlust out of their only child. Monk learned early in life never to complain to her because she always told his father what he had said. By the time he was ten, he hated both of them and would fall asleep at night dreaming of new ways to torture them.

His life had been claustrophobic. He stole money from the church safe — just a little here and there on Sundays. After he graduated from high school, he packed up his bag, a grocery sack actually, and left the farm. He went to college in Omaha. He had enough saved to pay for the first semester and received government loans to pay the rest of the tuition, loans he never intended to repay. Four years later, he left the state of Nebraska, vowing never to return.

To this day, he didn't know if his parents were dead or alive, and he didn't particularly care.

He'd never really cared about anyone — until now.

He told Jilly everything about himself. He told her he had committed his first murder at the ripe old age of twenty-two. He also told her he had once had dreams of working in the theater. He loved getting into costume and taking on different roles. And he was a good actor, he boasted, so good that he tried out for a major part in a summer stock play. Another actor mocked his performance and humiliated him in front of the director. Monk became so rattled by the heckling that he made a mess of his audition and, of course, didn't get the part. Vowing to get even, he bided his time, and two years later he went after the boy. He'd used his knife that time and had found the experience both exciting and liberating.

"When did you change your name?" she asked.

"The day I enrolled in college," he said. "I had a fake birth certificate, and I managed to make it look real enough to fool the administrator's office. It was really quite crude, but it got the job done."

"I didn't get to go to college," she told him. "I wanted to, but my mother didn't think I was smart enough. She took the money I'd saved and used it to pay for Carrie's education."

"What was your life like growing up?"

Jilly's eyes welled up with tears. "Loveless," she said. "I don't remember my father. He left when I was little. It was because of her."

"Your mother?"

"Yes," she said. "She drove him away. He ran

off with another woman, but looking back, I can't blame him. Mama was a cold and bitter woman. She never showed me any affection, and I think that's why I got into trouble . . . you know . . . got pregnant. I was looking for someone to love me. I shamed the family. I can't tell you the number of times my sister and mother shouted those very words at me." She shook her head and then whispered, "I was such an innocent fool. I was so sure that, once I had the baby, my mother and my sister, the golden girl, would forgive me and help me raise her. I wanted to do the right thing by my child."

"But that didn't happen, did it?"

She gripped his hand. "No, it didn't. It was so awful. Mama and Carrie came to the hospital. I thought they were going to take me and my daughter home."

"What happened, my love?" he asked when she was too overcome to continue. He leaned forward to pour more champagne into her glass.

"Carrie left the hospital room with my daughter. She never said a word to me. She just went to the bassinet, picked her up, and left. Mama grabbed my arm when I tried to go after my sister. I asked her where Carrie was going with my beautiful baby, and she said that she was taking little Avery home. 'Avery.' That's the stupid name my mama came up with for my daughter." She wiped the tears away from her face with her fingertips. "They wouldn't even let me name my own child. Carrie was making all the decisions, telling Mama what she ought to do, and Mama went along with whatever her golden girl decreed."

"And then what happened?"

"Mama told me I had to leave town and that I could never come home again. She said I had humiliated her and Carrie for the last time. I couldn't get through to her, and even though I begged her to forgive me, she wouldn't. I can still see that ugly, pinched look on her face. It was just like Carrie's. She called me terrible names, and then she opened her pocketbook and pulled out a hundred-dollar bill. She threw it in my face and walked out of the room."

"Wasn't there anyone who would help you?"

She shook her head. "Mama was real tight with the chief of police. She had him wound around her little finger. He used to drop by late every other night when Carrie and I were supposed to be sleeping, but one night I heard all this groaning and grunting going on, and I snuck down to see what was happening. I peeked in the living room, and there was the chief sprawled out as pretty as you please on our sofa with his pants down around his ankles. Mama was kneeling between his legs, servicing him. The fat pig was a married man," she added. "And he'd do anything to keep Mama from telling his wife about their sordid affair. Mama told me that the chief would lock me up in jail if I didn't leave town right away. I knew she had the power to make him do it."

She was sobbing uncontrollably now. He put his arm around her and held her close until she was able to calm down. Then he asked, "What happened to your daughter?"

"Carrie raised her and brainwashed her against me. My sister has always hated me. She wasn't . . . pretty the way I was, and she was eaten up with jealousy. Stealing my baby was her way of getting even with me, I suppose."

"How did you meet Dale Skarrett?" he asked.

"After I left Sheldon Beach, I worked odd jobs to support myself. I was trying to save up enough money to hire a lawyer and get my baby back. I didn't have any training to do much of anything, so I worked in bars and restaurants. I stole money a couple of times to help pay the rent, and I slept with men too. Twelve in all," she admitted. "I kept count . . . I don't know why, but I did, and I took every precaution so I wouldn't get any disgusting diseases. I hated doing it, but I needed the money. I was so desperate to get my daughter back." She turned away as she recalled the anguish. "Then, one night when I was working at a flea-infested bar down in Savannah, I met Dale Skarrett. God, he disgusted me," she said. "But he had money. He made sure I saw the wad of bills, and he wanted me. We lived together off and on for what seemed an eternity. I tried to move on with my life, but he kept coming back. And then one night he told me about this jewelry store he and his buddies, Frank and Larry,

135

were going to rob. Larry was shacking up with the daughter of the owner of the store, and she liked to talk about her family's money. Dale pretty much planned the robbery, but I helped with all the details."

"So you were an accomplice."

"Yes," she said. "The robbery went off without a hitch, but Frank had a big mouth, and he started talking about all the money he was going to get when Dale sold the diamonds. Dale had hid the uncut stones, and we had all agreed to wait at least six months before fencing them."

"But things went wrong, didn't they?"

"Oh, yes. An informant told the police about Frank's bragging. They picked him up for questioning, and he ended up making a deal with them. He gave them Larry's name, but he didn't give them Dale's or my name until later. He was holding out for a better deal, I guess. Larry called us and warned us in time, and we were able to get out of town. Larry didn't make it, though. There was a shootout, and Larry killed a policeman before he was killed."

Jilly started crying again. "I didn't care about the diamonds. Dale promised me that he'd help me get my daughter back. That was going to be my cut for helping him with the robbery. We drove back to Sheldon Beach, and he went to Mama's house to get Avery. I didn't look at it as kidnapping. I was simply taking back what my sister had stolen from me. I didn't know Carrie had made Mama go to court to have Carrie named Avery's legal guardian. The court took away all my rights as a mother and gave them to my sister. She stole my baby from me, Monk. She stole her . . ."

"I know your heart's breaking, my love."

"Avery was just a little girl when Dale went to get her, but Carrie had already turned her against me. Dale told me he tried to calm Avery down by telling her how much I loved her and that she would be happy with me. Avery became hysterical. God only knows what horrid lies Carrie had told her. She fought him like a tigress, kicking and trying to scratch his eyes out. He said he took off his belt to tie her hands together and that he gave her a couple of swats to get her to stop her tantrum."

Monk handed her another Kleenex so she could wipe her tears away. "Go on. You'll feel better after you get all that poison out."

She nodded. "Yes, you're right. Avery's screams woke Mama. She came running out with a gun in her hand. The chief of police had given it to her for protection. She tried to kill Dale. He told me he was backing away with Avery when she fired the gun. She shot my daughter by mistake." She shuddered. "Dale didn't tell me about that for a long time, so I didn't go to the hospital to see her."

"What happened with your mother?"

"When she saw what she had done, Dale said she screamed, then suddenly clutched her chest

137

and fell down. She was dead before she hit the floor . . . according to Dale."

"Heart attack?"

"Yes, but I didn't cry about her dying. She had turned against me, and I pretty much did the same to her. I didn't shed a single tear," she said proudly.

"I understand."

"Dale tried to keep his promise to me. He followed Avery when she went to live with my sister in California. He watched her school, thinking he could grab her when she came outside. She had a bodyguard, though, an FBI agent looking out for her. Carrie obviously convinced them that Dale would come after Avery. My sister is very clever," she added with a sneer. "She must have alerted the principal because he told the security guards that Dale was dangerous. There was always someone watching her. Dale tried to grab her as she was crossing the campus, but the FBI agent spotted him and tackled him to the ground. Dale wasn't armed," she added. "He was arrested and sent back to Florida to stand trial for my mother's death."

"And he was convicted."

"Yes. The autopsy report proved Mama had a heart attack, but the jury still believed Dale was responsible."

"And you don't?"

"I really don't care if he was responsible or not, but Mama did have a bad heart. I have something to confess now, darling. Please don't be angry. Let me explain before you react."

"I could never become angry with you. I promise," he said.

"Do you remember the money you gave me to pay off all my debts?"

"The thirty thousand?"

"Yes," she whispered. Her hand slid under his robe, and she began to caress his chest. "I gave most of the money to an attorney as a retainer."

"Why?" he asked. "Why did you need an attorney?"

"I hired him to help Dale. I want to get him out of prison, and now it looks like that might happen. When the attorney was going through the boxes of evidence, he found a bill from a cardiologist in Savannah. He went to see him," she continued. "And the doctor told him my mother's condition was fatal. More important, he said that he had come forward and told the prosecutor that he had treated Mama, but the prosecutors withheld that information from the public defender who had been assigned to represent Dale."

Monk was suddenly feeling insecure and angry, but he contained his emotions.

"Go on," he said.

"The attorney I hired did it," she said. "Dale's getting a new trial, and it's going to be soon. The judge was outraged when he heard that the prosecutor had suppressed evidence to help him win. It seems there's bad blood between the two men, and this was the last straw. Dale's attorney told me another case was postponed, and the judge gave Dale that opening. Carrie and Avery can't testify. Dale will stay in prison if they do."

"What about the parole hearing? Is that still scheduled?"

"Yes, but the trial should be over by then. If Dale doesn't get out of prison, I'll never get those diamonds. After all I've been through, I think I deserve them. Of course, whatever I get belongs to you too. Am I being too greedy?"

"No, I don't think so," he said. "But you must be honest with me now. Do you have feelings for Dale?"

"Oh, God, no," she cried. "I've always hated him, and I know how I can prove it to you."

"How?" he asked, intrigued by the sly smile of hers he found so titillating.

"As soon as Dale leads us to the diamonds, I'll let you watch me kill him."

All of his insecurities faded with that promise. She kissed him then and whispered, "I love you with all my heart. I would die rather than hurt you. Killing Dale will prove my love, but I want proof from you as well."

"What can I do?" he asked. He wasn't a man given to poetry, but he tried to be romantic as he vowed, "If you wish me to walk on water, I swear I'll find a way to do it. I'll do anything for you, dearest Jilly. Anything at all."

She snuggled up against him. "My sister and Avery both spoke at the last parole hearing," she said. "They're the reason he didn't get out then."

"And you want me to find a way to keep your sister and your daughter away from the trial and the parole hearing this time? Is that what you want?"

"Darling, I don't want you to just keep them away. I want you to make it impossible for them to testify. I want you to kill them."

# CHAPTER 7

Carrie woke up in a cold sweat. The nightmare
had consumed her, terrified her. Trembling like
a child, she wrapped herself in the down comforter and tried to calm her racing heartbeat.
She felt as if she were having a heart attack. She
put her hand to her chest and took a couple of
deep breaths. The nightmare had been so real.
My God, what had brought that on? She hadn't
thought about Jilly in years. Why was her sister
suddenly tormenting her sleep again?

Maybe she was just overly tired. Yes, that was
it, she thought, latching onto the possibility. It
made sense, didn't it? She had been working
seventy-, eighty-hour weeks for the past two
months, firming up and then nailing the incredibly lucrative Bliss account. The contracts were
all signed and delivered, and now that she could
finally slow the pace, her overloaded brain had
simply had a minor meltdown.

Rolling onto her back, she closed her eyes
against the piercing sunlight streaming in between the partially opened drapes and tried to

remember some of the yoga exercises Avery had taught her. Take deep, cleansing breaths. She remembered that much. Clear the mind and concentrate on relaxing every muscle of the body. Okay, it was coming back to her. First the toes. Then the legs. That's it, she thought. Now relax, damn it.

It wasn't working. Anxiety, like the boogeyman hiding in the closet, was still lurking, waiting to pounce.

For heaven's sake, it was just a nightmare. Vivid as hell, but still not real, so stop freaking out.

Carrie wished Valium were still in vogue. She would have taken a couple to soothe her nerves. Then she realized she was calming down. Her heart no longer felt as though it were trying to leap out of her chest like one of those creatures in *Alien*.

What she needed was a good long shower. Carrie threw the covers off and sat up. What time was it? Did the sun come up brighter here in the mountains than in L.A.? Of course it did, because there wasn't any smog.

Coffee, she thought. I'll ring for coffee. The caffeine will clear the fog in my head, and I'll be able to start thinking like a human being again.

Carrie was swinging her legs over the side of the bed when she saw them. There, pointed toward her on the nightstand, was a pair of shiny steel-bladed scissors. She froze, the scream lodged in her throat. She couldn't make herself look away, couldn't make the scissors disappear.

Her heart was slamming against her rib cage again. Could a person die of fright? Was this some kind of a sick joke? No. Whoever had put the scissors there couldn't possibly know about her nightmare. Think, damn it. Try to think.

Were they real? Carrie tentatively reached out to touch them, thinking she was having some kind of hallucination. When her fingers touched the hard, cold steel handle, she whimpered. Son of a bitch, they were real.

There had to be a reasonable explanation. Maybe the scissors had been there on the night-stand the night before, and while she hadn't consciously noticed, her subconscious had picked up on them. The possibility sounded desperate, but she clung to it. Then she spotted the yellow, invitation-sized envelope with her name handwritten in beautiful script propped up against the lamp. She was positive it hadn't been there the night before. Her hand trembled as she picked it up and opened it. The stationery was expensive, but there wasn't a Utopia seal or logo printed on it, or a return address.

"What the hell is going on?" she whispered. And then she pulled the two sheets out, unfolded them, and read the note.

Carrie:
Did you mourn me when you heard I died in that car crash so many years ago? Or did you celebrate? You always believed you were

so superior. I was just a stupid girl. Do you remember how you called me that? I've never forgotten. Your biggest problem was that you always underestimated me. Always. Surely you recall how I so loved to get even. That glorious day has finally arrived, and now you're right where I want you to be.

The house is wired, Carrie, and there isn't any way out. If you open a window or an outside door . . . boom. A simple push of a button and the house will disintegrate. Do you wonder how long I'll wait?

Tick. Tick. Are you scared?

Shall I tell you how I plotted and planned? I began by finding the man of my dreams. He loves me, of course, but then they all do, don't they? This one is very special. A perfectionist, actually. His name is Monk, and when I first seduced him, I must say he was terribly set in his ways. He's a hit man, my hit man, though he prefers to be called a professional.

He does whatever I ask him to do, and in return I've taught him how to have fun with his job. He's a proud man, proud of what he does, and he's careful and methodical, and so he won't let me make any mistakes. In the past, he only took on one job at a time, but I've convinced him to reach for bigger and better. He'd already contracted to blow up the house. It just took a little more planning to kill a few inconsequential women at the same time.

You know why you must die. You stole my dream from me and gave it away. You took my child from me too, and you turned her against me. Those are just two reasons, Carrie, but when all is said and done, your biggest sin is that you have made me un-happy.

Jilly

P.S. Don't worry about Avery. I'm going to take care of her too.

Carrie screamed once and began to sob. She was terrified. Shaking, she leapt from the bed and ran to the sliding glass doors. She grabbed a fistful of the drapes, ripped them out of her way, and looked outside. Then down. She saw the blinking red light protruding from the explosives, as evil and horrific as the devil's eye, and shouted, "Oh, God, oh, God . . ."

She ran for the bedroom door, tripped over her shoes and slammed her right foot into the bedpost. Pain shot up her calf. Cursing, she continued on. She stopped short in the hallway just outside her door and called out, "Is anyone there?"

Nothing. Not a sound. Too late, she realized she should have grabbed the scissors to use as a weapon just in case someone had been waiting, but Jilly had touched those scissors. Jilly, who had written the horrific, gleeful letter. Jilly, the psycho.

God help them all.

She edged along the wall to the spiral staircase. She was afraid to look down, afraid not to. It took her a good minute to get up the courage, and then relief, sweet, sweet relief, made her weak because no one was looking up at her. Maybe Carrie and Sara and Anne were all alone in the house. No, not a house now. A bomb.

She ran down the stairs, then raced to the judge's suite. She didn't bother to knock, but threw the door open and rushed inside.

The room was pitch black. Carrie couldn't even see her hand in front of her face. She felt her way across the sitting room, nearly knocking over a lamp when her elbow bumped into the shade. She grabbed it, and finally got it turned on.

Sara was in bed. Carrie could see a form huddled under the blanket, but she couldn't see her face. The drapes were tightly drawn. Carrie opened them and looked down. "Son of a bitch," she muttered. There it was, another blinking red light.

Turning, she slowly approached the side of the bed as she strained to hear the sound of Sara's breathing. She couldn't hear anything but the noise of the air conditioner as it kicked on.

Carrie gently shook her. "Wake up, Sara," she ordered.

She didn't move. She shook her again, much harder this time. "Come on, Sara. You have to wake up." Sara groaned.

She put her hand on Sara's wrist, feeling for a

pulse with her fingertips. When she finally found it, she felt like shouting with relief.

Carrie knew what had happened. The food they'd eaten last night had been drugged, but because she had thrown up, she'd gotten rid of most of the poison. How much had Sara and Anne eaten?

She grabbed Sara by her shoulders and started shaking her. "Open your eyes, damn it. Wake up, Sara."

Another groan was her only response. Carrie looked at the clock on the bureau and saw that it was already one in the afternoon. Then she turned to the nightstand, and just as she expected, there was another envelope propped against the lamp with Sara's name written on it. The handwriting was identical.

Should she open it?

"Go away."

Carrie jumped at the sound of Sara's gruff voice. She was struggling to open her eyes. Carrie stepped back as Sara rolled onto her back and told her once again to go away.

"No," she said. "Keep your eyes open. You have to wake up."

Sara heard her. She struggled to sit up but only made it halfway before she collapsed against the pillows. She focused on Carrie, awareness slow to penetrate.

"What . . . what are you doing here?"

"Listen to me," Carrie ordered. "You've been drugged. Do you understand what I'm saying?

Please, try to pay attention. We're in trouble."

"Drugged?" She shook her head. "No, I don't take drugs."

In her frustration, she shouted at the woman. "They put it in the food, Sara. Can you understand what I'm saying?"

"Yes. You're telling me the food was drugged?"

"Yes, that's right," Carrie said. "Keep your eyes open. I'm going to get a cold wet cloth. Come on, Sara," she coaxed. "Sit up."

By the time Carrie returned from the adjoining bath with a washcloth dripping with cold water, Sara had managed to pull herself up. Her shoulders were pressed against the headboard.

She looked at Carrie as though she was only just now seeing her. "Why are you in my room?"

Carrie tried to put the wet cloth on Sara's face, but the woman knocked it away.

"We're in trouble," she repeated. "I have to go wake Anne. So you have to listen to what I'm going to tell you. Okay? Can you concentrate yet?"

"Will you stop shouting at me? I'm awake now. What kind of trouble are you talking about?"

"The house is wired."

Sara blinked. "I don't understand."

"We're prisoners," Carrie said. "If one of us opens a door or a window, the house will blow up. Look at the glass door," she urged. "See the red blinking light?"

Sara wouldn't believe her. "This is just some kind of sick prank."

"No, it isn't," she said. Then she grabbed the envelope from the nightstand. "Open it," she said. "I got one too. Bring the letter with you down to the living room, and I'll bring mine. Even if you can't believe it, don't open any windows or doors. Okay? Now I've got to get to Anne before she wakes up and decides to open a window."

Sara nodded. "All right. I'll meet you downstairs."

She was opening the envelope when Carrie rushed out of the room. Anne's suite was at the opposite end on the same level. She ran to it.

Anne wasn't in bed. Carrie could hear her in the bathroom. She was throwing up. Carrie went to the door and knocked. "Anne, do you need help?"

She didn't answer her. Carrie tried again and again. She didn't know how long she stood there pounding on the door. Finally, Anne opened it.

The frail woman looked green. "What do you want?" she asked. She was swaying on her feet.

"Let me help," Carrie said. She put her arm around her waist, thinking it was the size of a pencil, and helped her back to bed.

"You should stay away from me," Anne said, her voice weak. "I've got some kind of a bug. Now you'll get it."

"No," Carrie said. "You don't have a bug." She was all but carrying the woman across the room. When she reached the bed, she pulled the sheet back and helped Anne sit down.

"I was up half the night, throwing up," she said. "Of course I have a bug. It's probably just one of those twenty-four-hour viruses.

There wasn't an envelope on Anne's nightstand. "You were up all night?" she asked as she helped the woman into bed. "Did you hear anyone . . . see anyone?"

"No, I didn't," she answered. "Let go of me. I don't want to lie down." She adjusted the pillows and slowly leaned back on one elbow.

"We were all drugged," Carrie explained. "The stuff had to have been in the food we ate."

"That's ridiculous. It was spoiled food, that's what it was. Am I going to give them an earful when I get to the spa. I could sue," she said. "And I just might. First, the inconvenience at the airport and now food poisoning. It's simply unforgivable."

Carrie didn't argue. She plodded ahead, telling about the envelopes she and Sara had received.

"The most important thing you need to know is that there are detonators on every window and door in this house. If we open one of them, the house will blow up."

Anne was looking at her as though she'd lost her mind. "Oh, for heaven's sake. What's the matter with you, trying to scare me like this?"

"I'm not trying to scare you. I'm telling you the truth. Did you find an envelope with your name on it?"

"No, I did not."

The answer was too quick, too angry. Carrie knew she was lying, but for the life of her, she couldn't understand why.

"Anne, we're all in this together. You have to tell the truth."

Indignant, she responded, "I am telling you the truth. Now get out of here and leave me alone."

"No," Carrie said. "I don't know how much time we have, and we have to find a way to get out of here without triggering the explosives."

Anne's pinched face was rapidly turning red. "I asked you to leave."

Carrie tried a different approach. "Sara and I . . . we need you, Anne. We have to work together to figure out what is going on."

Anne glared at her. "Why do you need me?"

"Because you're smart."

"You couldn't possibly know if I'm smart or not."

"You ran your own company, didn't you? That's what you told me."

Anne's chin came up a notch. As she smoothed the sheets around her waist, she said, "I started on a shoestring and turned my little hobby — that's what my father called my shipping company — into a forty-million-dollar operation. By next January, I'll have increased my profit margin to quadruple the amount my accountants anticipated."

Carrie didn't have time for this. To be forced to pander to the stupid woman's ego just to gain her cooperation was outrageous. Didn't Anne realize what they were all up against?

With effort, Carrie was able to control her temper. "Do you think you could join Sara and me downstairs in the living room to talk about our situation? We could sure use your . . . advice on how to proceed."

Anne tilted her head to the side and stared at Carrie for a long minute without saying a word. Then she shook her head. "You're really serious about this story of yours, aren't you? You believe —"

"It's true," she snapped.

Anne nodded. "What is your name? I've forgotten."

"Carolyn," she answered, trying not to shout at the obtuse woman. "You may call me Carrie if you like."

"All right, Carrie. I'll join you and Sara downstairs."

"If you don't feel strong enough, Sara and I could come in here —"

"What makes you think I'm not strong enough?" She sounded angry again.

"I heard you in the bathroom. You were throwing up."

"You said the food was poisoned."

"Yes."

"That's why I was throwing up. I'm not sick."

Who gives a damn if you're sick or not, she longed to ask. She took a deep breath, nodded, and said, "All right. Come downstairs."

"I still don't see what all the fuss is about."

Carrie completely lost it then. "Fuss?" she roared. "We're sitting inside a time bomb. Did you just not listen to a word I've been saying?"

"Yes, I listened. But isn't the answer right in front of you? Simply pick up the phone and call Utopia. Have them send someone to disarm the thing."

The phone. My God, why hadn't she thought to try calling for help? Carrie ran around to the other side of the bed and picked up the phone. Her excitement and hope were short-lived. The line was dead.

"It doesn't work," she said. She didn't bother to hang up the phone but dropped it on the bed.

"What about the cell phones?" Anne asked. "Do you think we'll be able to get a signal up here?" Glancing at the table beside her, she frowned and said, "Where's my cell phone? I had it sitting in the charger right over there, but now it's gone. Did you move it?"

"They took it," Carrie cried out. She ran to the sliding glass doors that opened to Anne's balcony, drew the drapes back, and said, "See that light, Anne? See it?"

"Stop yelling at me."

"See all the wires? The house is rigged," she said. "Do you understand yet?"

"Yes, all right," Anne said. She looked sullen now.

Maybe Sara could get through to the woman. Carrie took a breath and then said, "I'm going back to my room to see if they took my cell phones. Please hurry downstairs," she added, "And remember, don't open any doors or windows."

"I get it."

Carrie wasn't so sure about that. She didn't want to antagonize the woman, and so she pretended to agree. She paused in the open doorway and said, "Bring the letter with you . . . please. Sara and I are bringing ours."

"There wasn't any letter on my nightstand," Anne snapped.

Carrie turned around. "I never said anything about a nightstand."

Anne turned her head away from Carrie. "Shut the door after you."

What in God's name was the matter with Anne? Why was she lying? What could she possibly have to gain?

Carrie didn't have any answers. She went back to her suite but stopped short just inside the door. Her beautiful Gucci bags had been ripped open with a knife, and all of her clothes were strewn about the sofa and chair. Why hadn't she noticed the mess before? Just as she suspected, one of her two cell phones, her chargers, and the laptop were all missing.

She sprinted for the closet. "Please, God," she whispered as she threw the double doors open. Maybe Jilly hadn't been that thorough. Maybe she hadn't found the cell phone in her pocket.

Carrie started to cry when she saw her blazer

on the floor. Her sister had found the phone. She looked away, sobbing now as the magnitude of her situation overwhelmed her.

She let herself weep for a couple of minutes, then struggled to get her emotions under control. "I'm losing it," she said out loud. Wiping her face with the backs of her hands, she staggered to her feet and went into the bathroom. She stared at herself in the mirror. God, she was a mess. Her eyes were swollen, and her face looked haggard.

Carrie took the time to brush her teeth and wash her face. She lifted her robe off the hook behind the bathroom door and put it on. She felt better now, more in control. After she picked up the letter and the envelope her dear, demented sister had left for her, she went downstairs.

Neither Sara nor Anne was waiting for her. Carrie went into the kitchen and was surprised to find the pantry hadn't been stripped. There were boxes of unopened cereal, canned vegetables and fruit. She noticed the tops had dust on them, indicating they'd been there quite awhile. The refrigerator was empty, but there was a full container of Folgers coffee in the freezer.

Carrie kept going to the hallway to see if Sara or Anne had come down yet. What the hell was taking them so long? She went back into the kitchen, made a pot of coffee, and then carried a mug of the steaming brew into the living room. She deliberately kept away from the windows, just in case someone was out there watching.

She sat down in one of the easy chairs near the dining room and waited tensely. Her hand trembled, and hot coffee spilled over the rim, burning her fingers. Five minutes later, she saw Sara slowly making her way down the winding staircase. She was dressed in a royal blue floral silk robe. From the way she clung to the railing, she appeared to be woozy still.

"Do you need help?" Carrie called out when Sara stopped for the fifth time. She had a white-knuckle grip on the railing.

"No, I can make it. I'm a little dizzy. What in heaven's name was in that food?"

"I don't know what it was," Carrie said. "But it was powerful."

"It could have killed us."

Wouldn't that have been something? Carrie thought. To die from a canapé and never know about all the trouble Jilly had gone to. Her sister would have been enraged. Carrie smiled at the thought, as sick as it was.

"Would you like some coffee?"

"I don't think I can handle it just yet. How do you know that it wasn't poisoned?"

"It isn't," she assured her. "My letter was from my sister. She's gone to a lot of trouble to terrify me. She obviously wants me to suffer before I die, and poison would act too quickly."

"Then why did she drug the food?"

"To knock us all out," Carrie answered. She waited until Sara had taken a seat across from her, and then said, "She came into our rooms last night."

"Someone was here," Sara agreed. "He or she went through all my things. My cell phone and Palm Pilot are both missing."

"The phone line's dead too."

"Yes," Sara said. "I checked."

It suddenly occurred to Carrie that the judge was awfully calm. She asked her why.

"I don't see any reason to become hysterical. What would it solve? I'd rather exert my energy figuring out a way to get out of here . . . in one piece."

Carrie took another long drink of her coffee. It was tepid now and bitter, but she drank it anyway.

"My sister came back from her grave."

"Excuse me?"

"My sister . . . I thought she was killed in a car accident years ago," Carrie said. "My husband and I celebrated after my niece went to bed. I was told that her body was cremated in the inferno, but there were items from her purse that had been thrown clear during the impact, and those items convinced the police that the victim was my sister. I was a fool to believe it. Jilly was wanted for questioning by the police at the time."

"So she feigned her own death," Sara said, nodding. "Clever."

"Oh, yes," Carrie agreed. "Jilly was always sneaky and clever." She got up and handed the

158

letter to Sara. "She's hired a hit man. That's what she called him. Her hit man."

"Your own sister did this to you."

Sara didn't sound surprised, just intrigued. Carrie wondered at her reaction. In normal families, if there really was such a thing, sisters certainly squabbled. Some might even hate each other, but how many would go to the extreme of hiring someone to kill a sibling?

"You're not shocked," she said.

"No, I'm not."

Carrie shook her head. "Jilly isn't like anyone you've ever known."

"Want to bet?" Sara said dryly. "I've put away hundreds of men and women who committed heinous crimes. I believe I've heard and seen it all in the twenty-two years I've sat on the bench. Nothing can shock me now."

Carrie scoffed. "I wouldn't count on that. So tell me, Sara. Who wants you dead?"

Sara carefully adjusted the belt on her robe so that the bow was perfect, then folded her hands in her lap. "Who wants me dead? Oh, quite a few people, I would imagine."

She handed the letter to Carrie and watched as she unfolded the note and read it. It was short and to the point.

Judge Collins:
    I told you I would get even, and I'm a man of my word. Now it's your turn to suffer. I wish I could be there to watch . . . from a safe

distance, of course. You're going to die very soon now.

Rot in hell, bitch.

Carrie dropped the letter on the coffee table. Then she handed Jilly's letter to Sara.

"While you read her short but not-so-sweet note, I'm going to get another cup of coffee."

"I'd love a cup now," Sara said.

Carrie went back into the kitchen, and when she returned a minute later with two mugs, Sara had placed the note on the coffee table next to the one she'd received. Carrie handed her a mug, warned her the coffee was very hot, and sat down.

"Your sister hates you."

"Oh, yes."

"She accused you of stealing her child and turning her against her."

"That didn't happen."

"She seems to believe that all of her failures were your fault and that your success was stolen from her."

Carrie nodded. "Jilly always had the unique ability to rewrite history. Once she said it, in her mind it was real."

"She sounds like a psychopath."

"She is," Carrie said. "It was never officially diagnosed, but I'm sure that's what she is."

Sara began to trace the worry line in her forehead with her fingertip as she listened to Carrie. Back and forth, back and forth. She was so deep in thought she probably wasn't even aware of what she was doing. "What happened with the child?"

"Avery," she said. "Her name is Avery, and she's an adult now, not a child. Jilly left her in the hospital. She told my mother and me that we could keep her, sell her, or give her away. She didn't care what happened to her." Tears sprang into Carrie's eyes. She hated herself for showing such weakness in front of a virtual stranger, but she was powerless to do anything about it. "Jilly's going after Avery too. Oh, God, she could already have her locked away somewhere now. My niece was going to join me at the spa . . ." She covered her face with her hand. "We've got to get out of here soon. We have to find a way."

"Your sister has gone to quite a lot of trouble to hurt you," Sara said.

Carrie told her about Jilly coming into her room during the night and how she had believed she was having a nightmare. Sara was a good listener and so calm Carrie was actually comforted.

"Jilly could be very patient when she really wanted something, and, oh, how she loved complicated plans. Nothing could ever be simple."

Sara put her coffee cup down and leaned forward. "How much time do you think we have?"

"She's gone to a lot of trouble setting this up. She'll want to prolong my agony."

Both of them kept glancing at the spiral staircase, expecting to see Anne coming down the stairs.

"I've already checked every window I could reach. They're all wired."

"Yes, I would expect so."

"I wish I could be calm like you."

"I'm not calm," Sara protested. "I'm quite . . . discombobulated."

Her choice of words made Carrie smile. "So am I," she said.

"I'm thinking . . ."

"Yes?"

"How curious it is that the three of us are in this house together. What is it that we have in common?"

"I don't know," Carrie said. "And I don't know that we'll have the time to find out."

"We will get out of here."

Her resolve bolstered Carrie. "Yes, we must, and we will."

"I wonder what's keeping Anne."

"She's going to be a problem."

"Oh?"

Carrie nodded. "She won't admit she received a letter."

"Perhaps she's in shock."

Carrie thought Sara might be right about that. "And denial," she said.

"We're going to all have to work together, but I don't know how much help I can be. I'll do whatever I can. I'm sixty-eight years old." Sara shrugged. "And I'm terribly out of shape. When I received the invitation for a free two-week stay at the spa as a promotion, I thought to myself, why not? The experts say it's never too late to turn your life around. I decided to get into better shape. As you can see, I'm overweight, and once we get outside — and we will find a way to do that," she said with conviction, "I won't be able to walk far. I should have had both of my knees replaced several years ago. I'm walking with bone on bone now."

"Then Anne and I will hide you somewhere . . . somewhere safe in the woods while we go get help."

They heard a door close and both looked up. Anne had finally decided to join them. Carrie's mouth dropped open when the frail woman started down the stairs. She couldn't believe what she was seeing. Anne was all dressed up in a hot pink St. John pants suit. Her gold earrings matched the buttons. She had taken the time to put on makeup and curl her hair. When she reached the bottom of the stairs, she smiled, and then crossed the living room to join them. Her high heels clicked against the marble floor. Where in heaven's name did she think she was going? A formal brunch?

"Oh, dear," Sara whispered.

"Good morning, ladies," Anne said. "Or rather, good afternoon."

She sounded so cheerful. Had her mind snapped? Carrie wondered. She was about to ask the woman what the hell was the matter with her when Sara suggested Anne sit down.

"Did you sleep well?" Anne asked Sara. Then, before she could answer, Anne continued on. "I can't believe I slept so long. It must be this wonderful mountain air. Coming from Cleveland, it's a delightful change."

"Would you care for some coffee?" Sara asked. She was watching her closely, as though she were trying to interpret the woman's bizarre behavior.

"Not just yet. I'll ring when I'm ready."

Carrie turned to Sara. "I told you she was going to be a problem."

"I'm sorry. What did you say?" Anne asked. She carefully sat down and crossed one ankle over the other.

Carrie turned to her. "It wasn't the wonderful mountain air that made you sleep so long, Anne. We were all drugged."

"That's nonsense. Look where we are," she said. "Who would do such a thing in this beautiful —"

Carrie cut her off. "Did you bring your letter down?"

"I don't know what you're talking about."

"See what I mean?" Carrie asked Sara.

The judge took over. "Anne, Carrie and I each received a letter. They're there on the coffee table. Please read them."

Carrie noticed that Anne's hand was violently shaking as she reached for the letters. She picked them up and then quickly placed them back on the table. "I don't need to read these."

"Yes, you do," Sara gently asserted. "You'll see that we're in trouble here. Someone has wired this place to kill us."

"What rubbish," Anne muttered. "I will not have my day ruined with this ridiculous game you two are playing."

"We're locked inside this house," Sara told her.

"We are not."

"It's no use," Carrie said. "I tried to tell her all of this upstairs."

"You're lying," Anne said.

Carrie considered punching the woman. She thought she'd probably kill her if she did because Anne was so painfully thin and sickly. A good wind could have done her in.

"If any of us opens a window or door, the house will blow up," Sara patiently explained.

Neither she nor Carrie anticipated Anne's reaction. The woman bolted from her chair and ran across the living room. "You're only lying to get me upset. The house isn't wired, and I'm going to prove it to you."

She was headed for the front door.

# CHAPTER 8

John Paul had to hang around Utopia longer than he'd anticipated, but the wait was worth it. He was sitting, or rather sprawling, in an easy chair half hidden behind a couple of limp palm trees inside the lobby's bar when Avery Delaney walked inside. One hard look and he had her all figured out. She was a typical California blond. No, maybe not typical. She was unique, he'd give her that. But she was definitely all about her body. Why else would she want to spend a week at a spa? Why would anyone?

The Delaney woman wore a short white T-shirt that fit snugly across her full breasts, and tight jeans, obviously intending to show off her long legs and her tight ass. Her long, straight, blond hair shimmered in the light. It looked natural, but he doubted that it was. Probably came from a bleach bottle. Her sunglasses hid her eyes, but he figured she was probably wearing colored contact lenses. Her T-shirt hid her belly button, but he wouldn't have been surprised to find that she'd had it pierced. Wasn't that the fashion these days?

She was hot, all right. In fact, Avery Delaney was a beautiful woman, but she wasn't his type. She was a little too perfect for his tastes. Sexy as sin, though. As he watched her stop and take in her surroundings — pretending she didn't notice how the other guests had stopped to stare at her — John Paul wondered how much of her was real and how much had been cosmetically "enhanced." The breasts, definitely. And maybe even the ass.

She wasn't the kind of woman he'd want to have a lasting relationship with, but then he didn't want a lasting relationship with any woman. One night with her, however, sounded like a damned good idea. Hell, the woman probably had the IQ of a tsetse fly, but in bed, brainpower really didn't matter.

Miss Airhead couldn't seem to figure out where check-in was. Was she waiting for someone to take her hand and lead her across the lobby? She was looking up at the golden sphere slowly rotating like one of those old disco balls. Had the thing hypnotized her?

Avery knew she was gawking like a tourist. She couldn't help it; Utopia was incredible. The lobby was gigantic, the floors a shiny, ebony marble. Above her, hanging from the gilded dome was a glistening orb. She couldn't take her gaze off it. Was it real gold? It must have cost the owners a fortune, she thought.

She turned to her right and stopped again. One entire wall was a waterfall, and in the center of the gathering pool was a statue of Atlas. Another smaller sphere was perched on his shoulder. Both the sculpture and the bubbling waterfall were meant to impress the guests willing to pay a fortune to be pampered in such an environment, and in Avery's estimation, the owners got the job done.

Shaking her head over the expense of it all, she pulled up the strap of the old, hand-me-down Gucci backpack Carrie had given her, and crossed the lobby to the reception desk. A man about her age wearing a name tag labeled "Oliver" stood behind the granite counter waiting to welcome her. His smile was dazzling, his teeth astonishingly white. Freakishly so. He or his dentist had obviously overdone the bleach job, and his artificially tanned face only made his teeth more prominent. She tried not to stare as she gave him her name and leaned against the cool counter while he pulled up her reservation on the built-in computer screen.

Oliver's smile blessedly vanished. "Oh, dear."

"Excuse me?"

He wasn't looking at her now, but stared intently at the screen when he said, "Your reservation was canceled, Miss Delaney."

"No, that has to be a mistake. I didn't cancel."

"According to my computer, you canceled. It's noted right here," he added, pointing to his screen, which she couldn't possibly see unless she pole-vaulted over the countertop.

"That's wrong."

"The computer's never wrong. You called Utopia at . . ." He was trying to pull up the exact time she called in.

"Oliver," she said. Her impatience was brimming in her voice. "I didn't cancel. In fact, I called to tell reception I would be a day late."

"Yes, you did," he agreed, pointing to the screen once again. "But then you called again and canceled."

"No, I didn't," she insisted.

"But my computer —"

She interrupted him before he could tell her his computer was infallible again. "Why don't you just book me into another room. Anything will do."

She lifted her backpack and placed it on the counter. She began to dig through it looking for her billfold so she could give Oliver her credit card. Against her wishes, the week had been paid for by her aunt, but Avery wanted the charges transferred to her card.

Oliver, she noticed, had stopped typing. "Is something wrong?" she asked.

He coughed delicately and finally looked at her. "I'm afraid it won't be possible to book you into another room, and unfortunately, the room you canceled has already been assigned to another guest. We're at a hundred percent occupancy," he continued. "I'll be happy to put you on our waiting list, but I must warn you. There's little chance of an opening. Our guests book months in advance."

"I'm certain my aunt was able to reserve a room for me here," she protested. "If there had been a problem I'm sure she would have told me."

He was frantically typing again. Then he stopped and nodded. "Yes, we were able to accommodate you because of another cancellation. That is peculiar," he added. "Our guests rarely cancel at the last minute."

He frowned as he said the last, as though by canceling, he thought she had committed a terrible breach in etiquette.

"But I didn't cancel," she said. Lord, this was frustrating. "I'm joining my aunt here," she explained. "She checked in yesterday afternoon or early evening. Could you give me her room number? Her name's Carolyn Salvetti."

"I'm sorry, but we aren't allowed to give out the room numbers of our guests."

Of course he couldn't. She knew that. "Please call her room. I'm sure she'll be able to clear up this misunderstanding. She might have decided that I should stay with her."

Oliver looked relieved that the problem would be solved and he could get rid of her. Fortunately, there weren't any other guests waiting in line to check in. He flashed her another startling smile and said, "I'm sure that's what must have happened. Guests simply do not cancel at the last minute the way you did."

She had the sudden urge to grab him by his

shoulders and shake him until he admitted the spa had screwed up. Gritting her teeth to keep from saying something she would regret, she spelled the name Salvetti and waited.

"I know that name," he said.

"You do?"

He nodded. "A gentleman was in here yesterday asking for your aunt. He was very disappointed she wasn't here." He started typing, but a couple of seconds later, he was frowning again.

"Is there a problem?" she asked, knowing full well there was.

"There are no problems at Utopia," he said, and it was such a quick, automatic response she thought he'd been programmed to say those very words. "We do occasionally have minor inconveniences."

Give me a break. "All right. Explain the minor inconvenience."

"Mrs. Salvetti canceled."

"No, she didn't."

Oliver's shoulders slumped. She knew what he was thinking. Here we go again.

"I'm afraid Mrs. Salvetti did cancel. It is odd, I'll agree. It's so rare to get two last-minute cancellations like this. Of course, you're both members of the same family, so I guess we could say it was really only one last-minute cancellation for two rooms."

"Listen to me. My aunt didn't cancel. She called me from the Aspen airport yesterday."

"Perhaps something came up at the last minute

and she had to return home," he suggested.

"Something's very wrong."

"It's right here in my computer, Miss Delaney. Your aunt called yesterday afternoon."

What in the world was going on? As much as Avery wanted to continue to argue with Oliver, she knew it wouldn't solve anything. She wasn't sure what to do now. If an emergency had come up at work and Carrie had had to return to Los Angeles, she would have called. She wouldn't have left Avery hanging like this. Oh, God, what if something had happened to her or Uncle Tony? What if there had been an accident?

Calm down, she told herself. If anything bad had happened to either Carrie or Tony, one or the other would have called her.

Avery began searching her backpack for her phone. She would get hold of Carrie on her cell phone right this minute and find out what was going on.

She pulled out her Day-Timer and her billfold, clutched them in her right hand, and kept searching for her phone with her other hand. The damned thing always ended up on the bottom. "My aunt didn't cancel," she muttered. Then, more to herself than Oliver, she added, "There must have been a crisis at work. That's all I can think of to make Carrie turn around and go back home."

"Oh, your friend's back." Oliver didn't sound very cheerful.

"I'm sorry?"

"Your friend . . . he's coming this way. Maybe he can clear up this misunderstanding."

She didn't know what he was talking about. She didn't have any friends meeting her here. She turned around to see whom Oliver was watching, but there was only a man striding toward the counter, a big man, she corrected. Odd, but he seemed to be staring at her. And he didn't look happy.

"Are you referring to the gentleman coming this way?"

"Yes," he answered. "He was the one I was telling you about. He was here yesterday, looking for your aunt." In a low voice he added, "If anyone could benefit from our aroma stress-relief massage therapy, it's definitely your friend. I suggested the treatment to him, but he was quite . . ."

"Quite what?"

"Resistant to the idea. Actually, he was quite difficult about everything. I know I shouldn't say anything negative about a potential guest, but your boyfriend is wound tight inside. He should be practicing yoga on a daily basis. I mean, the man growled at me. He really did. Can you imagine? I told him you were scheduled to check in. It was noted in the computer under Mrs. Salvetti's reservation, and that's who he asked for when he came up to the counter. Your aunt called in and canceled. I had the unfortunate duty of telling him. Let me tell you, he wasn't happy about that news. He told me he'd come back today to see you, and he's been here since early morning. I noticed him when I came on duty. I hope he's in a better mood today."

She wasn't paying much attention to Oliver's prattling. She was busy watching the man crossing the lobby. He was something else. She'd never seen anyone like him, except maybe in the movies. The closer he came, the bigger he got. Tall and muscular, with dark hair and a weathered complexion. She guessed that he spent a good deal of his time outdoors or in a gym somewhere working on his abs. He was ruggedly good-looking, but he was too into the physical to appeal to her. She much preferred brains over muscle.

The man had great bone structure. That thought led to another, and she suddenly thought she knew who he was and what he wanted.

"You do know the gentleman, don't you?"

"It's okay. I'm sure he's a friend of my aunt's."

Carrie had probably used him in one of her commercials, and maybe, since he was in the area and had found out she was staying at the spa, he'd decided to stop by and say hello. It was either that, or muscle man was out of work and hoping that Carrie would take a liking to him and offer him a job.

Avery had great sympathy for actors because it was such a competitive field and so much of the decision-making process was out of their control.

The odds against making it in Hollywood were astronomical. She made up her mind to do what she could to help. She waited until he was about three feet away, then put her hand out and introduced herself. "My name's Avery Delaney." Oh, yes, he was definitely an actor. He had the dark, brooding look down cold.

He grasped her hand in his. "My name's John Paul Renard." His voice was deep and wonderfully southern.

Lordy, he had great eyes. The color of a gray dawn. She couldn't imagine him holding up a roll of paper towels in a commercial. Explosives, maybe, but not paper towels.

His body language intrigued her. He turned so that his back was to the counter; then his gaze slowly scanned the lobby. She got the odd feeling he was memorizing every face.

"You're a friend of my Aunt Carrie's?"

"Yes."

No further explanation, no embellishment whatsoever.

"You're an actor, right?"

The question so surprised him he smiled. "No."

"Oh . . . I thought . . . then what do you do for a living?" God, she hated it when people asked her that question, and it was really none of her business how the hunk, who couldn't even bother to look at her when she spoke to him, paid his rent.

"I'm a carpenter."

No way. "A carpenter?"

"Uh-huh." He drawled out the answer and stared into her eyes. She could feel the heat rush to her face and hoped to heaven she wasn't blushing. The man did have the strangest way about him.

Carrie was right. She really needed to start dating again. It had obviously been way too long. If a brute of a man like this one could affect her . . . way too long.

"A carpenter," she repeated. Then, "Okay." She'd go along. "And you've done some work for my aunt?"

"No." He was back to watching the people strolling into the lobby as he answered. "I need to talk to her," he said impatiently. "It's important. Where is she?"

"I'm not sure," she said. "But I'm about to find out." She turned around to search through her backpack again when a sudden, horrid thought occurred to her. She almost groaned out loud. "Did my aunt want you to meet me here?"

Carrie was up to her old tricks again, Avery decided, trying to play matchmaker. She was a little surprised at her aunt's nerve. She thought that her last talk with Carrie had done the trick. Her aunt had promised — vowed, actually — never to try to fix her up again.

Avery's voice was curt when she said, "Carrie isn't here today. If you're in the area, you could try back tomorrow."

He didn't take the hint and go away. Deciding

176

to ignore him — no small feat considering his size — she continued to hunt for her phone. She finally found it on the very bottom and pulled it out. Oliver began to shake his head. "Is there a problem?" she asked.

"There are no problems at Utopia, but the use of cell phones on the premises is frowned upon." Having said that, he pointed to a black-and-gold sign propped on the counter near the corner.

She flipped open the phone's cover, pushed the speed dial to Carrie's cell phone, and said, "Then I guess you better start frowning."

John Paul liked her response. Spunk, he thought. What a surprise. The plastic California girl with the too-blue-to-be-true eyes had a backbone.

Carrie's voice mail came on after the first ring, which meant the phone was either still being recharged or she was out of signal range. She called Uncle Tony next. He answered, and the second he heard her voice, he proceeded to give her hell because she hadn't called before her aunt left for the spa.

"You know how she worries when she doesn't hear from you."

"I'm sorry," she said. "Have you talked to Carrie since she left L.A.? Has she called you?"

"No, but I don't expect to hear from her. We said good-bye in L.A. She wouldn't let me ride to the airport with her," he said. "And I promised her I wouldn't bug her at the spa. She's there to relax and think about her . . . priorities. I'm sure she'll want to talk to you, though. Give her a call and be sure to tell her I send my love."

Her uncle didn't know she was at Utopia. Avery was about to explain her last-minute decision to join her aunt but then changed her mind. She didn't want to get Tony upset over what she still hoped was just a colossal screwup.

"If she doesn't answer her phone, don't fret. She's probably just getting a massage or something."

The lobby was becoming crowded. A raucous and loud group of twelve came into the hotel. Avery put her hand over her ear as she asked, "Tony, were there any problems at work? Has the office called you?"

"No," he said. "Are you expecting trouble? I talked to Jeanie this morning. Everything's good," he said. "Star Catcher isn't going to fall apart in two weeks. When you talk to Carrie, tell her to stop worrying."

"Yes, I'll tell her," she said. "I'll call you later, Tony. Love you."

She ended the call and looked at Oliver. "I'd like to speak to your manager."

Oliver looked offended by the request. He stiffened and his voice turned snippy. "I assure you Mr. Cannon will tell you the same thing I just did. We're booked to capacity. It's a misconception to think that we hold back rooms. I'll be happy to assist you in finding suitable lodging in Aspen. Nothing will compare to Utopia, of

178

course, but you could take advantage of our day spa treatments. I'm sure you'd enjoy our stress-relief hot-stone massage. It's quite invigorating."

His tone was grossly condescending. She wasn't interested in his damn massage. She wanted to find her aunt. Keeping her irritation in check was difficult, but she managed it. She had never used her job to get around obstacles before, and she wasn't about to start now, but the urge was nearly irresistible. Oh, how she would have loved to pull out her ID and flash it in front of Oliver's face. He'd sure as certain stop being so snippy then, wouldn't he? She couldn't do it, though, because it wouldn't be honest, acting like a full-fledged agent when she actually worked in the basement keyboarding all day. Besides, it wasn't a real FBI badge, and anyone with half a brain would know it.

She suddenly realized she was projecting her frustration and anger on the innocent clerk. Oliver was simply doing his job. Maybe Carrie had lost track of the time. She might have met a famous movie star at the mountain retreat and didn't want to leave.

That had to be it. Her aunt was busy networking and had forgotten to call. Avery clung to the possibility because it was all she had. Her anxiety didn't go away, though. Why had Carrie canceled her reservation at the spa?

"I really need to talk to your manager."

Oliver didn't move.

John Paul said quietly, "Do as the lady asks."

"Mr. Cannon went downstairs to the mailroom to see about a package."

"Go get him and tell him that John Paul Renard is back and wants to talk to him again. We'll wait in his office."

It wasn't what John Paul said but how he said it that got Oliver moving. He stepped back from the computer, turned, and jogged down the corridor.

John Paul didn't give Avery time to ask questions or argue. He started shoving her things back in her backpack, then grabbed her hand and pulled her along. "Come on. I know the way."

"I can handle this, Mr. Renard. You don't need to —"

"Call me John Paul." He led her behind the counter, then down a long, red carpeted hall.

She jerked away from him and dug in her heels at the door to the manager's office.

"All right. I want some answers," she demanded. "First of all, exactly how do you know my aunt?"

He had his own question. "Why didn't you tell your uncle that your aunt is missing?"

"I don't want him to worry. I'm not certain she is missing."

"Then where is she?"

Good point. Carrie was probably drinking mimosas on top of a mountain somewhere having a fine old time. And making Avery nuts worrying about her. No, Carrie would never be so thoughtless. Something was wrong.

"I don't know where she is, but I'm going to make some calls and find her."

"Why would she cancel?" he asked. "The clerk said a woman called —"

"The hotel must have screwed up our reservations. You don't need to hang around. If you'd like to leave your phone number, I'll make sure Carrie gets it. She'll probably come strolling into the lobby any second now with some outrageous excuse."

She didn't believe a word of what she'd just told him, but she hoped he would buy it and go away.

"Then I'll wait with you until she gets here."

She gave up. The man was more tenacious than she was. She would find out what his agenda was after she located her aunt.

Ten minutes later, she was sitting behind Mr. Cannon's art deco desk in his spacious wind tunnel of an office overlooking the serenity pool. The overhead ceiling fan was on low and making a clicking sound with each rotation. The noise reminded her of Mrs. Speigel. The sweet old woman made the same sound when she spoke because of her ill-fitting false teeth.

Cannon also had another fan perched on top of his black lacquered filing cabinet, but that one was going full speed. All the papers on his desk were weighted down with gold sphere-shaped paperweights.

"Cannon's taking too damned long. While you make your phone calls, I'll go find him," John Paul said. "You stay put."

Avery waited until he'd left the office and closed the door before she dialed her home answering machine. She hoped Carrie had left her a message explaining her absence, but that wasn't the case. Then Avery tried her office voice mail, and there wasn't a message from her aunt there either.

Now what? In desperation she called the pen. Maybe, just maybe, Carrie had talked to Margo or Lou or Mel.

Margo answered the main line. "I'm so glad you called, Avery. You're not going to believe this. I called your neighbor's caretaker like I told you I would —"

"Margo," Avery interrupted. "You can tell me later. I've got a problem here, and I need your help."

"You need to hear what I found out," her friend insisted. "Mrs. Speigel broke her hip."

Avery's nerves were nearing the breaking point, but she knew that she was going to have to wait until Margo finished talking about Mrs. Speigel before she'd let her get a word in.

"I'm sorry to hear that."

"She broke her hip two weeks ago, and then she got pneumonia. She almost died," she added. "But Marilyn, the lady who takes care of her, told me the antibiotics are finally working, and it looks like she's going to recover. That's pretty amazing considering the fact that Mrs. Speigel is in her nineties."

"Why are you telling me this?" She rubbed her brow as she asked the question.

"Don't you get it? Mrs. Speigel couldn't have snuck her car out. She was in the hospital. Someone stole her car, and whoever it was was in such a hurry to get out of the parking garage, he or she almost hit you." Before Avery could comment, Margo enthusiastically continued. "The car was abandoned on M Street. It was illegally parked, so they towed it. Marilyn told me that it would break Mrs. Speigel's heart if the family sold her car. Even though she never drives it, she feels independent having it in the garage. Marilyn uses it to take the old lady on errands. Aren't you happy to know Mrs. Speigel wasn't trying to kill you?" she added with a laugh.

"Margo, I need help. Stop talking for a minute and listen. My aunt's missing."

She filled her in on the information she had, then said, "There's a man here waiting to talk to Carrie. He won't tell me how he knows her or what he wants. He's the strong, silent type. Run his name through the computer, will you? There's something about him. His name is John Paul Renard."

"What do you mean, 'There's something about him'?"

"He says he's a carpenter, but he doesn't look like one."

"What's a carpenter supposed to look like?"

"Come on, Margo. See if there's anything in the system."

"I'm typing in the name right now. Are you looking for parking tickets or something?"

"I don't know what I'm looking for," she admitted. "He's got this air about him. When I first saw him across the lobby, I was sure he must be an actor, but later, I noticed the way he was watching the people coming and going. He might be . . . dangerous. I think he could be." She sighed dismissively. "I'm probably overreacting because I'm so worried about Carrie. It isn't like her to take off like this. Just look up the name, okay?"

"Jeez, Avery. You think he's a criminal?"

"I don't know . . ."

"Whoa."

"What? You found something?"

"Oh, boy, did I. Your John Paul isn't a criminal."

"He's not my John Paul."

"He used to work for the government. Wait, I'm scrolling down. Whoa. Get this. His file is classified."

"Classified?" She wasn't prepared to hear that.

"I'm trying to access . . . ah, here we go. I could lose my job for this, and so could you."

"I know. Just tell me what you see, okay?"

"Renard was in the Marines. Honorable discharge," she added. "He was recruited while he was still a Marine according to the file."

"Recruited for what?"

"I don't know. It just says 'special branch operations.' There's a bunch of numbers and initials, but I don't know what any of it stands for." She read the information to Avery as she scrolled down. She stopped suddenly, then said, "He's taken a leave of absence." Then, a few seconds later, she sighed loudly into the phone. "It won't give me any more information. That's all I can get because I don't have the necessary clearance. Hold on. I'm pulling up an old photo ID. Ah, here we go." She whistled.

"What?"

"I think I'm in love."

"Get serious," Avery said. She described John Paul to verify.

"I think it's the same guy. He's from Louisiana. He has family there. His brother-in-law is an attorney for the Justice Department." She read a few more personal facts and then said, "It looks like he went on quite a few missions when he was a Marine. Wait a minute, here's something interesting. It says one of the missions involved rescuing some hostages in the Middle East, but get this, Renard carried out the assignment despite the fact that he'd suffered a compound fracture of his left arm." Margo was silent as she scrolled through the rest of his record; then she said, "Beyond the Marine duty, it won't tell me anything. Do you want me to go to Carter? The man intimidates me, but I'll do it if you want me to. I'm sure he could get into Renard's file."

"No, don't ask him. At least, not until I think about it."

"What's going on?" Margo asked. "What does this Renard want with your Aunt Carrie?"

"I don't know. Listen, Margo, when Carrie called me from the Aspen airport, she said there was a driver there from the spa waiting to take her and two other women to a mountain retreat for the night. Carrie said the spa had trouble with a broken water pipe or something. The driver's name was Monk Edwards . . . or Edward Monk. I'm not sure which. I know it's not much, but it's all I've got. I remember Carrie also said the driver had a British accent. Run the name through, and if you find anything, call me on my cell phone."

"Do you have any idea how many Edwardses there are in the United States?"

"Monk isn't such a common name, though . . . unless it's just a nickname."

"Okay," Margo said. "Give me your room number at the spa in case I can't reach you on your cell phone."

"I'm not staying at Utopia because my reservation was canceled. I'm leaving anyway," she added. "Carrie said she was staying in a house owned by the spa. I'm hoping she's still there. If she's not . . ."

"Don't borrow trouble. Your aunt probably lucked into something much cooler than the spa. She'll get in touch with you. You'll see. And I'll get right on that search for a Monk Edwards or an Edward Monk."

Margo had just hung up the phone when it rang again. The call was from the department head reminding her that she still hadn't turned in her vacation forms. She spent ten minutes finding and then filling out the forms between interoffice business calls, then had to hand deliver the papers to Human Resources. She didn't get a chance to run the search for Avery until midafternoon.

After she typed the first name Avery had given her and hit the search key, she called out to Lou and Mel as they were heading to lunch and told them about Carrie. Each man had a theory as to what had happened to Avery's aunt. Lou was sure she went back to L.A. — they all knew the woman was a workaholic and obsessive to boot — but Mel thought she had probably hooked up with a business associate out in Colorado and called the hotel and left a message for Avery, but the spa had misplaced or erased the call.

"I never get my messages when I stay in a big hotel," he said.

"She probably found something better to do than sit in a mud bath all day and forgot about Avery," Lou suggested.

"Carrie wouldn't be so thoughtless," Margo argued. "She and Avery are really close." She happened to turn back to her computer screen and noticed the alert flashing. "What the . . ."

Scrolling down, she saw in big, bold letters, the priority code. She shouted to Mel and Lou again as she frantically read the information.

"Oh, my God."

Margo jumped up and started running to Carter's office.

# CHAPTER 9

Mr. Timothy Cannon, dressed for the tropics in a white Palm Beach business suit, stepped into the office and introduced himself. He was a dapper gentleman with a soft, prissy voice.

"Have you been able to locate your aunt yet?"

Just then John Paul walked inside. Avery watched him shut the door and then lean against it. When he folded his arms, she noticed the faint scar, about two inches long, on his left forearm. How could she have thought he was an actor? How could her instincts be that off base?

She forced herself to focus on the manager. "No, not yet," she said. "May I ask you a few questions?"

"Yes, of course."

Cannon sat down in the chair facing his desk, crossed one leg over the other, and began to straighten the crease in his pants with his thumb and forefinger.

"Do you always send a staff member to the airport to pick up your guests?"

"Yes, we certainly do. We don't want our

guests to be inconvenienced by having to find transportation on their own or carry their luggage."

"Did you send a staff member to the airport yesterday?"

Cannon smiled. "I see where you're heading. You're wondering about the rash of cancellations, aren't you? It's so unusual, you see, to have a last-minute cancellation at Utopia. The rooms are booked months in advance, but some of our more prominent guests do have last-minute schedule conflicts, and we try to be accommodating."

"What do you mean by a 'rash of cancellations'?"

He looked surprised by the question. He obviously thought she already knew about them. "I had scheduled three separate pickups at the airport yesterday afternoon," he said. "The guests were all ladies," he thought to add. "One flight, as I recall, arrived at three-fifty. Another came in at four-twenty, and the last was coming in at five-fifteen. I could check and tell you which time your aunt was scheduled to arrive."

"I'd like the flight information, credit card numbers, and anything else you've got on all three women."

"I couldn't give you that information."

Oh, yes, he could. And would, she thought. She didn't want to put the manager on the defensive yet. She had too many other questions she needed answered first, and Cannon was doing his best to be cooperative.

"If all three women were coming in within an hour or so of one another, why would you send three separate cars?"

"Because this is Utopia," he answered. "We pride ourselves on excellent service. None of our guests should be expected to wait for another. That would be an inconvenience. So, you see, I was going to send three separate cars, but when all three guests canceled at the last minute, I notified the staff members not to make the trip. As it turned out, we had unexpected guests arrive at our desk last night, and they were thrilled that we had openings for them."

She filed the information away and immediately asked another question. "Did you have a problem with a water main yesterday? Or a broken pipe?"

"Water pipe problems? At Utopia?" He scoffed at the notion. "There weren't any problems. We have an excellent maintenance crew here, and they anticipate problems before they arise."

"You have to get your water from outside the spa. Did one of those pipes break?"

"No."

"What about a mountain house . . . a retreat?" she asked. "Does Utopia own such a place in the mountains for guests to use when there is a problem?"

His jaw clenched. "We don't have problems at

Utopia," he insisted. "And the owners of Utopia don't have a mountain retreat. Clients who come to us stay with us. We don't parcel them out to other locations."

After he finished his explanation, he made a point of letting her see that he was checking his watch, then said, "If you don't have any other questions, I really must get back to work. Most of our clients who come for a week's stay are checking in today. It's going to become hectic. I wouldn't worry about your aunt," he added as he stood. "I'm certain she'll turn up soon."

He was blowing her off. Avery didn't budge from her chair. "May I have a list of your employees? All of your employees?"

"What do you want with it?"

"I'm looking for a specific name."

"I pride myself on knowing every one of my employees. Give me the name and I'll tell you if he or she works for Utopia."

"Edwards," she said. "The name is either Monk Edwards or Edward Monk."

Cannon didn't show any reaction to the name. He simply shook his head. John Paul, however, reacted as though she'd just thrown a fiery torch at him. He jerked away from the door and moved to the desk with the speed of light. Planting his hands on the blotter, he leaned toward her and demanded, "How do you know that name?"

The look on his face gave her goose bumps. They weren't the good kind.

A chill of dread settled around her heart.

"How do *you* know the name?" she countered.

"Answer me."

"My aunt called me from the Aspen airport. She left the message that she and two other women were being driven to a mountain house by a staff member from Utopia. She said his name was Monk Edwards. She also said the man had a British accent." Turning to Cannon, she asked, "Are there any employees —"

"With a British accent? No, I'm afraid not. Someone is playing a cruel trick," he said. "I did not dispatch a driver to the airport yesterday. Perhaps your aunt was . . . misinformed."

John Paul picked up the phone on Cannon's desk and began dialing. He turned away from Avery and spoke in a low voice, but she still heard every word.

"Noah, it's John Paul. Yeah, well, what can I tell you. Stop trying to interrupt and listen. I'm at a spa called Utopia just outside of Aspen. Monk's back. Looks like he's taken on three this time. Must be going for some kind of a record."

Avery pushed the chair back and stood. She was reaching into her backpack when John Paul said, "You better call in the troops. We both know they won't find anything, but you should probably go through the routine anyway. It's too late," he added, his tone antagonistic now. "He's already got them."

He hung up and started for the door but stopped when she called out, "Where are you going?"

He kept walking. "I've called in some people who will help you."

"What people? The police?"

"No, the FBI." He paused at the door. "Noah's a friend of my brother-in-law's. He knows Monk real well. I'll let him explain it to you when he gets here."

"Do you think the FBI will be able to locate my aunt?"

He didn't tell her that he thought her aunt was already dead and that the agents would eventually, with luck, be able to find the body . . . unless Monk had left her for the wild animals to dine on.

"Yeah, sure."

"Tell me the truth."

"Okay," he said. "I think they'll mess it up."

She was taken aback by the venom in his voice. "Why?"

" 'Cause they're FBI."

She left it alone. "Where are you going?" she repeated.

"I'll check out a couple of possibilities, but I doubt I'll find anything."

"And then?"

"Home. I'm going home."

If she had a gun, she would have considered shooting him in the foot. He was such a jerk. "You aren't leaving until you tell me what you know about Monk."

"Look, lady. There isn't anything I can do to help you now. I thought I had a head start, but I was still too late. I've called in help for you, so just hold tight and let them try to do their job."

As he left the office, Avery turned to Cannon. "I want the names, addresses, phone numbers, and any other pertinent information you have on those two other women traveling with my aunt . . . the two who canceled. If I don't get this information in the next two minutes, I swear to heaven I'll tear this place apart, and I'll make sure you're arrested for obstruction. Now get me that information."

She pulled out her FBI credentials and waved them in front of his face. Cannon blinked twice, then rushed to his computer to get what she demanded.

"This is highly irregular," he muttered as she grabbed her backpack, slung it over her shoulder, and went running after John Paul. "Highly irregular."

Avery caught up with John Paul as he was walking past reception. The lobby was crowded with incoming guests now, and she had to cut around three separate groups to get to him. When she finally reached him, she grabbed hold of his upper arm and tried to make him stop.

The creep didn't even slow down. He just kept going, pulling her along as she held tight. She noticed he didn't walk around people. They got out of his way. She dug in and tightened her hold. If she'd had long nails, she would have broken every one of them. His skin was warm, indicating he was human, but his muscle felt like rock.

"Will you stop? I need to talk to you." Then, when he still didn't slow down, she added, "Please, John Paul. I need your help."

Ah, hell. She sounded as if she was going to cry. There wasn't a damned thing he could do for her, but she was too naive to know that. She'd probably been sheltered from the real world all her life and couldn't possibly know how to cope. Like it or not, she was about to find out that life didn't always end happily ever after.

He felt sorry for her. Cursing under his breath, he finally turned to her. He thought about trying to soft-pedal the truth, but then decided she was going to have to deal with reality sooner or later.

"I can't help you."

"What did you mean when you said it was already too late? I heard you on the phone."

"I'll let the FBI explain. Do you have someone you could call to come and sit with you? Some family member or close friend who could take care of you?"

Avery stopped abruptly. God, he was callous. "You think my aunt is dead, don't you?"

He didn't immediately answer her, but the way he was looking made her think he was trying to judge if she was strong enough before he said anything. Was he worried she'd become hysterical?

"I'm not going to fall apart. Just answer me."

He took a step closer. "Yes," he said. "I do

think your aunt and the other two women are already dead."

She let go of his arm and stepped back. "Why? Why do you think that?"

"Isn't there anyone you could . . ."

"Call?" she snapped. "Aunt Carrie and Uncle Tony are my only family, and I'm not going to scare my uncle half to death the way you're trying to scare me until I have all the facts. Tell me how you know this Monk."

"Miss Delaney?"

Oliver was calling to her. She turned and saw the clerk holding up a house phone and beckoning her.

It couldn't be Margo, she thought. Her friend would have called her on her cell phone. Who then? Carrie . . . Maybe Carrie was on the line. Avery was suddenly so frightened, she couldn't catch her breath. Please, let it be Carrie.

She dropped her backpack as she sidestepped a couple. She was in too much of a hurry to pick it up. As she neared the counter, Oliver said, "The caller says it's urgent."

John Paul followed with her backpack. He saw her grab the receiver, then heard her say, "Carrie?"

"Sorry, darling girl. It isn't Carrie."

Jarred by the endearment and the whisper-soft voice of the woman on the line, Avery asked, "Who is this?"

"Who I am isn't important at the moment,

but your Carrie is, isn't she? We have her. Would you like to see her again?"

The voice was muffled. Avery didn't think she had ever heard it before.

"What have you done with her? Is she all right? If you hurt her . . ."

"Stupid girl, be quiet and listen," the woman ordered. "I'm only going to say this once, so pay attention. Three lives depend upon your co-operation. I've left a manila envelope on the counter with your name on it. It's right there, on your left. Ah, don't turn around," she said in a hushed croon that made Avery's skin crawl. "If you see me, all the rules will change and your poor, poor Carrie and her new best friends will have to pay the price."

Avery stiffened. "Where are you?" she whispered.

"Here," the voice answered. "I'm watching you. You want to look, don't you?" She laughed. "Don't be a killjoy and ruin my game. Pick up the map, Avery. That's my girl. See the nice watch? Put it on. Now."

Avery picked up the man's Swatch athlete's watch and quickly slipped the band over her hand.

"That's it," the woman said. "Now open the map and find the little red *X* I've marked for you. Hurry now."

Avery propped the phone on her shoulder, opened the map, and began to search for the mark. She dropped the phone as she leaned forward, trying to see a glimpse of a face in the reflection of the shiny granite wall behind the counter.

John Paul reached around her and picked up the phone. She grabbed it from him.

"Clumsy girl," the voice chided.

"I'm sorry."

John Paul watched Avery closely. The color had drained from her face, and she had a white-knuckle grip on the phone. He couldn't stop himself from putting his arm around her, concerned now that whatever she was hearing was going to be too much for her. He wasn't any good at comforting women — he'd actually never attempted it before — but he felt obligated to try.

"Oh, isn't that sweet," the voice was syrupy now. "Is he your lover?"

She was so rattled she couldn't think. "Yes . . . no."

The woman laughed. "Who is he?"

"No one."

"Oh?"

Avery said the first thing that popped into her head. "He's an actor. He worked . . . works for Carrie in commercials. I'll send him away."

"No, no, don't do that. He's in the game now, darling girl. By now he knows you're having trouble finding Carrie. We don't want him asking questions or calling the police. Besides, he'll have more fun on the treasure hunt with you. But no one else. You say one word to anyone, and we'll know it. From the time you hang up this phone, we'll be monitoring your progress. You're going to tell the manager Carrie called and everything's fine. Then you're going to take your cell phone out of your purse and drop it in the fountain on your way out of the hotel. Do you understand?"

"Yes."

"Take your boyfriend's cell phone. Let me see you do it."

She turned to John Paul. "Give me your cell phone."

"I don't have one."

She repeated what he'd said into the phone.

"We'll know if you're lying. It really doesn't matter, though. You won't be able to get a signal where you're going, but I still want to see you get rid of your phone."

"Yes, I will. Is Carrie all right? Is she —"

"She's fine . . . for the moment. Do what I tell you to do if you want her to stay that way." The tone of her voice turned hard and brittle, yet there was an underlying edge of excitement there as well. "Have you found the red *X*?"

"Yes, I see it."

"Follow the directions I've written at the bottom. You've got exactly two hours to get there."

"But it's at least a three-hour drive from here. It isn't possible. It doesn't look like there are any roads once we get —"

"I said two hours," the woman interrupted.

"One hundred and twenty minutes, Avery, and not one minute more. Didn't you hear me?"

"Yes, but what if we don't make it in time? What if we're late?"

The woman laughed. "Boom."

# CHAPTER 10

The woman sounded demented. She was laughing as she disconnected the line. Avery, shaken to the core, handed the receiver to Oliver, and as she did so, she leaned into the counter and, slipping her hand into her backpack, pushed the speed dial number that would connect her to the pen. She waited a second, then pushed the star to signal an alert. Cannon hurried toward her and dropped the printout of information she'd demanded on the counter.

"You were right," she said, her voice strained with what she hoped sounded like good cheer. "That was Carrie on the phone. It was all just a crazy mix-up. Now, if you'll excuse us, John Paul and I are going for a ride."

She was trying not to let them see how frantic she was. She shoved the papers Cannon had placed on the counter into her backpack before he could snatch them back, grabbed her cell phone and the map, and sprinted for the entrance.

She glanced at each face she passed, but there were so many people loitering in the massive lobby, it was impossible to get a good look at all the women. Where were the phone banks? There were palms and huge ficus trees everywhere. The caller could be hiding as she watched Avery now.

"Let's go," she shouted to John Paul before she realized he was right behind her.

"What's going on?"

She didn't answer. She rushed to the fountain, dropped her cell phone into the water, and then ran out the front doors and bumped into the bellman.

"Miss Delaney, if you'll give me your room number, I'll take your luggage up —"

Ignoring him, she ran down the stairs and stopped in the middle of the circle drive as she tried to locate her rental car. Where was it?

John Paul lifted the black duffel bag from the luggage rack. "This one hers?" he asked the bellman.

"Yes, sir. See, her name's on it. Has she checked in yet?"

"What have you done with my car?" she shouted at the same time.

She was running toward the valet stand when John Paul intercepted her. She wasn't going to go anywhere until he let her, and he wasn't going to do that until she told him what the hell was going on. She was shaking violently.

"Take a deep breath and calm down. You

aren't going to faint, are you?" he asked.

"No."

"Okay, tell me what happened. Talk to me, damn it. Who was on the phone?"

"It was a woman. I didn't recognize her voice. She said they have my aunt."

"They?" he demanded. "You're sure she said they?"

"Yes," she said. She was growing more frantic with each passing second. "Carrie's in trouble, and I have to get to her before it's too late."

"Did the woman tell you to get rid of your cell phone?"

Struggling to get away from him, she whispered, "Yes. Look, this isn't a prank. I could tell. She said that they would kill Carrie and two other women who are with her if we don't get moving. Please," she pleaded in desperation. "You have to go with me. She said you're in the game now. We have to hurry. She's given us two hours to get to a place she marked on the map, and I don't know how we'll make it in time. It's so far away . . ."

"You know this is probably a trap, don't you? You've got to know —"

"Yes," she shouted, no longer caring who heard her. "And once we're on our way, I'm going to try to think of a way to stay alive and help Carrie. Listen to me. I don't have a choice. If it were your mother or your daughter, would you stand here analyzing the situation? I know you wouldn't. You'd do exactly what I'm going to do. Play along and seize whatever chance you can. Now move it, Renard. Time's running out."

She was right. He would have paid the ransom or done anything humanly possible to keep someone he loved alive a little longer.

"Come on," he said. "We'll take my car."

Weak with relief because he wasn't arguing, she whispered, "Thank you."

He grabbed her hand and ran to the parking lot, with her stumbling along behind him. His SUV was illegally parked in front of a walkway. There was a security guard standing beside the hood shaking his head.

"Are you the owner of this —" He stopped when he saw the expression on John Paul's face, then quickly backed away, stepping into a bed of pansies.

John Paul ignored him. He pushed the security button on his keychain to unlock the doors and tossed Avery's bag into the back with his gear while she ran around to the front passenger seat.

She had the map out and was pointing to the red $X$ by the time he slid behind the wheel. "We've got exactly two hours. No, one hour and fifty-seven minutes now, to get to this spot. Let's go."

John Paul studied the map for about ten seconds. "It's going to be close," he said as he started the ignition.

"But we can make it?"

"Maybe," was all he would allow. "You navigate. Put your seat belt on."

He couldn't floor it until they were out of the parking area, but by the time they'd reached the gate at the end of the long, winding road, he was going fifty.

Avery was leaning forward, rocking, as though that motion would help them get closer to their destination. She realized what she was doing and forced herself to sit back while she concentrated for the moment on giving him directions.

He sped down the highway. "There," she shouted when she saw the sign. "Take the cutoff up ahead. It should be about a mile or so. You can stay on that two-lane for at least twenty miles, maybe thirty." Gripping her hands together, she watched the road until the turnoff came into view. "Slow down. There it is. You'll miss it."

"I see it," he said calmly.

He took the blacktop road on two wheels. Avery braced herself with her hand against the dashboard. Didn't these things turn over all the time? That was all they needed, for John Paul to wreck the car. Carrie would be doomed.

Calm down, she told herself. We'll make it. We have to.

She looked down, saw the masculine Swatch watch half on top of her little Timex, and quickly removed it. After she examined the front and the back, she carefully placed it in the cup holder between them.

The road straightened ahead, and he glanced

over. "Now you start talking," he said. "Tell me exactly what she said."

She told him what she could remember, and then she said, "She was there watching us. I tried to find her on my way outside, but there were so many people milling around."

"She might not have been inside. Didn't you notice all the security cameras?"

She shook her head. "No."

"All she had to do was hook into their system. She didn't have to be there to watch you at the counter. Was there anything to distinguish her voice?"

"No, nothing. She just sounded . . ."

"What?"

"Creepy. She told me not to be a killjoy, called what she was doing a game. She didn't want me to spoil her fun."

Avery remembered the papers she'd shoved in her backpack and pulled them out.

"What's that?"

"I asked Cannon to give me all the information he had on the other two women who canceled at the last minute. She told me there were two women with Carrie now. They have to be the same ones. The first name is Anne Trapp. She lives in Cleveland and owns Trapp Shipping Company. Then there's Judge Sara Collins from Miami. It appears that all three reservations were made on credit cards. Each with a different name on it." She read the names to him.

"Do the names mean anything to you?"

"No," she answered. "I don't think Carrie's ever mentioned any of them, and I don't know how she would know them. Carrie and my uncle live in Bel Air."

"I figured that was where you were from."

"For a while I was," she said. "I live in Virginia now." She picked up the watch and checked the time again. "Can't we go any faster?"

"I'm going close to eighty now. The speed limit is fifty-five. I just hope the highway patrol isn't around."

Oh, God, she hadn't thought about that. They would be delayed indefinitely if they were stopped.

"Slow down then."

"Make up your mind, sweetheart. Fast or slow? It's your call."

"We'll make up the speed on the access road. Slow down for now."

He did. "You're sure the woman on the phone said, '*We* have her'?" stressing the plural.

"You already asked me that, and, yes, I'm still sure she said they have her. Why is that important?"

He could barely contain his excitement. "Because just maybe Monk is waiting for you at that spot on the map, and that gives me a unique opportunity to kill the bastard. If I can figure out a way to get ahead of him . . ."

He didn't go on, but she noticed he increased their speed again. "I think it's time for you to answer some questions," she said.

"Like what?"

"Why were you looking for Carrie? How do you know her?"

He had to confess. "I don't know her."

"But you said . . ."

"I lied," he said curtly. "I know the man who . . ."

"Who what?"

He was going to say *the man who killed her* because, if Monk was continuing with his pattern, those three women were already dead and buried. He had changed one thing, John Paul acknowledged. He was obviously now working with a partner.

". . . who is after the women," he said. "The man calling himself Monk. I doubt that's the name on his birth certificate."

"Tell me what you know about him. Who is he?"

"A professional killer."

"A what?" she asked sharply.

He repeated himself, and then he glanced at her face to see how she was taking the news. Not well, he decided. Not well at all. She was rapidly turning green.

"Are you gonna get sick?" He asked the question without a bit of sympathy in his voice.

"No."

He didn't believe her. "Roll down the window and lean out if you think —"

"I'm okay," she said, even as she hit the

button to automatically lower the window. She took a couple of deep breaths. The air was heavy with an earthy, musty scent. It made her want to gag. No, fresh air wasn't helping.

A professional killer. My God, she thought.

She exhaled and tried to clear her thoughts. Deal with what you know as fact, she told herself. Think it through.

Anne Trapp. Sara Collins. Those two women were throwing a wrench in her analysis. What was the common denominator?

"There has to be a connection," she said, and as soon as the words were out of her mouth, she shook her head. "No, I can't assume that."

He concentrated on the road. He had increased the speed once again because there weren't any other cars around, and he was betting the highway patrol was busy monitoring the more congested areas. He eased up on the gas pedal when the needle hit seventy.

"Road ends in five miles."

She grabbed the map. "How do you know?"

"I just read the sign."

"We're supposed to take the access road."

"I'm looking," he said.

She glanced at the watch for what had to be the hundredth time and saw that a full twenty minutes had passed. Then she measured the distance in her mind to the red *X*.

He glanced over at her. "Without good roads, it's going to be close. We might not make it, Avery."

"We'll make it," she insisted. "We have to make it."

"Ah, here we go," he said as he swerved off the road onto an access. Gravel spit up over the tires and hit the windshield as he fishtailed up the winding road. It was only wide enough for a single car, and the branches of the evergreens scraped the sides of the SUV as it zoomed past.

"We're headed in the right direction, and that's all that matters," he said.

"If we're lucky, maybe farther up we'll hook into a better road."

"Or no road at all."

"How exactly do you know Monk?"

"I've never met him, if that's what you're asking. He's become a hobby of mine. He went after someone close to me."

"Someone hired him to kill this friend of yours?"

"No," he answered. "But she got in the way. It was my sister. He was hired to get some information she had, and he tried to kill her to get it. Fortunately, his plans got all screwed up, and he ended up going to ground."

"So you've been tracking him for some time."

"Yes," he answered. "The man I called from Cannon's office also has a vested interest in Monk."

"Who is he?"

"Clayborne," he answered. "Noah Clayborne. He's FBI," he added with a note of disdain.

"But he's a friend of yours?"

"I wouldn't call him that."

She tilted her head as she studied him. What was his problem? He turned her attention then when he said, "Like I said, Monk went underground for over a year. Couldn't find more than a hint of his work . . . until now."

"How did you know he was in Colorado?"

"He used a bogus credit card he'd used before in Bowen . . . that's where I live," he said. "Bowen, Louisiana."

"Then the FBI knows he's in Colorado too," she said.

"No, they don't."

"But if you tracked him with the credit card receipt, surely the FBI —"

"They don't know about the credit card receipt."

"You didn't notify them?"

"Hell, no."

There it was again, that surly edge of hostility. "Why not?"

"Because I didn't want them to screw it up."

"The FBI does not screw up investigations. They're experts and extremely efficient in their —"

He cut her off. "Spare me the platitudes. I've heard all the propaganda before. I didn't buy it then, and I don't buy it now. The Bureau has become too glutted with bosses all trying to break the backs of the agents working under them so they can get to the top. There isn't any loyalty these days. It's just dog eat dog. They're

". . . bureaucratic," he added with a shudder.

"You're cynical."

"Damn right."

She looked out the side window. "Thank you anyway."

"What are you thanking me for?"

"Coming with me. You could have refused."

"Just so you understand. I'm not doing this for you or your aunt. I want to get Monk before he kills anyone else."

"In other words, you have your own agenda, and you aren't doing me any favors. I understand," she said.

She didn't understand, though. How could anyone be that hardened? She found herself wondering if he ever went out of his way to help anyone in trouble. Probably not. He was the type of man who drove past accidents and stepped over heart attack victims.

They rode in silence for several minutes, and then Avery said, "Tell me what you've learned about Monk. He must have a pattern. They all do."

He thought it was odd she'd know about such things. "Actually he did have a pattern, but it's obviously changed."

"How has it changed?"

"Monk always kept a low profile. In and out as fast and as clean as possible."

"You sound like you admire him."

"No, I don't admire him," he said. "I'm just saying his pattern never varied much before. In the beginning, the murders he committed all took place within a two-week span every year. That didn't change for seven years. I have a theory about that."

"You think he holds down a full-time job somewhere? That he's living two separate lives."

"I think he used to," he corrected. "Murder obviously pays a hell of a lot more, so I'm guessing he probably quit his other job. Couldn't you just picture him sitting at his desk, diligently working. He would have been the nice guy. You know, the one who draws the chart for the football pools, and because he was so well liked, people would tell him their troubles. I'll bet you this, Avery. When he gets caught, the people he worked with will be shocked. They'll all say the same thing. Bob was such a sweet, charming man."

"So was Ted Bundy."

"Exactly my point."

"How do you know the early murders were his work? Did he leave a card or something so he'd get credit?"

"Sort of," he answered. "He likes roses. He leaves a long-stemmed red rose."

"That's eerie," she said. "So he used to be a nine-to-fiver, and killing people was his idea of a great vacation, but now he's strictly a professional killer . . . any time of the year. What else is different about him these days? You seem to have studied his work closely."

He nodded. "He's never tried anything like

this . . . taking three victims. He isn't a show-man. And he's always acted alone before. Now it appears that he's hooked up with a woman. Maybe he's showboating to impress her."

They struck a bump in the road. Avery grabbed the dashboard again as the top of her head hit the roof.

"Are we still headed north?" It was impossible to tell. The trees hid the sky, and it was ominously dark in this stretch of forest.

"Northwest," he said.

She heard a scream in the distance. No, it was more like an animal's screech. The sound gave her chills.

"How does he get his contracts? Do you know?"

"No, but I'm guessing the Internet," he answered. "It's easy. It's anonymous, and up until now, he's been careful and discriminating in selecting his targets. He probably has enough work to keep busy for the next fifty years. You'd be surprised how many husbands want their wives dead and how many wives would pay through the nose to get rid of their husbands."

"My uncle Tony had nothing to do with this."

"You're sure?"

"I'm sure," she answered emphatically.

He let it go for the moment. "You said there had to be a connection between the women . . ."

"I was analyzing what we know, trying to put it together. I made the assumption that one man or woman hired Monk to kill all three women, so that's why I was trying to think of something they all had in common. But my premise might not be valid."

"Meaning?"

"We have to allow for the possibility that three different people hired Monk, and that, for whatever reason, he decided to kill the victims all at the same time."

He had to admit she was right. "One thing is certain. Monk was paid a hell of a lot of money to kill these women. He doesn't come cheap. If he has lumped them together, the real question is, who wants your aunt dead?"

He expected her to immediately tell him what a sweet, lovable woman her aunt was and that she didn't have an enemy in the world.

"Lots of people dislike my aunt. Some, I would imagine, hate her."

He wasn't prepared for that. He actually smiled. "Yeah?"

"Carrie can sometimes be . . . abrasive."

"Is that right?"

Avery nodded. "She's in a cutthroat business."

"Oh? What business is that?"

"Commercials."

"Excuse me?"

"She makes commercials."

He laughed, the sound harsh in the confines of the car.

"However," she continued, ignoring his reaction, "none of her business associates would go to such extremes to get rid of her."

"How can you be so sure?"

"I just am," she said.

"Okay, then that brings us back to your uncle Tony. How strong is their marriage? Any problems you know about?"

She was suddenly feeling sick to her stomach. "Carrie thinks Tony's cheating on her."

"Ah."

"They've been seeing a marriage counselor."

"Is that right?"

"Tony loves Carrie," she said.

"How well do you know your uncle?"

"Not as well as I should," she admitted. "I went away to boarding school and was only home during the summer, and then I worked in Carrie's office. Still, I think I'm a good judge of character. Tony would never be unfaithful."

"Wives usually know."

"Carrie isn't your typical wife. She's got a very suspicious nature. I think, deep down, she can't believe any man could love her. She's . . . insecure, and that's why she's often abrasive. She doesn't want anyone to see her vulnerability."

"So that leads us right back to . . ."

"If they are separate contracts, and one person hired Monk to kill Carrie and me, then . . ."

"Then what?"

"I know who he is."

# CHAPTER 11

The first hour was a nightmare, and then it got worse.

The crazy woman had almost blown them to kingdom come. Anne's hand was on the doorknob when Carrie tackled her to the floor. She was so skinny she went down hard, and Carrie landed with a thud on top of her. Both of them were screaming. Carrie had her hands full, and it was impossible to get the woman to listen to reason. Twisting and turning, Anne tried to claw Carrie's eyes with her long, tapered, acrylic nails. She made it to her knees and nearly got away from Carrie when Sara grabbed her by her ankles and dragged her from the door.

As thin and frail as Anne appeared, her rage gave her almost superhuman strength, but fortunately it was quickly spent. Panting from exertion, Carrie kept the woman pinned to the marble floor by sitting on her spine. She held Anne's head down with both her hands pressed against the back of her neck.

"Find something we can tie her up with,"

Carrie shouted to Sara so she could be heard over Anne's screeching.

Ten minutes later Anne was sitting in a chair at the round table in the breakfast nook. Her wrists were tied to the arms of the chair with two phone wires.

"How dare you treat me this way. You're not going to get away with this. You just wait and see. I'm going to report you."

Carrie, exhausted, fell into the chair adjacent to Anne's. She covered her brow with her hand, her elbow propped on the table, and calmly asked, "How do you plan to do that, Anne?"

"You bitch," Anne railed. "I'll call the police."

"Be my guest. Use the phone. Oh, wait. You can't because the damn phone's dead."

"You're lying."

Carrie turned to Sara, who was leaning against the counter, watching. "Is she just on another planet? I think her mind's completely snapped."

"Perhaps," Sara said. "Shock will sometimes make a person . . . irrational."

"What in God's name are we going to do?" Carrie whispered.

Sara pulled out a chair and sat down across from Anne. She folded her hands on the table-top. "Now, Anne, it won't do for you to continue to pretend that everything is all right. We're all in trouble here, and we need your co-operation."

Anne's immediate response was a glare. "Leave me alone, you fat pig."

"Charming," Carrie muttered.

"Bitch," Anne shouted at the top of her voice.

"If you continue to scream every word, Anne, I'm afraid I'm going to have to gag you," Sara warned. "Are you going to calm down?"

Anne's glare grew even stronger.

"Anne, where's the letter that was left for you?" When Anne turned her head away, Sara asked, "Are you giving us the silent treatment now?"

"Wouldn't that be a blessing?" Carrie scoffed.

Sara leaned back in her chair, adjusted her silk robe to cover her gown, and said, "You know, Anne, if you didn't get a letter . . ."

"I didn't," Anne snapped.

"Then you could be an innocent bystander who just got caught up in our . . . dilemma."

Dilemma? Carrie was about to take issue with Sara's poor choice of words. For God's sake, they were sitting inside a bomb. But then she caught Sara's eye and decided to keep quiet when the older woman gave a quick shake of her head.

"You see, Anne," she continued in a calm tone. "As a judge, I put away a good number of hardened criminals over the years. I had a reputation for giving harsh sentences, but in all of those cases, the men and women who came before me were career criminals. I don't have any regrets."

Anne finally looked at Sara with icy disdain. "Why are you telling me this?"

220

"Because it's important. Over the years there have been numerous threats against my life, but I've never given any of them a second thought."

She went into the living room to get the letters she and Carrie had received. She returned to her seat at the table and read her letter to Anne. When she was finished, she held the paper up in front of Anne's eyes so she could see she was telling the truth.

"And you think one of those criminals is making good on his threat?"

"Yes, that's exactly what I think. Either there's an ex-con behind this, or someone still in jail has gotten outside help."

"Where would an ex-con or a prisoner get the money to hire a killer?"

"Who cares where he got the money," Carrie interjected.

"I'm not talking to you, bitch," Anne hissed.

Sara raised her hand for silence. She didn't want Carrie's temper to trigger another tantrum.

"It's a valid question," Sara said. "I don't know how he got the money. Perhaps a relative came into an inheritance or . . ."

"And maybe you put away an innocent man, and those relatives know it."

"Yes, that might be how it happened."

Carrie was gritting her teeth to keep from interrupting. She wanted to tell both women that right now they needed to find a way to get out of the house, and then, once they were safe, they could speculate on the who, how, and why until the cows came home.

"Carrie's letter wasn't like mine," Sara said. "Hers was signed."

Anne looked intrigued. "So he wanted you to know how much he hated you before you died?"

"Not 'he,' " Sara corrected. "She."

Carrie nodded. Anne still wouldn't look at her, but Carrie didn't care about that. "My letter was written by my sister, Jilly."

The announcement so shocked Anne she couldn't continue her stony silence with Carrie any longer. "Your own flesh and blood wants you dead?"

"Yes."

Appalled, she asked, "What kind of a family do you come from?"

Carrie held her temper. "Dysfunctional, Anne. I come from a very dysfunctional family. My sister's crazy."

"Good heavens," Anne said. "Wait a minute. Are you lying? I mean, if your sister is really crazy, why hasn't she been locked away?"

"I was told years ago that Jilly died in a car accident. The funeral home wanted to send me her ashes. Jilly, it turns out, was much smarter than I thought. She's waited and planned all these years to get even with me."

"Why? What did you do to her?"

"She thinks I stole her child."

"Did you?"

"No, Jilly abandoned her when she was a

baby. My mother and I raised her."

"And your sister never came back?"

"Oh, yes, when Avery was five, Jilly came back with a sleazebag of a boyfriend named Dale Skarrett. She thought she could just waltz in and take Avery away. She'd already used extortion to get money out of my mother. That's true," she said when Anne looked so appalled. "My mother had to pay to keep Avery. I was home when they came, and while I physically tried to shove Jilly out of the house, my mother called the police. When Dale Skarrett heard the sirens, he grabbed Jilly and took off. I moved to California the following morning. While I was off building a career, Avery stayed with my mother. Then, when Avery was eleven, Jilly sent Skarrett to the house to kidnap her. Avery wasn't going to go quietly. She fought him tooth and nail, and he used his belt to beat her within an inch of her life. She was so young . . . and helpless. I guess I sort of thought of myself as her mother, but when it mattered, really mattered, I wasn't there to protect her the way a mother should."

"What about your mother? Didn't she do anything?"

Carrie looked down as she continued. "The police chief was a friend, and he had given Mother a gun, taught her how to use it too. She was in the backyard and didn't hear the screaming until she came into the house. My mother had become hard-of-hearing," she added. "From what the police were able to ascertain, Mother tried to shoot Skarrett. She must have given him warning because he grabbed Avery just as she fired. The bullet struck my niece."

The words came out in a monotone, but there were tears in her eyes. "I left an old woman to take care of my niece, knowing that Jilly was out there."

"But surely you couldn't have anticipated . . ."

"Oh, but I did know what Jilly was capable of," Carrie said.

"What happened to your mother?" Sara asked.

"She suffered a massive heart attack. She was dead by the time the police got to the house, and Avery was hanging on by a thread. I caught a flight from L.A. to Jacksonville. By the time I got there, Avery had already had surgery and was in ICU. The first thing the doctor told me was that Avery would recover, but he didn't give me time to rejoice because he said she wouldn't be able to have children. A hysterectomy at age eleven. That has to be some kind of record," she said bitterly.

Sara looked startled, and Carrie assumed she was reacting to her morbid account of that awful day.

"That poor child," Anne said. She sounded genuinely compassionate.

"I remember her," Sara whispered.

"What?" Carrie all but shouted.

Sara nodded. "The names . . . there were so many over the years; it isn't possible to remember all of them. And I didn't remember

Avery until you mentioned the hysterectomy at age eleven. I'll never forget reading the transcripts of the trial."

"I don't understand," Carrie said. "Why would you read the transcripts? Judge Hamilton was the judge at the trial."

"Yes, but Hamilton died before the sentencing date. He had a massive stroke, and the case was given to me. I'm the judge who sentenced Skarrett, and he has every reason to want me dead. I gave him the maximum."

Astounded, Carrie sat back. "So *there's* the connection between the two of us. Dale Skarrett . . . and Jilly."

"Jilly was never charged with any of it, was she?" Sara asked.

"There wasn't any proof to go after her. Besides, she had vanished," she explained. "It was Avery's sole testimony that got Skarrett convicted of second-degree murder. A few weeks after his sentencing, I got a call from a funeral home in Key West asking me what I wanted done with Jilly's ashes. That's how I found out she was dead."

"Except she isn't dead," Anne said.

"No, she definitely isn't. I saw her in living color last night," Carrie said emphatically. "She hasn't aged much at all. She's still beautiful . . . and still frickin' nuts."

Sara went to the kitchen cabinet and took down a cup and saucer.

"I always wanted to have a daughter, but my

husband didn't want children. He convinced me that it would cramp our lifestyle," Anne said.

"What was your lifestyle?" Sara asked as she poured the hot coffee.

"Work. Just work. I felt guilty about that," she confessed. "And so I gave in to my husband on all the little things."

Anne considered having children a little thing? "I see," Carrie remarked.

"Eric is ten years younger than I am," Anne continued. "But age never mattered to him. He loves me very much."

"I'm sure he does."

"He's taken over operations. You know, the mundane office managerial tasks, and he's so clever. He found a new health insurance carrier with a group rate that was less than half of what we had been paying."

Carrie couldn't understand why Anne wanted to talk about this now. Sara untied Anne's left hand and placed the cup of coffee in front of her. "There isn't any milk," she said. "But I found some sugar if you want it sweetened."

"No, thank you."

Carrie couldn't put up with the nonsense a second longer. The two were acting as if they were at a tea party. "What the hell are we going to do?"

"Find a way to get out," Sara said. "We're three smart women. We should be able to think of something."

Anne didn't seem at all interested in that topic. "Sara? What did you mean when you said I could have been an innocent bystander?"

Sara refilled her cup and sat down. "If you didn't have a letter on your nightstand . . ."

"I didn't," Anne rushed to assure her.

"Then I think I know what happened. Your plane landed just a few minutes before mine did, remember?"

"Yes."

"And didn't you tell us that you were irritated because the driver from the spa was waiting for me at my gate, but there wasn't anyone waiting for you? In the car you said that, if you hadn't seen the man holding up the sign for Utopia, you would have had to carry your own luggage and get a taxi."

Anne nodded. "Yes, I certainly do remember, and I was extremely put out. I'm still going to register a complaint with the manager. There should have been a driver waiting for me at my gate."

"Therefore," Sara continued as though Anne hadn't gotten sidetracked, "perhaps you weren't meant to be part of this. However," she hastened to add before Anne could interrupt, "the fact remains that you are going to die when this house blows up."

"But why? I didn't do anything wrong."

"And we did?" Carrie asked.

Anne shrugged.

"Answer me," Carrie demanded. "Do you

honestly think we deserve to die like this?"

"I don't know," Anne said. "You must have done something pretty awful to make your sister so mad, and, Sara, you might have sent an innocent man to prison."

Carrie had thought that Anne was going to be sensible, but her comments indicated she was still in Lala Land.

"I still don't understand why he brought me here," she said.

"Because you saw his face," Carrie muttered. "How could you have run a business? You ask such stupid questions."

"I don't like you." Anne took a dainty sip of her coffee after making the childish remark.

"I don't give a damn if you like me or not."

"Ladies, this isn't getting us anywhere," Sara interjected. "Anne, the killer couldn't leave you behind. You had also met me, and if you had gone to the spa, you would have complained to the management, and that would have signaled an alarm . . . since they obviously didn't send a driver to the airport."

"You also could have given a description of the man to the police. It was much too risky for him to leave you behind," Carrie explained. "And you could have told the police where he was taking us," Sara added.

"Oh, I'm sure he lied about where we were going. He lied about everything else, didn't he?" Sara asked. She suddenly looked weary, and her voice trailed off.

"No, he didn't lie about that."

Both Sara and Carrie frowned at Anne. "How do you know?" Carrie asked.

"Because I saw the sign. It was a tarnished brass plaque in the center of the iron gate. The driver pushed the button on that remote control gadget, and I read the sign as the gate was swinging open. Land Between the Lakes. So he didn't lie about that."

"That was very observant of you," Sara said.

"For all the good that does us," Anne said. "We can't tell anyone."

Carrie's head snapped up. "Oh, my God, I did tell."

"What did you say?" Sara asked.

"I called my niece from the airport. I was in the ladies' room, and I remembered I had my cell phone in the pocket of my blazer, so I called her. Her voice mail picked up and I left a message telling her where we were going to be spending the night. What a fool I am. I went on and on about the famous guests who had stayed here before. Monk — if that is his real name — must have done his research." Tears flooded her eyes as she whispered, "That's why he was telling those stupid stories about movie stars. He knew I'd be impressed. I'm such a shallow fool."

"He played all of us," Sara said. "Did you tell your niece the name of the property?"

"Yes," Carrie answered. "I don't know if she got the message because she might have already left for the airport. What if he was there waiting for her?" Her voice broke on a sob.

Sara reached across the table and patted Carrie's hand. "If he had been waiting for her, wouldn't he have driven her here? Maybe that's what they're waiting for," she added. "Maybe that's why they haven't . . ."

"Haven't what?" Anne asked.

"Killed us," Sara said bluntly.

"But you said they left us food in the pantry and in the freezer, so they obviously want to keep us alive a little while longer," Anne argued.

Sara disagreed. "The food . . . that's what's so alarming. Doesn't it seem more frightening to you that they didn't empty the cabinets?"

Carrie hadn't thought of it that way, but now she agreed with Sara. "I think that means they're going to blow the house soon. They're not going to let us sit in here until it's all gone. They left the water on too," she pointed out. "We have to get out of here." She buried her face in her hands and whispered, "I've got to get to Avery. If that monster has her . . ."

"Concentrate on finding a way out, Carrie, so that you can help your niece."

Anne straightened in her chair and nodded. "As long as you both agree I'm innocent, I'll help and I won't do anything crazy, like opening a door. I promise, but you have to say it."

Carrie lifted her head. "Say what?"

Anne straightened in her chair. "That I'm innocent."

230

She was, of course, implying Sara and Carrie weren't. It was infuriating, her holier-than-thou attitude, but Carrie caught Sara's nod and decided she had to get along with Anne if she wanted her cooperation. "Yes, you are innocent," she said.

After Sara concurred, Anne turned to Carrie. "You should try to make amends with your sister, fix the wrong you did."

Oh, how Carrie hated the woman. She held her tongue as Anne preached on. "Family is the most important thing of all. I recently learned that truth. Being able to lean on someone . . . like my husband when times get difficult . . . that's very important. I'm very fortunate," she continued. "My husband adores me."

She was excited when she turned to Sara. "He'll sound the alarm. My husband calls every single day. He's never missed. I told him not to bother while I was at the spa because I'd be doing all those treatments, and it would be difficult for him to get hold of me, but he wouldn't listen. He said he couldn't go to sleep at night unless he talked to me. So don't you see? If we can just wait it out, my husband will have the police tearing Colorado apart looking for me."

"We can't wait," Carrie objected.

Sara shook her head at her for losing her cool. "You sound like you have a wonderful marriage," she told Anne.

"Yes, I do. We're blissfully happy." There was a note of defiance. "And he will search for me."

"Yes, I'm sure he will," Sara placated. "But we might not have time to wait for the police to find us. Colorado's a big state."

Anne nodded. "Yes, you're right. We have to help ourselves. All right," she said as she untied the cord around her right arm. "What can I do? I don't know that I can be much help because I'm just getting over a long bout of illness. I've lost weight, and I don't have my strength back yet. I'm an excellent cook, though. I could fix us something to eat."

"That would wonderful," Sara said. "Thank you, Anne."

Carrie wasn't as trusting. Maybe Anne had come to her senses. Then again, maybe she was simply playing them. The stakes were too high to trust her. Carrie decided that either she or Sara had to keep an eye on the woman at all times.

"Is anyone hungry now?" Anne asked as she stood.

"I am," Sara said.

Anne didn't seize the opportunity to make a sarcastic remark about Sara's weight this time. In fact, she apologized for what she had said earlier, and damn if she didn't sound sincere.

"I never should have called you a fat pig. I was overwrought, but that is a poor excuse for hurting your feelings."

"Sara, why don't you stay here and keep Anne company while I search the house again," Carrie said. "I'll start at the top and work my way down. I've got to be missing something."

She was actually beginning to feel a little optimistic as she ran up the stairs. She hurriedly dressed in her designer sweats and then methodically rechecked each opening. There was a tiny window high up in the corner of her bedroom. It took her a long time to move the bureau over to the wall and then climb up, but she still wasn't tall enough. She ran downstairs to get one of the dining room chairs. She noticed Sara was standing on a chair in front of the double-pane living room windows. She had a lipstick and was printing the word "help" across the glass.

Carrie stopped her. "If Monk, or whatever the hell the bastard's name is, has put a triggering device outside . . ." She didn't have to finish her thought.

"The house will blow when help arrives."

"It's a possibility," Carrie said as she lifted the chair and started back up the stairs.

"I'll stop," Sara said. She got off the chair and went to get a towel to wipe off the letters she'd just written.

"What about trying to cut through the glass?" Carrie heard Anne ask as she continued on up the spiral staircase.

Carrie's arms ached from the exertion of lifting the chair on top of the bureau. It took her three tries, and she was panting because she was so terribly out of shape. She fell trying to climb to the top, but fortunately, she landed on the bed. She propped the chair against the wall and tried again. When she was finally able to reach the window, she burst into tears. The son of a bitch had wired that tiny little egress too.

She wouldn't give up, no matter how hopeless their situation was. Maybe Anne's suggestion would work. Maybe they could cut through the glass without disturbing the wires. Wiping the tears from her eyes, she gingerly scraped her diamond ring against the sliding glass door. Fifteen minutes later she stopped. All she had managed to do in that time was make a small scratch on the glass.

Carrie walked down a flight to the next level and proceeded to examine Anne's room and then Sara's. She spent hours trying one thing and then another before she finally gave up. She'd wasted the afternoon and part of the evening on the impossible.

# CHAPTER 12

Jilly walked around the stone bench nestled in the grotto facing the serenity pool. She paused to watch an instructor dressed in white tai chi clothing lead his students in an ancient exercise. The teacher was quite graceful, but his students were obviously novices, and their movements were stiff and awkward.

She continued on to where Monk had parked the all-terrain Mercedes. Flowers were in full bloom wherever she looked. There were even large patches of flowers along the back parking lot. Utopia was enchanting, and perhaps when this business was concluded, she could come back here for a full week of pampering.

Her phone rang just as she slid behind the wheel of the new car. She had been waiting for Monk to call from his satellite phone, and she answered before the first ring ended.

"Hello, darling."

Monk smiled. He loved the sound of her throaty voice and the way she whispered the endearment. "Has she arrived yet?" he asked.

"Yes, I've just sent her on her way, and I'm leaving now. I'll take the shortcut you found for me, and I'll be there a good forty minutes ahead of her."

"Did you enjoy talking to your daughter?"

"Oh, it was lovely," she gushed. "She's afraid. Thank you, darling, for letting me do this. There is one little worry, however."

"Yes?"

"Avery wasn't alone."

"What?" he asked sharply. "Who was with her?"

"A man," she answered. Adjusting her phone against her ear, she started the car and pulled out of the parking lot. "Her lover, no doubt," she speculated. "I had to include him because he knows that Carrie is missing. He went into the manager's office with Avery. Did I do the right thing? Did I?"

He knew she needed reassurance. "Yes, of course you did the right thing. Did you happen to get his name? Do you know anything about him?"

"No," she answered. "I thought about asking the clerk or the manager, but then I decided to wait and talk to you first. Do you want me to go back and find out who he is?"

"No, no, don't do that," he said. "You'd only draw attention to yourself. You're so beautiful, people will remember you . . . and you do look like Avery. I'll find out who he is."

"Yes, all right. Are you ready for both of them?"

"The plan's changed."

"Oh?"

"The river store is open, and business, I'm afraid, is booming. It's been busier that a 7-Eleven since early morning."

"How can that be?" she cried. "You checked. The owner was mauled by a bear and won't get out of the hospital for at least another week. You checked," she repeated.

She was becoming upset. He hurriedly tried to quiet her fears. "It's going to be okay."

She wouldn't let it go. "But how can the store be open?"

"The owner's cousin from Arkansas opened the store this morning. The owner must have called him. It doesn't matter," he stressed. "We're simply going to plan B. You remember, I told you I always have a contingency plan in mind whenever I take on a new assignment."

"I remember," she said, relieved. "You're so clever, darling."

The least little praise made him want to please her all the more.

"Wait," she said urgently. "The package with Carrie's red scarf. Is it still there on the counter?"

"No, but that doesn't matter now," he said. He had already thought the matter through. The original plan had been to lure Avery into the store by placing a large manila envelope with her name on it on the counter by the window so she would see it when she looked inside. She would be desperate and break in. Monk would be waiting for her, and after he had killed her, he would bury her in the forest about a hundred yards behind the store. He'd already gone to the trouble of digging her grave. The hole was deep enough to accommodate her lover as well, he supposed, but now that the store was open and there was a steady stream of customers coming and going, Monk knew he couldn't kill them there.

"Do you have Carrie's wallet with you?" he asked.

"Yes, it's in my purse."

"Good," he praised. "We'll use it, then."

"Do I get to help? You promised me," she reminded him.

How could he deny her? It would have been so much easier if she'd agreed to stay at the spa and let him do his job. Jilly complicated his life, made him scramble to get everything done the way she wanted it done, but she was such a joy to be with, he didn't mind. He had tried to talk her into blowing up the house before they left it last night, but she wouldn't hear of it. She wanted her sister to wake up and know who was killing her and why.

Monk didn't like leaving the women, but he couldn't be in two places at once, and Avery's unexpected arrival had thrown him a curve. He hadn't let Jilly know how unsettling and worrisome those last-minute changes were, but now that he'd worked it all out in his mind, he was feeling in control again. He wished he had more time to go over the plan, but that wasn't possible.

"Darling, did you hear me? I get to help, don't I?"

He pushed his concerns aside.

"Yes, of course you can help. How would you like to talk to Avery again?"

She laughed. "Oh, I'd love to," she said. "I'm hurrying to you. I'm already turning onto that little road you found. I won't be long. When I get there, you have to tell me exactly what you want me to say to her. I don't want to mess up again like I did in Virginia when I took that old woman's car."

"Hush now. Don't fret about that. It's water under the bridge. Besides, you're a rookie," he said with a chuckle. "You were bound to make a few mistakes."

"I only wanted to please you, and I thought that, if I could immobilize her, I would make your job so much easier for you. You could have broken into her apartment and killed her there. I thought you could make it look like a robbery."

They had been over this topic at least ten times, and each time he tried to reassure her that he had forgiven her misjudgment. She never should have gone after Avery with that car, not only because of the danger to herself, but also because she very well might have killed her. Jilly had been so proud of her careful research. She'd done her own surveillance, discovered the dusty old Cadillac was owned by a woman who never drove it, and had been so

239

clever in the way she'd gotten into the apartment and stolen the keys. She'd had fun too, dressing up as a policewoman collecting for the widows' fund.

Still, Jilly hadn't thought the plan through. When he gently pointed out that if she had killed Avery, Carrie certainly would have canceled her vacation plans, Jilly was mortified. Now she always checked with him first so that she wouldn't do anything rash. He liked the way she looked up to him, trusted him to know what was best.

"I'll meet you at our designated spot. Now, here's what I want you to do," he began.

She listened, growing more excited as he explained the details. When he was finished, she giggled. "It's perfect, darling. Absolutely perfect."

# CHAPTER 13

"His name is Dale Skarrett," Avery said, "and he's in prison now."

"Where?" John Paul asked.

"Florida," she answered. "He came up for parole a couple of years ago, and Carrie and I went to the hearing. We each spoke to the board, and they listened to what we had to say. We're the reason he didn't get out."

"So he has a real good reason for wanting both of you dead."

"Yes."

"What'd he do?"

She hated bringing those memories back to the surface. It made the wounds fester again.

"I'll explain later," she said, buying herself time.

"What'd he do?" he calmly repeated.

She turned away from him to stare out the window. "He murdered my grandmother," she answered. She anxiously looked at the watch. "We have twenty-three minutes left to get to God only knows where. What should we be looking for?"

He knew she was trying to make him focus on the problem at hand so that he wouldn't ask her any more questions. Eventually she would tell him what he wanted and needed to know if they were going to get through this alive, but he didn't press her now for the grim details. Like she said, they had only twenty-three minutes to go.

"We look for anything that doesn't belong."

They were still climbing higher and higher as they wound around the mountain. Avery had lost her sense of direction, but thankfully, John Paul hadn't.

Sunlight was streaming in through the branches again, and the area wasn't quite as thick with evergreens. She thought they were getting closer to an open area or a summit. Would they be sitting ducks?

"We're going to get nosebleeds if we keep climbing. Are you cold?" he asked.

"No."

He knew she was. He'd noticed her rubbing her arms a minute ago. He reached over and flipped on the heater. Avery immediately adjusted the vents so the hot air would blow on her arms.

"What do you think she meant?"

"What?"

"When the woman said 'boom.' I keep picturing those women tied to chairs with explosives."

"Maybe," he said. "Or maybe they're inside something that's wired."

"There are caves and old shafts around here, aren't there?"

"Yes," he said. "There are hundreds of them."

She checked the time again. "Twenty-one minutes."

"I'm aware of the time," he snapped.

"Can't you go any faster?"

"You want to drive?"

"No," she said. She realized her frustration and fear were misdirected. "Sorry, I didn't mean to criticize. I know you're doing the best you can."

It occurred to her then that she didn't know much about the man she had so eagerly jumped into the car with. No, that wasn't true. She knew enough to trust his ability. He had proven himself capable when he was in the military. Hopefully, the skills he'd learned would come in handy, if he still remembered them.

She decided to find out. "Were you any good at what you used to do before you took a leave of absence?"

The question jarred him. "What are you talking about?"

"You were in the military."

He gave her a sharp look. "How do you know that?"

"I had a friend look you up in the computer where she works."

She waited for a reaction. She was ready with a good reason for invading his private life if he asked. He didn't, though. In fact he didn't say anything for awhile.

"When did you do that?"

"Look you up? When I was in the manager's office at the spa. You had left to go find Cannon."

"You did a background check on me." He seemed to be having trouble believing her.

"Yes, I did."

The glare he cast her should have scalded her face. "Where does this friend of yours work?"

"Quantico."

Uh-oh. He didn't take the news well at all.

"Son of a . . ." he began.

"You were a Marine," she blurted.

She watched him take a breath and knew he was trying to keep his temper under control. Oh, yes, he was angry; his neck had turned pink. It didn't matter to her, though. She had done what she had to do, and he was going to have to deal with it.

The muscle in his jaw flinched. Lord, he was good-looking. The thought came out of nowhere. Jeez, Avery, get a grip. For all she knew, the man could be paying alimony to eight ex-wives. She quickly discounted the Henry VIII notion right away. There couldn't possibly be eight women in the United States willing to marry him. No way.

"You were a Marine," she repeated.

"So?"

She had to grab hold again when he swerved to avoid a tree trunk. There were deep ruts in the dirt from other cars or trucks that had ventured up this road, but it was so isolated, so . . . quiet she was a little unnerved. She felt completely out of her element. She was a big-city girl who fell asleep to the music of car horns and police sirens. The silence now seemed almost deafening.

Swarms of gnats scattered as they hit the windshield. Avery picked up the watch and checked the time again. Seventeen minutes left.

John Paul kept glancing over at her. She thought he expected her to finish what she'd started.

"So that was good to know," she said.

"Why?"

"Marines are trained in combat, and that could be helpful." He didn't respond to her observation. "I also found out you were recruited by covert —"

He didn't let her finish. "Look, I know what I was. You don't have to go into it."

Damn. She had been hoping he would finish for her and tell her what she didn't know. Had he been in special ops or covert operations? And what exactly had his expertise been?

She looked at the map while she gathered her gumption. She couldn't find out unless she asked, could she?

"So what exactly did you do?"

"Don't you know?"

"Your file was classified."

"I would bet so."

There it was, that snide tone of voice again.

"Did they teach you to be obnoxious, or were you born that way? You've got that alienation thing down pat."

"Avery, leave it alone."

"You don't scare me."

His eyes narrowed as he looked over at her again. "Yeah, I do."

"Oh, brother."

He smiled in spite of his bad mood. Maybe he didn't scare her. Interesting, he thought. And different.

"Do you think the two of them are together? Monk and the woman who called me?"

"I don't know. If the missing women are still alive and if he's tied them up or hidden them somewhere that's really isolated, then he could be with her. He's got a lot going on," he said. "*If* the women are still alive."

"He has to keep his eye on them. And he has to follow us."

"I don't think he's following us."

"But he's tracking us, isn't he?"

He almost smiled. "How?" he asked. He already knew the answer, but he was curious to know if she had figured it out.

"There's some kind of device inside the watch."

"Yes," he said. "He knows exactly where we are."

She shivered. The killer was monitoring their progress. "Shouldn't we get rid of it?"

"No, I don't want to do that. I think we

should use it to our advantage. Let's wait and see what happens when we get near the X."

Avery picked up the watch and looked at it carefully. "There isn't a single scratch or mark on it to indicate someone's tampered with it."

"Monk's a professional. He wouldn't leave any marks."

"So he knows all about transmitters? He understands that technology?"

"Yes, he does."

"How do you know so much about him?"

"I read his file."

"The FBI file?" Her eyes widened. "If you're on leave, that's got to be illegal."

"I'm sure it is."

"John Paul, you could get into serious trouble."

She sounded worried about him. She was just chock full of surprises, and what a piece of work she was turning out to be. If he didn't watch out, he would start to like her.

"I've got connections who could bail me out," he said.

"Like your brother-in-law?"

"How'd you know about Theo?" he asked.

"When my friend pulled up your file for me, she told me."

"Having a relative working in the Justice Department comes in handy."

"You don't like your brother-in-law?"

What an odd question. "Sure I do. My sister loves him, and they're happy together. Why would you ask me that?"

"You sneered the words 'Justice Department.' "

He smiled. She was a quick study. "I didn't sneer."

She decided not to argue with him. "Do you think the woman who called me hired Monk?"

"Could be," he said, "but I don't think so. From what you said about her, he's letting her call the shots. I think she might be more like a partner. It's so damn odd. Monk never played games before. So why the treasure hunt?"

"I don't know."

"We might catch a break if the woman is making some decisions. Maybe she isn't quite the perfectionist he is."

"She's someone who knows Carrie and me."

"Because?"

"The way she talked. Her tone was mocking when she said Carrie's name. She doesn't like her."

"That's a given."

"Which means she's interacted with her."

"What about you?"

"She called me stupid. I've got to assume she doesn't like me either," she said dryly.

"No kidding."

"Maybe it's just that Skarrett has told her about us. But the way she talked . . . it sure sounded like this was personal to her."

Avery picked up the Swatch watch again and then gingerly placed it back in the cup holder. She could almost visualize a red light inside, pulsating like a heart. The image creeped her out.

John Paul was a good driver. She decided to let him worry about getting stuck in the mud and nicking a tire on a rock. Closing her eyes, she leaned back and let her mind move from one possibility to another. What was she missing? She felt as though she had the answer to this crazy puzzle in the back of her mind, but she couldn't quite reach it.

"How much time's left?" As soon as she told him, he said, "I don't know what we're going to barrel into, so listen up. You do whatever I tell you. If I tell you to get down, don't argue. Just do it. Once I figure our where the X is, I'm gonna try to bypass it some way and then circle around. You'll stay in the car."

"I have to show."

"No, you don't."

"Are you crazy? Of course, I have to," she argued. "The woman said they would kill Carrie and the others if we're late. If I don't show my face . . ."

"Did this woman offer you any proof that they're still alive? Did you ask for any?"

"No," she said. "I should have, but I didn't. The conversation was short, and she wouldn't let me ask questions."

"Then you should have said no."

"Tell her I wouldn't play her game?"

"Yeah," he said. "That's what I would have done."

She shook her head. "I don't believe you. But, I'm sorry I didn't ask for proof. I should have."

"Should have, could have . . . it's too late now. I figure we've got a ninety percent chance of walking into a trap, so I want —"

She wouldn't let him finish. "I told you, I don't have a choice. I have to show. I'm hoping I can figure out a way to placate the madwoman."

"Placate a madwoman? That's a contradiction, isn't it?"

"Don't be a smart . . ."

He raised an eyebrow. "Smart ass? Is that what you were going to say?"

"No."

"Then what?" he challenged.

She became defensive. "Look, if you want to bail, that's fine with me. Just get me to the *X* and take off."

"I'm not going to bail."

"Okay, then," she replied, irritated she'd sounded so relieved. "I know there's a good chance Monk has already dug our graves, but if you think I'm going to hide in the woods and hope for the best, then you're out of your mind."

"All I'm trying to say is that, if I'm lucky, maybe I'll spot him and be able to get close."

"And you don't want to worry about me. You want blind obedience."

"Exactly."

"Two heads are better than one."

"How much survival training have you had?"

Point taken. "None, but I could still help."

"Yeah, sure."

"Get rid of the attitude, John Paul. I can help. I have a few moves of my own."

"I'll bet you do."

"What's that supposed to mean?"

"Never mind."

She was doing a slow burn. Out of all the people in the world, she had to be stuck with the most obnoxious one. "You think you've got me all figured out, don't you?"

"Just about," he drawled.

Avery concentrated on the road. Thankfully, Jungle Boy didn't have any other sarcastic remarks to make. His scowl could have been chiseled in stone.

She thought she heard something, quickly rolled her window down, and strained to listen. "Do you hear that?"

John Paul flipped off the heater blower, rolled his window down, and then nodded. The sound of running water was faint, but there. "We went farther than I thought if we're close to the river. Maybe it's a tributary. It sounds like a waterfall."

They came to yet another crossroad. This one was traveled more than the last. And there was a sign nailed to a tree: *Last Chance Country Store. Beer and Raft Rentals.* Below the sign was an arrow pointing to the west.

The road curved downward. They hit a deep rut and lurched forward as they once again broke through the trees.

"The store's got to be around the bend down

there," he said as he shot across the road and up into the trees on the other side. There was just enough room to turn the car around. Satisfied that they were concealed from the road, he put it in park and turned the motor off.

"How much time do we have left?"

"Twelve minutes," she said. "You think that's the spot?"

"It's gotta be the place. It sticks out, doesn't it?"

He was right. Please, God, let him be right. She could just make out a small rustic building through the trees. It sat on the bank of a river and was a place where river travelers could stop for supplies.

He unhooked his seat belt, reached under the seat, and pulled out a SIG Sauer. When she saw the gun, her mouth dropped open.

"I'm leaving the keys," he said, ignoring her reaction to the gun. "If you hear gunshots, you get the hell out of here. You hear me?"

She wasn't about to leave him, but she thought he'd want to argue if she told him the truth, and so she simply nodded.

"Is it loaded?" she asked as he opened the door.

"Hell, yes."

Stupid question, she thought. Of course it was loaded. "Be careful." She moved into the driver's seat.

"Hand me the watch."

"You're taking it?" she asked.

"You think I'm going to leave it here with you and let Monk know exactly where you are? Give it to me."

"What are you going to do?"

"Go hunting."

# CHAPTER 14

Time had run out. Avery had just decided to go after John Paul when he opened her door. She never heard him coming. "Monk isn't close. He could be on his way, but he isn't here now."

"Are we driving down or walking?"

"I'll drive."

She scrambled back into the passenger seat, bumping her knee on the dashboard. He slid in and started the engine.

"How do you know he isn't hiding behind a tree or a bush somewhere?"

"Because I looked. There weren't any signs."

"You would have seen them?"

"Of course I would have seen them."

She was reassured by his arrogance. "Okay, then."

"There's a trailer behind the store about thirty yards to the south, and next to it is an old beat-up truck. No one was inside the trailer."

"You went in?"

He didn't answer. "There's a man and a woman inside the store. The woman's in the

254

back office using the phone, and the man's in front, working the counter. He keeps looking out the window like he's expecting company. While I was there, a milk truck pulled out and another guy was unloading cases of beer. There are three or four customers."

He drove onto the road and continued down the slope. His gun was in his lap.

"Do you see that man looking at us?" he asked. "He's on the right by the door."

They watched a young couple herd their two little boys out the front door, then saw the man inside slam the door.

"What the hell?" John Paul muttered when the man turned the sign over in the window. "Closed, my ass."

He parked close to the side of the building so that she would be protected when she stepped out. He turned the motor off, slipped the keys into his jeans, and as he sprinted around the hood of the car, she saw him tuck the gun into his waistband.

They heard rap music blaring as a car pulled into the parking lot. John Paul went to the corner of the building and looked out front. Four young men in their late teens piled out and stood laughing and guzzling their beers. On top of the old Chevy were two kayaks roped to the roof.

John Paul motioned to Avery to stay put, retraced his steps, and said, "I'm gonna check out the back again."

He let the man at the window watch him walk into the woods, then circled around, swung over the railing at the back door and looked inside. The woman was hunched over the desk, still talking on the phone.

Even though she was much too young, she reminded him of Ma Kettle from the old movies he used to watch on television when he was a kid. Dressed in dirty overalls and a muted plaid flannel shirt with the sleeves rolled up, she was rattling off numbers into the phone as she turned the pages of a Sharper Image catalog. She didn't notice him watching her. He stepped back as the swinging door opened. A man poked his head in the room and braced the door with his hand to keep it from hitting him.

"Chrystal, we got us a problem," he said in a thick hillbilly accent. "There's two cars out front now. Four drunks just got out of one car. They're most likely stoppin' to stock up on more beer, I expect, but I'm most worried about that gal in the other car. She's gonna be knockin' on the front door any second now. I think maybe she spotted me peekin' out the window at her 'cause that car she was in is parked on the side of the building now. Think she's the one?"

"Can you hang on a minute, hon?" Chrystal said into the phone. She turned in the swivel chair and frowned at the dark-haired man. "Most likely she is, but I'm not finished with this catalog yet, and you promised me I could —"

He interrupted. "Maybe she ain't the one.

Maybe she just needs to use the facilities. There was a big fella with her, but he went off into the woods to find his own facilities, I expect, like those four drunken boys. One of them is peein' on the petunias."

"Can't you see I'm busy here, Kenny? If that gal wants to use our facilities, you make her buy something first, and don't let her wander back here. I've still got a good ten pages to go."

"Don't know why you didn't think about doin' that earlier. Had to wait till the last minute, didn't you?"

John Paul went back to the entrance and was on the porch by the time Kenny unbolted the door.

Avery slipped around the corner of the building and ran to stand next to him. He pushed her behind him. He was being protective, and she didn't mind. She was so worried that they might not be in the right place, she couldn't think about anything else.

"Can't you read the sign? We're closed," the man said.

Avery stepped to John Paul's side. "It's an emergency," she blurted.

"Then you got to buy something first."

"Excuse me?"

"You heard me. You got to buy something, and after you pay, I'll let you use the facilities."

Kenny was snarling at her like an attack dog. He was a thoroughly unpleasant-looking man with blue-black dyed hair and bushy brown eyebrows. He wore a dark plaid shirt tucked into his faded black jeans. His gut hung down over his belt.

"Did you hear me?" he asked when she didn't respond. "I ain't gonna budge until you agree."

He changed his mind when John Paul stepped forward. If Kenny hadn't gotten out of the way, he was sure the big man would have walked right over him.

Up close, Kenny was much younger than John Paul had estimated. He couldn't have been more than thirty-five or forty years old. He was also agile. He warily kept his eye on John Paul and hurried around the counter as though the barrier would protect him.

Planting his big hands on the counter, he leaned toward Avery and smiled. One of his eyeteeth had a gold cap that gleamed in the sunlight streaming in through the dirty window. "All right, little lady. I'll tell you what I'm gonna do. Since you're so pretty, I'm gonna break the rules for you. You don't have to buy nothin'. Nothin' at all. The bathroom's right over there," he said, pointing to the door in the far corner.

She shook her head. "My name's Avery Delaney, and this is John Paul Renard. Has anyone come in here asking for us?"

"No," he answered, a little too quickly.

He was lying. All the telltale signs were there. He couldn't look her in the eye, and he was becoming more and more agitated by the second.

Hostile too. He kept glancing up at John Paul as he shifted his weight from foot to foot.

The door crashed into the wall when it was thrown open. Avery and Kenny turned to see who was coming inside, but John Paul kept his attention on Kenny. He wasn't going to trust the bastard for as much as a second.

Three of the four boys sauntered in and staggered to a stop when they spotted Avery. She could hear the fourth boy. He was leaning over the porch railing throwing up.

"Hi there," one of them called out. Another tried to whistle, but he couldn't get his lips to work. Spit sprayed out of his mouth instead.

Two of the boys were obviously brothers, for they looked alike and sported identical eagle tattoos on their forearms. The oldest-looking one of the group had a scraggly goatee and a pierced eyebrow with a silver ring.

"The store's closed," Kenny shouted.

"No, it ain't," Goatee said. "You let *them* in," he added, pointing to Avery and John Paul. "We only want some beer."

"Yeah, beer," one of the brothers parroted.

They staggered toward the cooler against the back wall. One of them tripped into a display of cans and sent them careening everywhere. Goatee thought that was hilarious.

Kenny wasn't amused. He looked as if he wanted to kill someone. "You pick up every damned one of them cans and put them back like I had them. You hear me?"

A brother snickered while Goatee gave Kenny the finger.

"Get the hell out of my store," Kenny bellowed. He turned his wrath on Avery next. "If you ain't gonna use my facilities, and you ain't gonna buy nothin', then maybe you folks ought to leave."

"What about phone calls?" she asked, sounding as desperate as she was feeling. "Have you gotten any calls for me?"

"No."

One of the brothers was standing about three feet away from Avery and was fixated on her as he swayed on his feet. His stare was unnerving.

"Stop staring at me."

He grinned stupidly at her, then lunged with both arms outstretched with the obvious intent of hugging her.

John Paul was about to pull Avery into his side, but she was already moving. She lashed out at the drunk with a kick that was quick and effortless. Her foot struck him square in the stomach and sent him flying into the wall. He hit with a loud thud, slid down, and landed on his butt.

She pointed a finger at him. "You stay there."

And still the stupid grin remained on the drunk's face. He was too far gone to feel any pain.

She turned her attention to Kenny again. "May I use your phone?" Out of the corner of her eye she spotted Goatee and the other brother coming around the corner. Each of them had two six-packs of beer and a bag of ice. She didn't mince words. "Over there, both of you. Sit down next to your friend and be quiet until I'm finished."

Goatee shook his head. "You can't tell me what to do, sweet cakes."

"We don't have a phone," Kenny muttered at the very same time.

"Sure you do," John Paul asserted as he stepped toward Kenny.

"What happened, Mark?" the other brother asked.

Goatee strode forward, thinking he could elbow his way between Avery and John Paul.

"My turn," John Paul drawled a scant second before he sent Goatee sailing headfirst into the wall. He dropped the beer and the ice on top of Mark, then fell down next to him.

They didn't have to tell the third drunk to join his friends. He staggered over, put the beer down, and sat. Leaning back, he opened one can and took a long swallow.

Kenny realized John Paul was looking at the phone on the counter. "What I meant to say is that we got a phone. Of course we do, but it ain't workin'. Line's down and it takes weeks and weeks to get a repairman to come all this way. In case you haven't noticed, we're sittin' out in the middle of nowhere." He was talking so fast the words were tripping over each other.

Kenny could see John Paul wasn't buying it,

and so he turned to Avery. The phony smile was back. "Your mister have a problem?" As he continued to smile at Avery, he slowly reached underneath the counter.

He looked down and too late realized he never should have taken his eyes off John Paul. He heard a click and jerked up to find the barrel of John Paul's gun pointed at his forehead.

"Now hold on. No need for that," Kenny stammered.

"John Paul, we need this man's cooperation," Avery said.

"And this is how we get it," he replied. "Kenny, turn around and put your hands on the wall behind you. Avery, get his gun from under the counter."

She walked around the counter and immediately spotted the Magnum on the shelf underneath. She slowly picked it up and then checked it. The weapon was loaded and ready. She engaged the safety, noticed a box of cartridges, and grabbed that too. She put both in a plastic sack with a picture of a squirrel on it.

"What are you doing with a Magnum? Do you have a permit?" she asked Kenny.

"That's none of your damn, nosy business."

The good-old-boy façade was gone now. True colors were finally spewing out. Kenny's face twisted with rage as he snarled, "I can refuse service to anybody I want to, and if I want to keep a loaded gun on the premises, then that's what I'm gonna do. Can I turn around now? I'm getting a crick in my neck. You can use the phone. I was just . . . worried you was gonna make a long-distance call, and my cousin George, he's the man who owns this place, well, he would see the bill and then he'd say to me, 'Kenny, you're gonna pay for this.' "

"Where is George?" Avery asked.

"He got hisself attacked by an old brown bear. He didn't know she was there until he saw one of her cubs," Kenny said. "Can I turn around now and put my hands down? You can see I'm cooperatin' and you got hold of my gun."

"Yeah, sure," John Paul said.

Avery was heading for the phone when, out of the corner of her eye, she saw a lady's billfold sticking out between two sales slips in the trash can next to the cash register. She leaned down to pick it up. Then she caught her breath. It was a new, black Prada billfold. Carrie owned everything Prada made.

Kenny was watching John Paul. "If you're gonna rob me, you might as well know I don't have much cash. Maybe two one-hundred-dollar bills and forty some in change."

"Where'd you get the hundred-dollar bills?" John Paul asked.

"A customer."

"We didn't come here to rob you," Avery said. She opened the billfold, saw that it was empty, and held it up for John Paul to see. "I think this belongs to my aunt."

Kenny grabbed her from behind. He wrapped

his big arms around her in a bear hug and lifted her up so he could use her as a shield. His arms were like bands of steel, but his chest was soft, almost mushy.

"Let go of me," she ordered. "I don't have time for this."

Kenny was trying to duck down behind her so John Paul couldn't get a clear shot. "Not till your mister puts that gun down."

John Paul was surprised Avery wasn't frightened. If anything, he thought she looked put out. "That's not gonna happen," he said. "Avery, you'll have to change your clothes."

That remark got her full attention. She stopped squirming and asked, "Why?"

"Because I'm gonna get blood all over you when I blow this mother —"

"No," she said. "Kenny, I know this billfold belongs to my aunt, and I don't care that you took the money. But you're going to have to tell me where you got it. Now let go of me."

"No way," he snarled close to her ear and tightened his hold.

His fingers were interlocked around her waist. She took hold of one of his little fingers and jerked it back hard. At the same instant, she lowered her chin, then slammed the back of her head into his face. She heard a crunch as he gasped in pain and let go.

"Ouch," she whispered. Damn it, that hurt. She stepped away from Kenny and rubbed the back of her head as she walked over to John

Paul. Not as simple as it looked in the movies, she thought. Lesson learned.

She noticed the incredulous look on John Paul's face. "What?" she asked.

His smile was slow and easy. "Not bad."

She rolled her eyes in exasperation and looked at Kenny, who was leaning into the counter. "I need to know where you got that billfold."

"It belonged to my wife, Chrystal. She got tired of it and tossed it in the trash."

"Stop lying. This is a matter of life or death," she said, her voice hostile now. "I really don't care if you took any money out of the billfold," she repeated. "But I need to know where you got it."

"I just told you . . ."

He wasn't going to admit anything. Avery's initial panic had dissipated as soon as she'd spotted the billfold because now she knew she was in the right place. The tightness was still in her chest, however, and she was becoming infuriated over the man's uncooperative attitude.

Kenny's nose was bleeding. He held a Kleenex against his nostril and squinted at her. "I'm gonna sue you, bitch. That's what I'm gonna do."

"John Paul, I think you're going to have to shoot him after all," she said.

Kenny didn't seem worried until John Paul asked Avery, "How about the kneecap?"

Fortunately, Kenny had become a true believer. "Okay, okay," he said. "When we opened up this morning, me and Chrystal found a package with her name on it." He pointed to Avery. "It was just sittin' there on the counter, so Chrystal decided to have a look inside."

"And?" Avery prodded.

"And it was just a red scarf. It had a perfume smell to it Chrystal didn't care for, so she stuffed it back in the envelope and tossed it in the trash."

"How did you get the billfold?" she asked.

"I was gettin' to that," he said, resentment brimming in his words. "A woman came in just a little bit ago. She held up a brand-new hundred-dollar bill in exchange for that package with the scarf, and we took it, of course. Then she grabbed another manila envelope from our shelf. Just helped herself to it. She turned around so we wouldn't see what she was doin' and put that billfold inside. After she sealed it, she wrote your name on it and told us she'd give us another hundred if we'd promise to tell you that she was gonna call and for you to stay here until she did."

"But you opened the envelope as soon as she left?" John Paul asked.

"No, not that second. It nagged at Chrystal, though. She just had to have herself a peek inside, and when she saw the billfold filled with money, she helped herself. Anybody would've done the same thing."

Avery didn't waste time arguing ethics with him. "What exactly did the woman with the hundred-dollar bills say?"

"I already told you what she said."

"Tell her again," John Paul ordered.

"She's gonna call you. That's what she said. She told me she knew just about the time you folks would be coming into the store and said you was supposed to wait until she called."

"But you weren't going to tell us any of that, were you?" John Paul said. "You were going to send us on our way and never mention the billfold or the woman."

Kenny didn't answer. He shrugged and then said, "There wasn't much money in the wallet. Just a bunch of twenty-dollar bills."

"Hardly worth getting your nose broken?" John Paul said.

"Look, I should have told you, and now I'm sorry I didn't," Kenny said. "When my wife gets off the phone, I'm sure that lady will call. You're just gonna have to wait."

"Where is your wife?" Avery asked.

John Paul answered. "In the back office."

He grabbed her arm when she started in that direction. "Do you know how to use a gun?"

She pulled away from him and hurried to the back of the store. "I'm not going to shoot anyone, John Paul."

"Be careful," he ordered.

She took the warning to heart. When she reached the swinging door, she slowly pushed it open and looked inside. A woman was sitting with her back to the door. She was bent over with the receiver to her ear as Avery quietly walked forward. She heard the woman say, "No,

I want five of them. That's right. Five. Now the last item is number A3491. The silver stereo with all them CD holders. I want eight of them. No, make it ten. That's it, hon. Are you ready for my credit card number? What? Oh, my name's Salvetti. Carolyn Salvetti. I'll be using my American Express card to pay for all this merchandise, but I want them shipped to my Arkansas home."

Avery was furious. She came up behind the woman and snatched the phone from her hand. Chrystal lurched out of her chair, sending it crashing into the wall. "Who do you . . ." she sputtered.

Keeping her eye on Chrystal, Avery spoke into the phone. "Cancel the order. She's using a stolen credit card."

"No," Chrystal shouted as Avery hung up the phone. "You got no right to come barging in here. No right at all. This is my private office. Now give me that phone back."

"You and Kenny are going to jail."

"Hold on there a minute. We didn't do nothin' wrong."

Chrystal's eyes were set a little too close together and her moon-shaped face was twisted in anger. Not pretty, Avery thought as she watched her step forward threateningly. Her brown eyes darted back and forth like a cornered rat's as she considered her options. "There's no reason to call the police."

The woman towered over Avery and outweighed her by a good sixty pounds. When a sudden gleam came into her eyes, Avery knew what she was thinking, that her size gave her the advantage.

"Don't even think about it," Avery said.

"This is private property," Chrystal half shouted. And then she lunged.

Avery didn't need to defend herself. She simply stepped to the left and watched as the large woman fell on top of the desk. Her precious catalog ripped open and flew to the floor.

What a klutz. "Behave yourself," Avery scolded like a teacher disciplining a child with a harsh warning. "Now get up and go into the store. Move it," she shouted when Chrystal didn't move.

Carrie's driver's license and all of her credit cards were on the desk, except the American Express card. She saw Chrystal slip the card into her pocket. "You just don't give up, do you? Give me the damn card."

Chrystal threw it at her. Avery caught it in midair and then nodded toward the swinging door again.

Chrystal shoved the door open and hurried ahead. She tried to push the door back in Avery's face, but Avery used her foot to block it.

"Bitch," Chrystal growled. Then she saw Kenny and took her wrath out on him. "I told you we'd get into trouble, but you wouldn't listen to me."

John Paul slipped his gun into the back of his

jeans and then looked at Avery, waiting for an explanation. She took a step closer to him as she said, "Chrystal was doing a little early Christmas shopping with my aunt's American Express card."

"Aren't they a pair?"

"Yet another good reason I'm never going to get married," she said.

"I don't see any need to get the police involved," Chrystal muttered.

"Who said anything about the police, Chrystal?" Kenny demanded. "Why'd you have to go and bring them into this?"

"I didn't, you old goat. Blondie did," she added, pointing at Avery. "And all this is your fault, Kenny. If anyone's gonna go back to jail, it's gonna be you. I already got one strike against me. Didn't I tell you you shouldn't let me open that package? Didn't I?" she screeched like an irate hen. "You made me do it."

"Shut your trap," Kenny told her.

Chrystal finally noticed her husband's condition. He was sitting on the counter, swinging his legs back and forth while he held a torn Kleenex to his nose. She gave John Paul the once-over too. "Who's he?" she demanded. "And why are you pickin' at your nose?"

"I ain't pickin' nothin'. That gal behind you broke my fuckin' nose. I'm gonna get me a lawyer and sue her."

"From jail?" Chrystal bellowed. "You moron. You aren't gonna sue nobody."

270

John Paul had about had it with the happy couple. He went to the front door and stood to the side looking out. The teenager who had been throwing up was now curled up on the porch sound asleep.

"Stop arguing," Avery demanded. She was a little surprised that Kenny and Chrystal actually obeyed her.

"No reason to scream at us, missy. You can see we're cooperatin'," Chrystal said.

"Fine. You're cooperating. Where's the envelope?"

"You mean the one the billfold was in?" Chrystal asked.

"Yes."

"I threw it in the trash by the facilities," she said. "There was just the billfold, but I'll get it for you so you can see for yourself."

She took her sweet time crossing the store and returned a minute later with the yellow envelope. Thrusting it at Avery, she said, "See. It's empty."

Kenny's nose had stopped bleeding, and he tossed the Kleenex toward the wastebasket behind him but missed. "I told you everything that gal said to me, but she was pretty chatty with Chrystal."

"That's right. She sure was chatty. She told me you folks were goin' on a treasure hunt. Kinda' old to be playin' games like that, aren't ya?"

Avery was close to pulling her hair out in frustration. These people were driving her crazy.

271

"When she came in, did you see her car? Was there anyone waiting?"

"Had a nice new Mercedes," Kenny said. "But there wasn't nobody inside it. Just the gal."

"Did she tell you where she was sending us?"

Her obvious anxiety gave Chrystal a surge of power. She said snidely, "Depends."

"Depends on what?" Avery asked.

Chrystal rubbed her fingers together, the universal sign for money. Avery didn't have the patience to negotiate.

"The woman left instructions too, but Kenny and me aren't sayin' another word until you make it worth our while."

"Okay, John Paul. We're back to doing it your way. You may shoot one of them. That should get the other one talking."

He liked the way she thought. The gun was out, the safety off less than two seconds later.

"Got a preference?" he asked.

Chrystal put her hands up. "Hold on there. No need for violence. Kenny and me is peace-lovin' folks, aren't we, Kenny? We'll tell you what you want to know. The woman said a gal would be comin' in. Said the gal's name was Avery." Turning to her, she asked, "You're her, aren't ya? You got to be her."

"Yes. What else did she say?"

"That she'd be callin' and that you'd be leavin' in a hurry, but she was sure wrong about that, wasn't she? I mean, you're still here."

Kenny snorted. "They can't be leavin' in a

272

hurry until after she calls, you twit."

"Avery, I really want to shoot these people. Put them out of their misery," John Paul said.

She understood how he felt. "Put the gun away, John Paul."

The second he lowered the gun, Chrystal cheered up and managed a smile. "Kenny, they'll need supplies for where they're headed. You carry what they want out to their car while I total it up in my head." Turning to Avery she asked, "You got cash on you, don't you?"

"We don't need supplies," she said.

"You want directions to where she's sendin' you?"

Avery understood. In other words, buy the damn supplies. "Yes," she answered.

"Don't you be givin' them no discounts, Chrystal. And no credit cards. These folks ain't gonna live long enough for the receipt to go through."

Chrystal nodded. "The woman's sending you to a fiver."

What in God's name were they talking about? Then Kenny said, "Don't know how you think you're gonna do the river. Since all the rain we've been having, only fools would try to raft it. You're gonna drown before you make it over the first rapids." The possibility so tickled him he chuckled. "Don't matter how experienced you are."

"That's right, hon," Chrystal said. "You're gonna get yourself drowned, all right. Now, that gal said you'd see a sign with writing on it and you'd find what you're lookin' for right by it."

"Did she tell you what's on the sign?"

"Coward's Crossing. All the locals use that name too, for that little area where you can look down at the river if you're too afraid to go in. Years ago, there used to be a rope bridge, which is why they called it a crossing."

"You'll have to hike to get there," Kenny said. "I know the lay of the land 'cause I've been comin' up here ever since I was a boy, and there ain't no path up there."

Chrystal didn't agree and began to argue with her husband.

Avery reached for the phone and then stopped. One quick call to Margo, she thought, to tell her where she was and what was going on. Should she chance it?

Kenny finally won the shouting match, and while Chrystal sulked, he gave Avery detailed instructions on getting to Coward's Crossing. She pulled the map from her pocket and asked Kenny to mark the area.

John Paul had two plastic sacks full of bottled water and food. He grabbed two more protein bars, shoved them into the smaller sack, and headed to the car. Kenny hopped off the counter to chase after him just to make sure he wasn't going to try to drive away without paying.

Avery grabbed a piece of paper and wrote down Margo's number. "Chrystal, I want you to drive to another phone and call this number.

Tell whoever answers that I was here and where I'm headed. There's a lot of money in it if you make the call," she promised. "But don't use this phone."

"How much money?"

"Five thousand dollars." She said the first figure that popped into her head. "And when we capture the man we're after, there will be twice that amount, and you'll get all of it."

"How much exactly?"

"Ten thousand." The lies were getting easier.

Chrystal looked suspicious. "How do I know you aren't gonna help yourself to that money?"

"Because I'm FBI," she said. "My ID is in the car. Would you like me to go get it?"

"I should have guessed it," she snorted. "You bein' so bossy and all. You don't have to show me your badge. I believe you. You got that FBI look about you, and that fancy karate move you did on me in the office got my suspicions up. I should have paid attention to the warnin' bells goin' off in my head."

What fancy move was she prattling about? All Avery remembered doing was stepping out of the woman's way.

"That's very astute of you," she said dryly.

"Now, tell me again about that money. Would it be fifteen thousand in all?"

"Sure."

Chrystal squinted at Avery. "And you're saying all I got to do is make that call?"

"Yes, and will you —"

Chrystal cut her off. She'd glanced at the number on the paper and blurted, "Wait a minute. This here is a long-distance call. Can I reverse the charges?"

"Yes."

"Okay, I'll do it, but I got to tell you, I still don't get it. You could use the phone right there," she said, pointing to the counter. "What's the catch?"

She didn't waste time telling Chrystal she couldn't take the chance the line might be tapped. "You just can't use this phone. Wait about twenty minutes, then get in your pickup and drive to the nearest phone."

"Will you pay for the gas?"

Avery felt like screaming. "Yes."

John Paul had just walked back inside the store when the phone rang. Avery flinched at the sound.

"That's probably her," Chrystal said. "We haven't gotten a single call since we reopened the store this morning, so that's got to be her. Want me to answer it?"

Avery grabbed the phone and answered on the second ring.

"You were late," the caller said.

"No, we weren't. We were right on time. The woman you left the package with was using the phone when we arrived."

"Yes, she was."

Avery then knew she had been monitoring the line. Thank God she hadn't tried to call Margo.

"Did you get the directions to where you're going?"

"Yes. I want to talk to Carrie."

"No, that isn't possible."

"Then how do I know she's still alive?"

"Carrie is alive . . . for now anyway. It's up to you to keep her and her friends that way, isn't it?"

"Why are you doing this?"

"No more questions," she hissed. "Or I'll hang up the phone right now. Do you understand me?"

"Yes."

"You're on a lovely treasure hunt, and you're winning points as you move along. The prize is Carrie. You do want to see her again, don't you?"

"Yes."

"That's good." She laughed. "You're so eager to please. You'd better hurry, Avery."

"How long —"

"Hurry now."

The woman disconnected the call. Avery's heart was pounding. She put the phone down as Chrystal asked, "Was it her?"

"Yes," she answered. "Chrystal, describe her to me."

"You mean you want to know what she looked like?"

"Yes."

"She was older than you, but not as old as me, and not as heavy as me. Kenny?" she shouted, "How old would you say that woman was?"

Kenny walked inside. He scratched his stubbly jaw while he considered his answer. "I don't know. Never could judge a person's age real good. She sure was a looker, though."

Chrystal nodded. "Had yellow-colored hair, and it's kind of funny really, you askin' me what she looked like."

"Why?" Avery asked.

"Well . . . 'cause . . ." Chrystal shrugged. "She kinda looked like you."

# CHAPTER 15

Chrystal told Kenny they would receive a big reward if he drove to town and made a call for Avery. Kenny didn't believe his wife, and he didn't want to do it. Avery thought it might be because his nose had started bleeding again.

Unlike Avery, John Paul wasn't interested in trying to coax them into cooperating, because he understood how their twisted pea-sized brains worked. He had had enough of the Bonnie-and-Clod pair. He shoved Kenny into the wall and calmly told him that he would hunt him down and skin him alive if he didn't do what Avery asked. Simple as that. Kenny believed him, and so did Chrystal. The look in John Paul's eyes indicated he wasn't the type of man to make idle threats.

Chrystal jumped back when John Paul walked past. She knocked the phone off the counter and quickly picked it up. Instinctively putting the receiver to her ear to make sure no one else was on the line, she hung up and said to Kenny, "The phone isn't workin'."

279

"Are you sayin' the line's dead?" Kenny gasped the question, still trying to recover his breath.

"Didn't I just say it was broke?"

"She did it," Kenny decided, glaring at Avery. "She must have broke it after she finished talkin' to that woman and hung up. You saw her slam it down, didn't you, Chrystal? You're gonna have to pay for repairs," he told Avery.

Avery picked up the phone to see if Chrystal was telling the truth. The line was dead. That was quick, she thought. They must have been ready.

John Paul stood by the door waiting to get Avery's attention. "Avery . . ."

"Just a minute." She walked over to the teenagers sprawled out on the floor. Two of them were curled up like cats, sound asleep, but the droopy-eyed boy named Mark was still sitting upright and watching her every move with the stupid grin still plastered on his freckled face.

"Who's the driver?"

"Huh?"

She nudged his foot. "Who's driving the car?"

"Me."

"Give me the car keys."

The grin didn't falter. "I don't have to," he slurred even as he dug into his pocket and pulled out his key ring. He dangled the keys in front of his face. Then he giggled.

She snatched the keys out of his hand and tossed them on the counter. "Chrystal, you make sure those boys don't get into that car. You understand?"

"I'm not gonna be a baby-sitter. You expect me to stand here and watch them?"

"Make them sleep outside, but don't give them the keys." She turned to leave, but John Paul raised his hand for her to stop.

"More customers," he said. He glanced out the window and watched two older women, dressed in hiking clothes, get out of a Ford. He pushed Avery's hand away from the doorknob. "You're not going with me."

"Oh, yes, I am," she insisted.

"Listen to me," he ordered. "You go back to town with those women and get to a police station. Keep the gun just in case."

"While you go ahead to Coward's Crossing?"

"Yes. If I can get there quick, I might be able to find a good spot to ambush him."

She shook her head. "If you kill him, we won't be able to find Carrie and the others."

"The woman knows where they are."

"She'll disappear, and you know it. It's too risky. Besides, if Monk or the woman finds out I'm not with you —"

"They won't know."

"You have to take me with you."

"No. It's too dangerous for you, and you'll slow me down."

"Then I'm going to follow you. Kenny gave

both of us the directions. I can find Coward's Crossing. I'll take the teenagers' car. Simple as that, John Paul." She poked him in his chest. "You need me to get him. Now get out of my way."

He didn't want to waste any more time arguing. He decided he'd have to find a place to dump her on the way. Someplace safe. Yeah, that's what he would do.

He opened the door. "You stay close," he whispered as he stepped back so the gray-haired women could come inside.

The ladies walked right past the teenagers and didn't seem to notice them when they headed for the facilities, as Kenny so quaintly called the bathroom.

Avery turned back to Chrystal, who, at this point, was the more agreeable of the two. "How long do you think it will take to get to Coward's Crossing?"

"You aren't gonna make it before nightfall," Chrystal answered. "What with all the rain, those little roads got all washed out."

John Paul was opening the door but paused when Kenny shouted, "Hey, wait a minute. You ain't gonna take my gun, are you? I've got to have something for protection, being out here with just the missus."

"Let it go, Kenny," Chrystal said. "George never got a permit for that thing."

Kenny's face turned red. "Why'd you have to open your big mouth and bring that up?"

"She would have wanted to see it," Chrystal argued. "They always do."

"Who's 'they'?"

"FBI." She pronounced each letter as though it were a profanity.

"What?" Kenny screeched. "You're saying that gal's FBI?" His eyes bulged at the news.

Mark groaned. "Ah, man, we're gonna get busted."

Ignoring the drunk, John Paul closed the door in Avery's face and asked softly, "You're an FBI agent?"

Uh-oh. One quick glance at his expression, and she inwardly cringed. He looked so offended that she didn't think it would be a good idea to explain it all to him now. Maybe later, she thought, when he was asleep.

"Answer me," he demanded. "Are you an FBI agent?"

He wasn't going to budge until she responded. She swallowed, then whispered, "Sort of."

Then Chrystal, who, Avery decided, really did have a big mouth, said, "She told me she left her ID in the car, but she'd go get it if I wanted to see it."

"I'm leaving," Avery announced. She used every ounce of strength she possessed to push John Paul out of her way so she could get out the door.

He didn't move an inch. "We'll be talking about this later."

She waited until he stepped back, then

brushed past him. Childishly wanting to have the last word, she muttered, "No, we won't."

The SUV fantailed out of the lot onto the dirt road when John Paul floored it, the tires spitting up pebbles and dirt clumps. He headed toward the river and was driving like a lunatic.

"Slow down," she ordered.

He eased up on the pedal while Avery went over the directions. "I should have asked Chrystal to give me a guess as to how many miles Coward's Crossing was from the store."

"We're going to be hiking," he said.

"I'll keep up with whatever pace you set."

"We'll see. Tell me, what did the woman on the phone say?"

She repeated the conversation and added, "I demanded to talk to Carrie, but she said that wasn't possible."

He shook his head. "And yet you *still* believe your aunt's alive?"

"Yes, I do. I think the woman wants to keep Carrie around . . . for a little longer anyway." She didn't have a valid reason for why she felt that way. Maybe it was just desperate hope on her part. "You know what I don't understand?"

"What?"

"Why are they going to so much trouble if they want to kill me? Why make it complicated? There was ample opportunity to ambush me on the way to the spa, before you were even involved. It would have been so much simpler." She slapped her forehead. "Of course. They didn't know I was going to drive to the spa. When I missed my flight, they had to improvise. You were another complication. You were hanging around the spa asking questions. Now it makes sense."

She shook her head. She must be tired. It took so long for her to figure it out. She closed her eyes for a moment and thought about the phone call again.

"The woman . . . she's having fun."

"I'm sorry?"

"I could hear it in her voice. She was excited, even when she was hissing at me and calling me stupid. She doesn't want this to be over too soon. She wants to drag it out." She thought it over for a long minute and then said, "She likes giving orders, and as long as we play her little game, or treasure hunt, as she called it, she might prolong it even more."

He drove as fast as the dirt roads would allow while she gave him directions. Avery kept replaying the conversation in her mind, analyzing what little data she had. It was so frustrating.

John Paul interrupted her. "Okay, Avery. It's later."

"I'm sorry?"

"I said it's later, and we're going to talk about it now. Why the hell didn't you tell me you were an FBI agent?"

"You made it very apparent you didn't particularly like the Bureau."

"Yeah? When did I do that?"

"When we were in the manager's office at Utopia, you called your friend Noah. I heard you tell him to bring in the troops."

"And?"

"And then you told me they'd mess up the investigation. When I pressed you on your attitude, you became quite hostile. Besides . . ." She could feel herself blushing. "I'm not really an agent, not yet anyway."

He slowed the car. "Yeah? Then why are you telling people you are?" He shook his head and said, "Who in his right mind would want to impersonate an FBI agent?"

Avery hated being put on the defensive. God, he was such an obstinate, opinionated jerk. "I don't usually tell people I'm an agent. I just told Chrystal, in hopes of gaining her cooperation. Unlike you," she added, "I don't use coercion and brute force to get what I want."

John Paul ignored the criticism of his tactics. Why fix what wasn't broken? Brute force had always worked. "I do what I'm good at doing. That's my motto."

"Watch out," she warned as he turned the corner and nearly ran into a deer. John Paul hit the brakes and swerved off the road, narrowly avoiding the animal. The car rocked and bounced but held the ground.

It was too dangerous to try to maintain a high speed. He slowed the car and said, "Chrystal's right. We aren't going to make it before nightfall."

"Think positive."

"Why?" He sounded genuinely perplexed.

"Maybe we'll get a decent road soon," she said.

They drove around another sharp curve. Down below to the west was a road that looked well traveled. He decided to go for it.

"Hang on," he said as they started down the hill. The slope was steep, and he had to be mindful of jagged rocks.

Avery flattened her hands against the seat as they bounced along.

"So," he said, "were you lying about having a badge?"

"I have credentials in my backpack."

"But you're not an agent?"

"No."

"Then what the hell are you doing with credentials?"

"I do work for the Bureau. I'm just not a field agent."

"That's good."

"Why? Because you hate the Bureau?"

"No, because you're not any good at it."

"How would you know what I'm good at?" she said. Lord, he was irritating. Every time he opened his mouth, he said something that rubbed her the wrong way. No man had ever been able to get under her skin the way John Paul did.

"You don't have the instincts," he said. "And before you get all hot and bothered and argue, answer a question for me, and be honest."

She folded her arms and frowned at him. "What?"

"Did you anticipate that Kenny might have a loaded weapon under that counter? Did you even for a split second consider the possibility?"

"No."

"There you go."

"I haven't been trained to be a field agent. I didn't go through the academy."

"That's no excuse. You've either got it, or you don't. You've got some good moves," he added. "The way you kick-boxed that kid was impressive. But you'd still make a lousy field agent."

She refused to comment on his assessment.

"What exactly do you do for the Bureau?" he asked.

John Paul could see the blush was coming back. She was either embarrassed or so mad at him her face was turning a fire red. She sure was pretty. Ah, hell, where had that come from? He had no business thinking about such things, especially now that he knew she represented everything he detested.

"I type," she said. She heard how defensive she sounded and quickly added, "There isn't anything wrong with being a typist."

"I didn't say there was."

"I'm part of a very important team."

"Ah, jeez."

"What?"

"You bought it all, didn't you? A team player. You're probably a damn liberal too, aren't you?"

"As a matter of fact I am," she said. "And I'm certainly not ashamed of being a typist . . . it's an honorable job, after all."

"Okay."

"Quit being so condescending. I wasn't hired to be a typist, but that's what I pretty much do anyway, all day, every day. I transfer information into the database. Now, can we let the matter drop?"

"Yeah, okay," he said.

He seemed preoccupied now. "What are you thinking?" she asked.

"This is a good road. Maybe we will get close to Coward's Crossing before it gets dark. We'll hike a couple of miles, find a secluded spot for you to hide, and then I can —"

That was as far as she'd let him get. "Not gonna happen," she said. "I'll tell you what. You drop me off, find another good road, and with any luck, you can make it back to Aspen before dark."

"And why would I want to drive back to Aspen?"

"I've been thinking . . ."

"Uh-oh."

She ignored the insult. "I think you should get out while you still can. You can tell the FBI where I'm going."

He blinked. "You're kidding. Right?"

She began to fold and unfold her hands. "No, I'm serious. What can they do if you leave? Nothing," she said, answering her own question.

"Frankly, you don't need to be involved. You said it yourself. They want me, not you. Besides, you called Noah, and he's FBI. I'm sure he's alerted the local team, and they're most certainly on their way. When you get to a phone, you can call him again, and tell him exactly where I'm headed."

"I've got an opportunity to get Monk, and you think I'm gonna . . ." He was so angry he was sputtering. He shook his head. "Let me get this straight. You really believe I'll drop you off in the middle of nowhere and take off?"

"Wasn't that your plan?"

"Hell, no," he argued. "I was going to find a safe place for you to hide until I got back, someplace Monk would never find you."

"In other words, you'll drop me off in the middle of nowhere and take off." She didn't give him time to think about it. "You're not dropping me off anywhere, unless you plan to go back to Aspen."

"You're nuts, you know that? You're just plain nuts."

"I gather that's a no?"

He didn't respond to her sarcasm.

She brushed her hair away from her face with her fingers and laid her hands on top of her head. "I wish we could get out of this car. I need a quiet place to think."

"You can't think in a car?"

She knew he wouldn't understand. When she was in her cubicle at work, she felt the same way she felt when she was doing yoga. She'd perfected the technique of clearing her mind and then slowly entering data one clue at a time while her hands worked the keyboard. No, he couldn't possibly understand, and she couldn't explain.

"So who looks like you?"

"I'm sorry. What did you ask?"

"Back at the store," he said. "Chrystal said the woman looked like you. So I've gotta ask if you happen to have any crazy relatives trying to kill you."

"No. There's only my aunt Carrie and her husband, Tony. No other relatives."

"Parents dead?"

She turned in her seat and stared at his profile when she answered. "I don't know who my father was. I don't think the woman who had me knew who he was either," she said.

She watched him closely to see if she had shocked him. His expression didn't change.

"She died in a car crash quite a few years ago. There isn't anyone else."

"Chrystal said —"

"I heard what she said, John Paul. Do you know how many women her description fits?"

He glanced at her and asked, "So is it real?"

"Excuse me?"

"Your hair. Is it real?"

She blinked. "Are you asking me if I wear a wig?"

"No, I'm asking about the color. Are you a

real blonde, or did you get that from a bottle?"

"Why do you care about the color of my hair?"

"I don't care," he said, growing irritated now. "But the woman looked like you, so I gotta wonder if you —"

"No, I don't color my hair."

He was surprised and didn't hide his reaction. "Yeah? What about your eyes?"

"What about them?"

"Colored contacts?"

She shook her head. "No."

"No kidding."

"Are you deliberately trying to be a jerk?"

"Look, I'm just trying to put it together, okay? Kenny said the woman was beautiful. A real knockout."

"And?" she pressed.

He shrugged. "Have you looked at yourself lately? You've got to know . . ."

"Know what?" she pressed when he didn't continue.

He frowned at her. "Hell, woman. You're pretty, damn it."

It was the most hostile, backhanded compliment she'd ever received, and the odd thing was, it didn't upset her. For the first time ever, she didn't feel the need to launch into her favorite lecture about how appearances weren't the least bit important.

She forced herself to consider the problem at hand. "The data isn't sufficient to form a conclusion."

"Jeez, you sound like a computer. A lot of things aren't adding up."

She agreed with a nod. Her stomach was hurting. She felt as though she had a hot coal lodged in her esophagus. She picked up her backpack, found her antacid, a bottle of water, and two energy bars. She opened the bottle, popped the pills, and swallowed. Then she handed the bottle to John Paul and opened one of the energy bars for him.

"Thanks," he said after he took a long swallow of the water. He took a bite of the bar and washed it down with another gulp. "It tastes like cardboard."

"You're welcome."

His smile lasted for half a second, but she still saw it and reacted. She surprised herself. She couldn't stand the man an hour ago, but now she didn't think he was so awful. He had a beautiful profile . . . and was sexy as hell. No reason for her to pretend she didn't notice, even though she wasn't going to do anything about it.

He was also protective. The way he tried to boss her around in the store when she went running to the back office. He acted . . . worried. Worried about her safety. Nice, she thought. He wasn't such a cold duck after all.

"It's gonna rain," he remarked.

"Rain will slow us down."

"It's still coming. The sun's going to be setting soon," he said. "I'm going to plant the watch about a mile or two from here. Then we'll go on for as long as we can."

He parked the car and picked up the watch. "What'd you do with that gun we took?"

"It's in the sack on the floor."

"Get it out and keep it on your lap. Have you done any target practice?"

"No."

He gave her a disgruntled sigh. "Keep the safety on." He got the gun for her. "I won't be long."

He disappeared before she could tell him to be careful. A fine drizzle began to fall, covering the windshield. It seemed an hour had passed before he came sprinting down the hill toward the car. When he opened the door, a blast of cold air filled the interior.

The second he turned the motor on, she flipped on the heater. "Where did you leave the watch?"

"I hooked it to a tree branch by a crossroad to the west. If he's tracking us now, I'm hoping he'll think we took the other road."

He drove on, thanking God he had a four-wheel drive. He zigzagged up the side of the mountain, slowly weaving in and out of the trees. When the terrain became too dense to go any farther, he maneuvered the car into a cluster of thick pines, turned it around, and then backed in until he was assured the car couldn't be seen from the road below.

Night rushed in on them, closing them in together. The drizzle had turned into rain. A booming clap of thunder sounded. She flinched.

"You've got a weapon just in case, food and water."

"What do you mean I've got food and water? You think you're going to leave me here?"

He reached for the door.

# CHAPTER 16

By the time Carrie plopped down on the living room sofa, she felt doomed. Jilly and Monk had thought of every possible way out. Oh, yes, they'd wired every window . . . except, perhaps, one. She looked up at the skylight that loomed over the spiral staircase. The bubbled rectangle was over thirty feet above them. She shook her head. Even if they stacked table upon table upon wardrobes, they still wouldn't be able to hack their way through.

Anne had prepared a dinner from the contents of the pantry, and the three women ate in dejected silence. The sun had gone down and the house was dimly lit by the candles Anne had found. None of them wanted to turn on the lights, fearing Jilly and Monk were watching, and there weren't any drapes to cover the massive windows. Sara had brought up the possibility that Monk had hooked up a video camera to observe them. That so freaked out Carrie, she once again scoured the house, this time looking for a camera.

Anne was reclining on the sofa, and Sara sat in an easy chair waiting for her when she came back downstairs.

"I couldn't find anything," Carrie said. "I looked everywhere. I even searched the light sockets, the ones I could reach," she added. "I don't think anyone's watching us."

"What difference does it make if they can see or hear us?" Anne asked.

Carrie thought the question was stupid but didn't say so. "Because if we're digging our way out of the basement and they can see us, they'll push the button and kill us right then and there."

Digging through the basement was, of course, out of the question. The door to it was locked, and there was a big sign taped to it. One word, but quite enough to keep the three women from trying to break the lock. "Boom."

Exhausted and frightened, Sara and Carrie sat in silence as they stared out the windows at the deepening shadows on the beautiful landscape.

Anne struggled to sit up. Carrie noticed a stack of papers on the sofa next to her.

"What's all that?" she asked.

"Newspaper clippings I found in the chest in the foyer. One of the owners of the house must have saved them. Here they are," she said, handing Carrie a picture of a bride and groom on their wedding day.

"They look happy."

"I imagine they were," Anne said. "But now they're getting divorced and fighting over this house. Here, take all of the articles," she said, thrusting them at Carrie. "It's quite sordid. Is anyone ready for dessert?"

She sounded like a hostess of a party. Carrie found the question hilarious and laughed until tears came into her eyes. Sara was also tickled. She began to giggle.

"Oh, I don't know if I have room for dessert," Sara said. "After that gourmet dinner of baked beans and canned beets, I'm quite full."

"Don't forget the creamed corn," Anne reminded. "I worked hard to get just the right amount of pepper mixed in."

"It was very tasty," Sara said.

"I've taken inventory of the pantry," Anne said. "I thought we could have canned peaches for dessert. Shall we eat in the kitchen by candlelight? I've closed the blinds so no one can see in from the driveway."

Anne was sounding so chipper that Carrie became alarmed. Her own burst of laughter had been due to near hysteria, but Anne wasn't hysterical. She was acting as though she were having a lovely time getting together with old friends.

"After dessert, I have a surprise for you," Anne said. Her wry smile reminded Carrie of the cat who'd just eaten the canary.

"You aren't going to try to open the door to the garage, are you? That one is wired too," Sara said. "I checked it myself."

"In other words, you read the sign on the door?" Carrie said.

"Well, yes," Sara answered sheepishly.

Carrie put her hand out and helped pull Sara up from the easy chair.

"I'm a little stiff," Sara said.

Anne had already gone into the kitchen. They could hear her singing. Carrie, picturing Anne climbing up on the granite counter to open the window above the sink, rushed ahead of Sara. Blessedly, the image wasn't real. Anne was opening the can of peaches.

Carrie couldn't stop worrying. The woman had yet to grasp the futility of their situation. "Anne, you're not getting loopy on us again, are you?"

Anne laughed. It was a high-pitched noise, like china breaking. "I don't think so. Now sit down and relax."

At this point, Carrie knew she would have done anything Anne or Sara told her to do. She was feeling so beaten down. She was sick with worry for Avery, and though she was loath to admit it, she missed Tony.

"I miss my husband." She was surprised she'd said the thought out loud. "I guess I do love him."

"You don't know?" Anne asked. She placed the fluted ice cream bowls on the table and scooped peaches into each one.

"I thought he was cheating on me. He said he wasn't, but I didn't believe him. Some woman was calling at all hours of the night. The phone's on my side of the bed, and I always answered. She'd ask for Tony, but when he'd take the phone, he told me she hung up. What if it was Jilly calling?"

"You didn't trust your husband."

"No, I didn't."

The three women ate in silence while Carrie continued to wallow in self-pity. "You know what I hope?"

"What's that?" Sara asked.

"When it happens, I hope we're all sound asleep so we don't know it."

"That's grim," Sara said.

"Will the sound of the explosion wake us up before the pain of being incinerated —"

"Stop it, Carrie," Sara demanded. "We don't have time for such negative thoughts."

"Listen, if I want to —"

"Ladies, please," Anne interrupted. "Are you ready for my surprise?"

"You are loopy," Carrie muttered. "You found some Froot Loops?"

Anne didn't acknowledge her ridicule. "I've built two houses in the last ten years. The second one was over three thousand square feet. Cedar siding," she added. She nervously laughed as she qualified. "I hired a contractor, of course, but I was there every single day making sure everything was done the way I wanted it done. I drove the builder crazy."

"I'll bet you did," Carrie said.

"Why are you telling us this?" Sara wanted to know.

"I was leading up to my surprise," Anne said. She took a breath and then whispered, "I found it."

"Found what?" Carrie demanded.

Anne beamed with self-satisfaction. "A way out."

# CHAPTER 17

"You'll be okay here," John Paul told Avery.

"What do you mean, I'll be okay? You're thinking about hiking to Coward's Crossing now? In the dark . . . in a rainstorm? Are you nuts?"

"Avery," he began.

She grabbed his arm. "Okay, if your mind's made up, I'm going with you."

She knew he'd argue, and he did exactly that. He was almost civil as he told her she would slow him down, and he didn't want or need to have to worry about her out there. When that didn't work, he tried intimidation, even going so far as to threaten to tie her to the steering wheel.

She let him go on and on as she climbed into the backseat, found her black jogging jacket, and put it on, and then dug through her bag until she located her baseball cap.

Scooping her hair up under the black-and-orange Orioles cap, she adjusted the brim, sat back, and kicked off her tennis shoes. Her goal was to try to blend in with the night, and white tennis shoes would be seen.

Thank God she'd decided to bring her hiking shoes. She knew he was watching her every move as she carefully repacked her duffel bag.

"I think it's crazy to hike in the dark . . . only an idiot would try it, but if that's what you want to do, then I'm right behind you," she said.

"You're staying here," he said between gritted teeth.

She pretended she hadn't heard him. "We won't get far, and one of us might break an ankle or something walking into a hole we can't see. If I were making the decisions," she added as she carefully placed her tennis shoes, soles up, on top of her clothes and rezipped the bag, "I'd say we should stay in the car until dawn. Then we hike at a fast clip."

"Yeah, well, you're not making the decisions. I am."

She pushed the duffel bag to the floor, stacked her hands on the headrest, and leaned forward until she was just inches from his face. "Why?"

He couldn't hold on to his glare or his bad mood when she smiled. Hell, she even batted those big baby blue eyes at him.

"Are all the typists at the Bureau smart-asses like you?"

He was trying to put her on the defensive so she'd stop arguing with him and let him do what he was trained to do. It was a great plan, he thought, but unfortunately she was having none of it.

"Are all burnouts as obnoxious and stubborn as you are?"

He caught himself before he smiled. "Probably," he allowed.

"Are we going or not? Time's a-wasting, John Paul."

"We're going to wait until dawn," he said. "Don't give me that smug look, sugar. I had already decided to wait."

"Uh-huh."

He was smart enough to know it was time to stop arguing. Honest to God, she was more stubborn than he was, and in truth, that impressed the socks off him. She wasn't going to let him win this round, but he already had another plan in mind. He'd sneak away a little before dawn. When she woke up, she'd have to stay in the car and wait for him to come back.

And if he didn't make it back . . .

"I'm gonna leave the keys in the car."

"Okay."

"Get in the front seat so I can fold down the back. I've got a sleeping bag," he added. "You can use it."

"We'll both use it."

"Yeah?"

She rolled her eyes. "Don't get any fancy ideas, Renard."

"Fancy?" He laughed.

Avery had already found the latches and unhooked the seat backs. When they were flat, she spread out the sleeping bag. She tucked her hiking shoes under the seat, removed her jacket, and tossed it on the floor. John Paul stretched out on his back with his feet against the dashboard. He looked comfortable, his hands stacked on his chest, his eyes closed.

Shivering from the cold, she had to climb over his legs to get to the other side. Her teeth were chattering as she stretched out beside him. She couldn't reach her jacket. It was under the seat below him. A gentleman would have put his arms around her to warm the shivers away. He wasn't a gentleman, she decided, when he completely ignored her.

It had always been a point of pride with her never to complain. She was usually quite good at suffering minor and major ailments in silence. But John Paul brought out the worst in her. She really wanted to whine now, and she was more disgusted with herself than with him. He couldn't help being a jerk. She could.

Suck it up, she told herself. Then a minute later, when she was sure her toes were frostbitten, she whispered, "Screw this."

"What?"

"I said it was cold."

"Huh."

"Huh, what?"

"I could have sworn I heard you say, 'Screw this.'"

He really liked being rude, she supposed, and

no wonder, he was so very good at it. She smiled in spite of her misery. "Don't you think it's cold?"

"No."

Ignoring his answer, she said, "We should share our body heat." He didn't move a muscle. "Put your damn arms around me, Renard. I'm freezing. For God's sake, be a gentleman."

He still didn't move. She was half on top of him now, trying to steal some of the warmth his body generated. The man was like an electric blanket.

"Move it." She grimaced after giving the order. She sounded like a drill sergeant.

He was trying hard not to laugh at her. "If I put my arms around you, sugar, I might not remain a gentleman."

Oh, brother. "I'll take my chances, *sugar*," she drawled back.

She leaned up so he could put his arm out, and the second he did, she cuddled up against his side. John Paul rolled over and enveloped her with his arms.

He felt as if he were hugging an ice cube. The bottom of his chin rubbed the top of her head. Damn, she smelled good. Like peppermint, maybe, he thought as he began to rub her back.

"You're one big goose bump."

She didn't have the energy to talk. His warmth was so comforting, she closed her eyes and let him caress her. Her T-shirt had ridden up above her navel, and too late, she felt his hands slip under the fabric. His fingers splayed wide across her back.

She lurched upward at the same instant he felt the scar tissue, her head slamming into his chin.

"Damn," he muttered as he dropped back. "What the hell did you do that for?" he asked, rubbing his jaw.

Avery frantically pulled her shirt down and rolled away from him. "Go to sleep."

She'd closed up on him quicker than he could snap his fingers. He rolled onto his back and closed his eyes. What in God's name had happened to her back? He knew what he'd touched was scar tissue. Who had done that to her?

"Leave me the hell alone," Avery whispered.

She was coiled for a fight. She waited tensely for the questions to start, holding her breath. She expelled it loudly. Why was he silent? Why wasn't he asking questions?

She told herself she had nothing to be ashamed of or embarrassed about, but very few men had ever seen or touched her back, and she had memorized their reactions. The look of shock, and in one instance, disgust. Mostly she remembered how one man she had actually believed wasn't superficial had visibly shuddered. Then, of course, the sympathy and the questions came . . . the hundreds of questions.

John Paul wasn't talking, though. She couldn't stand his silence long. She rolled toward him, propped herself up with her elbow, and glared down at him. The jerk's eyes were closed, and he looked as if he were sleeping. She knew better.

"Open your eyes, damn it."

"My name's John Paul, not Damn It."

What the hell was the matter with him? Why wasn't he asking her questions . . . or flinching? She knew he'd felt the knotted scars. "Well?"

He sighed. "Well, what?"

She was getting angrier and angrier by the second. "What are you thinking?"

"Trust me, sugar, you don't want to know."

"Oh, yes, I do. Tell me."

"You sure?"

"Answer me," she demanded. "I want to know what you're thinking."

"Okay. I'm thinking that you're a real pain in the ass."

Her mouth dropped open. "What did you say?"

"You heard me. I said you're a real pain in the ass. You damn near broke my jaw when you jerked up. One second you're letting me warm you, and the next you're trying to kill me."

"I was not trying to kill you."

He rubbed his jaw. "I could have chipped a tooth."

Oh, brother. "Look . . . I'm sorry, okay? I was just startled, and I . . . Wait a minute. Why am I apologizing?"

He flashed a devilish grin. Her heartbeat immediately quickened. " 'Cause you should," he drawled in his seductive southern accent.

The big jerk was so aloof and impassive, so why were her senses going berserk now? With the bursts of lightning, she could see his face clearly. The day's growth of whiskers should have made him look scruffy, but it didn't. She had to resist the urge to touch his cheek. His wonderful scent was driving her to distraction too. He smelled like wintergreen and musk and fresh wood shavings. And when he had held her in his arms to warm her, his body had felt like a smooth block of sculptor's marble. Everything about him was sexy, damn it. He was so masculine, so . . . Get a grip, she told herself. Remember, you're in charge.

Yeah, right. She put her forefinger and her thumb up in front of his eyes about a half-inch apart and said, "I'm this close to really hating you."

She'd used just the right amount of anger in her voice. She nodded too, just to let him know she meant every word.

He wasn't impressed or intimidated. He simply closed his eyes and lazily said, "I can live with that."

# CHAPTER 18

"We go through the wall." Anne made the announcement and then waited for the women's reaction to her suggestion. Sara looked incredulous; Carrie looked irritated.

"Yeah, right," Carrie muttered. "I'll use my superhuman karate kicks and my X-ray vision . . ."

"Now, Carrie, let's hear what Anne has to say," Sara chided.

"I'm telling you, it could work. When I got out of the car, I walked over to the stone wall and looked down. The mountain slopes on this side of the house. It's not a sheer drop like it is outside the living room windows."

"Go on," Sara urged.

"I also noticed the sides of the house are cedar boards, not stone like the front," she said. "There's an outside wall in the pantry that's just on the other side of the stone wall. I suggest we punch a big hole in the Sheetrock near the floor, so that when we do kick the cedar boards out, we won't be seen from the front."

"But Anne, there's more than just Sheetrock and cedar boards," Sara said.

"I know exactly what's between those walls," she boasted. "There's insulation, but that won't be difficult to tear out, and maybe wiring too, which we could work around, and a layer of sheathing . . ."

"And what else?" Sara asked. She leaned forward while she considered Anne's idea.

"Two-by-fours," Anne said. "Studs are usually about sixteen inches apart. We should all be able to squeeze through."

"How do we make a hole in the Sheetrock? With our fists?"

"We use the poker from the fireplace," Anne said. "And knives to widen the hole. I took inventory, and the kitchen knives are still in the drawers. If we started now, who knows? We might be out of here by morning."

"Time's running out," Carrie said. "I say we try to break a window and hope we don't . . ." She stopped when Sara shook her head.

"Too risky," Sara said. "I say we go with Anne's plan."

"What about the cedar boards?"

"It won't be as difficult as you think," Anne said. "They're nailed in, but if we hit them hard enough or kick them, they'll eventually pop right out."

"My goodness, we've got a plan," Sara said. She slapped her hand on the table and smiled. "I'm sure we won't be able to find any rope to use to climb down, but wouldn't sheets work?"

"In the movies, they always use sheets to get out," Carrie said.

"Really?" Anne asked.

Carrie nodded. "You honestly don't watch television, do you?"

Anne shook her head. "I could work on the sheets. Maybe instead of tying knots, I could figure out a way to braid them together . . . or something."

"That's good," Sara said. "While you're doing that, Carrie and I will work on the wall. Anne, you're brilliant. I never would have thought to go out through a wall. I think this is doable."

"We have to leave during the night," Carrie said. "I don't relish the idea of tromping through the wilderness in the dark, but if we make our way downhill until we estimate we're past the fence, then we could get to the road and follow it back to town."

She'd made it all sound easy. Was she being naive, or could it be that simple?

"We should probably take a couple of sharp knives with us," Sara suggested. "Just in case we run into any wild animals."

"Or Monk," Carrie said. She shivered then. "I think I'd prefer fighting off a wild animal than running into him. Do you know . . ." She suddenly stopped, embarrassed at what she had almost confessed.

"What?" Sara asked.

"You'll think I'm gross, but I thought he was handsome."

Sara snorted with laughter. "I did too. I loved his accent. Do you think it was real?"

"I thought so," Carrie said. "I thought he was sexy."

Anne had been listening quietly to the conversation until Carrie made that comment. She couldn't keep silent any longer; her disapproval was evident. "Shame on you, Carrie. You're a married woman."

Carrie defended herself. "I'm married, yes, but I'm not blind, and there isn't anything wrong with appreciating a great-looking man. Surely you've —"

Anne cut her off. "Absolutely not," she insisted. "I would never insult my Eric by lusting after another man."

"Did I say I lusted after him?"

"Will you stop bickering," Sara begged. "You make me want to open a door."

# CHAPTER 19

John Paul retrieved the watch then hiked over twelve miles. He made a wide circle around the perimeter of the location marked on the map looking for signs — anything out of the ordinary, like a sniper hunkered down in the scrub. When he was satisfied he was alone, he planted the watch and backtracked four miles to Coward's Crossing.

There wasn't any doubt about being in the right place. There was a crude hand-painted sign nailed to a stake that had recently been pounded into the ground. The white paint with the words "Coward's Crossing" wasn't weathered and, therefore, couldn't have been more than a couple of days old. The arrow on top of the sign pointed to a boarded-up, abandoned mine shaft. There was a woman's bright red silk scarf nailed to another board above the entrance.

Dawn had arrived, and the mist was being burned by the rising son. John Paul was safely concealed by the trees and bushes. From where he was positioned, he could see the entrance to the shaft. He didn't relish the idea of climbing down inside. Were the women there? Doubtful, he thought. Monk wouldn't have kidnapped them and then given Avery a map showing their location. No, Monk was isolating his prey. No doubt about that.

When would he take his shot? Maybe he thought they would want to go into the shaft. How had Monk planned to kill them? Explosives, he guessed. Yeah, that's what Monk would do. Clean and neat, an underground explosion no one would hear, and he wouldn't have to worry about burying what was left of their bodies.

Come on, John Paul urged. Show yourself. There was a good thirty yards of open space between the cover of the trees and the shaft. Check it out, Monk. Let me get one clear shot. He would try to immobilize him so he could question him and, hopefully, find out where the women were.

Someone was out there. The silence in the woods confirmed it. No birds singing, no squirrels scurrying about as they foraged for food. Nothing but the wind whistling a forlorn melody through the branches and an occasional rumble of thunder in the distance.

John Paul was patient. He could wait it out for as long as he needed. But what about Avery? How long would she sleep? And when she woke up and found him gone, would she try to come after him? The possibility sent chills down his back. He pictured her walking into a trap and had to force himself to block the image of her being gunned down.

He thought he heard something and tilted his head, straining to listen. The sound didn't come again.

What was Avery doing now? Was she still asleep? He'd left her snug as a bug in his sleeping bag with the gun next to her.

Damn, he'd hated leaving her. Knock it off, he told himself. She's fine. The car's well-hidden and over ten miles away. Yeah, she was okay. Ah, hell, try as he did, he couldn't convince himself.

How in God's name had she worked her way under his skin so quickly? And what the hell was the matter with him to be attracted to her? She was a damn liberal, he reminded himself, one of those "Let's save the world" types. Worse, she was a team player, and the team she obviously loved playing for was the Bureau.

They were completely, thoroughly, absolutely unsuitable for one another. And yet here he was, worrying himself sick about her.

Monk could have tracked them . . . a twig snapped behind him. Without making a sound, he turned, trying to pinpoint the location. He thought it was maybe thirty or forty feet away, but with the rising wind it was impossible to be accurate.

For over five minutes he didn't move a muscle. Then he heard another sound, a faint rustling of leaves. Ever so slowly, he eased back on his haunches, zeroed in on the exact spot where the noise had come from, and took aim.

Then he saw those blue eyes staring at him between two little branches she had so painstakingly parted.

He was suddenly livid. He had damn near killed the woman. What could she have been thinking to sneak up on him like that? If she hadn't stayed perfectly still and let him see her face, if she had made one more little sound, he might have blown her away. Son of a bitch, he silently cursed as he eased up on the trigger. Son of a bitch.

Thank God he hadn't hurt her. An odd thought, given the fact that he was now contemplating wringing her neck.

He strained from the effort he exerted not to shout at her. He held up one hand, motioning for her to stay put. She slowly shook her head and held up one finger. Then she pointed behind her.

He moved through the brush toward her.

Avery knew he was furious. His jaw was clenched so tight she thought it might shatter. She slowly got up on her knees, leaned into him until her mouth was touching his ear. Then she whispered, "He found the car."

John Paul heard movement and saw the glint of steel through the trees about fifty feet away. Like a lion, he sprang.

Avery didn't have time to react. One second

she was whispering into his ear, and the next she was flat on her stomach on the ground, her face smashed into dead leaves with John Paul covering her as he fired. The dirt around her head was spitting up into her hair.

He rolled, fired again and again as he jerked her to her knees. "Move it," he ordered.

After the first shot, he knew Monk had a high-powered rifle. Probably with one of those fancy nightscopes too. All the bastard needed was one clear shot. No, make that two.

He figured Monk was trying to get them to run into the clearing by shooting at their only other way out.

Avery inadvertently cooperated. She veered to the right, away from the hail of bullets, but John Paul threw his arm around her and lifted her off the ground as he pushed her in front of him, using his body as a shield against the bullets flying around them.

"Go, go, go," he whispered, urging her on.

A branch came flying at her face. He blocked it like a football player with his forearm and shoved her ahead. She stumbled back against him, righted herself before he could try to jerk her arm out of its socket again, and kept going. They were running uphill now through a maze of trees. She heard a roaring in her ears, thought it was her heart pounding.

She was wrong about that. She reached a boulder. The surface was wet and slick. She scrambled up on her hands and knees, and then came to a hard stop. Good God, there was a sheer drop of at least fifty feet, and at the bottom was white, foaming water.

The hell with that. In her mind, they were out of options. The rapids were below them, but the killer was behind them and rushing toward them. As Avery peered over at the white water, she thought they had a better chance of surviving if they faced Monk head-on.

She unzipped her windbreaker pocket and pulled out the gun. John Paul emptied his gun, released the clip, and snapped another in. Then he flipped the safety on, glanced over the boulder to see what was below, and shoved his gun into Avery's pocket. After he zipped it up, he took her gun, put it in her other pocket, and zipped it closed.

She didn't like where this was leading. "We stay and fight," she said.

He shook his head. She frantically nodded. They could both hear Monk crashing through the brush. He was firing wild now, but nonstop. John Paul wrapped his arms around Avery's waist, holding her tightly in a bear hug. As he leapt from the rock ledge, he asked, "Can you swim?"

# CHAPTER 20

Could she swim? He had the gall to ask her that question after he'd lunged off the ledge with her locked in his arms. Avery didn't scream. Her life didn't pass before her eyes either on that endless flight down into the water below. She was too busy trying to punch him so he'd let go of her. And too scared to make a sound. Oh, Lord, don't let us drown.

They hit hard, plunging feet first into the icy water. It felt as if a thousand needles sliced through her feet and traveled at the speed of light all the way up into her brain. The impact was paralyzing.

He never let go of her. Not when they were sucked under by the raging water, and not during their frantic search for the surface as they were plummeting down the roaring rapids. Just when she was certain her lungs were going to burst, they finally clawed their way to air, but they had only enough time to fill their lungs before they were pulled under by the current.

She saw a brown bear watching them from the bank. She could have sworn he was grinning at them and didn't want that image to be her last before she died. She wanted to survive so she could give John Paul hell for trying to drown her. As if something had hold of her ankles and was tugging her down, she sank again. She would damn well have to fight harder to make it. She'd grown up swimming in the ocean, first in Florida and then in California, and was a stronger swimmer than most, but this wasn't swimming. They were bobbing like corks.

They reached the surface again. Gasping to take in as much air as possible, she spotted a big old gnarled tree branch bouncing from one white-water crest to another. With both hands, she grabbed hold when it came roaring past.

The river zigged and zagged, but they were getting closer to the bank. She started kicking with all her might. John Paul hooked one arm over the branch and steered their lifeline in the same direction. When they finally reached shallow water, he stood and pulled her to the bank.

Sprawled out side by side on the grassy slope, they were both too exhausted to move. Avery was gulping in air and shivering so much her teeth were chattering.

"You okay, sugar?" he panted.

She suddenly bolted upright and gagged. She thought she might have swallowed half the river.

"Can you swim?" she said between gasps. "Is that what you asked me after you shoved me off that ledge?"

"So you heard me, huh?" He reached over and gently pushed her dripping hair out of her eyes.

She looked back at the raging river. God surely had a hand in their survival, she thought. There simply wasn't any other explanation possible.

"Okay, so now we know what a fiver is," she said.

He sat up. "Yeah?"

She smiled. "They obviously rate the rapids," she explained. "This one was the big mother. A fiver."

He shook his head. They had just been through hell together, and all she wanted to do was tell him how they rate rapids?

"Did you hit your head or something?"

"No, I just figured out the rating system. That's all."

"Want to go again?"

"Been there, done that," she said. Squinting up at the cliffs above them, she said, "I think we lost him."

"I'm not sure," he said. Reluctant as he was to move, he forced himself to get up. He shook himself like a dog who'd just had a bath, then offered her his hand.

She made the mistake of clasping hold. He yanked her to her feet, pulling on her socket again. The man didn't know his own strength.

Now what was he doing? He'd turned and was surveying the area they'd just vacated.

"What?"

"Grab some brush and throw it over our imprints. No, never mind. You'll only make it worse. I'll do it."

She walked into the protection of the trees and watched him pull several small branches over the soft earth. "Why is it that you automatically assume I'm incompetent? Is it just me you have a problem with, or are you that way with every woman?"

"Just you."

She saw him grin before he turned away. He got a kick out of irritating her, she decided, but she was too weary from near heart failure in the rapids to rise to his bait.

"Do you have any idea where we are?" she asked. Her words sounded slurred, and she was shaking almost violently now.

"No."

It wasn't the answer she was hoping for. "So I guess you weren't a Boy Scout?"

"I can get us where we need to go."

"Back to the car?"

"No. It would take too long trying to find a place to cross over the water."

"We need to get to a phone." And a hot shower and dry clothes she silently added.

He finished covering their footprints, stepped back to survey his handiwork, and nodded with satisfaction.

"A phone's a given," he said as he walked closer to her. "Damn, babe, you're freezing, aren't you?"

"You're not?" she asked as he took her into his embrace and began to vigorously rub her arms.

"I'm okay," he answered. "I've got ice water in my veins, or so I've been told."

"Who would say such a thing?" she asked.

"My sister."

"Oh." Then, "She ought to know."

"Do you have any strength left?" He was unzipping her windbreaker so he could get to his gun. His weapon was just a little damp. He shoved it into the back of his jeans and zipped her pocket closed again.

"I have as much strength as you do."

"Then start jogging. You'll get warm in no time."

"Which way?"

"We have to go up before we can go down."

She looked at the mountains surrounding them. "It would be easier to follow the river, but Monk would anticipate."

She turned around and started jogging at a fast clip through the woods. Water sloshed between her toes as she ran. The sensation of ice cubes melting around her feet wasn't pleasant.

John Paul kept pace with her for over an hour. They neither stopped nor spoke to each other.

He was impressed with her stamina. Once she had established the rhythm, she didn't slow down. She didn't complain either, and she wasn't clutching her side. He already knew she was in shape. One look at her body and he could tell she worked out. Still, the way she kept moving, so steady and sure, was proof that she did more than take a one-hour aerobic class once a week at some little spa back home.

He spotted the clear-water creek ahead and thought they should stop to catch their breath.

"Let's stop for a minute."

Thank God, thank God. "Are you sure you don't want to keep going?"

If he had said yes, she thought she would either burst into tears or keel over from exhaustion. The stitch in her side felt like someone was holding a hot coal against her ribs, and it had taken all she had not to grab hold and double over.

She noticed he didn't appear to be the least winded. Avery stretched her legs so they wouldn't cramp on her before she collapsed to the ground. Scooping up water with cupped hands, she greedily drank.

"Do you think he's tracking us?" she asked a minute later.

"Probably," he answered. "But he'll have to find a place to cross over those rapids, so we have some time. Tell me what happened at the car." He had been silently cursing himself for leaving her.

She sat down in the grass and leaned back against the tree. "I woke up and you were gone," she said. "So I decided to follow you."

His shoulder rubbed against hers as he sat beside her.

"I didn't get far," she admitted. "I had just started up the hill when I saw the headlights through the mist. Honest to Pete, I almost ran out to flag it down, but thankfully, I came to my senses and decided to wait until the car came closer."

"Ah, man," he whispered. "You could have walked right up to him before you . . ." He couldn't go on. The thought of what could have happened to her made him sick.

"He parked his car down below, then got out. He had a flashlight and a rifle tucked under his arm as he climbed the hill to where your car was hidden. He must have pinpointed the location before you moved the watch. I knew it was Monk, of course, so I stayed hidden."

"Then what happened?"

"He checked out the car."

"Did you see his face?"

"No. I could have if I'd moved, but I was afraid I'd make a noise, and he'd know I was there, watching. He opened the hood of your car, pulled something out, and threw it into that gully on the side of the hill. I could find it if we go back. He had the hood of his windbreaker up, so I couldn't see his face or the color of his hair, but he was at least six feet. He wasn't thin, though. He was quite muscular, not heavyset. He reminded me of a bodybuilder."

"He's good with disguises," he said. "Noah's

326

description is what the FBI is using, but he didn't get a clear look at him either. From what I've heard about Monk, he could be in the same room with Noah today, and I doubt he would be recognized."

"I don't know if he was alone or not. He was driving a Land Rover, but when he opened the door and got out, the light didn't go on, and he parked it a good distance away. I couldn't see inside. Do you think the woman was with him?"

"I don't know."

"He's very good at what he does, isn't he?" She sounded disheartened.

"Yes, he is," he said.

"He stood there a long time, maybe five minutes," she said. "He didn't move a muscle. It was creepy."

"He was probably listening to the sound of the forest, hoping to hear something."

"Like me."

"Yes." He put his arm around her and pulled her close. "Thank God you didn't try to run."

"I thought about trying to get my gun out of my pocket, but I was so close to him I worried he'd hear the sound of the zipper."

"If you had been asleep, Monk . . ."

Before he could finish his bleak thought, she interrupted. "He'd shoot me? I'll tell you what, John Paul. If you ever leave me behind again, that's exactly what I'm going to do to you."

Since she was all but clinging to him so that

she could borrow some of his warmth, the threat didn't carry much weight.

"I won't leave you again," he promised in a gruff whisper. "I never should have left you. Hell, I guess I've been away from it too long. My instincts are all screwed up."

She homed in on what he'd just said. "You've been away from it too long? What exactly is *it*, John Paul?"

"Come on, sugar. We should get moving. Time's a-wasting."

In other words, leave it alone. She decided to accommodate him now and try again later. She was stiff and sore when she stood. Groaning, she rubbed her backside, not caring that she appeared less than ladylike.

"You know what I need?"

"Food, dry clothes . . ."

"Yes, that too," she said. "But what I also need is to get into my yoga position, relax, and do my free-association exercises."

"Your what?" He was sure he hadn't heard correctly.

She repeated. "You let the fragments drift in your mind; then when you're completely relaxed, you take hold of one at a time and you analyze it. You can't do it, though, until you reach total relaxation."

John Paul watched her stretch her long legs. "So how do you reach total relaxation?" he asked.

"Visualization," she said. "I go to a place

where I feel completely safe and free, like a real home. You know, I go to my . . . happy place."

"You're kidding."

"No."

He laughed. "You do know you sound insane, don't you?"

She wasn't joking when she answered. "It runs in the family."

She clasped her hands behind her back and twisted her torso, then shook her arms and legs to loosen them and started running again, her pace slower this time, but just as determined. Once again, he fell in right behind her and stayed there until she was panting for breath. They'd been climbing steadily since they'd left the river, and so far they hadn't seen a single sign of civilization. Where in thunder were they? Were they even still in Colorado?

She suddenly stopped, doubled over, and took a couple of deep, gulping breaths. Then she put her hands on her hips and slowly straightened.

"You okay?" he asked.

Why wasn't he winded? He was human, wasn't he? She made up her mind that, no matter what, she wouldn't utter one word of complaint. Not one frickin' word.

"Can't see the forest for the trees." She tried to sound flip. Cheerful was simply too much to ask for.

John Paul was sympathetic. "Do you want to rest?"

Is the Pope Catholic? Does it always rain on picnics? Hell, yes, she wanted to rest.

"No," she said weakly. Then, more forcefully, "I'm good to go . . . unless you want to . . ."

"No," he said. "Let's keep moving."

"Are we still heading north?" she asked, stalling for another minute to catch her breath. The air was so thin, she felt lightheaded. "I can't seem to get my bearings. If the sun were out . . ."

"We're going northeast."

One foot in front of the other, she told herself. Steady as you go. Come on, Delaney, pick up the pace. Time's a-wasting. Suck it up.

She kept up the steady barrage of psychological nagging as she ran through the forest. She tried not to think about her soggy underwear sticking to her skin or the fact that she was lugging around at least a pound of mud on each of her hiking boots.

She didn't quite clear the dead branch she tried to jump over, tripped, and would have gone headfirst into a tree trunk if John Paul hadn't grabbed her. The terrain was getting steeper, more treacherous. As she raced along, the muscles of her calves began to burn, and she was finally forced to slow down when they broke through the trees.

She suddenly stopped. They had reached a shelf of rock that hung out over the side of the mountain. Spread out before them was a panoramic view of the lower hills. Lush green meadows were tucked in between towering peaks with hundreds and hundreds of trees, their branches stretching toward heaven. Everything was so green, so alive. And not a soul was around. People surely flocked to this paradise, didn't they? So where were they all hiding?

"Isn't it picturesque?"

"Yeah, yeah, it's picturesque," he mumbled.

Desperately trying to stay positive, she said, "Is your cup always half empty? Can't you appreciate —"

He cut her off. "Have you noticed where we are? It's going to take us a couple of days to get back to civilization." He studied the lay of the land below looking for roads, but he wasn't having any luck. He had, at least, gotten his bearings back.

"We don't have that much time," she said. Her shoulders slumped, and as she looked around her, the beauty suddenly turned menacing, and the realization of their predicament sank in. Could it get any more bleak? She wanted to cry, but she didn't give in to the urge. Suck it up, she told herself. "It'll be okay," she asserted.

"Yeah? What makes you think so?"

She had to think about it for a minute before she could come up with anything. "Because we're due for a break."

And that was when it started raining again.

# CHAPTER 21

Anne was one of the most uptight, rigid women Carrie had ever met. She was certain the woman wouldn't be at all helpful, but she was proven wrong. Anne more than held her own. After she finished tying together the sheets, she helped them with the wall. She was a hard worker, with surprising stamina. She didn't have any sense of humor, but then, there really wasn't anything to laugh about, was there? As long as Anne's sacred marriage wasn't discussed, she was almost pleasant to be around.

She was also the woman in charge, giving them orders as they worked side by side. Punching a large hole through the Sheetrock with a fireplace poker didn't take any time at all. The insulation was messy but not difficult to remove. They filled a leaf bag with the stuffing. Luckily, there weren't any wires or pipes in the area they uncovered. Next, they sliced through the sheathing with kitchen knives.

Then they got to work on the boards. That was a bitch. Carrie had to take a break when her thumb started bleeding. While Anne removed the splinter with her tweezers and bandaged the cut, Sara took over.

By three o'clock in the morning, they were all worn-out.

Sara and Carrie had Band-Aids on every finger. Anne still looked like a fashion plate. Her nails weren't even chipped.

"How's the sheet rope coming?" Sara asked. She pushed the sleeves of her striped blouse up to her elbows and fell into the chair.

"It's ready to use," Anne said. She placed a bowl of tomato soup in front of Sara and then went back to the stove to fill Carrie's bowl.

"I'm too tired to eat," Carrie said.

"You'll need to keep up your strength," Anne told her as she placed her bowl on the table.

Sara noticed Anne take two pills out of her pocket. She turned her back on them when she put them in her mouth and drank a glass of water.

"What did you just take?" Sara asked.

"Oh, nothing," Anne answered as she took her seat across from Carrie.

"Aspirin?" Carrie asked.

"Yes," Anne said just as Sara shook her head.

"Not aspirin. They were pink capsules."

"You're very observant," Anne remarked. "They're prescription medication for nausea. I'm just getting over a bout of illness."

Carrie was barely listening. She had one elbow propped on the table, resting her head in her hand. She was too beat to care about table etiquette.

"What kind of illness?" Sara asked. She was swirling the soup with her spoon.

"Nothing much," Anne said. "I found this tiny little bump about eighteen months ago, and I told Eric about it. He went with me to the doctor," she explained. "As it turned out, it was no big deal."

"Thank goodness," Carrie said.

Sara was watching Anne's eyes. "Where did you find this little bump?"

"In my right breast," she said. "I had the biopsy and then got on with my life. Like I said, it was no big deal."

"So it wasn't malignant," Sara said.

Carrie wondered why she was persisting with the subject. Hadn't Anne just told them everything was all right? She thought Sara was being nosy.

"She just said . . ." Carrie began.

Sara didn't look at Carrie as she nudged her under the table. "But it wasn't malignant?" She repeated the question.

Anne looked at her soup when she answered. "Just a little bit."

Carrie straightened. "Is that what the doctors said?"

"Oh, you know how doctors are," Anne said. She waved her hand as she added, "They're all alarmists. Eric said they only make money if they can do a lot of procedures . . . and surgeries . . . when it isn't at all necessary."

Carrie glanced at Sara before she asked, "Did they recommend surgery, then?"

"Of course, but Eric said they would, and of course he was right. They thought they could talk me into having my breast removed. Can you imagine what that would have done to our insurance premiums?"

"No, what would it have done?" Sara asked.

"The rate would have gone sky high. Besides, the insurance company wouldn't have paid for the little procedure anyway."

Removing a breast was a little procedure? Carrie was too stunned to speak. She picked up her spoon and pretended to eat.

"Eric had made some wonderful investments with our cash surplus. He's so clever," she said. "They were good, sound investments that I, of course, approved when he told me about them."

"After he made the investments?" Sara asked. "He told you then?"

"Yes, of course," she said. "He has carte blanche. I mean, he is an equal partner in the business."

Carrie and Sara could see Anne's spine stiffening. She was becoming defensive. Sara took a taste of the soup and then said, "Good choice for dinner, Anne. I love tomato soup."

Anne smiled. "I do too."

"So why do you think the insurance company wouldn't pay?"

"Preexisting condition," Anne explained. "The

old insurance policy had lapsed, and the new one Eric found that had a much more reasonable premium didn't begin for thirty days. I had the biopsy during that period where they could say it was preexisting. Eric told me to wait, but I was foolishly anxious. We had the money to pay for the procedure," she hastily added, "if we had believed it was necessary. He did a lot of research on the Internet, and we decided to explore alternative methods. Your soup is getting cold, Carrie."

"About this —" Carrie began. Sara kicked her under the table.

"Yes?" Anne asked. That guarded look was back in her eyes.

"Are there any crackers?"

"No, I'm afraid not."

"You're very lucky to have Eric," Sara said.

Carrie choked on her soup. "Yes, you are," she lied. "It's a shame he couldn't go to the spa with you."

"I tried to talk him into it," she said. "He gave me the week's stay as a surprise for my birthday. He wanted me to rest and relax, and when I got back home, we were going to go back to the doctors and see what needed to be done. I was worried about what all this would cost, but Eric wouldn't listen. He said that if we had to spend every penny to get me well, then that's what we would do."

That son of a bitch, Carrie thought to herself. He was getting rid of her, but Anne, perhaps still in shock, couldn't accept the truth, and so she painted this lovely picture of her adoring husband. Had he left her a letter, or did he want her to die without knowing he was responsible?

"We should be on our way before dawn," Sara said, interrupting Carrie's thoughts.

"My hands are raw, and so are yours. Getting down that rope . . ."

"We can manage it."

"Anne, did you bring any workout clothes?" Carrie asked. "You can't go tromping down the mountain in high heels or the slippers you're wearing now."

"No, I didn't."

"Between Sara and me, we'll be able to outfit you properly," Carrie said.

Her whole attitude toward Anne had undergone a radical change. She found herself feeling protective and hoping that Anne stayed in denial until they reached civilization.

"Why don't you pack us some food to take along," Carrie suggested to Anne. "And a first-aid kit."

"You could use my fanny pack," Sara said. "It's on my dresser, but I don't have the energy to go upstairs to get it."

"Oh, I'll get it. I love being useful. Don't touch those dishes," Anne ordered as she hurried out of the kitchen. "I'll wash them later."

The second Anne was out of earshot, Sara whispered, "That bastard."

Carrie nodded. "Now I've got another reason for wanting to get out of this alive. I'm going to kill that son of a bitch."

Sara nodded. "You hold the gun, and I'll pull the trigger."

# CHAPTER 22

Something was growling, and it definitely wasn't human. Avery scooted closer to John Paul. Promising her she could have twenty minutes to rest, he had found shelter for them under a jutting rock. The ground was dry, and the area was wide and deep enough for him to stretch his legs.

Avery had lobbied for finding a cave. John Paul had vetoed that idea because he didn't want any unexpected company, like mountain lions or bears, sharing the space.

She suggested a fire, but he vetoed that idea too. The smoke could be seen from miles away.

She heard the growl again. It seemed closer. She nudged John Paul and whispered, "Do you hear that?"

"Uh-huh."

He sounded half asleep. He was sitting up with his back against the rock, his long muscular legs stretched in front of him, one ankle crossed over the other. He put his arm around her and told her to relax.

Her head was down on his shoulder, and every now and then his chin would rub against the top of her head. She couldn't decide if he was being affectionate or if the day's growth of whiskers made his skin itch.

Another rustling noise came from below them. She tensed in reaction. Then she thought she heard something growl again. What in heaven's name was it? A bear? A mountain lion? What?

John Paul had his gun on the ground next to him, and his hand rested on the handle.

She took a deep breath and tried not to think about how uncomfortable she was. Think positive, she told herself. Keep that cup full. Be an optimist.

Oh, God, we're gonna die out here. She sighed then. So much for being an optimist. He must have felt her shivering because he began to rub her arm. She thought that was sweet. She really did try to relax, but anxiety was keeping her mind revved up. Could a body be too exhausted to rest? When she'd sat down, she had been close to collapsing, and she knew she had to rest if she wanted to be able to run again.

What would the woman do about Carrie and the others now? Was John Paul right? Were they already dead?

She forced the thought aside and once again tried to get comfortable. Every muscle in her body ached, and her toes throbbed. She tried to take her boots off, but John Paul stopped her.

Her feet needed to acclimate to the wet boots, and all she had to do was walk off the cramps. He acted like an authority, and since she knew he'd had survival training while in the Marines, she acquiesced. Besides, she'd been too weary to argue.

Avery was determined that, no matter what, she wouldn't turn into a cynic like her aunt and John Paul. When the rain had begun and John Paul had teased her because she'd boasted that they were due for a break, she pointed out that the rain was a lovely, soft drizzle that brought with it a hazy fog, which, she insisted, was enchanting. Yep, that's what she'd said. She'd smiled too. Then the drizzle turned to a deluge. And still she tried to maintain her positive attitude. What more could happen? she reasoned. They were already wet.

And that's when the deluge turned into hail the size of golf balls, pelting their bodies as they ran into the protection of the trees.

More rustling noises pulled her back to the present. Had he heard the sound? She lifted her head from his shoulder and strained to hear. Fingers of gray light curled down through the branches as the rain continued.

His eyes were closed, but as she stared at him, they slowly opened. His gaze locked on hers. She was so thankful that he was there with her. She felt safe with him. She wasn't having to go through this nightmare alone, and his strength comforted her and gave her hope.

"I want . . ." She couldn't get the rest of the words out, couldn't tell him how much she appreciated his help. She couldn't stop looking at his mouth.

"Yeah, I do too."

Later, she wasn't so certain who initiated the kiss. She knew she'd leaned into him, and then his head had tilted down toward hers. Or had she pulled him close and had he merely accommodated her? She couldn't remember. Their mouths had just . . . merged.

And, oh, it felt wonderful. His mouth was so warm against hers, and, Lord, did he know how to get rid of a woman's defenses. He made her want much, much more. He was gentle and giving, yet rough and demanding at the same time. His hand cupped her chin, and he pressed it gently to let her know he wanted her to open her mouth for him.

She scooted up on his lap and wrapped her arms around his neck. When he began to caress her, she let go of her inhibitions, and her bones felt like Jell-O. She got quivers in her stomach. His tongue was driving her wild, making her want to be bolder.

The warmth of his touch radiated through her body. When he ended the kiss, she realized his hands were under her T-shirt. She knew he was as affected by the kiss as she was, for she could feel his heart beating rapidly under her fingertips.

She tried to get off his lap then, to retreat, but

he wouldn't let her. He held her tightly against him, then gently pushed her head down on his shoulder.

"You know what would be real nice now?" he whispered in that gruff, sexy tone of voice.

She was still trying to catch her breath. The taste of him lingered on her lips, and she was replaying every second of that powerful kiss in her mind.

The question suddenly penetrated. "For Pete's sake, John Paul."

"What?" he said.

"You want sex."

He didn't say a word for a long minute, acting as though he was taking his time to think it over. "Well, yeah. That would be nice too, I guess. Sugar, if you're offering, I'm not gonna turn you down." She wasn't looking at him, so he knew it was safe to smile. "But what I really want is a cheeseburger."

Her head snapped up. He got his chin out of her way in the nick of time. "What?"

"I was thinking a cheeseburger would be nice about now. And french fries and a cold beer," he added.

"The shrubs weren't enough for you?"

He laughed. "They weren't shrubs. Those were edible leaves and berries I made you eat. They'll give us energy," he added. "But I still want a cheeseburger. My brother-in-law got me hooked on junk food."

"You were really thinking about food?"

He grinned. "Yeah. I was, but if you're desperate to have sex, I guess I could accommodate you."

"I do not want to have sex."

"You said you did."

He was exasperating. "No, I didn't."

"And you kissed me," he pointed out. "So I just assumed . . ."

"Oh, for Pete's sake."

"It's obvious you can't keep your hands off me, sugar."

No wonder love and hate were so closely linked. Right now, she wanted to strangle him. He enjoyed making her squirm, seemed to be getting a real kick out of it.

She really wanted to have the last word. "It was just a meaningless kiss."

"Then how come you got all hot and bothered?"

"I did not."

"Liar."

Only he could make the insult sound like a caress. "Did you get all hot and bothered?"

"Hell, no."

She laughed. "Now who's lying?"

"The first rule in any operation is to tell as few lies as possible. Now try to rest. Ten more minutes and we're moving."

She couldn't rest, not until she relaxed, and there was only one way to do that. She moved away from John Paul, assumed the lotus position she'd learned from her yoga instructor, put her hands on her knees, palms up, straightened her back, and closed her eyes. She concentrated on her breathing, deep cleansing breaths, forcing herself to block the noises of the forest and the thoughts rushing through her mind. It took a good five minutes before she could feel her muscles easing.

"What are you doing?"

His question pulled her back. "I'm doing my relaxation exercise."

"Yoga?"

"Sort of. I clear my mind, then I go . . ."

"What?"

She sighed. Home, she thought, I go to my imaginary perfect home. She answered, "I go to my happy place. Okay?"

He didn't laugh. "Yeah? So you were serious about that? I thought you were joking."

"I picture a place that makes me feel good. It's a porch," she said. "And I see myself sitting on this swing. I can smell lilacs, and I can hear water in the background. It's . . . soothing, and it frees my mind. Then I start filtering through the data I've collected."

"Whatever works," he drawled.

He didn't understand, but then she didn't expect him to. She closed her eyes again, ignoring him now, and once again concentrated on her breathing.

Another couple of minutes passed, and she began to let the bits and pieces of the puzzle come together. Ironically, it was something that

John Paul had said that got her mind racing.

"What did you mean?" she asked.

"About what?"

She stretched her legs and then turned to him. "The first rule of an operation is not to lie?"

"No, I said tell as few lies as possible."

"Yes, that's what I meant. Why is that a rule?"

"Lies can come back to bite you . . . trip you up. So . . ."

She took it from there. "So, if you stick to the truth on all the little things that don't matter, you won't get tripped up. Oh, my God, of course."

She was suddenly as excited as a kid in a toy store. She unzipped her jacket pocket and pulled out a soggy map.

"I'm such an idiot. Monk could have read about the property in the paper, and when Carrie asked him where he was taking her, he came up with that name. I assumed he was lying. Why wouldn't I assume that? He'd lied about everything else, but John Paul, what if he was telling her the truth?"

Her babbling worried him. "Are you getting punchy?"

She smiled. "Yes," she said. "But it still all makes sense anyway."

"What are you trying to tell me?"

"I think I know where Carrie and those other women are."

Her announcement gained his full attention. "You think you know? How?"

"Carrie told me where Monk was taking her."

One eyelid dropped. "And you're only now mentioning that fact?"

"Hear me out," she said. "I thought he'd lied to her. I told you my aunt left me a message on my machine, and I erased it, and you heard my question to Cannon, didn't you?"

"I heard you ask him if there was a water problem."

"And Cannon said, no, not at Utopia. I also asked him if the spa owned a house in the mountains."

John Paul nodded. "I remember his answer was no."

"Because he said no, I didn't ask any other questions about the house. Carrie called it a retreat. I assumed that everything Monk told her was a lie. But what if it wasn't?"

"Why would you think he was telling the truth about their destination?"

"It's what you said. Why lie when you don't have to? Lies have a way of coming back to bite you." She repeated his very words. "Monk already had grabbed her, right? And he'd already told her his name. She was meekly going along, probably without a care in the world. But she called me on her cell phone from the ladies' room. And I doubt she would have told Monk she'd made the call. There wouldn't have been any reason."

"If Monk had told her where he was really taking her, he wouldn't have let her out of his sight."

"He couldn't go with her into the ladies' room," she pointed out. "And he might not have known she had one of her cell phones with her."

"One of her cell phones?"

Avery nodded. "She carries two at all times. Carrie's a workaholic, and it makes her crazy if the battery runs down. Besides, she uses one for personal and the other for business."

"She could just carry an extra battery."

"Oh, she does," she said. "So what do you think?"

"The truth? I think you're reaching."

"No, I'm analyzing the data, and I think we have at least a fifty percent chance I'm right. We have to check it out."

"You know where this house is?"

While he opened the map, she told him about the old gentleman who sat with her in McDonald's.

"Yeah, I see the circle he made."

Avery then told him about the couple who were fighting over ownership. "The judge is supposed to decide soon which one of the thoroughly unpleasant couple gets the house. He also told me the place has been vacant for weeks."

John Paul slowly nodded. "Okay, it's worth a look. Break's over. Time to move."

"We've got to get to a phone. That's the first order of business."

"No," he whispered. "The first order of business is staying alive so we can get to a phone."

And that, he knew, was easier said than done.

# CHAPTER 23

Now that the three women were finally ready to leave, they were immobilized with fear.

It was four o'clock in the morning, and they estimated that they had approximately two hours before dawn. They huddled together at the kitchen table, dressed for the forest in layers of clothes, sipping hot tea to fortify them against the night air. A frigid breeze poured into the kitchen from the hole in the pantry wall.

"What if Monk put down trip wires or something?" Carrie asked. "What do we do then? We won't see them in the dark."

They all worried about the possibility, and then Sara said, "I don't think he'd take the time to climb up the side of the mountain. I'm sure he thinks he's got us locked in tight."

Carrie was so scared, she was trembling. "Listen," she whispered. "If I don't make it . . ."

"Don't talk like that. We're all going to make it," Sara said, but her voice lacked conviction.

"Let me say this," Carrie insisted. "If I die, I

want you two to promise me you'll make the police find Avery and protect her. Call my husband," she added. "Tony will want to help keep Avery . . ." Her voice caught on a sob, and she couldn't go on.

"Focus on one worry at a time," Sara suggested.

"That's right," Anne said. "Concentrate on climbing down the rope."

Carrie nodded. "Yes, all right." She pushed her teacup away and stood. "We should go now. No more stalling."

Anne grabbed Carrie's hand. "Everything is going to be fine. You'll see."

Smiling, Carrie squeezed her hand. Uh-oh. Anne's eyes were getting that glassy look. She had probably taken one of her pain pills. When Carrie had searched the upstairs for a way out, she'd noticed the bottles of medications lined up on Anne's vanity. There were enough to start a small pharmacy.

"Did you remember to put your medicines in your jacket?" Carrie asked.

"Yes, of course I remembered."

"I could put some of the bottles in my jacket."

"No need," Anne assured her.

"What about the letters," Sara asked Carrie. "Did you zip them in your pocket?"

"Yes, I've got them."

"Okay, then," Sara said. "Let's do it."

They had already decided that Sara should go first. One end of the sheeted rope was anchored to the kitchen table, which couldn't be pulled through the doorway, but Carrie and Anne were still going to hold the rope while Sara lowered herself to the ground. Anne had tied big knots twelve inches apart so they would have something to grab.

Carrie was the second one to go because Anne had argued that since she weighed the least of the three, she stood the best chance of getting down on her own if the rope came loose from the table.

Carrie had wanted to go last, but Anne wouldn't hear of it. "If the rope doesn't hold or I fall, you and Sara could maybe catch me, but I couldn't help catch you or Sara. I have to go last."

"Oh, God, don't think about falling. You made a good, strong rope, Anne. It's going to hold."

"Yes, we'll all be just fine."

Anne sounded obscenely cheerful. Was she getting nuts again, or was the pain pill responsible?

Sara led the way into the pantry. Carrie and Anne watched as she picked up the end of the rope and tied it around her waist. "I hope this is long enough."

Sara got down on her knees, then scooted to the opening. "Get down on your stomach," Carrie whispered. "And go out slowly, feetfirst."

"Did you put the penlight in your pocket?" Anne asked.

"Yes, I've got it."

Carrie sat on the floor and braced herself with her feet against the two-by-fours. Anne got behind her to help hold the rope. Just when Carrie thought Sara was never going to reach the ground, the sheet went limp. Carrie fell back against Anne. Recovering her balance, she took a deep breath and said, "Guess it's my turn."

She rolled onto her stomach and scooted to the edge.

"Wait," Anne whispered. She grabbed Carrie's jacket, shoved a thick envelope in the pocket, and zipped it closed.

"What are you doing?"

"You're the strongest of the three of us, so if Sara and I don't make it, you make sure . . ."

"Yes?" Carrie prodded. "Come on. What?"

"Just make sure. Now go."

Carrie didn't waste time arguing. She would find out what Anne meant after they'd gotten away from the house.

Her hands were bleeding and raw, and she was too frightened to cry. She slowly lowered herself down. Anne tried to help, but when she tried to pull up on the rope so she could get a better grip, she almost went out the opening headfirst.

Carrie made it to the ground.

The rope went slack and Anne fell back. Quickly straightening, she looked down, trying to see the two women. She stayed on her hands and knees for a moment and listened to the soft calls from below.

Then she pulled the rope up. She backed

away from the opening. *"Three blind mice, three blind mice,"* she sang. *"See how they run, See how they run . . ."*

She stood up, brushed the dirt off her borrowed sweatpants, and walked into the kitchen. *"See how they run,"* she sang. Odd, that that particular melody had popped into her head and wouldn't let go. She and Eric had decided never to have children, yet now she was singing a silly nursery rhyme. Her father used to sing that song to her. How did the rest of it go? Was it "They all ran after the farmer's wife, she cut off their heads with a carving knife"? Or was it, "They all ran away from the farmer's wife"? And why couldn't she remember the rest of the song?

*"Three blind mice,"* she sang softly as she knelt down and tried to get the knots out of the sheet. Realizing she could break a nail, she got up, went to the counter to get the scissors Carrie had brought down, and cut the rope from the table leg.

*"Thre blind mice."* She stood again, paused to take a drink of her lukewarm tea, and then, because she knew that Carrie and Sara were anxiously waiting for her, she walked to the opening in the pantry and dropped the sheets down. They surely couldn't misinterpret what that meant, for she'd tossed away her only lifeline. She heard one of them cry out, thought it must be Sara, for, of the two women, Sara seemed a tad more tenderhearted.

"*Three blind mice*. My goodness, I can't get that silly tune out of my head," she said as she shut the pantry door. Noticing the messy kitchen, she went to the sink, filled it with soapy, hot water, and did the dishes. When she was finished, she straightened the table and chairs, put fresh place mats in front of each chair, then blew out the candles and headed for the stairs.

She was feeling so tired and old and haggard. A good long nap would fix that, she thought. But first things first. She simply had to do something about her sorry appearance. She couldn't understand how fashion-minded women with money, like Carrie and Sara, could ever wear sweatpants. Why, even the name was offensive. Ladies shouldn't sweat. They shouldn't even perspire. Only common, coarse women did such disgusting things as sweating and belching and body piercing . . . or letting others, like doctors, mutilate their bodies for them. Hadn't her loving Eric told her that was how he felt? He adored her body and couldn't stand what the surgeon wanted to do.

Feeling a bit light-headed, Anne gripped the banister as she slowly made her way upstairs. After she took a long, hot shower, she curled her hair with her curling iron, then brushed it and lacquered it in place with hairspray. It seemed to take an hour to decide which of her new St. John knit suits to wear. The mint green with the adorable silver clasps won because she thought it was both elegant and chic. Slipping into her silver pearlized high heels, she picked up her favorite platinum-rimmed diamond earrings and put them on. The diamonds were a gift from Eric on their last anniversary.

She'd walked all the way down the hallway before she remembered she hadn't put on any perfume. Retracing her steps, she squirted a dab on each wrist. Sighing with contentment, she hurried downstairs but stopped on the bottom step. The rising sun had turned the living room into a golden temple. The color took her breath away. Eric should be here to see this, she thought. Yes, he should.

Anne didn't know how long she stood there. Ten minutes might have passed, or twenty, maybe more. The effects of the second prescription pain pill had finally caught up with her, and she zigzagged across the living room, giggling because she found it so amusing that she couldn't walk in a straight line. Was this what it felt like to be stoned? Was she stoned? Trying to focus, she reached the sofa and plopped down. She fell asleep seconds later.

Although she hadn't realized such a thing was possible, she knew she had wept while she slept because, when she awakened, her face was wet with tears. She struggled to sit up and wiped the dampness away with her fingertips. Noticing the makeup on her hands, she'd decided to go back upstairs to powder her face again when she thought she heard the sound of a car coming up the drive. Still somewhat disoriented, she staggered to her feet, adjusted the lapels of her jacket, and walked into the dining room to look out the window at the circle drive. Her gait was stiff and unsteady.

A silver Cadillac DeVille came screeching around the curve. "Now, who could that be calling at such an early hour?" Anne asked. She checked the time on her Bulgari watch — another gift from her beloved Eric — and was astonished to see that it was after nine in the morning.

Anne stepped back into the shadows as the car came to a rocking stop. The door opened and a woman with the most frightful look on her face leapt out. She slammed the door shut, then opened the back door.

The woman looked vaguely familiar, but Anne couldn't remember where she might have seen her before. Her face was contorted with rage, and though Anne couldn't hear what she was saying, she knew she was talking because her lips were moving.

Was she Jilly? The stranger did have blond hair, and she was tall and shapely, as Carrie had described, but she certainly wasn't what Anne would consider beautiful by any means. Perhaps, if her expression weren't so hostile and if she were smiling instead, she might be pretty. But not beautiful.

Her complexion was lovely. She'd give her that. From a distance it looked almost flawless, and Anne decided she really must find out what kind of facial cleanser the woman used to get such perfect skin. Or was it heavy makeup? Anne made a mental note to find out.

Her haircut was a little too short and spiky, but the color was wonderful. Highlights, Anne thought, and she wondered if the unpleasant woman would give her the name of her stylist. Why, she'd kill to have highlights like that. Suddenly feeling self-conscious about her own appearance, she patted her hair down, certain she'd gotten it mussed during her little nap.

"My goodness," Anne whispered when she saw what the woman was carrying. She had a red gasoline can in one hand and an ax in the other. "What does she think she's doing?"

The woman's head was down, and she hadn't spotted Anne yet, but as she strode to the steps, Anne remembered where she'd seen her before. She was pictured in one of the clippings she'd found in the chest. Oh, yes, she remembered now. The woman and her ex were fighting over ownership of this house.

Anne rushed to the foyer and stood in front of the elongated beveled glass panes that framed the door. She could hear what the woman was saying now. She was spewing filth. Anne's hand went to her throat. She was appalled by the vulgarity. The woman must have said the "F" word a good ten times, enraged at a judge for giving her house away.

Ah . . . now Anne understood. The house had

been awarded to the husband. Anne didn't have any sympathy for the crude woman. She obviously hadn't been a good wife. Shouldn't the husband make all the important decisions? He'd paid for the house. He should keep it.

The woman rushed up the porch steps, screaming now. "That son of a bitch thinks he's going to take my house and leave me penniless? Screw the prenup. He thinks I'm bluffing. I told him he'd never live here. Surprise, surprise, bastard. When I'm finished redecorating . . ." She spotted Anne and came to a dead stop. Then she roared, "Who the hell are you, and what are you doing in my house?"

"Hello there," Anne called out. "What are you doing with that ax and that can?"

"None of your fucking business."

"I really would appreciate it if you wouldn't use obscenity in my presence. It offends me."

The woman put the can of gasoline down, dropped the ax, and reached into her pocket to get her key out.

"Did the bastard hire a housekeeper?" she yelled loudly enough so that Anne could hear through the door.

"I assure you I'm not a housekeeper."

"Open the fucking door."

"Oh, I don't think that's a good idea."

The woman shoved the key in the lock and tried to turn it. When she realized it wouldn't work, she screamed, "Damn him to hell. How dare he change the lock. How dare he. He knew . . . He had that judge in his pocket. Well, fuck him."

She pulled the key out of the lock, threw it down and glared at Anne. "If you don't open this door, I'm going to use this ax. You don't want to mess with me, bitch. Not today."

"Are you threatening me?"

"Open the damned door."

The sneer was the last straw. Tears flooded into Anne's eyes as she swung the door open and forced a smile. "Won't you come in?"

There was a second's delay, long enough for the woman to shove Anne back and step over the threshold.

The explosion blew half the mountain away.

# CHAPTER 24

Keeping up with Jilly was a full-time job, but Monk found it thoroughly exhilarating. He hadn't felt this alive in years. He was the cautious one, of course, while she, with the enthusiasm of a novice, planned her grand schemes, never worrying about the little mundane things, like the FBI tracking one of the credit cards she'd used.

Monk couldn't fault her for making that mistake. He blamed himself because he should have destroyed the cards after he'd used them. He kept all of his credit cards under various names and addresses in his attaché case, and Jilly had simply helped herself to the first ones her hand touched.

The result hadn't been as bad as it could have been, though. John Paul Renard was now involved, and Monk was absolutely delighted about that turn of events. He'd known that Renard was trying to track his movements for over a year. He'd intercepted several inquiries Renard had made to various law enforcement agencies in Europe. Now Monk had the opportunity to get rid of the pest before he caused real trouble, and Monk could humor Jilly at the same time.

Before they'd settled on using Utopia to bring the women to Aspen, his beautiful fiancée had had the time of her life, sitting at the table hour upon hour, poring over her notes. Oh, how she loved the intrigue, the excitement, and most of all, the danger, and she was trying to teach Monk how to have fun too. Whenever he did anything to please her, such as agreeing to last-minute changes in her complicated plans, she aptly rewarded him in creative ways. All of them of a sexual nature. Just thinking about some of the things she'd done to him and allowed him to do to her made him blush like a teenager.

She was turning him into a true romantic, but he didn't view that as a weakness, for his obsession was with Jilly and no other. He believed with all his heart that, if the erotic games they played in bed didn't kill him, they would grow old together.

Oh, yes, she was an obsession. His every waking minute was spent thinking about her, protecting her from harm. As long as he maintained his vigilance and cleaned up her mistakes, they would be safe.

Monk had had to talk Jilly out of one scheme. She had briefly toyed with the idea of kidnapping Avery and sitting down with her to tell her the truth about Carrie. Jilly was such an innocent. She believed she could convert her daughter. Monk gently explained that, after all the years of brainwashing by Carrie, Jilly would never be able to convince her daughter that she was, in reality, a loving mother.

Jilly wasn't perfect by any means. She had a twisted view of motherhood, for she believed that because she had brought Avery into this world, she owned her. She spoke of Avery as her possession, not a person, and Carrie had taken that precious treasure away from her. For years her anger at her sister had festered, but Jilly was patient when it came to vengeance. No matter how long it took, she would get even.

She insisted on being the one to push the button that would blow the house apart. She promised Monk she wouldn't shed a tear over her sister's death. Carrie had brought this on herself. She was the reason Jilly hadn't succeeded in life; she was the reason Avery hated her. She was the reason for every one of Jilly's failures. And so it was only fair that Jilly get to watch her sister die.

Monk wasn't put off by Jilly's brutal honesty. How could he cast the first stone? She had accepted him with all his sins, and he could do no less for her.

Now he was trying to clean up the mistakes at the abandoned mine. Jilly had been sure they would climb down into the shaft to find the next clue as to Carrie's whereabouts, and then Monk could have dropped a couple of explosives into the hole, sealed it, and followed Jilly back to the retreat.

Monk hadn't believed Renard would go into the shaft, and he had been proven right. He had thought, however, that he could get a clear shot at the two and toss the bodies down the hole, but he missed his chance when they scrambled up the rocks and leapt into the river.

He was methodically tracking them now. He'd lost precious time backtracking to his vehicle and crossing the river, but with his car he'd been able to make up some time by speeding down the mountain road and cutting back to where he anticipated they'd be heading.

Renard hadn't left any tracks, but then Monk knew all about the ex-Marine and hadn't expected less. When he'd done his research on his stalker, he'd read his history, and he'd been impressed. He believed that under different circumstances they could have become friends. They were, after all, very much alike. They were both professional killers. Monk had murdered for money, while Renard killed for honor. That didn't make him superior, however. If anything, Monk believed it made him a fool.

Still, he would have liked to have had the opportunity to sit down with him, share some cold beers and talk about their past exploits. But Renard would never go for that. The man was too honorable for his own good. According to his sealed file, which Monk had gotten unsealed, Renard was suffering from burnout. Monk didn't believe such nonsense. He thought Renard had left the job when he realized he was beginning to enjoy the power he felt every time he pulled the trigger. Honor be damned.

Was Renard as curious about him? Did he fantasize about sitting down to discuss the thrill of the hunt, the exhilaration of the kill? Monk wished he could find out. Maybe if he was able to wound him, paralyze him, then Monk could sit down beside him and chat it up like old friends until Renard bled out. Wouldn't that be something, to talk to an equal, to commiserate, to boast?

Monk chuckled. Now who was fantasizing? He checked the time and then shook his head. If he didn't spot the couple soon, he would have to get to his car and drive to where Jilly waited. She was anxious to get back to the little mountain retreat to see how her sister was holding up. By now, the three women had probably turned on one another like polecats, each one slowly going out of her mind with terror. That was what Jilly hoped anyway.

Stop daydreaming and get back to business, he told himself. He lifted his highpowered binoculars and scanned the terrain once again. He was turning toward the north when he saw the observation tower in the distance, maybe a mile away. Climbing down was a forest ranger. Monk watched until the man was standing on the ground.

"Well, well," he whispered as he calculated. "Just my size."

Exactly one hour later he was leaning over the

rail at the top of the tower, scanning the hills. Looking down at the bushes below he saw the white T-shirt of the forest ranger he'd shot in the temple and then stripped.

He was just about ready to give up the chase when he suddenly spotted the couple. Avery's blond hair, so like her mother's, shimmered gold in the sunlight. Monk couldn't believe his good fortune. There they were, all right, walking down the mountain as pretty as you please, looking as ragged and worn-out as any two people he'd ever seen. His burst of laughter echoed around him. Wait until he told Jilly. He knew what she would say. She'd tell him he was an exceedingly lucky man.

He'd agree, of course, even though he knew luck had very little to do with finding his prey. After poring over his map, he'd anticipated that if they survived the white water, they would get out before that tremendous drop below Coward's Crossing.

Monk decided to meet them head-on. He climbed down the ladder and walked around to the path, his head down, the bill of his cap concealing his face.

When he reached the wide open space between the trees, he ever so slowly turned and pretended to notice them near the peak. He raised his hand to wave.

Avery heard John Paul behind her. "Fall down, Avery. Do it now."

She didn't hesitate. Pretending to stumble,

she went down on one knee. John Paul caught up with her and dropped to put his arm around her shoulders to steady her.

"Act like you hurt yourself."

Rolling to her side, she clutched her ankle and gave an exaggerated grimace. She wanted to cry from disappointment. "He's not a forest ranger, is he?"

"No."

She kept rubbing her ankle. "How do you know?"

"I saw his rifle. Forest rangers don't have scopes on their rifles."

She looked up at him. "You saw the scope from this far away?"

"The sun caught it just right," he explained. "I think it's him. I'm not saying it's Monk, but . . ."

"Thinking he might be is enough for me," she said.

"Okay, I'm gonna help you stand. You lean against me, and we start down the hill again, but we'll angle toward the west. When he reaches the trees, we run like hell."

"He'll come after us."

"Ready?"

He didn't give her a chance to answer, but hauled her up, lightly bracing her against his side.

"Limp," he ordered gruffly as they once again started down the hill. They were walking like two drunks, staggering toward the west as they moved along.

He was deliberately keeping them out of Monk's range. He was sure now that the man dressed as a forest ranger was the killer because he hadn't moved from his spot at the base of the trail. Rangers were helpful, weren't they?

"He's waiting for us to get within firing range."

"Oh, God."

"You scared?"

"Duh . . ."

Her response made him smile. "That's good," he said. "Okay, sugar. Start running."

She immediately bolted toward the safety of the trees. John Paul was right behind her, but he dared a quick look down below and saw Monk running toward them. They had a good head start. Avery led the way steadily downhill, hoping to intercept the road below Monk, all the way praying there would be campers or real forest rangers around who could help them.

Her ears were ringing. What was that sound? The wind whistling through the trees? Or was it the sound of gunfire sizzling? No, that wasn't it.

The noise stopped as suddenly as it had begun; then it started up again, but it was louder, shriller this time. It sounded like a whistle.

"Hear . . . that . . . ?" she panted.

"Yeah."

Then she heard a trumpet. Was she losing it? She kept running, her feet pounding into the soft earth as she raced along, still panting from her exertion.

The muscles in her legs were burning. Suddenly she lost her footing. She would have hurled headfirst into a gulley if John Paul hadn't reacted instinctively, lifting her off her feet as he kept stride.

He slowed as he let go of her, then kept pace just in case she went down again. All at once, they broke through the trees, crossed the road . . . and ran into the middle of Boy Scout Troop 183. Before he could stop, John Paul bowled over one pup tent and mowed down the troop master, who got the wind knocked out of him. The trumpet he was holding went flying into another tent.

"Cell phone," Avery shouted at the man sprawled on his back. "We need your cell phone."

"No signal up here," he answered as he came up on his elbows. His face was red with anger. "Who in thunder do you people think . . ."

John Paul was frantically searching the road ahead of them. Monk wouldn't have any qualms about taking a couple of kids out as long as he could get his primary targets. One of the boys shouted when he saw the gun tucked into the back of John Paul's jeans. One blistering look from John Paul shut the boy up.

Avery dropped down on her knees next to the leader. "Listen to me. We need help. There's a killer coming this way. Where's your transportation? Answer me, please," she begged.

Her terror got through to him. "We've got a

camper here, but my Ford four-wheeler is parked about half a mile down the road. The keys are in my jacket in that tent over there, the one with the troop numbers painted on it."

John Paul was lifting Avery to her feet. "Get in that camper and get your boys out of here," he yelled back at the man as he pulled Avery toward the next slope, staying well hidden in the trees.

"Get to a phone and call for help," she shouted.

Her legs were trembling, and she didn't think she had it in her to run much longer. Concentrating on putting one foot in front of the other, her heart feeling as though it were lodged in her throat, she suddenly remembered they hadn't gotten the keys.

"We have to go back . . . the car keys."

"We don't need them," he said. "Now move it, sugar. You're starting to drag."

She fantasized about hiding somewhere and waiting for John Paul to come back with the car. She could find a spot where Monk wouldn't find her, couldn't she?

Suck it up. Damn it, I don't want to. I can do it. I can do it. She kept up the drill until the pain in her side became excruciating. She wondered if she could die upright. Sure she could.

Tears came into her eyes then, for she saw the old SUV parked in the gravel near the curve in the road. John Paul raced ahead of her. He broke the back window, reached in, and unlocked the front door.

Avery ran around to the other side as he unlocked the door for her. It took less than forty-five seconds for him to hot-wire the car, throw it into gear, and take off.

She was impressed. "Were you a juvenile delinquent growing up?"

The second they rounded the curve, she fell back against the seat and allowed herself to fall apart. A sob caught in her throat.

"Are you crying?"

"No."

"Sure sounded like you were." He gave her a sharp look.

"I'm joyful." She hastily wiped the tears of relief from her cheeks.

He grinned. He had the very same feeling, but it didn't last long. "Hell," he muttered.

"What hell?"

"The road's winding back around . . . he might be coming down, getting into position . . . ah, hell, that's what he's gonna do, and there isn't any way we can go off-road here."

He leaned forward, pulled his gun out, and dropped it into his lap. He rolled down his window, then picked up the gun.

She frantically got her weapon out and then rolled down her window. "What the hell are you doing?" he asked.

"Getting ready just like you."

"No. Get down and stay down. If he's coming at us, you'll be on his side."

She ignored his order. "Just tell me when to

start shooting. We'll keep him down until we get past."

It sounded like a great plan, and she'd said it with gusto, but that was only because she didn't believe Monk could have gotten down the hills that quickly.

She was wrong about that. She spotted him before John Paul did.

"Get the hell down," John Paul shouted.

Her response was to flip the safety off. Leaning against the door, she put her arm out the window, steadied the barrel of the gun on the side mirror, and waited. She ducked down as much as she could.

When Monk crouched down and swung the rifle up, John Paul shouted, "Now!"

They fired simultaneously, again and again as they sped toward the killer. Monk dove for cover, then scrambled to roll over and get his weapon up. Avery kept firing, pinning him down as they flew past.

The road suddenly curved up the mountain. There was a dirt road that angled sharply to the south that would have taken them farther down the mountain, but John Paul knew that, at the speed he was going, the SUV would roll if he tried to make the turn.

"I'm out," he said as he emptied the magazine.

She was turning to look when John Paul grabbed the back of her neck and shoved her down. "Get on the floor," he ordered as the back window shattered.

They were still climbing and had reached another sharp curve when Monk blew out the left rear tire.

The car went into a spin. They careened off the road into the brush, narrowly missing a tree head-on, but finally stopping when they hit a rock.

"Move it," he shouted as he leapt out of the car and raced around to the other side. Avery had no sense of where they were, only knew they were once again climbing. Her heartbeat, like the turbulent white water, was roaring in her ears. She raced up the steep slope, then skidded to a stop.

"No," she cried.

John Paul stopped beside her. "Ah, hell."

She wanted to weep as she stared down at the swirling water below. No. Not again. Shaking her head, she said, "I won't do it. I can't. You can't make me."

He looked genuinely sorry when he grabbed her. "Sure I can."

# CHAPTER 25

Picturesque, my ass. If Avery saw another white-water anything, she thought she just might start screaming and never stop. At the moment, she was feeling malevolent toward pine trees too. Hated every one of them. She wasn't real fond of John Paul either. He had tossed her over the cliff like a discarded candy wrapper, and on the way down she had vowed that, if he survived, she'd kill him, just for the sheer joy of it.

She knew she was being irrational. She didn't care. Her bad mood intensified when she cut her leg on a jagged rock. If they'd been in the ocean, the blood pouring from her cut would have sounded the lunch bell for the neighboring sharks. Trying to stay positive as she fought to stay afloat, she told herself to be thankful there weren't any sharks around. And her leg didn't hurt all that much compared to the searing charley horse in her calf that nearly caused her to drown. John Paul hauled her onto the bank, half carried her into the trees so they wouldn't be seen, and then dropped her. She landed with a thud on her backside.

He dropped beside her. "That wasn't so bad, was it?"

Since she'd taken in more than enough water to fill a backyard swimming pool, she was too waterlogged to answer the absurd question. Shoving her hair out of her eyes, she glared at him.

"It wasn't as bad as the first jump, was it? I don't think that drop was more than twenty feet," he said.

"You pushed me over a cliff."

Actually, he hadn't pushed her. As he recalled, he'd thrown her so she wouldn't hit the rocks jutting out from the base of the cliff. He didn't think it would be a good idea to mention that now, though. "Did I have any other choice?"

She wasn't ready to admit that there really hadn't been any other alternative. Their guns were useless against a high-powered rifle, and Monk was hot on their trail.

"I don't want to talk about it."

He grinned. "Cup half empty, sugar? Where's that optimistic attitude?"

"At the bottom of the river."

He stood and offered her his hand. "Come on. Let's get out of here."

She didn't know if she had enough strength to even stand. She was so tired and cold and wet. Suck it up, she told herself.

"Right," she said as she grabbed hold. When

he jerked her upright, she fell against him. He put his arm around her and held her tight while he made up his mind which direction they should go.

"Aren't you tired?" she asked.

"Yeah, I am."

She looked back toward the river. "Maybe he'll give up now."

John Paul shook his head. "That isn't gonna happen. He's a professional. He's taken the contract, and he won't stop coming after us until . . ."

"He succeeds?"

"Or until I kill him."

"I vote for the second option."

They both heard the sound of children's laughter. Avery pulled away from him and started running toward the noise. "I hope they have a phone."

"Doubt you can get a signal."

She actually smiled. "There's that negativity I so love. You had me worried, John Paul. For a minute there you were . . ."

"What?"

"Cheerful."

"The hell I was."

He sounded as though she'd just insulted him. She was laughing as she ran toward the sound. The reason for her sudden good humor was either joy or hysteria. A family of five was setting up tents near a little stream.

After a brief explanation, everyone piled into

the father's minivan and headed toward a town the man remembered he'd driven through on the way up the mountain.

Thirty minutes later they reached the sleepy little community of Emerson. Downtown consisted of four streets. The father stopped the van in front of a two-story stone building. The second they got out of the van and closed the sliding door, the father sped away.

"I think maybe you scared him," Avery remarked.

"The faster he can get his family away from us, the safer they'll all be."

There was a police station, which was surprising, considering the size of the town. Sharing the same building, the police station was squeezed in between the volunteer fire department on one end of the building and Bud's Burgers on the other. There were three doors facing the street with signs above each one. They walked through the middle door into a wide hall. Swinging doors were on both sides. One connected to the restaurant, and the other to the fire department. The police station was directly ahead.

The aroma of hamburgers and onions and french fries filled the air, but the smell didn't spur Avery's appetite. It actually made her nauseous. The lack of food, running for miles and miles, the cold, and the terror had taken their toll. She felt all used up. Getting from the door to the counter was suddenly more challenging than surviving the currents. Her feet felt as though they weighed a hundred pounds, and it took every ounce of stamina she had left to move at all.

John Paul could tell she was having trouble. She seemed to wilt before his eyes.

"You okay?" he asked as he put his arm around her waist.

"I feel like rigor mortis has set in," she said. "I'm not dead, am I?"

Smiling, he said, "You're still breathing."

He looked through the glass window and saw the police chief sitting behind his desk. There was a stack of papers on the blotter, and he was poring over them. Every couple of seconds he would glance up at a television mounted to the wall behind the counter. Dressed in navy pants and a white shirt with the name *Chief Tyler* on the pocket, the middle-aged man was frowning as he picked up a sheet of paper.

A woman in her late sixties stood behind the counter with her back to the door. Her hair was as white as Avery's face. She seemed mesmerized by the program on the television.

John Paul could hear her talking as he pushed the door open. "Didn't I tell you something bad was going to happen? Didn't I tell you, Bud?"

"Yes, Verna. You told me."

"And didn't I tell you he brought this on himself?" she asked. "Tearing out all those beautiful trees and digging away at the mountain just to build himself a fancy monument. It looks like

377

Mother Nature decided to get even, didn't she?"

The chief wasn't paying much attention. "Yes," he drawled as he continued to scan the sheet of paper in his hand.

"If you ask me, he's the villain. I feel sorry for his wife."

"You mean ex-wife, don't you?"

"That's right. He got rid of her so he could move on to a younger model. It's criminal, if you ask me. Poor thing. He got her used to living the high life, and then he yanks the rug right out from under her."

The chief was clearly exasperated. He dropped the paper on the desk and looked at the television. " 'Poor thing'? Didn't you see that interview they did with her last month? They had to bleep out every other word she said. I think he was crazy to ever marry her."

"But how is she going to get along now?"

"She can get a job and work like the rest of us. Nobody put a gun to her head when she signed that prenup," he pointed out.

John Paul and Avery had been listening from the doorway. They walked inside as Verna was telling the chief it was all a terrible shame. The chief spotted them, did a double take, and stood.

"What happened to you two?"

"It's a long story."

"I'll be happy to listen," he said.

Avery pulled away from John Paul and walked over to the counter. Verna gasped, and her brown eyes widened as she approached.

"My name's Avery Delaney," she said.

"You're soaking wet. What in heaven's name happened to you? You look like something my cat dragged in."

Avery didn't know where to begin. She saw John Paul shake the policeman's hand and sit in the chair he offered. She decided she'd let him do the explaining.

"May I use your phone?" she asked. "I need to call the FBI."

Verna's eyes now looked as if they were going to pop out of her face as she called over her shoulder, "Bud? The lady wants to call the FBI."

"Let her use the phone," the chief said. He was leaning into the desk, listening intently as John Paul explained the situation.

Verna placed an old-fashioned black phone on the counter. "There are showers on the second floor above the fire station and nice clean cots too. While you make your call, I'll go get a couple of blankets for you folks. Your lips are trembling. You're gonna get hypothermia if you aren't warmed up soon."

"Thank you," she said. "You're very kind."

Avery picked up the phone and then put it back down. Exhausted, she couldn't remember the phone number to the pen. She closed her eyes to think about it. Was it three-nine-one or nine-three-one?

Maybe she could call Carter. What was his

private number? Then she heard John Paul ask the chief if he had ever heard of a property called Land Between the Lakes.

"Everyone in Colorado has heard about that property."

"How far away is it?"

"Quite a distance from here," he said. "And with all the Lookie-Lous out there, you won't be able to get close. By now, the police have the area sealed off. The best way to see it is on television."

John Paul didn't know what he was talking about. He glanced at the screen.

Nine-three-one. That was it. Avery picked up the phone and started dialing. The receiver was halfway to her ear when she happened to look up at the television. She froze, the phone number once again forgotten.

A local newscaster announced that they had new footage of the disaster from a hiker just outside of Aspen who had captured the explosion with his video camera.

"The judge's decision was announced at eight-fifteen this morning, granting ownership of the mansion to Dennis Parnell. For those of you who just tuned in, we repeat, late this morning, the Parnell mansion known as Land Between the Lakes was ripped apart by an explosion."

The phone crashed on the floor as Avery collapsed.

# CHAPTER 26

Numb with shock and despair, Avery couldn't move. Carrie was dead. Carrie, who had given her unconditional love, always, no matter how crazy Avery made her with her career choices.

And Avery had failed her. Carrie would still be alive if Avery had been faster or more clever. All that time wasted running from point to point for the demented woman on the phone who taunted her with lies that Avery could save Carrie. She should have found a way to rescue Carrie and the other women. Now it was too late.

John Paul held her in his arms and let her ramble as she told him over and over how she was to blame.

Verna made soup and all but force-fed Avery, then led her upstairs and stood like a prison guard outside the bathroom while she showered. The old woman, hearing Avery's sobs, kept whispering, "The poor dear."

When she was finished, Verna handed her one of the chief's gray T-shirts to put on, then gathered up her clothes to wash.

She hovered over Avery like an anxious mother hen. She sat Avery down on one of the cots and knelt on the floor with her first-aid kit. The cut on her leg wasn't deep, but it needed to be cleaned. She applied a liberal amount of iodine and wrapped the wound in gauze.

When she was finished, she tucked Avery into bed and headed downstairs to fix a cup of hot tea for her. When she turned back at the doorway to ask her if she wanted a dab of milk in her tea, Avery was already fast asleep.

John Paul was waiting at the bottom of the stairs. "Is she okay?"

"She's sleeping, and that's the best thing for her now. She's all tuckered out."

Nodding agreement, John Paul went back into the station. The chief was on the phone verifying that John Paul was who he claimed he was. When he'd gotten the information he needed, his attitude became more open and friendly.

"The troops are on their way," he said. "I know you've got to be hungry, so I called over to the restaurant, and one of the employees is bringing some food for you."

"Thanks," John Paul said.

"I checked you out," he said then. "You were a Marine."

"Yes."

"I was in the army," he offered. "Went through West Point, then did some duty in Germany. My best friend was a Marine. He died last year, and I sure do miss him. He was a good man."

John Paul wasn't sure why he was telling him his history. "I hear you're good with a gun," Tyler continued. "Do you think trouble's coming this way? Until the FBI gets here, we're on our own."

"If Monk knows where we are, then maybe he'll try to end it here. I don't think he knows, though, and I'm guessing he's gone to ground to reorganize. That's what I'd do."

"We can't be taking any chances," Tyler countered as he stood and crossed to a cabinet on the other side of the room. He pulled a key from his pocket and unlocked the padlock. When he opened the doors, John Paul smiled. Chief Tyler had an arsenal at his disposal.

"You like to be prepared for just about anything, don't you?" he asked with approval.

The chief grinned. "Sometimes we get a cranky bear I have to go after."

"You go after them with an M1911?"

"No, that's just a leftover from my army days. Take your pick," he said. Turning to his assistant, he said, "Verna, you go on home to your daughter and stay there until this is finished."

"I don't want to leave that girl alone upstairs. She needs comfort now. I'm worried she might be going into shock."

"She's tougher than she looks," John Paul said. "I'll com . . . I'll watch out for her."

He'd damned near said he'd comfort the woman, but he'd caught himself in time. What was the matter with him? He didn't have a clue how he was supposed to make Avery feel better, only knew he didn't want her crying on anyone else's shoulder. None of this made any sense to him. She confused him, turned his thinking upside down, and put all sorts of crazy, impossible thoughts into his head. He couldn't understand how or why she had become so important to him, only knew he was driven to keep her safe from harm . . . at all costs.

Protect and serve. If he kept thinking like this, he would end up on the side of law and order again. He shuddered at the possibility.

The chief interrupted his thoughts. "I've got good strong doors with double-bolted locks. There's a back door out of this area, and that has a glass window, but I put in an alarm because of all the firepower I've collected, and the whole town will hear the noise if anyone tries to get in."

John Paul checked out the perimeter. Fifteen minutes later he and Tyler were satisfied with the lockdown. He ate, then went upstairs, showered, and put on the sweats and T-shirt Tyler had given him. When he stepped out of the bathroom, Verna was waiting with a plastic trash bag to collect his wet clothes.

"My son-in-law will drop these off with Avery's after they've been laundered," she said as she started down the stairs. "You take care of her. You hear?"

"I will," he promised.

She left a few minutes later with her daughter.

Tyler had insisted that he could hold down the fort while John Paul caught some shut-eye.

He hadn't argued. He tried not to make any noise as he walked into the dormitory where Avery slept. There were four cots, all with clean bedding, lined up against one wall. The chief had told him that when the building was constructed, the town believed they would have a full-time fire department, but when the town didn't develop the way the city planners thought it would, the budget couldn't afford salaried firefighters. It was volunteer now.

John Paul noticed the window was unlocked. It overlooked the alley behind the building, and there was a fire escape ladder just a couple of feet to the left. He locked the window and then sat down on the cot next to Avery's.

She was sleeping on her back. Her face was scrubbed clean; her hair was still damp from washing, and he thought she was the most beautiful woman he'd ever seen. She looked like an angel, but she had a little vinegar in her disposition, the way she tried to boss him around. He liked the fact that she stood up to him, held her own. He liked her attitude too. She viewed the world the way he used to when he had been naive.

He was tired, and surely his fatigue was the reason he was thinking such foolish thoughts. When the FBI arrived, he'd leave. Simple as that. Avery was the ultimate team player, he reminded himself, so he'd let her team watch out for her.

"Hell," he muttered as he rolled onto the cot.

He got in two full hours of sleep before Tyler woke him. John Paul had heard him coming up the stairs and had the handgun aimed and ready when he opened the door.

The chief waited until John Paul put the gun down. Then he walked inside. "We've got company," he whispered. "The FBI's here, and the man in charge wants to see you."

Avery was still out cold. She'd kicked off the sheet, and one leg was hanging off the side of the bed. There was a bandage wrapped above her ankle. Spots of dark blood dotted the gauze. When had she hurt herself? he wondered as he carefully lifted her leg and tucked her back under the sheet. And why hadn't she told him?

He knew the answer to that one. She would never think to complain.

Fighting the urge to kiss her, he went into the bathroom to splash cold water on his face.

He became angry thinking about the interview he'd have to suffer through with the Feds. If the team leader turned out to be like so many others John Paul remembered, then he'd be an arrogant, opinionated, we-do-it-my-way-or-no-way prick.

By the time he'd dried his face and hands, he was ready for a fight. Fact was, he was looking forward to it. He found himself hoping the guy did turn out to be a prick because he was suddenly in the mood to kick some ass.

Unfortunately, Agent Knolte was neither a prick nor a know-it-all. The freckle-faced agent was intelligent, eager, and sincere, and seemed to know what he was talking about as far as strategy went. He'd certainly done his home-work on Monk, knew almost as much about him as John Paul did.

There were only two problems with Agent Knolte. One, he looked like a twelve-year-old. And with a cowlick and braces, no less. What were they doing in the Bureau these days? Re-cruiting from grade school? The second problem was monumental. Knolte was a by-the-book agent.

"Mr. Renard, it's an honor to meet you," Knolte said, extending his hand as four other eager agents crowded around. "We all heard about the hostage rescue down in South America, and I want you to know we consider it a privilege to be able to work with you."

John Paul stared into Knolte's brown eyes. "I was never in South America."

"But I talked to —"

"I was never there."

"Yes, sir. If you say so," Knolte hastily agreed.

Another agent stepped forward. "Sir, we un-derstand the Agency was elated to hear you de-cided to come back to work after your long leave of absence."

John Paul didn't look at the man when he re-sponded. "I didn't take a leave of absence. I re-tired and I'm still retired." Then without missing a beat, he asked, "How old are you, Agent Knolte?"

The question didn't seem to faze the man. "Older than I look," he answered. "Let me introduce you to my team."

John Paul suddenly found himself surrounded by agents wanting to shake his hand. The attention didn't sit well. Chief Tyler observed the spectacle from the back hallway. When John Paul caught his eye, the middle-aged man shook his head and muttered something about a damn fan club.

"We'll need to question Miss Delaney," an agent named Brock said.

"Not until she's had some sleep," John Paul said. "You can talk to me."

The interview lasted an hour. There were constant interruptions as Knolte kept getting updates from another agent at the explosion site. He told John Paul that they'd brought in the dogs and were searching for bodies. Thus far, two had been found. From the remains of the vehicle near the site, they knew that one of the women was the former wife of Dennis Parnell, the owner of the house.

The wait for the discovery of the other bodies was grim and tense. Then Knolte got another call and thrust the phone at John Paul. "You'll want to hear this."

A minute later John Paul bounded up the stairs. Knolte could have sworn the brooding man actually smiled for a second there.

The door to the dormitory banged against the wall when he rushed inside, but the noise didn't disturb Avery.

He shook her awake. "Sweetheart, open your eyes. Come on, Avery, wake up."

She was slow to respond. She felt drugged and disoriented. She finally opened her eyes and struggled to sit up.

"Is it time to go?"

"Carrie's alive."

She squinted up at him, shaking her head as she tried to comprehend what he was saying. "Alive? How can she be alive? The house —"

"She got out before the explosion. I don't know how she managed it, but she's okay."

Avery burst into tears. John Paul sat down next to her and pulled her onto his lap. He held her while she cried all over him.

When she was finally able to calm down, she asked, "Did everyone get out? Where's Carrie now? Have they called Uncle Tony? The poor man will be beside himself. First, they tell him she's dead, and then they tell him she's alive. I hope to God he has a strong heart."

John Paul wasn't sure which question to answer first. "Carrie's in a hospital in Aspen."

She jerked away from him. "Why is she in the hospital? You told me she was okay."

"She is," he insisted. "But the other woman was hurt. The judge tore up one of her knees when they fell into a deep ravine," he explained. "Carrie twisted her ankle, and fractured her arm, but she was still able to drag some dead branches over them so they could hide the rest of the night. One of the police dogs found them," he added. "They were taken to the hospital, and the judge is in surgery."

"But what about the other woman? There were three . . . weren't there?"

"Anne Trapp. She stayed inside the house."

"Why? Why would she stay?"

"I don't know. You'll have to ask Carrie, or maybe Knolte knows the reason now."

Avery stood and nearly tripped over her backpack and duffel bag. "How did these get here?"

"The chief called a friend. He got my car working and drove it here."

Avery was so relieved and jubilant about Carrie, she felt limp and giddy. She wanted to laugh and cry, and kiss John Paul. Oh, she really wanted to kiss him, and a whole lot more. What was wrong with her? Maybe it was the endorphins. Yes, that's what it was.

She mentally shook herself. She needed to concentrate on Carrie now. And Uncle Tony. "Did anyone call my uncle?"

"Yes," he answered. "He's a happy man right now, but scared too. He wants to get on the next flight to Aspen."

She nodded approval. "Who's downstairs?" she asked as she knelt beside her duffel bag and unzipped it.

"FBI," he said. "There are five of them downstairs, all talking on their cell phones. They've taken over the police station, and Chief Tyler isn't real happy about that. Tyler's an okay guy," he added. "He doesn't much like the FBI either."

She rolled her eyes. "Your prejudice is juvenile, John Paul." She pulled out a pair of khakis. "I should go down and find out what they have so far. Any word on where Monk might be?"

"No," he answered. He was staring at her legs, noticing how long and shapely they were. One thought led to another, and another, and before he could stop himself, he was picturing her legs wrapped around his thighs.

He looked at the wall behind her head. "You can't go downstairs like that."

"Like what? I'm going to put on slacks," she said. "And since when do you care what I look like?"

"I don't care," he answered gruffly. "But I can see through that threadbare T-shirt."

She looked down, whispered, "Oh, God," and grabbed the sheet from the cot, tugging with all her might to get the end out from under John Paul. She dropped her slacks as she wrapped the sheet around her.

"Why didn't you say something sooner?" She was blushing.

"Now, why would I want to do that?"

His grin was lecherous. Shaking her head, she said, "I need to go to Carrie as soon as possible. She must be crazed after what she's been through."

His smile vanished. "Not a good idea," he said. "Sit down, Avery. We need to talk."

His tone of voice indicated it was serious. She sat down beside him. "You don't think I should go see Carrie?"

"No, I don't. Talk to her on the phone if you need proof she's okay, but don't go to her."

"Why not?"

"Because that's what the FBI wants you to do," he said. "The agent calling the shots from Aspen told Knolte —"

She interrupted. "Who's Knolte?"

"The kid agent downstairs running the show here," he explained. "He told me the game plan. They want to put you and Carrie and the judge together in protective custody until they get Monk, and that's not a good idea."

"John Paul, they're good at what they do."

"Yeah? Well, so is Monk," he said. "And staying together is gonna make it real easy for him."

Avery didn't say a word. She silently agreed, but she felt it would be disloyal to the Bureau to admit her reservations.

She tried to get up, but he put his hands on her shoulders.

"What are you doing?"

"Bracing you so you won't hit your head if you faint."

"Listen," she said. "Downstairs . . . when I lost it . . . that was the first time in my life I ever passed out. I'm not a weakling. I was sleep-deprived and stressed . . . really stressed out. I

392

won't faint again. Now let go of me. I want to get dressed and go downstairs to talk to Agent Knolte."

"In a minute," he promised. He tightened his hold as he said, "There's something else you need to know."

"Yes?"

He was suddenly at a loss for words. He was searching for the best way to tell her. "It's going to be difficult . . ."

"I can handle it. Just tell me." She relaxed her shoulders then and said, "Sorry, I didn't mean to snap at you. What is it?"

"Carrie knows who the woman with Monk is."

She tilted her head. "She knows her?"

"Yes." He took a breath. "You know her too."

"Come on, John Paul. Stop fencing. Just tell me," she demanded.

"Jilly. Carrie said her name is Jilly."

Avery's reaction stunned John Paul. She didn't faint; she didn't cry; she didn't argue, and she didn't go into full-blown denial.

She roared.

# CHAPTER 27

"Get me a gun, John Paul. I want a gun now. A big one."

She looked like an avenging angel as she paced around him. She stopped just inches in front of him, poked him in the chest, and made her demand again.

Chief Tyler stood just inside the doorway of the dormitory, shifting from foot to foot as he waited for one of them to notice him.

"She'll stay dead when I get finished with her," Avery railed. "I want a gun."

The chief couldn't stop himself from trying to reason with the distraught woman.

"Now, Miss Delaney, you shouldn't be talking crazy. What if someone does shoot your mother? With you making threats, who do you think the police will come looking for? I understand you're overwrought, but . . ."

She whirled around to confront the policeman. "Jilly is not my mother. She's the woman who gave birth to me, but she has never been nor will she ever be my mother. Are we clear on that?"

Tyler hastily nodded. Her wrath was blistering, and he was so surprised by the change that had come over her he didn't know how to proceed. She'd been such a sweet, appreciative little lady when he'd first met her, but now she was a spitfire.

The chief turned to John Paul for help. "This can't be the same woman I met downstairs. She wouldn't happen to have a twin, would she?"

"Sorry, no twin," he said. "She's just got a temper." He made that comment sound like a compliment.

The chief thought it was an understatement. "Can't you reason with her? She can't go running out of here with a gun, thinking she can shoot her moth . . ." He stopped himself in time. "If she isn't your mother —"

"She isn't."

"Then what should I call her?"

Avery didn't hesitate. "A frickin' maniac," she snapped. "A deviant sociopath, a psychopath. Take your pick. Just don't call her my mother."

"Yes, ma'am."

Mollified, she clutched the sheet to her neck, picked up her duffel bag, and walked with her head held high toward the bathroom.

"John Paul?"

"Yes?"

"Get me a damn gun."

The door shut before he could answer.

Tyler scratched his jaw and asked, "What are you going to do about her?"

He shrugged. "Get her a gun."

Tyler stepped into the room and shut the door behind him. "Are you going to let them take her to Aspen? You heard them talking. They want to put her, her aunt and that judge in a safe house until they catch the man hired to kill them."

"Yes, I heard," he said.

"If you ask me, they're putting all their eggs in one basket, and I figure the reason must have something to do with their budget. Less manpower if they keep them together, but if this professional killer . . . what's his name?"

"Monk," John Paul said.

"If he's any good, he'll find them. All he'd have to do is wait around that hospital and follow the judge. That's what I'd do."

John Paul agreed. "I heard Knolte say they were going to keep them together."

"But you didn't hear the rest of their plans because you had already gone upstairs to tell Avery her aunt was alive. Did you know there's an important trial coming up?"

"No, I didn't know."

The chief lowered his voice as he continued. Even though he could hear the hair dryer humming in the bathroom and doubted Avery would hear them talking, he moved closer to John Paul.

"They're going to retry a man named Skarrett. You familiar with him?"

He tensed. "Yes," he said. "So he's getting a new trial? When is it?"

"It starts three weeks from today," he said. "Knolte was on the phone arguing with another agent who's giving them orders. Anyway, when he hung up, he noticed me watching him, and he closed up tight, until I told him I was coming up here to check on the girl." He smiled as he added, "Of course, I didn't come right up. I made a little noise going up a couple of steps, then snuck back down and lingered in the hall so I could hear what he was telling the others."

He glanced at the bathroom door before continuing. "If they haven't nabbed Monk by the time the trial starts, they aren't going to let Avery or her aunt testify, and from what I could gather, the man in charge didn't think it would be so bad if Skarrett got off."

John Paul was astonished. "Are you serious?"

"Oh, yes," he drawled.

"Why in God's name would they —"

"They're hoping that Skarrett will lead them to a big stash he's got hidden away. It seems Skarrett robbed a jewelry store and stole several million in uncut stones. They're hoping to get them back."

"So they're going to make it easy for Skarrett to walk?"

"Avery's a key witness," Tyler pointed out. "And if she doesn't testify . . ." He left the sentence hanging. John Paul was staggered by the endless possibilities of what could and would go wrong. His voice reeked with sarcasm as he said,

"Now, that's a plan guaranteed to get screwed up."

Tyler was in full agreement. "That's the way I see it too. Are you going to tell Avery? Once they've got her in that safe house, she won't be able to get out."

"I'll let Knolte tell her," he said. "Avery works for the FBI, so she's a believer in teamwork."

"An idealist, huh?"

"Afraid so."

"That's not good. What about you? What are you going to do?"

"I guess I'll take off," he said. "No reason to hang around here."

"You think this Monk has backed off?"

"Yeah, I do," he said. "But not for long. He's taken the contracts, and when he hears that Carrie and the judge are still alive, he'll hit again. He has to. His reputation is on the line. He's going to continue to go after Avery too."

Oh, yes, he'll strike again and again and again. Until he gets the job done.

It was as though Tyler had just read his mind. "So you think it's okay to let those boys downstairs watch over Avery? You think she'll be all right?"

"She's a smart, tough woman. She can handle herself."

Tyler looked disappointed in him. "If you think that's the right thing to do, but if you don't and you decide you might want to do something on your own, I thought I'd mention I've got this nice little cabin tucked away in the mountains. I was going to go up there for a couple of weeks, and I just stocked the kitchen. Only needs the refrigerator foods, like milk and eggs, and you'd be all set. If you're heading toward Denver, it won't be much out of your way. It would be a good place to hide out until you and Avery decide what to do . . . about the trial and all."

John Paul tried to interrupt him, but Tyler rushed on. "There's a barn where I keep my car, and I'll write out directions for you and tell you where the key to the cabin is hidden . . . if you're interested. You think about it and let me know before you leave. I'll go down and write those instructions just in case."

Having had his say, he turned around and went back downstairs. John Paul didn't know what the hell he was going to do. He stood there thinking about the situation for several minutes, then muttered an expletive as he picked up his gear and carried it down to the car. The chief's assistant had dropped off his clean clothes. They were folded next to Avery's on the bottom step. He shoved his in the bag, ran back up the stairs, and placed hers on one of the cots, and then headed outside.

The chief's friend had parked John Paul's car in the alley between the buildings, just below the windows in the dorm. He threw the bags into the back of the SUV and then decided he should say good-bye to Avery. He couldn't just take off, could he? Saying good-bye and wishing her luck was the decent thing to do.

If she asks me to stay, then I will, he told himself. But if she doesn't ask, then I'm out of here. Simple as that. She doesn't need me. But if she asks . . .

He walked into the room and stopped cold. He nearly tripped over his own feet when he saw her. She was standing by the window with her arms folded, waiting for him.

"Why are you glaring at me?" he asked with a defensive scowl of his own.

"I saw you putting your bags in the car," she said, nodding toward the window. "Are you leaving, then?" She took a step toward him but stopped when she noticed his back stiffened. "I would appreciate an answer."

"Do you want me to stay?"

"Do you want to stay?"

"What kind of an answer is that? I'm not in the mood to play games, Avery." Then, before she could respond, he squinted at her and asked, "What happened to your face?"

Her hand went to her cheek. "What's wrong with my face?"

"Nothing. It just looks . . . different."

"I washed it, put on some moisturizer and a little makeup. That's all."

"Makeup? Why would you do that? Do you want to look nice for your FBI buddies?"

Oh, brother, was he in a mood. "What's the matter with you?"

He couldn't answer because he couldn't possibly put into words what was going on inside his head right now or how he was feeling. Why he was suddenly itching for a fight was beyond him. He only knew he was furious with her and with himself because she had been able to do to him what no other woman had done before. She had tied his stomach into knots. What was worse was that he had let her.

What was next? His heart? The hell with that.

"Have you talked to Agent Knolte yet?"

"No, I was waiting for you to come upstairs. Were you going to leave without saying good-bye?" The big jerk. She would not cry, no matter how angry he made her. She took a breath to steady her resolve, walked across the room, and thrust her hand out. "Thank you for all you've done."

He ignored her hand. "Avery . . . if you want —"

She interrupted. "Chief Tyler came upstairs looking for you. He wanted to talk to you, said it was important."

"I just talked to him not five minutes ago."

She shrugged. "He must have something else to say to you. He's waiting in the restaurant."

"Yeah, all right."

"Have a safe trip home," she said. She turned around and walked back to the window. "Good-bye, John Paul."

He couldn't believe she was blowing him off. He stared at her back for a minute, then abruptly turned and went downstairs. Her cold farewell had been that of a stranger, and he was too pissed off to try to figure out why her attitude had changed.

Fortunately, he didn't get swamped by agents as he walked through the police station. Knolte and a couple of other young hotshots were studying maps and talking·on their cell phones. One agent did try to engage him in conversation, but he ignored him, shoved the swinging door open, and crossed over to the restaurant. The front was deserted, but he could hear whistling coming from the kitchen. He walked behind the red Formica counter and spotted the chief at the grill. The aroma of sizzling meat filled the air.

"You ready to take off?" the chief asked.

"Just about."

"You want to take a hamburger for the road?"

"No thanks. Where is everyone?"

"My restaurant crew? I sent them home a while back. If Knolte and his friends want something to eat, they can fix it themselves."

"Did you want to see me about something?"

Tyler frowned. "I already said what I had to say. I went ahead and put that sheet of directions in your car just in case you change your mind and decide to take me up on my offer to use my cabin. You ought to think about it," he urged. "I can't get up there for another month, thanks to my wife's relatives. She informed me last night we have two weddings and a reunion to attend."

"Yeah, I'll think about it," he said. "Thanks for your help, Chief, and for the food and bed."

"Glad I could help," Tyler said. He unlocked the back door and stepped into the alley with John Paul.

"You take care of yourself."

"I will," he said as he opened the car door and slid behind the wheel. He noticed the folded paper the chief had placed on the seat next to him and picked it up with the intent of handing it back.

"You sure that little girl's gonna be all right?"

That was the third time the chief had asked him that question. John Paul gave him the same answer. "She'll be okay."

He didn't believe that nonsense, not for one second, and he could tell from Tyler's expression, he didn't believe it either.

"I'll be seeing you," Tyler called, raising the spatula he was holding in farewell.

John Paul put his key in the ignition, dropped the paper on the seat, and then sat there, brooding. His conscience wouldn't quiet down. Avery had made her choice, he reminded himself. Yeah, she had let him know in no uncertain terms that she didn't want or need him.

There was only one problem with her decision. He wanted and needed her.

He thought he'd gotten rid of his feelings years ago when disillusionment had taken root, but now he realized he'd only been fooling himself with his hate-everyone, don't-need-anyone attitude and that he was as human and flawed as everyone else. Who would have thought?

Did he even like Avery? Yeah, he did, he admitted. The woman was a real smart-ass. How could he not like her?

He shook his head and turned the key in the ignition. The engine purred like a well-fed kitten as he put the gear into drive.

God knows he tried, but he couldn't summon up the strength to drive away. Damn it, she was making him nuts. She was just like a chigger, itching and irritating. She wanted him to leave. Right? Hell, yes. She was sure she was going to be fine and dandy with that super-duper team watching out for her safety. . . . God help her.

Avery was a fighter, and she could certainly handle anything that came her way. But could she control the actions of the agents assigned to protect her? Could she prevent them from screwing things up? And while she was watching them, who would be watching her?

He put the gear back in park and turned the motor off. What the hell was he going to do?

Let the FBI worry about her. Damn right. That was definitely what he was going to do. He started the motor again, but this time he didn't get the gearshift into drive. He sat there like a lump of ice, frozen with indecision, while the car idled.

What a game player he was turning out to be. He was now desperately trying to convince himself he didn't care what happened to her.

She made him laugh. She made him want things he thought he could never have.

Hell, she humanized him.

John Paul fought the good fight, but when all was said and done, he lost the battle. He bowed his head in submission as the truth sliced through him. Son of a bitch.

Face it, Renard. You aren't going anywhere without her.

He turned the motor off and reached for the door.

The voice stopped him. "Will you get going? Move it, Renard. I'm suffocating back here, and your sleeping bag smells like dead leaves."

He swung around. "What do you think you're doing?" he asked.

"Don't start with me, John Paul. Put the damn car into drive and get us out of here. Don't make me tell you again."

His smile was slow and easy. The tension eased out of his shoulders, and his stomach stopped aching. The world was suddenly right again. Avery was snarling at him like a mountain cat, definitely giving him attitude.

He started the engine and changed gears, but he didn't accelerate. "If you go with me, sugar, I'm calling the shots, and you're going to do what I tell you to do. Can you deal with that?"

She didn't hesitate in answering. "When I jumped off the fire escape ladder, I landed on the roof of your car and dented it. You deal with that."

He grinned as he drove down the alley. How could he not be crazy about her?

# CHAPTER 28

Jilly was anxiously waiting to hear the body count. She paced around her hotel bungalow while the television, tuned into a local Colorado station, droned on and on, but each time that wonderful film clip showing the explosion of the house came on, she hurriedly sat down on the edge of the bed. Enthusiastically and greedily, she devoured every second of the magnificent footage.

How fortuitous that a hiker just happened to be filming the landscape at the exact second the house disintegrated. His lens had captured every bit of the back of the house. Had Jilly not been able to watch it on television, she would have been irate. Admittedly, she was still a little irritated because she had been looking forward to pushing the button, but this clip that the station kept showing over and over again was almost as good.

The phone rang just as the clip ended. She hit the mute button before she answered.

"Hello, darling."

A second's pause followed. "Did you see it on television?"

He sounded so eager to please, yet nervous at the same time. "Yes, of course I saw it. Wasn't it marvelous?"

"Yes . . . yes," he replied. "Two bodies so far."

"One to go," she said. "You sound nervous, darling. What's wrong?"

"I was worried that, after the fact, you might feel bad. I'm glad to know you're okay."

"Feel bad about Carrie? She ruined my life and stole my daughter from me. I'm overjoyed," she said.

"I miss you," he said. "I want —"

Her voice dropped to a throaty whisper. "I know what you want. Are you in the car now?"

"Yes," he whispered back.

"You'd better pull over," she said. And then in the most erotic detail she told him what she would do to him when they were together. His breathing amused her. The rapid panting of a dog in heat, she thought. The power she had over men excited her.

"Will you like that?" she asked breathlessly so he would think she was as out of control as he was.

And then she gave him more until he was whimpering with his need. A sudden silence followed a low groan. She knew what was happening and smiled with satisfaction. She could have had a wonderful career doing phone sex, she thought, but she certainly wouldn't make the kind of money she wanted. Still, it was nice to know she had options.

"Are you feeling less lonely now, darling?"

"Yes," he answered with a sigh. "I'll be with you soon. I love you, Jilly."

"I know you do, darling. I love you too."

She hung up the phone and began to pace again. Would the police be able to tell who was who from what little was left of the bodies? She knew that skulls and teeth were one way of identifying victims, but what if those had also been blown to smithereens?

Umm. What would they do then?

The film came on the television again. Jilly rushed to the bed and sat down to watch. Oh, it was lovely, so lovely.

When the news bulletin ended, she went to her overnight bag and took out her precious videotape. She carried it with her wherever she went. She popped it into the VCR and knelt in front of the TV to watch. How many times had she seen it? A hundred? A thousand? And yet, she never grew tired of it . . . or the feelings it provoked.

"Now do you see why you have to die?" she whispered to the screen.

She happened to notice one of her nails was chipped and rushed into the bathroom to repair it. Checking the time, she realized that Monk would be arriving soon. She needed to get ready to greet him properly. And reward him, of course. Like a dog who'd performed a difficult trick, Monk would be anxious for his treat.

Virginal white, she decided as she pulled the negligee from her overnight bag. He'd like that. But then he liked everything she did to him, didn't he?

She mustn't forget to put on red lipstick. Oh, how men loved pouting red lips.

They loved her perfect body. They loved her angelic face.

They all loved her.

# CHAPTER 29

The paramedics told Carrie she was in shock. She didn't agree, but she understood how they had reached their diagnosis. Granted, there was something a little peculiar about her behavior. When they'd lifted her out of the ravine, she had been sobbing uncontrollably and incoherently. She knew the words she wanted to say, yet she couldn't seem to get them out in the right order or at the right time. Still, their conclusion was a bunch of nonsense. They weren't doctors. What the hell did they know? Her mind was working just fine, thank you very much.

Camera lights glared in her face as she was carried on the stretcher and placed inside across from Sara in the waiting ambulance. Carrie struggled to sit up until she realized one of the paramedics had rudely strapped her down. She was able to move one of her arms, though. Reaching across the narrow aisle, she took hold of Sara's hand.

Her friend was in terrible pain. Both paramedics were working on her leg. "Is she going to be all right? Is she going to be all right?" The question became a chant she couldn't stop. Even though both men tried to assure her that yes, yes, she was going to be fine, Carrie felt compelled to keep asking.

One of them gave Sara an injection, and she closed her eyes seconds later. Her hand went limp in Carrie's. After they finished immobilizing her leg, one of them checked her blood pressure again while the other worked on Carrie.

"He's going to kill Avery. Make them stop him. Do you hear me? He's going to . . . going to . . ."

Carrie passed out. The terror of what she had been through, added to sleep deprivation, had finally caught up with her. Her body simply rebelled and shut down.

When she next opened her eyes, she was in a hospital bed. And, oh, how she ached. It seemed every muscle in her body throbbed. Had someone taken a stick to her?

She desperately tried to clear the fog in her mind. Avery. Oh, God, she had to find Avery before it was too late. She saw the call button pinned to the sheet on her left and tried to reach for it. Pain shot up through her elbow and she cried out. Looking down, she saw the cast on her arm and let out a low curse.

How had that happened?

The ravine, of course. She'd fallen headfirst into that deep pit, and she remembered putting her arm out to try to brace against the fall. She knew she'd injured her wrist, but she thought she'd just sprained it. It hadn't hurt all that much at the time, had it? She couldn't remember. Maybe it had gone numb, as numb as the rest of her at that point. She did remember landing on top of Sara, though. Her friend had been writhing in agony, and Carrie distinctly recalled putting her hand over her mouth to stifle her cries, terrified that Monk was lurking in the dark waiting to catch them.

Where was Sara? Carrie could hear men's voices in the hallway, and she couldn't reach the call button. She was about to shout when the door opened and a young doctor dressed in blue scrubs and a white lab coat came inside. He was holding a chart in his hand.

His name was Dr. Bridgeport, and he looked as if he hadn't had any sleep in a week. That can't be good, she thought. Then she noticed his hands. They were huge, as though he'd had them transplanted from a bigger body, along with the new row of dark hair plugs in his scalp.

"Are you my doctor?"

"I'm a neurologist. I've reviewed your X rays and CAT scan," he began.

"I had those tests?" she interrupted.

He nodded. "You suffered a mild concussion. I'm going to keep you overnight for observation. I didn't see anything alarming on the scan," he added.

"What about my arm?"

"You broke it."

"Obviously," she said.

He was writing in her chart and, without looking up, said, "Your primary physician will be in to check on you in a little while. Meanwhile, you've got quite a few eager law enforcement officers waiting to talk to you. I'm going to allow two in the room . . . if you're feeling up to it."

"My head hurts. May I have something for pain?"

"In a little while," he promised.

She knew what that meant. When Avery was little and wanted something Carrie didn't want her to have, she used the very same phrase. It hadn't worked on Avery then, and it wasn't working on Carrie now.

"I want something."

"You've suffered a concussion, Mrs. Salvetti, and I would rather —"

She cut him off. "Oh, never mind. Doctor, a friend of mine rode with me in the ambulance. Her leg was all torn up. Where is she? Do you know?"

The doctor nodded. "Judge Collins is in surgery," he explained.

There was a hard rap on the door. The doctor closed the chart, smiled at her, and turned to leave. "You need to rest," he said as he opened the door and let two men in dark suits rush inside. "Ten minutes," he said to the agents, "then she needs to get some sleep."

They moved like soldiers on parade, arms stiff, heads high. They were also dressed alike, except for the choice of tie colors. One wore a gray-and-black-striped tie, and the other had on a muted plaid.

An agent named Hillman was in charge. There was a sharpness about his eyes she found comforting. She didn't think he would miss much.

The other, younger agent pushed the button to elevate her back, poured her a glass of water, and hovered at her side while Hillman questioned her. He led her through the sequence of events, rarely interrupting when she paused to collect her thoughts. She wanted to tell him everything at once, impatient to ask questions of her own, but Hillman was tenacious and made her keep to his agenda.

She turned to the more cooperative agent and asked him to find her jacket.

"The letters are in the pocket."

Hillman found the jacket hanging in the built-in closet. He pulled on a pair of gloves and dropped the envelopes into a Ziploc bag the other agent held out for him.

"Anne gave a letter to me. I want to read it."

"We'll let the lab dust it for prints," the sidekick told her.

She'd thought he was more malleable than Hillman, but now she realized he was just as tenacious.

"I want to know what that sick bastard of a husband wrote to her. He hired Monk to kill her, you know. You have to arrest him."

Ignoring her demand, Hillman resumed his questions. Carrie had had enough. "No, it's my turn. I want to know where my niece is."

"We're searching for her . . ."

"Find her."

Seeing how distraught Carrie was, sidekick offered her a sip of water by holding the straw under her nose. She turned her head.

"Tell me what you know about . . ." Hillman once again tried to get her back on track.

"I want an update on Judge Collins, and I want it now."

The agents exchanged a glance, and then Hillman answered. "She's out of surgery and in ICU."

"So far, so good," the other man said.

She glared at him. "What's your name?"

"Bean, ma'am. Agent Peter Bean."

No wonder he hadn't introduced himself. Saddled with a name like that, she wouldn't have told anyone either. Bet they called him string bean in grade school, she thought.

Hillman started the questions all over again. For an hour he kept it up, grilling her, going over the same facts again and again until she began to feel as if she were the criminal they were trying to get to confess.

Her head was pounding. "That's it," she said. "I can't answer any more questions now."

Hillman looked disappointed, but he agreed to let her rest for a little while. She wasn't in the mood to be cordial. She told them not to come back until they had news about Avery. To calm her down — she was shouting now — Hillman let her call her husband. Bean dialed the number for her. The second she heard Tony's voice over the phone, she burst into tears.

"I need you, Tony. You have to come to Aspen."

His voice shook with emotion as he replied, "Sweetheart, they told me I couldn't. They said as soon as you're discharged from the hospital they're going to move you and the judge to a safe house somewhere. Carrie, love, are you all right? I wish I could be there with you. I wish . . . I'm sorry you're going through this alone."

"Have you heard from Avery?"

"No," he answered. "I didn't know she was planning to join you at the spa. One of the agents who came to talk to me told me she missed her flight."

"I don't know where she is," she sobbed.

"We'll find her," he promised. "Nothing's going to happen to her. I promise you. And I'm keeping the line open. She'll call. I know she'll call."

"Tony, I didn't realize . . . I'm so sorry about everything. You can have Star Catcher. You can run it any way you want. I don't care about any of that anymore. I should have trusted you. I've been such a fool."

She was sobbing now and angry because the agents were listening to every word.

"I love you," she whispered. "I do, Tony. I love

you very much. Please . . . tell me it isn't too late."

"No, no, it isn't. I can . . . I love you too," he stammered. "I'll get on the next plane. We'll make our marriage work again. Anything is possible with your love. Anything."

# CHAPTER 30

Any hope that the FBI would be able to keep the names of the survivors out of the papers and off the television had been squelched when a news crew filmed Carrie and the judge being carried into the ambulance near the site of the explosion.

Avery heard about it on the radio as she and John Paul were driving through the mountains. As soon as they'd left the sleepy town, she'd climbed in front, clipping him on the shoulder with her left foot when she fell into the passenger seat. Her shoe fell in his lap. Shaking his head over her awkwardness, he handed her the shoe while she apologized.

They continued to listen to the broadcast until the signal faded. "Does everyone in the United States carry video cameras now?" he asked. He sounded disgusted. "Some people just love invading other people's privacy."

"Film crews from television stations usually carry cameras," she said.

"No need to be sarcastic, sugar."

"I wasn't being sarcastic. I was simply pointing out a fact. Carrie must have hated having a camera in her face. Someone from the FBI should have grabbed the film. The crime-scene investigators must not have gotten there in time."

"Should've, could've," he drawled. "That's the Bureau's motto."

"You're not going to rile me."

He laughed. "I wasn't trying to."

She rolled the window down and let the cool night air in. "Yes, you were," she said. "I've finally gotten you all figured out."

"You think so?"

She smiled. "When I first met you, I thought you must have some kind of grudge against the FBI, but now that I know you better, I realize that isn't true at all. Your phobia is much bigger than that."

"Oh?"

She nodded. "You don't like any government agency."

"That's not true."

"When we talked about your brother-in-law working for the Justice Department, you sneered."

"Justice has too much power."

"What about the CIA? I know you worked for them."

He didn't argue or deny. "Their priorities change on a whim, leaving agents and civilians out there to hang."

"What about the IRS?"

"Everyone hates the IRS."

She'd give him that one. She kept on naming government agencies, and he continued to tell her what was wrong with each one of them.

"I think I've made my case. You know what your biggest problem is?"

"No, but you're going to enlighten me, aren't you?"

"Uh-huh," she said. "You don't like anyone in a position of authority."

He wasn't offended by her analysis. "You know what they say. Absolute power corrupts absolutely."

"The FBI doesn't have absolute power."

"They think they do."

"You know what I say?"

"What?"

"Therapy. You need intense therapy to help you get rid of your hostility."

Before he could tell her he hated therapy too, she changed the subject. "I need to get to a phone and call Carrie."

"Why didn't you call her from the police station?"

"Because you would have left without me. I still can't believe you were going to abandon me. I get mad every time I think about it."

Should he tell her the truth or not? He clenched his jaw while he thought about it. She'd sounded so disappointed in him, even hurt.

"Look . . ." he began, and then stopped.

"Yes?"

"Maybe I was going to stay."

"Maybe?" She poked him in his arm. "What does that mean?"

"It means I was gonna stay. Now it's your turn to squirm. How come you decided to leave your super team?"

"Stop calling them that. I'm sure Agent Knolte and the other agents are quite capable of doing a good job."

"Yeah? Then, I repeat, why did you decide to go with me?"

She shrugged. "I thought about what you said, and I agreed. It isn't smart to put all of us together in the same safe house."

"And?"

"And what? Are you waiting for a compliment?"

Before he could tell her the thought hadn't crossed his mind, she said, "Okay, fine. I think I have a better chance of surviving with you."

"What made you cross over to the dark side?" he asked, grinning. "Did Knolte say or do something that turned you into a rogue agent?"

"I'm not an agent. I'm an analyst, and he didn't say or do anything. I still have complete faith in the Bureau. No one is more loyal than I am."

"Uh-huh," he said. "So why'd you leave?"

She had to think about it for awhile. "I'm taking initiative. We're taught to do that at the Bureau."

"Yeah, right," he scoffed. He nodded toward a

sign on the side of the two-lane road. "There's a restaurant five miles ahead," he said. "I need to make a call too and get us some help."

Mr. Loner was going to ask someone for help? That was a shock.

"Then what?" she asked.

"You can call Carrie, but don't tell her where we're headed."

"How can I? I don't know where we're going."

He picked up the folded paper. "Chief Tyler has a cabin a couple of hours away. It's got a barn, and I can hide the car inside. We'll stay there tonight."

She glanced out the back window once again to make sure they weren't being followed. They hadn't seen another car in a long time, and she realized she was probably being a little paranoid, but she continued to stay on guard. One couldn't be too cautious, she reasoned.

"Do you have any guesses where Monk might be?"

"He's probably still in Colorado, and by now he's heard that your aunt and the judge are still alive."

"The FBI will be looking for us too," she said.

"Not us, sugar. You. They'll be looking for you."

"I turned the shower on in case one of the agents came upstairs, and I locked the dormitory door, but eventually Knolte will find out I'm gone, and he'll sound the alarm."

And then all hell was going to break loose.

When Carter found out about the situation, he'd have her ass on a platter. She already had her argument rehearsed. She'd insist it wasn't insubordination. Carter was tough, but he was also a reasonable man. Surely he would see the merits of her taking initiative . . . again.

"Will the chief tell Knolte he offered you the use of his cabin?" she asked.

"No, he won't," he said. "Did he know you were going out the window?"

"No."

John Paul took the exit and pulled into the tarred parking lot adjacent to the restaurant. The neon letters were blinking *Open*.

"Are you going to tell me about Jilly?" He had avoided bringing up that subject until now because he had seen how Avery reacted when Tyler called the woman her mother. She didn't answer him. "You're going to have to tell me what I'm up against."

"What *we're* up against," she said. "Yes, I'll tell you what I know, but not on an empty stomach. Tomorrow," she promised, "I'll tell you everything."

"Okay."

He took her hand as they walked into the diner. The colors inside made both of them squint. The walls were painted a neon purple and orange as a backdrop to the white Formica countertops. A jukebox sat just inside the door. Elvis Presley was singing "All Shook Up" as they made their way down the narrow aisle.

John Paul chose a booth against the wall so he could watch the parking lot. He waited until Avery slid into the orange vinyl seat and then sat down across from her.

The waitress was a teenager, but she shuffled like a ninety-year-old. Her tongue was pierced, which gave her a speech impediment when she spoke.

"What can I git ya?"

They ordered turkey sandwiches and iced tea. As soon as the waitress went behind the counter, Avery dug some change out of her bill-fold and headed for the telephone she had spotted at the end of the aisle, between the men's and women's rest rooms.

The conversation with Carrie was mostly one-sided. Her aunt was in a state. "Where are you?" she demanded. "Why aren't you here? Are you all right? Did you hear? Jilly's alive. The demon faked her own death. I didn't think she was that smart. She's like a cat, Avery. Yeah, that's what she is. Do you realize, if you had shown up at the spa when you were supposed to, you'd have been inside that house with us?"

"Carrie, slow down," Avery said when her aunt finally paused.

Carrie took a deep breath and then told her some of what had happened from the moment she'd gotten into the car with Monk and the other women. Avery didn't say a word while she listened to the grisly highlights.

"When I see you, I'll tell you everything,"

Carrie promised. "How are you doing?"

"I'm fine."

"I was so scared and worried about you, but you're okay."

"Yes, I am," Avery said, her gaze locked on John Paul. "Carrie, who's the agent in charge of watching over you?"

Her aunt spoke at the same time that Avery asked the question. "They said they're going to put us in protective custody. I'm assuming they'll fly us to Florida."

"Why Florida?"

"Because of the trial."

"What trial?"

"Oh, Avery, you didn't know? That bastard Skarrett has a trial date set. Didn't anyone notify you? They sure as hell didn't call me."

Avery was stunned by the news. She had known that there was a possibility of a new trial, but she hadn't thought it would happen this soon.

"No, I wasn't notified."

Carrie was beside herself. "They told me this killer Jilly hired won't stop until we're dead."

"Or until we get him," she said. "And we will, Carrie. Now, please, try to calm down. Have you talked to Tony yet?"

Carrie's voice mellowed. Sniffling, she whispered, "He's beside himself with worry. He wants you to call him as soon as possible so he can hear your voice. I want to go home, Avery, and I want you to come with me, but they won't let us. I don't even know if they'll let Tony come stay with me. I'm trying to cooperate —"

Avery interrupted. "How is the judge doing?"

"What? Oh, Sara. Her name's Sara. She's hanging in there. She trashed her knee and had to go to surgery, but she's doing okay now. They're keeping her in ICU for another couple of hours because of her age, but that's just a precaution. The doctors already let me sit with her and talk to her for a few minutes. Oh, my God, I forgot to tell you. Sara Collins is the judge who sentenced Skarrett."

"No, that can't be right. I remember the judge. His name was Hamilton."

"Yes, Judge Hamilton heard the case and convicted Skarrett. We went back to Bel Air once the verdict was in, remember?"

"I remember."

"But Skarrett hadn't been sentenced yet. Anyway, Hamilton died, and when Skarrett came up for sentencing, Sara was the judge."

"So that's the connection," she said. "But what about the other woman?"

"Anne Trapp wouldn't go with us. It's a long story, and I'll tell you everything as soon as you get here. Are they going to bring you to the hospital, or will I meet you at the airport? If they want us to fly to Florida, I'm not going without you. We'll have three full weeks to catch up before they decide if they're going to let us testify or not. If Monk is still on the loose —"

Avery interrupted. "Three weeks? You're telling me the new trial will start in just three weeks?"

"Yes," she said. "I'm sure they'll put us in a safe house near the courthouse so that, if we do get to testify, it will be easier getting us there."

Avery couldn't compute the information in her head. "And you're saying there's a possibility we won't be allowed to testify?"

"Honey, what's the matter with you? Aren't you listening? Yes, there is that possibility that we won't get to testify. Okay? We'd be sitting ducks, and it would be a perfect opportunity for Monk to hurt us."

Avery gripped the phone. "No one is stopping me from testifying."

"Be reasonable."

"Do you want Skarrett to walk?" Her voice shook with her fury.

"Your safety is more important to me."

"I'm not letting him walk."

"We'll have plenty of time to talk about the trial," Carrie said. "Why aren't you asking me about Jilly?"

"I don't want to talk about her."

"I hope when they catch her, I get to have five minutes alone with her."

"She'd annihilate you."

"But not you, not with all that tai chi and karate stuff you learned." Carrie sighed. "Don't be afraid of her."

Avery felt like laughing. After all the hellacious stories she'd heard about Jilly over the years, she would have to be as crazy as Jilly not to be afraid.

"Did you see her? Was she inside the house?"

"Yes," Carrie answered. "I'll tell you everything when I see you."

"I want you to promise me that you'll do whatever the agents tell you to do. Okay, Carrie? Promise me."

"Yes, of course I will."

"Don't make their job . . . difficult. You know how you can get when you're upset or scared."

"I'm not scared; I'm angry. Very, very angry. Why the hell couldn't Jilly stay dead?"

"She never died," Avery pointed out.

"They better not put us in a flea-infested shack while they're protecting us. The house is in Florida, so I want something on the beach."

"Carrie, that isn't your decision."

"If it's not nice, you can pull some strings for us. I can't wait to see you."

Avery braced herself. Her aunt had a very short fuse when things weren't going her way, and Avery was about to ignite it.

"I'm not going to be joining you. I'm not going to the safe house with —"

That was as far as she got. Carrie's scream made her cringe, and she had to move the phone away from her ear.

From where John Paul was seated, he could hear the aunt shouting. The color left Avery's face as she listened. He got up, walked to the phone, and gently took it from her.

"Say good-bye, sugar."

"She's very upset."

"Uh-huh."

"I love you, Carrie, and I'll see you soon," she said. "Bye now."

She heard Carrie shouting, "Avery Elizabeth, don't you dare hang up this —"

John Paul placed the phone back in the cradle. "She sounds nice," he managed with a straight face.

The waitress was watching them as she placed their plates on the table. Avery pulled away from John Paul and went into the ladies' room to wash her hands. By the time she sat down in the booth, he had already devoured his sandwich and was finishing his iced tea.

"I don't want you to get the wrong idea about my aunt. Granted, she can be difficult, but I'm sure, once you got to know her, you'd love her as much as I do."

He grinned. "I don't see that happening."

She took a bite of her turkey sandwich, thought it tasted like pressed sawdust, and picked up her glass of iced tea to wash it down.

"You want this?" she asked as she pushed the plate toward him.

He pushed it back. "You need to eat that," he said as he helped himself to one of the limp potato chips.

She noticed him watching the highway beyond the parking lot. "They don't get much business here, do they?"

"They're closing in fifteen minutes. Maybe that's why we're the only customers. Tell me something, Avery. When you filled out your application to work for the Bureau, was it your goal to become an agent?"

"Yes."

"Then why didn't you?"

She was about to give him her standard answer, but then decided to be completely honest with him. Besides, she was pretty sure he'd cut through the bull and know she wasn't telling him the truth.

"I thought I should want to be an agent. An FBI agent saved my life, and I think that was when I got it into my head that I wanted to be just like him. You know, save people."

"So you were going to save the world. How old were you when you made this momentous decision?"

"Twelve. I'd just turned twelve."

"That's amazing."

"Why?"

"That you didn't change your mind, that you held on to that goal all through high school and college."

"Do you remember what you wanted to be when you were young?"

"I don't remember how old I was when I decided it would be pretty cool to be an astronaut. Maybe ten or eleven."

"That plan didn't work out?" she asked, teasing.

"Life got in the way," he said. "I ended up in engineering at Tulane, graduated, and joined the Marines."

"Why the Marines?"

"I was drunk."

She didn't buy it. "Tell me the real reason."

"I thought I could make a difference. I liked the discipline, and I wanted something different than Bowen, Louisiana."

"But you live in Bowen now, don't you?"

"Yeah, I do," he said. "I had to go away to realize what I really wanted in life. I actually live outside of Bowen, in the swamp."

"You really did drop out of life, didn't you?"

"I like solitude."

"Guess you don't get much company in the swamp."

"I like that too. Where did you go to college?" he asked.

"Santa Clara University," she answered. "Then Stanford." She took another bite of her sandwich and could barely get the horrible food down. The bread was soggy; the lettuce was wilted, and the turkey was dry.

"Neither one of us went very far away. We both stayed close to home. Carrie wanted me to go to college in L.A. so I could work part-time for her company."

"Doing what?"

She blushed. The instantaneous reaction made him all the more curious.

"She was pushing me to do more commercials. I got roped into doing one for her when she was in a bind."

"So what'd you have to do in this commercial?"

"Hold up a bar of soap, bat my eyelashes, and sing a silly jingle."

He didn't laugh but he came close. "Sing it for me."

"No," she said. "I was awful and I hated it. I guess I'm an introvert," she added with a shrug. "Since I'd had this dream of becoming an agent for so long, Carrie gave in and stopped nagging me. We both gave in actually."

She pushed her plate to the side, and John Paul reached over and took a couple more potato chips. "How did you give in?"

She folded her paper napkin just so and placed it on the table. "I did a project at a grade school in San Jose for one of my classes, and I really enjoyed working with the children, so much so that I considered becoming a teacher. I was good with them," she added, a hint of surprise in her voice. "I even went so far as to take a couple of the classes I would need to get a teaching certificate. I thought I could teach history. I didn't tell Carrie, though."

"Why not? What does she have against teachers?"

"Nothing. She just didn't want me to become one."

He leaned back and stared at her. "Avery, what aren't you telling me?"

Ignoring the question, she called out to the waitress to please bring them their bill.

"Come on, babe. Answer me. Why didn't she want you to teach?"

"The pay's terrible."

"What else?"

"Teachers don't get much respect. You know what they say. Those who can do, and those who can't teach. Carrie didn't think there was much . . . status in teaching. My aunt isn't a shrew," she said. "I know I've made her sound terrible, but she isn't like that. Honest."

"So was that all? That was your reason for not teaching? There wasn't enough status?"

"Carrie didn't think it would be a good idea for me to be around kids."

"Why not?"

He wasn't going to let it drop. "She thought it would be too difficult for me."

"Ah."

"What does that mean?"

He homed in like a pigeon. "You can't have kids, can you?"

She wanted to tell him. She felt an overwhelming need to tell him everything, to spill her guts, as her uncle Tony would say. She'd never felt this need before, but John Paul wasn't like any other man. He didn't give a hoot about silly things like status. He wasn't a game player, and he didn't have a hidden agenda. What you saw was what you got. Maybe that was the reason she was so attracted to him. And so comfortable.

"I don't know how you made that leap."

"You told me you weren't ever going to get married, which I thought was a little odd."

She jumped on his comment with a vengeance. "Why? Because all women should want to get married? You can't really believe that. Lots of women are very happy living the single life."

He put his hand up. "Whoa," he said. "I don't disagree, but when you told me you weren't going to get married, you were damned defensive about it. That's what I thought was odd. Now I understand why. You can't have children, and that's the reason Carrie doesn't want you working with them. I'm right, aren't I?"

"Yes."

She was primed for a fight. She'd let him see her vulnerability, and she knew that if he gave her an ounce of sympathy or was the least bit compassionate, she would lose it. She'd either pull his hair out or her own. Worse, in her estimation, she might cry. She knew her reaction was a defense mechanism, but she didn't care. Staring into his eyes, she waited, daring him to be nice to her.

He stared back. "Well?" she finally demanded when he didn't say a word.

"That's just damned stupid."

She blinked. "Excuse me?"

"You heard me, sugar. You love working with kids, so that's what you ought to do. Listening to your aunt and trying to please her is just damned stupid."

"But I'm good at my job in the Bureau."

"So what? You've got more than one talent, don't you? You can be good doing a lot of different things."

He got up to pay the bill and then made a phone call, but all the while, he never took his gaze off the parking lot. Avery looked over at the waitress who blew a bubble twice the size of her face and then leaned on the counter and stared at him.

Five minutes later he hung up the phone. "Come on. We need to get going."

She followed him to the car. He was about to open the door for her when she asked, "What are you good at doing?"

"Lots of things."

"I know you worked for the CIA. What was your talent then?"

He didn't deny it. "Shooting. I was a good shooter. No, that's not true. I wasn't just good. I was great. Eyesight of an eagle."

"Anything else you're good at doing?"

"Yeah," he drawled. He put his arm around her waist and began to slowly pull her toward him. "I'm real good at a couple of other things too."

"Like what?"

He drew her closer and put his lips to her ear. "If things go the way I plan, you'll get to see firsthand," he whispered.

"Oh, brother," she answered breathlessly.

Could he feel her goose bumps? Probably, she

thought as she sighed and turned to look into his eyes.

Smiling gently, he kissed her warm, soft mouth, taking his time coaxing a response. She was becoming impossible to resist. The dazed look in her eyes made him feel arrogantly pleased with himself. "We'd better get out of here before I get carried away and show you right now."

He opened the door for her and then got behind the wheel. They drove out of the lot and once again headed toward Denver. "We need to put some distance between us and that diner," he told her. "The waitress will remember you."

"You think so?"

"Yeah. You're definitely memorable."

"News flash, sugar," she drawled, trying to imitate his sexy southern accent. "Bubble Gum was staring at *you*."

He shrugged. "It's going to take us at least another hour or more to get to Tyler's cabin. If I see a store on the way, we'll stop and get some supplies."

"I doubt anything will be open this late."

"And that's important because?"

"Shame on you. You're going to break in?"

"They'll never know I was there."

She didn't try to dissuade him. She was too busy thinking about his earlier remark. What would happen if things went the way he planned?

Thirty miles down the road, they found a fish-

and-tackle/grocery store. It was dark inside.

John Paul's skills seemed endless. He got the door unlocked without making a scratch, charmed the black Doberman guard dog, and shopped to his heart's content. She helped him carry two gallons of milk and four grocery sacks to the car.

He calculated the expense as he sacked the items and left four twenty-dollar bills sticking out from under the cash register.

"How long are we going to be staying at Tyler's place?" she asked when they were once again on their way. "We've got enough food for a month."

"We'll stay at least one night, maybe two," he answered. "Tyler told me there's a little town about fifteen miles from the cabin. I've got Theo checking on a couple of things, and when I find out what is going on, we'll decide what to do."

"I'm not going to miss that trial."

"I understand. May I ask you something?"

"Yes?"

"Is Skarrett the reason you can't have children?"

"Yes," she said. "A bullet hit just right, but you know what? I would never have had children anyway. I wouldn't take the risk that what's wrong with Jilly is genetic. So, you see, it doesn't matter."

"Yeah, it does," he argued. "Skarrett took that choice away from you. That's what matters."

He couldn't keep the anger out of his voice,

but she didn't become upset. What he'd said was true.

She changed the subject to a less stressful one, talking about silly things that had happened to her when she was growing up. He told her stories about his life and his family, and when he talked about his father, she laughed several times.

"People really call him Big Daddy?"

"Yeah, they do. You'll like him," he predicted.

He was assuming she would meet his father someday. She'd like that. She wanted to know about his family and his home and his work. She wanted to know everything about him. Before she could continue the conversation, they saw two pairs of headlights coming up the road toward them.

He swerved onto a side road and turned his lights off.

They silently waited until the cars passed by.

"When you asked your brother-in-law to help, were you worried he might tell the FBI where we're going?"

"Because he's with Justice?"

"Yes."

"Family comes first, sugar. Always."

"Still . . ."

"He won't tell, and he will help. I told him what I needed done, and he agreed."

"Good. I'm glad we can trust him."

They waited in the dark for a few minutes before he felt it was safe for them to go.

Avery's mind wandered and then circled around and around what he'd whispered in her ear. Maybe if she stopped staring at him, she could think about something else. It had been such a long time since she'd been intimate with a man, and she thought she had become an expert at blocking those thoughts and urges.

She *had* been an expert anyway, until he came into her life. Now the floodgates were wide open, and all she could think about was touching him. Everywhere.

For thirty more minutes she battled to think about something other than sex. She mentally balanced her checkbook, then calculated how long she could stay in her apartment without a paycheck coming in. Three months or four? If she got fired.

She started tapping her foot on the floor. Who was she kidding? Of course she was going to get fired. They couldn't arrest her for being insubordinate, but would Carter charge her with hindering an investigation?

John Paul put his hand on her knee. "How come you're so jittery?" Then, before she could come up with a good lie, he said, "There it is."

He pulled onto a dirt road. His night vision was better than hers. She hadn't even noticed the little curve. "You're sure?"

His hand was still on her leg, and she wasn't inclined to move it. She stared straight ahead, pretending to watch the road as she thought about ripping his clothes off him.

Was she turning into a slut? She shook her head. No, she was simply having normal urges, like any other woman, but because she hadn't had those urges in so long, she wasn't handling herself well.

"What are you thinking about?" he asked.

Sex, damn it. I'm thinking about sex. "Nothing much."

"Yeah?"

Even his voice was sexy. Threading her fingers through her hair, she realized how tense she was, and how horribly unsure of herself.

They drove around a bank of trees, and then the road flattened into what she thought might be a field. It was impossible to tell in the dark. She began tapping her foot on the floorboard again. She was nervous about being alone with him in the secluded cabin.

He pulled up to the steps in front. When he turned the motor and the lights off, it was pitch black. She couldn't even see her hand in front of her face.

"You stay put until I get the key from under the porch step."

She couldn't have moved if her life had depended on it. Her legs felt like rubber, and she thought she just might start hyperventilating. Fortunately, she had her wild thoughts under control by the time he'd unlocked the front door and turned the lights on inside the cabin. She got out and helped him carry in the bags.

The cabin was charming and smelled of pine

and Lysol. A stone fireplace faced the front door and was flanked by two wicker chairs with red-and-yellow-checked overstuffed cushions. The hunter green sofa had seen better days, for the arms were frayed, and the fabric was faded, but it looked very comfortable. To the right of the front door was a round pine table and four single ladder-back chairs.

Beyond the table was a narrow kitchen with a back door. She placed a bag of groceries on the counter, then walked through the living room to the other side of the cabin. There were two doors along the short hallway. The one on the left opened into a bathroom. At the end of the hall she opened the other door and stepped inside. Soft light spilled into the spacious room. A double bed with an old iron headboard was covered with a multicolored quilt.

The longer she stared at the bed, the faster her heart beat. She could hear John Paul putting the groceries away, knew she should probably help, but couldn't seem to make herself move.

"It's just a bed, for Pete's sake. What's the big deal?"

Disgusted with herself for being so nervous, she grabbed her duffel bag and went into the bathroom to take a shower.

She hadn't bothered to pack a pretty nightgown or a robe. After she dried her hair and brushed her teeth, she put on a pair of skimpy pink panties and her ratty old Santa Clara T-shirt. It was at least three sizes too big for her. It hung like a tent and ended just above her knees.

Staring into the mirror, she took inventory and decided she came up lacking in the feminine wiles department. For the first time in her life, she wanted to look pretty. Boy, wouldn't Carrie have a good laugh now? She was always criticizing the way Avery dressed, and for once, Avery had to agree.

There wasn't anything she could do about her appearance now. With a sigh, she put her bag in the corner of the bedroom so she wouldn't trip over it, then walked into the living room just as the front door opened and John Paul came inside. He shut the door, bolted it, then turned around and froze.

"What happened to you?" she asked. He didn't answer her. "You look like you showered in the dirt. What happened?" she repeated.

John Paul couldn't make himself stop staring at her legs. Fantasies were raging in his mind. "I put the car in the barn, and I thought . . . the oil . . . the tires . . ."

"Yes?"

"What?"

He finally forced himself to look into her eyes, knowing he probably resembled a buck caught in the headlights. When he'd noticed her standing in the doorway, his knees damned near buckled. That well-scrubbed look was intoxicating. She was simply gorgeous. Did she have any idea of the power she had over him?

"What about the oil and the tires?"

"That's right."

He was blathering like an idiot, and she was fully responsible for his radical drop in IQ. He strode past her, muttering incoherent words as he went into the bathroom and shut the door.

She took a bottled water out of the fridge, turned the lights off in the kitchen and the living room, and then went into the bedroom. She kept telling herself to relax as she folded the quilt. She found clean sheets on the closet shelf and put them on the bed with a lightweight blanket she pulled out of the cedar chest. She climbed on top, scooted to the middle. Straightening her back, she folded her legs in the lotus position. She tried to clear her mind and concentrate on her breathing. Just as she was about to sit down in her imaginary porch swing without a care in the world, she was interrupted.

"Going to your happy place?"

Her eyes flew open. John Paul was standing in the doorway watching her. He wore a pair of shorts and nothing else. He hadn't even bothered to button them. He had taken the time to shave, she noticed, and he'd washed his hair too. There were big drops of water glistening on his tanned neck and shoulders.

Sitting on the bed definitely put her at a distinct disadvantage. If they were going to approach their situation as adults, she wanted to be on equal footing. She scrambled to get off the bed.

"Yes, I was," she said. "I was trying to relax."

He yawned loudly. "Avery?"

"Yes?"

He leaned casually against the doorframe, one ankle crossed over the other, his arms loosely folded across his chest. She tried not to stare at the dark swirl of hair around his navel.

"Am I sleeping on the sofa or in the bed?"

Did she have the courage to be completely honest with him, to tell him what she wanted? Put up or shut up time, she thought a little frantically. She cleared her throat, then whispered, "In bed . . . with me, if that's what you want."

Damn it, she sounded vulnerable, maybe even a little afraid. She couldn't quite manage to look into his eyes. "If you want," she repeated hoarsely.

"Yes, I want."

John Paul took a step toward her but stopped when she put her hand up. "Not so fast, Renard."

"What?" he warily asked.

"There are a couple of ground rules we need to go over first."

She wasn't kidding. He would have laughed if she hadn't looked so nervous. "Ground rules? Like no hitting below the belt? That kind of rule?" When she didn't immediately answer, he asked, "Are we going to box, or are you going to let me —"

"I'm keeping my T-shirt on. Agreed?"

"Okay, if you want to, but if you change your mind and want to take it off, that's fine too."

"If I want to, I will, but I don't want to, and I probably won't. Agreed?"

At this point he'd lost track of what she was negotiating. "Yeah, sure."

He took another step toward her. "I'm not finished."

He grinned. "I didn't think so. Okay, what else?"

"You have to use protection. I can't have children, but we haven't had blood tests, and we . . ."

"I planned on using protection," he said when she stammered to a halt.

"You planned?"

"Uh-huh." He pulled the condom out of his pocket and tossed it on the bed. "Anything else?"

"That was pretty presumptuous."

"Avery, if I don't touch you pretty soon, I'm gonna go nuts, so hurry up and finish the rules."

Her heart was racing. "If you're disappointed . . ."

"I won't be."

"But if you are, you keep it to yourself. Don't complain to me."

"Honey, are you always this uptight before sex?"

"Do you agree?"

"Okay. I won't complain."

"This isn't funny, John Paul. I'm serious."

He'd waited for as long as he could. "Now it's my turn," he said as he grabbed a wad of her T-shirt and pulled her toward him. "You are underneath here somewhere, aren't you?"

He let go and put his arms around her waist. His hand slipped up under the fabric and splayed wide across her back. She didn't try to wiggle away when his fingers touched her scars. He leaned down and kissed the side of her neck just below her ear.

Shivers raced down Avery's spine. Her hands had been balled into fists, but as he tickled her earlobe with the tip of his tongue, she began to relax. His sweet warm breath against her sensitive skin only made her shivers intensify. She could feel the strength, the power of those hard, steely muscles under her fingertips. How could anyone this strong be so very gentle? She sighed into his neck and dropped her head on his shoulder.

"Pay attention, sweetheart. I've got some ground rules too."

She lifted her head and stared into his eyes. Why hadn't she noticed how incredibly beautiful they were? When he smiled, they lit up.

"Yes?"

"Do you trust me?"

Trust him? She was falling utterly in love with him. Of course she trusted him. She was terrified of admitting it, though. "That's not a rule."

He wouldn't let her dodge the question, and when she tried to distract him by pressing against his groin and kissing him, he shook his head. "I already know the answer, but I want . . .

no, I need to hear you say the words."

"You are the most opinionated, obstinate, exasperating man I've ever known, but almost from the moment we met, I felt this strange connection. It's as though I've waited all my life to feel so safe . . . and free. I can't explain it," she whispered.

He tilted her chin up, brushed his mouth over hers, and then whispered, "Then trust me. That's my rule. You have to trust me."

She thought she understood what he was asking. And he was right. Love and trust went hand in hand.

It was now or never. Please, God, don't let him be repulsed. She stepped back into the soft light from the bedside lamp, waited until he had let go of her, and then, before her courage completely deserted her, she pulled the T-shirt over her head and tossed it on the floor. She turned so that he could see her ravaged back.

Most of the damage had been done to her lower spine. The angry, ugly scars puckered her skin. She was afraid to turn around, to look into his eyes.

"Sugar?"

There was laughter in his voice. Confused by his reaction, she stood as stiff as a corpse with her hands at her sides staring at the wall.

"Yes?" she whispered.

He put his hand on her shoulder. "I'm a little more interested in the front right now."

"What . . ."

He gently turned her around and pulled her up against him. Her soft breasts pressed against his chest. He squeezed his eyes shut and whispered, "Damn, I've been dreaming about this. It's better than the dream, though. Much better."

"But my back . . . You saw . . ."

"We'll get to that," he promised. "I've got a lot of territory to cover," he whispered as he kissed a tear away from her cheek. "But in my present condition, I've gotta prioritize."

Before she could argue, or worry, or cry, his mouth took absolute possession of hers in a kiss that was sinfully carnal. His tongue slid in and out of her mouth in a ritual of lovemaking until she was trembling with desire.

His hands were everywhere, caressing, stroking, teasing, as his mouth slanted over hers again and again. He rid her of her inhibitions, and she eagerly kissed him back. She stroked his chest, loving the feel of his coarse, dark hair under her fingertips.

He growled low in his throat with pleasure when she tweaked one of his nipples between her fingertips, and so she did it again.

They were both panting for breath when he ended the kiss and stepped back. He let his shorts drop to the floor, staring into her eyes, reveling in the passion he saw there.

Avery held his gaze as she slid her hand down to remove her panties. The look of surprise when she realized they were on the floor made him smile over his handiwork.

She let him have his moment. "You're good," she whispered shakily.

He followed her onto the bed. Bracing his arms on either side of her, he leaned up and said, "You haven't seen anything yet."

His face was taut with passion. The way he was looking at her made her feel bold. "Neither have you," she whispered back. She moved restlessly against him, her hands slowly easing down his sides. His body was as hot as his gaze.

John Paul loved the way she touched him. Hell, he loved everything about her. She made him crazy. She pulled him down for another kiss, and this time he let her be the aggressor. Their tongues dueled as their hands learned the secrets of each other's bodies.

When she touched his erection, he thought he might just lose it then and there, and he tried to get her to stop, but she wouldn't. He could barely breathe because of the ecstasy she evoked. His hand slipped down between her thighs, his fingers caressing her intimately until she arched off the bed and cried out.

He held off as long as he could until he was desperate to be inside of her. He hungrily kissed her soft, sweet mouth as his knee nudged her thighs apart. Gripping her derriere, he leaned up so that he could watch her. In one slow push, he entered her, then plunged deep.

She arched up against him at the same time, crying out in rapture as she wrapped her legs around his thighs and squeezed him tight.

Capturing the sides of her face with his hands, his mouth covered hers and his tongue sank into her warm sweet mouth. He took his time. Long, slow thrusts that cost him dearly. Beads of perspiration covered his brow, and as he made love to her, he realized it had never been this incredible before. Never.

Avery was overwhelmed by the sensations rushing through her. They were so intense, so new. She couldn't let him slow the pace any longer. She came undone in his arms, wild, more demanding, her nails scoring his shoulders as she met his thrusts with equal passion.

Driven to please her and give her fulfillment before he claimed his own, he tried to slow down, but she would have none of it. Their lovemaking turned uncontrolled, primitive, almost savage. He was consumed.

Avery could feel her control vanishing, but she wasn't afraid. It was the most amazing feeling to be so uninhibited and to let herself go without fear or worry. She knew she was safe in his arms, and as she reached the precipice and her body began to shiver for release, she arched up against him. Wave after wave of undiluted pleasure coursed through her body as she clung to him.

Impossible to hold back, his orgasm was triggered by hers, and he climaxed deep inside of her, clenching his jaw in ecstasy.

They stayed joined together as one for long, blissful minutes. Their breathing was ragged, and neither one of them had the strength to move. Their hearts pounded in unison. He buried his face in her silky hair, closed his eyes as he inhaled her wonderful fragrance.

"Damn," he whispered. She'd taken every ounce of his strength. His bones felt like liquid as he tried to move so he wouldn't crush her.

She obviously didn't mind his weight because she squeezed him when he shifted his position, and whispered, "Not yet."

Had he been too rough with her? The thought popped into his head and anchored there. He could have been more gentle, but she'd been so wonderfully uninhibited, he'd gone a little crazy.

"Avery? You okay?"

She smiled because of the worry she heard in his voice. And then she whispered, "So that's what all the fuss was about."

And then she laughed with such delight, he smiled in spite of his exhaustion.

With a sigh, he rolled away, then got up and went into the bathroom.

She pulled the sheet up, adjusted her pillow, and fell back. She was still a little overwhelmed by what she had just experienced. Sex, she decided, sex with John Paul anyway, could definitely become addictive.

The bed springs groaned when John Paul stretched out beside her. She opened her eyes and smiled. He looked so arrogantly proud of himself. He was on his side with his head propped up staring at her.

She looked thoroughly ravaged. Passion lingered in her eyes, and her lips were swollen from his kisses.

She knew she'd satisfied him, but she still needed him to tell her so. Silly how she could feel so powerful a minute ago and now the old insecurities were creeping back. No, she hadn't disappointed him. Why wasn't he telling her so?

He could see it happening. In her eyes. They were clouded. He didn't think she was regretting anything . . . just worried maybe.

He knew he'd guessed right when she said, "What are you thinking?"

He tugged on the sheet, pulling it down to the tips of her breasts. She pulled it back up.

"Bet I can get this off you faster than a prom dress," he drawled.

"Oh, brother. You're pretty happy with yourself right now, aren't you?"

"Damn right I am," he said as he leaned down and kissed her. His tongue slipped inside and tickled the roof of her mouth. When he pulled back, she was breathless. But then, so was he.

Oh, how she loved this man. He was so completely perfect for her. She reached up to brush his hair off his forehead, an excuse to keep touching him. She couldn't seem to get enough.

" 'Heavens to Betsy'?" he drawled. "That's what you said, sugar, when you were coming apart in my arms. Actually, you screamed it."

She laughed. "I did not."

"Yeah, you did."

"I know what you shouted, but I'm not going to repeat it."

His grin was lecherous. "Guess what."

Her fingers trailed down the muscled cord on the side of his neck, then crossed his shoulder. She gently traced it with her fingertips.

"What?" she asked lazily.

"Prom dress is gone."

Startled, she lifted her head and looked down. The sheet was around her ankles. "You *are* good."

He leaned down and kissed each breast. His fingers slowly circled her navel. A jagged scar crisscrossed the lower part of her abdomen. The raised, puckered center indicated a bullet had done the damage. Probably .38, he thought. Or maybe a .45.

Damn, it was a miracle she had survived. He leaned forward and took his time kissing every inch of her stomach, smiling as she inhaled sharply. He rolled back on his side so he could watch her face as his hand slid down into her soft curls.

Avery was having trouble catching her breath. "Do you want . . ."

"Oh, yeah. I want."

Moaning softly, she moved restlessly against him, her toes rubbing his lower legs.

She tried to touch him, but he grabbed her hand. "Relax, sugar. Let me . . ."

It was as far as he got. She was surprisingly strong. And bold. She pushed him onto his back and leaned over him. "Relax? I don't think so, John Paul. This is a team sport, isn't it?"

He couldn't answer her. Her hands had captured his arousal, and she was slowly driving him wild with her caresses.

"And . . ." she whispered as she straddled his hips and kissed him passionately.

"And what?" he asked, his voice as coarse as sandpaper.

Her eyes sparkled when she answered. "I'm definitely a team player."

# CHAPTER 31

The man was insatiable. Avery woke up at noon. She didn't usually sleep so late, but John Paul hadn't let her get much rest during the night.

She was on her stomach with one arm hanging over the side of the bed. He was tickling her back. His fingers were as light as feathers. Was he trying to drive her crazy, or was he being so very gentle because of her scars?

Oh, God, her scars. Even Carrie, who loved her like a mother, couldn't stop herself from grimacing when she looked at her.

"You awake yet?" he asked. "Avery?"

She didn't say good morning. She blurted, "What do you think?"

"About what?"

"My back."

"Can you handle the truth?"

Uh-oh. She didn't like his tone one bit. She could feel her defenses building inside her. "Yes, I can handle it," she said tightly. "What are you thinking about?"

"Your sweet little ass."

She rolled over and looked up at him.

"It's the first thing I noticed about you when you came strutting inside the lobby of that spa."

Smiling, she said, "I didn't strut."

"Sure you did."

"You're a pervert."

"You're a liberal. I figure that makes us even. About the scars . . ."

She was still smiling when she asked, "Yes?"

"They're just scars. They don't define who you are. Now get up. Breakfast will be ready in ten minutes. Move it," he said as he rolled off the bed.

He was stark naked and seemed thoroughly happy about it. He was gorgeous. All muscle and male.

"Put some clothes on for Pete's sake."

"Why?"

"Do you go around like that in the swamp?"

"I wish I could, but I can't, not with the gators and snakes."

He grabbed his jeans from the chair and went into the living room. Avery took a quick shower and put on a pair of navy shorts and a pale yellow blouse. Her hair was tucked behind her ears when she padded barefoot into the living room.

John Paul went into the kitchen to fix her plate and placed it in front of her. Then he handed her a bottle of Tabasco sauce.

He'd prepared scrambled eggs with lots of pepper. She took a bite and quickly washed it down with orange juice.

"You like spicy food," she said, smiling.

"In Louisiana, spicy food is a way of life."

"What was it like growing up in Bowen with a father everyone in town calls Big Daddy Jake?"

"Interesting," he answered. "My dad's quite a character, always got something going, if you know what I mean. He's a bit of a con, but he's got a good heart."

He told her a couple of funny stories about the mischief that he and his brother, Remy, got into when they were boys. He mentioned his father and his younger sister often, and each time, she noticed, his voice softened.

"Mike's as bossy as you are." His smile indicated he thought that was a good thing. "She's a surgeon," he added proudly. "Her name's Michelle, but everyone calls her Mike, everyone but her husband. They're expecting their first baby in September."

"Theo," Avery said. "She's married to Theo, and he's an attorney with Justice."

"That's right."

He told her another story while she ate her breakfast, and then she helped him do the dishes.

"It rained hard early this morning. Thunder shook the rafters."

"I didn't hear a thing."

"I wore you out."

He sounded cocky. She decided to let him have his due. "Yes, you did," she agreed as she folded the tea towel and put it on the counter. "We have to make plans."

"I know," he agreed as he followed her into the living room. She curled up on the sofa. He sat down in a chair, kicked his shoes off, and propped his feet up on the opposite end of the sofa. He was such a big man he swallowed up the chair.

"But not today," he said. "Today we rest and talk. Tomorrow we plan."

"What will we talk about?"

"Not what, but who," he said. "We need to talk about Jilly."

She had put it off as long as she could. Nodding, she said, "Carrie kept a diary. She was very young, around eleven, when she started writing in it. The diary wasn't filled with her hopes and dreams and crushes, though. No, it was all about Jilly. Every single page was filled with one horrific incident after another involving her sick sister. Carrie told me she wanted to have some kind of record . . . proof, I guess, in hopes that one day Jilly would get caught, be put away. She thought that if the doctors read her diary, they would realize how dangerous Jilly was and make sure she stayed behind bars for the rest of her life, but I think there was more to it than that. I think that deep down Carrie believed that one day Jilly would kill her."

"That was a hell of a way to grow up," he said.

Avery agreed. "Carrie stopped writing in the diary when Jilly left town, but she always kept it, just in case Jilly came back. I knew where it was hidden, but Carrie wouldn't let me read it."

"But you did read it, didn't you?"

"Yes, I did. I wish to God I hadn't, though. I was old enough to think I could handle anything, but there was such scary, sick stuff in there . . ."

"How old were you?"

"Fourteen. I read every word, and I had nightmares for months. Carrie had put in a lot of details, and I learned all the twisted facts about Jilly."

She was hugging a throw pillow to her chest in a death grip. The sadness in her eyes was heartbreaking.

"I hate talking about her," she whispered.

"I know."

Her shoulders slumped. "There really arc monsters in this world. Predators," she said. "Jilly's one of them. Do you know what scared me the most after I read that diary?"

"What?"

"That I would wake up one morning and be just like her. You know, Dr. Jekyll–Mr. Hyde. Genetically, I'm forever linked to her."

"That isn't going to happen, Avery."

"How can you know that?"

"You have a conscience. That's not going to go away. You're nothing like her."

"That's what Dr. Hahn told me," she said.

"Who's Dr. Hahn?"

"A psychiatrist. I was waking up screaming every night, and in desperation, Carrie took me to Dr. Hahn." She added, "Carrie made me promise not to tell anyone because she didn't want people to think I was crazy."

"She was worried about what other people thought?" he asked, trying to keep the censure out of his voice.

"Dr. Hahn was wonderful, and he helped me . . . cope, I guess you could say. Carrie didn't know why I was having the nightmares because I hadn't told her I'd read the diaries, and I think it was the third or fourth session when Dr. Hahn asked her to come in and I told her then what I had done. She had a fit, of course, but when the doctor had gotten her to calm down, he asked her if he could read the diary, and she agreed. She would have done anything to help me get over what she called my night terrors."

She smiled at John Paul as she swung her legs down from the sofa. "I think the doctor had nightmares after he read them. I grew up knowing that Jilly was crazy, and Carrie did tell me stories, but they paled in comparison to what was in the diary."

"What did Hahn say about Jilly after he read it? What was his reaction?"

"He was excited."

"Excited?" he repeated, not understanding.

"He was sure Jilly was a pure sociopath, and he wished he'd had the opportunity to study her. Based on what he read, he concluded that Jilly was morally and emotionally stunted, which was why he believed she was incapable of

460

feeling guilt or remorse. Other people's pain certainly didn't make her feel bad. On the contrary," she explained, "she enjoyed hurting people for no apparent reason. She just liked it. She was a master at blaming others and rewriting history, and she was very deceptive."

John Paul put his feet down on the floor and leaned forward, bracing his arms on his knees.

"She was . . . amazing, the way she could manipulate people. Everyone loved her, no matter what she did. She was so damned clever."

"Give me an example."

"When she was quite young, she started having fun with pets. She tortured and killed Carrie's cat with gasoline and a match. She told Carrie what she'd done, but in front of their mother, she cried because, she said, she so loved that cat. One of the neighbors took her to get an ice cream cone to make her feel better. By the time she was a senior in high school, she was into bigger and better. She was the most popular girl in school, of course. Everyone loved Jilly. A girl named Heather Mitchell was voted homecoming queen, and Jilly was voted first attendant. According to Carrie, Jilly was gracious about it at school, but when she came home that afternoon, she went into a rage that lasted for hours. She nearly destroyed the house. Carrie's bedroom suffered the most damage. Not Jilly's room, of course. Then, after dinner, she became real quiet and got that sly look in her eyes and pretended to accept it."

Avery took a breath. The muscles in her arms were aching, and she realized she was gripping the pillow. She let go.

"The next day a beaker of sulfuric acid was missing from the chemistry lab. After school, Jilly got Heather alone, but Carrie saw her take her arm and lead her down the street. Jilly told Heather that she'd better not show up for homecoming weekend or she'd be sorry. Heather was a sweet girl, and she was going through a terrible time. Her mother had died two weeks before of an aneurysm, and the poor girl was still reeling from the shock. When Jilly got through tormenting her, Heather locked herself in her bedroom, but her father finally got her to tell him what was wrong. He said that Jilly had admitted stealing the acid. She threatened to wait for Heather one day after school when she was all alone in her house and throw the acid in her face."

"Good God."

Avery nodded. "What Carrie wrote wasn't hearsay. She talked to Heather."

"What did Heather's father do?"

"He went to the principal the next morning and demanded that Jilly be expelled. He also went to the police."

"And what did they do?"

"Nothing," she said. "The chief of police was a close friend of my grandmother's, and he wasn't going to do anything that would upset her. Besides, it was one girl's word against the other's.

Jilly, of course, denied the incident. My grand-mother and Jilly were called into the principal's office that afternoon. Grandmother made Carrie go with them."

"Was Jilly expelled?"

"No," she said, scoffing at the notion. "Did I mention that the principal was a man? His name was Mr. Bennett, and he was a very unhappily married man. His wife was a cold woman and very difficult to get along with, or so Carrie wrote."

"What happened?" John Paul asked, bringing her back to the story.

"Carrie watched Jilly seduce Bennett. Jilly be-came hysterical. Lots of tears flowing, but it was all a calculated act. The principal rushed over to the sofa where Jilly was and sat down beside her. He put his arm around her to comfort her, but it was Jilly's body language that . . . fascinated Carrie . . . and Bennett's reaction."

She shook her head. "Have you ever seen a woman move like a cat? Carrie said Jilly was like that. When Bennett put his arm around her, she rubbed up against him in an obscene way."

"What did your grandmother do?"

"She was as clueless as ever, according to Carrie. She'd gone out to the front desk to get Jilly a glass of water, but even if she had stayed, she wouldn't have noticed anything because she didn't want to notice. Carrie wrote that Jilly was clinging to Bennett while she cried. She had her head on his shoulder, but she looked up at

Carrie, who was standing behind the principal, and Jilly had this Cheshire cat smile on her face. When it was over, Bennett threatened to suspend Heather for making up the lie."

"Jeez."

"Like I said, Jilly had a way with men. Some of them became obsessed with her. They would call at all hours of the day and night. Every once in a while, Carrie would sneak upstairs into Grandmother Lola's bedroom and listen in on the extension. She wrote that the men cried and pleaded, and after Jilly hung up, she could hear her laughing. Oh, how she loved the power she had. She loved manipulating, and she used sex to get what she wanted. Her specialty was destroying married men. I'll bet you can guess who one of those men was," she said.

"Bennett."

"Yes."

"My God," he said. "And all this was going on while she was in high school?" Before Avery could answer, he asked, "What happened to Heather?"

"She didn't go to homecoming, and Jilly was crowned queen, but that wasn't enough for Jilly. Heather had upset her, and so she had to be punished. Jilly tormented her. A month passed, and just as Heather was beginning to think Jilly had moved on, she came home from school one day and went up to her room. She had this old teddy bear she kept on her bed. Someone had poured acid all over it. That someone, of course, was Jilly."

John Paul rubbed his jaw and waited until Avery continued.

"Carrie heard about it at school the next day. She went to see Heather's father. He had to stay home with his daughter because she was so distraught, and Carrie told him Jilly wouldn't stop going after Heather and that he needed to get his daughter out of town and not tell anyone where she had gone. Heather was close to a nervous breakdown. She was seeing a therapist," she explained. "And the therapist thought it would be good for Heather to get away from Sheldon Beach. She left during Christmas vacation and didn't come back."

"Did it ever end?"

"Oh, no," she said. "Heather's father filed another report with the police two months later. He said that someone was stealing his mail. One Saturday afternoon, he happened to look outside and saw Jilly opening his mailbox. She was looking for letters from Heather so she could find out where she was."

"She doesn't give up, does she?"

"No, she doesn't. She never had sex with any of the boys in her high school. All her friends believed she was sweet and wholesome. Carrie heard a couple of rumors about Jilly, but not from anyone at school. Heather was the one who was ostracized, not Jilly. She was that good at being bad."

She stood and stretched her arms above her head. "Do you want something to drink?"

After the story she'd just told him, hard liquor sounded good to him, but he settled on a Diet Coke instead. She got herself a bottle of Evian water and handed him his soda.

He opened the can, took a swig, and asked, "Did your grandparents try to get her some help when she was little, or did they know then that something was wrong with her?"

"Grandfather left when Carrie and Jilly were little girls, and Grandmother Lola lived in what Carrie called a fantasyland. She had an excuse for every atrocity Jilly committed."

"When did Jilly get pregnant with you?" he asked.

"Her senior year. Carrie thought her pregnancy saved Heather because Jilly had other things to think about. Jilly tried to get an abortion, but the doctor wouldn't do it because she was too far along. She gave birth and left town three days later. And that was the last entry in the diary," she added.

"Leaving me behind was the last straw for Grandmother. She dragged all of Jilly's things out to the curb for the trash collector. When she was packing up her things from the closet, she found a shoe box full of mail from Heather's house, and guess what else she found?"

"The acid."

Avery nodded. "The beaker was only half full, but it would have been more than enough to kill Heather. I think Jilly didn't forget about that girl. I think she was biding her time."

A clap of thunder jarred her. She flinched in reaction, then got up and walked to the window to look out. Dark angry clouds loomed overhead. Lightning sliced across the sky, and then there was another booming blast of thunder.

She didn't turn around as she said, "Carrie didn't think Jilly was very smart. She used her body to get what she wanted. She's obviously become more devious and clever over the years. Carrie said there wasn't a man alive who was immune to her charms."

"Do you believe that?"

"Skarrett obviously became obsessed with her, and look where he ended up. When I was five years old, Jilly and Skarrett came to the house. Jilly told Grandmother she had to pay to keep me. Fortunately, Carrie was home. She told Jilly she didn't have any legal rights to me and pushed her out the door. It was a horrible fight, but Skarrett kept his distance . . . then. Jilly kept screaming, 'You're dead, Carrie. You're dead.' "

"Where were you while all this was going on?"

She turned around and looked at him. "I don't remember any of it, but Carrie told me she found me hiding under my bed. After they left, Carrie promised me they would never come back."

She took a gulp of her water, put the lid back on, and stared down at her hand. There was a deep indentation in her palm from where she'd been gripping the bottle cap.

"But they did come back, didn't they?"

"Yes."

He watched her closely as she closed her eyes and told him what had happened on February 14, all those years ago.

When she was finished, she said, "Skarrett's her puppet. And I think she's got Monk doing her bidding now too. She's playing both of them to get what she wants."

She put the bottle down on the table and took a step toward John Paul. "So now you know."

"Now I know . . ."

"So?" she demanded. "Tell me what you think."

He shrugged. "I think you're right. Jilly is a maniac."

She threaded her fingers through her hair and took another step toward him. "No, that's not what I was asking."

"Then what?"

She stopped a foot away from him. "Aren't you sorry?"

He felt as if he were playing twenty questions. In exasperation, he asked, "Sorry about what?"

"Getting involved with me. It's a temporary situation, but even so . . ."

"Hell, no."

She stepped back. "John Paul, you've got to be a little repulsed . . ."

"Afraid not."

She glared at him. "Why not? I don't come from a normal family. Genetically speaking, I'm a mess."

"Sugar, no need to be so melodramatic and no need to shout at me either. I can hear just fine."

"How can you smile after what you just heard? How can you —"

"Avery, you didn't do any of those things. Jilly did."

He thought he was being extremely logical, but she wasn't the least bit interested in being reasonable. "Now do you understand why I won't ever get married?"

Before she could take another step away from him, he reached for her. He put his hands on her hips and slowly pulled her toward him.

"No, I don't understand."

She tried to push his hands away, but they were cemented to her body.

"You're going to have to explain it to me. Are you afraid you'll sneeze and turn into a sociopath?"

"No, of course not, but I can't have children, and even if I could . . ."

"I know," he said softly. "You wouldn't risk it."

"Men want children."

She stood between his knees, frowning at him while she shifted from foot to foot.

"Some do," he agreed. "Some don't."

"Do you?"

He wasn't going to lie to her. "I always figured I'd settle down one day and have a couple of kids. I still might," he said. "But, Avery, there are a lot of children out there who need good homes."

"Do you think after doing a background

check on my family that I would ever qualify?"

"Yes, I do."

"I won't get married."

The defiance was back in her voice. She was trying to hide her vulnerability, but it wasn't working. He knew she was hurting inside.

"Did I ask you to marry me?"

"No."

"Okay, then. I think we've had enough heavy talk for a little while. And I also think you need to lighten up a little."

It occurred to her that he was behaving the same way he had when she'd shown him her back. The scars hadn't seemed to faze him. Obviously, neither did the stories she'd told him about Jilly.

What the hell was the matter with him?

"You need to relax," he told her. He worked her blouse up over her navel and leaned forward to kiss her stomach.

"That's what yoga is for. It helps me relax."

"I've found a better way to unwind."

He unbuttoned her shorts and reached for the zipper. She grabbed his hand.

"What do you think you're doing?"

His smile made her heart race. Her hand dropped to her side, and she watched him unzip her shorts. As they fell to the floor, he finally answered her.

"It's simple, sugar. I'm going to *my* happy place."

# CHAPTER 32

Secrets were best shared in the bedroom. They made love, and after he had kissed and caressed every inch of her beautiful body, she was exhausted.

"I told you I'd get around to your back," he said as he rolled away from her.

She laughed because he'd sounded so smug. Still breathless from their lovemaking, she whispered, "You're insatiable."

He grinned arrogantly. "With you I am."

It was a lovely thing to say, almost a compliment, she thought. "Move over," she told him. "I'm falling off the bed."

The double bed didn't give him anyplace to go. "We're gonna need to buy a king-size bed."

Her mood changed as swiftly as the wind. "Why?" she asked tensely.

"Because I'm too big for a double bed," he answered. "My feet hang over. What's the big deal about a king-size bed?"

"We both know we can't have any kind of a lasting relationship."

"Did I ask?"

"No, but you implied . . ."

"Sugar, you worry too much."

She silently agreed. Of course, she worried . . . about everything. But what terrified her more than anything was ruining things. Admitting to herself that she loved John Paul had already put her in a mild panic. What was going to happen when they parted? Would she ever recover?

"I don't believe in marriage. Look what it does to some people."

"What people?"

"People like the Parnells . . ."

"Sugar, those aren't what you'd call typical people."

"What about the divorce rate?"

"What about couples who have stayed together?"

"I'd ruin things," she blurted out.

When he didn't respond, she propped herself up with her elbow, leaned over him, and waited. Had he fallen asleep?

"Did you hear what I just said?"

He was wearing an adorable smile and nothing else. He oozed self-confidence, probably because he didn't give a hoot what anyone else thought. She'd lived her life trying to please everyone. He was the complete antithesis. He didn't want to please anyone.

"You don't have much faith in yourself, do you? It's okay," he added before she could answer. "I've got enough for both of us."

She put her hand on his flat, hard stomach and circled his navel with her fingertips. He made everything sound so easy.

She couldn't stop touching him. She could almost see the strength radiating from his muscles, but she wasn't the least bit intimidated by him. When she was in his arms, she didn't feel overwhelmed or diminished. On the contrary, he made her feel powerful. It was the most incredible sensation, not worrying about pleasing him, just knowing that whatever she did was all right, being that free, that liberated. Her trust in him was absolute, and she realized what a wonderful gift he'd given her.

"John Paul?"

"Ummm?"

"Are you sleeping?"

"A little."

"I want . . ."

"Okay, sweetheart. Just give me a couple of minutes, and I'll be able —"

Her body was still tingling from the last time. She laughed. "Not that," she said. "I want you to tell me something."

He yawned. "You were perfect, Avery, but you've got to know —"

She pinched him. "I'm not asking for a review. I want to know why you walked away."

Before he could deliberately misinterpret, she said, "I've told you my secrets, most of them any-

way, and now it's your turn. Why did you retire?"

"It's boring stuff."

She pinched him again. "Tell me."

He opened his eyes and looked at her. The de-
termination he saw told him he wasn't going to
be able to finesse his way out of this one. Besides, he figured he owed her.

"It wasn't any one big assignment that went
wrong," he said. "Just a lot of little screwups
that made me . . . reevaluate what I wanted out
of life. I had a bad problem."

"What was it?"

"I started thinking too much. I had a lot of time
to do that while I waited in hellholes for the next
assignment. They were usually generals," he explained nonchalantly. "Little prick dictators who
surrounded themselves with thugs. I didn't mind
killing them, for the greater good," he added sar-
castically. "And I liked going in after hostages.
There was justice in that action, but one night,
while I was freezing my ass off, I noticed I was
getting a callus on my finger. My trigger finger,"
he added softly. "That really freaked me out."

"So what did you do?"

"I finished my assignment, told them I was
done, and went home."

"Was it that easy? Didn't they try to change
your mind?"

"Yes and no," he answered. "At the time, it
was easy because I worked for a good, decent
man. He knew I'd had it. I think the way he got

474

around all the red tape was to give me an extended leave."

"But they're still trying to get you to come back?"

"Every once in a while," he agreed. "I won't, though." He closed his eyes again and said, "I did some badass things, Avery."

"I would imagine so," she whispered. "And you didn't believe that what you were doing made any difference, did you?"

She'd hit the mark dead center. "No, I didn't. Dictators are like weeds. You rip one out of the ground and two more pop up overnight."

He opened his eyes again and watched her as he recounted one of his bloodier assignments. When he was finished, he noticed she hadn't pulled her hand away. She was still stroking his chest. Her touch was soothing.

"So now you're a carpenter," she said.

"Yes."

"Are you any good?"

"Yeah, I am. I'm still using my hands, but now I build things that will last. I don't break necks. It's odd."

"What is?"

"The urge to kill. I never had that before. I do now."

Her eyes widened. He'd made the confession so casually. "Oh? Who do you want to kill?"

"Skarrett."

She shivered in reaction. "No," she said. "I don't want him to die."

"You've got to be kidding."

"I'm serious. I want him to live the rest of his life behind bars."

"Yeah, well, if I get the opportunity . . ."

"No," she said firmly.

"Okay," he said when he realized she was getting upset.

"I mean it."

"I said okay," he said.

"I won't mind if you kill Monk," she said then. "But I hope someone brings him in alive. Can you imagine the things he could tell them?"

He shook his head. "He won't talk. He's not the kind of man who likes to boast. Maybe, if the interrogators work him, treat him like a professional, he might give them a little insight, but I honestly don't see that happening." He shrugged and added, "I think they ought to squash him like a bug."

"And Jilly?"

"You call it."

"She needs to be locked up in an institution for the criminally insane, and she needs to stay there for the rest of her life."

"You don't want her dead?"

"No, I don't," she said. "I don't think she can help being the way she is. I just want to make sure she can't hurt anyone anymore."

He brushed his thumb across her lips. "You've got a gentle heart," he said.

"So do you."

"The hell I do," he grumbled. "But I've got

great hands," he added as he reached for her.

She slapped his hand away. "I already know you're good with your hands," she said.

She got an impish gleam in her eyes as she rolled on top of him. He locked his legs around her to keep her from making a eunuch out of him.

"Now I'm going to show you how good I am," she cooed.

It wasn't an idle boast. Avery had a vivid imagination, and what she did to him with her hands and her mouth was magical, and probably illegal in some states, but of course he wasn't about to mention that to her.

That night they slept entwined in each other's arms even though both of them knew that the interlude would be over in the morning. They couldn't push reality away any longer.

Avery awakened before John Paul did and quickly showered and dressed in the bathroom so she wouldn't disturb him. Then she went into the living room, softly closing the bedroom door behind her, and checked the time. There was a digital clock on the wall above the table. She hoped it was accurate. Five forty-five Colorado time, which meant it was seven forty-five in Virginia.

She thought she heard the shower running as she reached for the phone. "Stay predictable, Margo," she whispered. "Don't get spontaneous now."

She dialed information, got the number she needed, then hung up and waited, her gaze locked on the time.

At exactly seven-fifty, Avery dialed. The phone was answered on the third ring.

Avery made up a name, told the employee it was an emergency and that he needed to put Margo on the phone. She described her friend and added, "She comes in every morning at seven-fifty."

"Yeah, the short lady, right?"

"Yes."

"She just left."

"Go after her," Avery shouted. "Hurry. Get her back. Go."

The phone clattered against the wall when the employee dropped it. She heard him shouting Margo's name, and then a minute later, she could hear Margo arguing.

"No one knows I'm here. What do you mean it's an emergency? Hello," she said.

"Margo, it's me, Avery."

"Oh, my God, Avery. How did you know I would be here . . . how did you . . ." She was rattled.

"You always pick up doughnuts on your way into the office."

"Do you have any idea how much trouble you're in?"

"I haven't done anything wrong," Avery countered.

"Why did you leave that police station in Colorado? The agents are there to protect you."

"I have protection."

"Renard?"

"Yes," she answered impatiently. "Tell me what you know."

The bedroom door opened, and John Paul stopped in the doorway, staring at her incredulously. She put her hand up when he started toward her.

"Hold on, Margo." Cupping the receiver with her hand, she said to John Paul, "Trust me." Then she raised the phone to her ear again. "Okay, Margo. Start talking."

"The trial begins July tenth," she said. "But Avery, the parole hearing is still on too. Skarrett might pull it off this time. He could get out."

"Over my dead body."

"Jeez, don't talk like that."

"Is the hearing still scheduled for the sixteenth?"

"I think so."

"Are you sure or not?"

"I'm sure," she said. "Don't get all hostile on me, Avery. They know about Jilly. Your aunt told them. That had to have been a hell of a shock. I'm so sorry —"

Avery interrupted. She didn't want sympathy. "Do they have any idea where Jilly and Monk might be?"

"Not a clue."

"What about my aunt? Have they moved her from the hospital yet?"

"No, not yet. Don't worry about her. A gnat couldn't get into that hospital. Security's unbelievable."

"I'm not worried," she said. "Monk can't be in two places at once."

"What does that mean?"

"I'm going to keep him busy. He's going to have to try and stop me from testifying at Skarrett's trial."

"What does he care about Skarrett?"

"He doesn't," she said. "But he's working for Jilly now, and she wants Skarrett out of prison. I'll bet, if you check the records at the prison for visitors over the past year, you'll find that Skarrett had a female visitor listed more than once. I think she's made some kind of deal with him."

"For the millions in uncut stones that he stole," Margo said.

I'm sure Skarrett thinks they'll share the loot and that he'll live happily ever after with Jilly. But when they have what they want, Jilly will let Monk kill him."

"Avery, you're in over your head."

"Maybe," she whispered. "I can't stop now, though. About the trial . . ."

"Yes?"

"Find out who the prosecutor is, and make sure I'm on his witness list."

"Okay," she said. "Can I tell Carter I talked to you?"

You're going to tell him anyway, she thought. Margo was her friend, but Avery knew she would believe she was being helpful by filling Carter in.

"Yes, please do."

"Where are you now? He's going to ask."

"Alabama," she lied. "I've got to go now. Tell Carter I'll call him."

"Wait," Margo cried. "What are you going to do?"

Avery knew what she wanted to do. She just didn't know how yet. The conversation with Jilly popped into her head. What had she called her? Oh, yes, how could she forget?

"I'm going to be a killjoy."

John Paul trusted her. Otherwise he would have ripped the phone out of her hand and hung it up. He'd sat down on the sofa beside her and impatiently waited for her to finish her conversation. He looked relieved when she told him she'd caught Margo at the doughnut shop.

"Clever," he said with approval.

"She's a creature of habit."

She told him what Margo had said. "I promised I'd call Carter," she added, "when we get to Florida."

"But not before."

"You better think hard before you agree to go with me, John Paul. It could get . . ."

"Bloody?"

She nodded.

"I'm in," he said. "For the long haul."

He reached over, cupped the back of her neck

481

with his hand, and drew her toward him. He kissed her possessively and said, "Did you hear me? I'm in it for the long haul. And like it or not, babe, so are you."

"Until we get Monk and Jilly."

He let go of her. "That's not what I mean, and you know it."

She pulled away and went into the kitchen. She fixed breakfast, cereal and toast, and then, because she was feeling restless, did the dishes while he looked over the map, figuring their route to Sheldon Beach.

She was putting the bowls back into the cabinet when he called out to her.

"We've got company."

She dropped the tea towel and ran into the living room. John Paul was standing by the front window, cautiously looking out. He held his gun at his side, pressed against his leg.

He saw the car when it came around the grove of trees and relaxed. "Better get packed," he said as he flipped the safety back on the gun and tucked it into the back of his jeans. "Our ride's here."

What ride? "You were expecting someone?"

He nodded. He couldn't see the driver yet because the sun bouncing off the windshield obstructed his view, but the make and model were right. It was a new, gray Honda.

"Who is it?"

He shrugged. "I told Theo I needed transportation. The police will be looking for my car, and I figured you didn't want them to hold us until the FBI took you into custody."

"The FBI wouldn't do that unless they had my permission."

He snorted. She assumed that meant he didn't agree. "They would not trample all over my rights as a citizen."

"Sure they would," he said. "And they'd tell you that they were only doing what they felt was best for you."

She wasn't going to get into a full-blown argument about the Bureau now. Besides, deep down, she was concerned that there was a kernel of truth in what he'd said. She wasn't willing to risk it.

"Theo drove all this way from Louisiana?" she asked.

"No," he answered. "He wanted to come, but I talked him out of it. I reminded him that he's going to be a father and that he's a lousy shot. If he gets himself killed, then I'll have to become the kid's father figure. Said I'd raise his son or daughter to be just like me."

"And that gave him chills?"

"Yep," he replied. "And like I said, he's a lousy shot. He'd probably shoot himself getting his gun out of its holster."

"And you don't want him to get hurt. You better watch it. You're beginning to sound nice."

He squinted against the sunlight trying to see the driver. "Theo said he knew someone who could keep quiet and help. Who wouldn't mind breaking some rules. Ah, hell," he groaned when he finally saw who was behind the wheel. "Not him. That son of a . . ."

"Who?"

"Theo. My brother-in-law has a sick sense of humor."

"John Paul, what are you talking about?"

"Theo sent *him*," he snapped, stabbing at the air with his finger.

"Who?" she demanded. She was beginning to feel like an owl.

"Clayborne. He sent Noah Clayborne." He spat the name out as though it left a foul taste in his mouth.

She was thoroughly confused by his attitude. "But you called Noah from the spa. I heard you on the phone. Why are you angry now?"

"Yes, I did call him, but I didn't think I'd have to see him," he muttered. He turned to her, gave her a quick once-over from head to toes, and barked, "Put some damn clothes on."

She looked down at herself. Yes, there were clothes. White tennis shoes, navy shorts, white T-shirt. "What's the matter with what I have on?"

"Too much skin showing. Ah, hell, it wouldn't matter if you were dressed like a nun. He's still gonna hit on you. Then I'm gonna have to shoot the bastard." He stomped to the door, all but pulled it off the hinges when he opened it, and went out onto the porch. "Just see if I don't."

Oh, brother. "He's bringing us a car." She

called out the reminder. "Stop complaining about him."

"Yeah, you're right," he called back. "We'll make him stay here or take my car. He doesn't need to go with us."

Avery stepped back to the window. John Paul had made her curious about Theo's friend. She knew Noah couldn't possibly be as obnoxious as John Paul had implied. No one could be that awful.

The car stopped in front of the house, and Noah Clayborne opened the car door and emerged into the sunlight.

Avery felt like whistling. Tall, broad-shouldered, with sandy blond hair, the man was dressed casually in jeans and a gray T-shirt. He wore the old-fashioned shoulder holster and a pair of Ray-Ban sunglasses. John Paul scowled at him, but Clayborne smiled back, as though the joke were on Renard. The man had a dimple and definitely oozed sensuality.

She wasn't interested in him, of course, not in that way. John Paul was sexier — everything about him appealed to her — but Noah, in appearance anyway, could be a close runner-up. Of course, her analysis was strictly clinical. She had never taken the time to notice such things about a man before, or if she had, she hadn't been able to admit it to herself. Had finally having sex again turned her mind into mush?

"I'm going to need therapy when this is over,"

she whispered. "Big-time therapy."

Straightening her shoulders, she went outside to meet him. He'd reached the steps but stopped when she walked onto the porch.

John Paul's social graces definitely needed work. She waited a couple of seconds for him to introduce her, then realized he wasn't going to. She would have stepped forward, but John Paul put his arm around her shoulders and jerked her close to him.

Noah's response to the ridiculously possessive action was to widen his grin. He removed his sunglasses and looked directly at her. Blue eyes. The man had intense blue eyes. Bet he breaks a lot of hearts, she thought, as she felt John Paul tighten his hold.

Was he married? She hoped not because she could think of at least three friends to fix him up with, providing, of course, he wasn't just a body without a mind. Margo wouldn't be bothered by that, but Peyton, her childhood friend, would definitely want a man with a brain.

"What the hell are you staring at, Clayborne?" John Paul barked.

She put a stop to the pissing contest. She pushed his arm away and walked to the edge of the porch.

"Thank you for coming," she began. Extending her hand, she added, "My name's Avery Delaney."

Noah came up the stairs and shook her hand.

He didn't let go as he introduced himself and then said, "I gotta know."

"Yes?"

He glanced at John Paul and said, "How'd a sweet thing like you get hooked up with him?"

"She's lucky," John Paul snapped. "Now let go of her."

Noah smiled at Avery and continued to hold on to her hand. He was enjoying himself by deliberately provoking John Paul. He seemed to know what buttons to push to get John Paul riled. Come to think of it, it didn't take much.

"We appreciate your help, don't we, John Paul?"

She had to elbow him to get him to answer. "Yeah, sure."

"Please, come inside. Are you thirsty?" she asked as she led the way into the cabin.

"If he's thirsty, he can get his own damned drink," John Paul said. "You don't have to play hostess, Avery."

She whirled around. "Stop being a jerk," she ordered. "I was being polite, something you know precious little about. Now stop acting like a rooster and get rid of the attitude."

He immediately backed down. "Yeah, all right."

Noah tried not to laugh.

John Paul looked a bit sheepish as he said to Noah, "She's got a temper."

"Uh-huh," Noah drawled.

"Look, it's not what you —"

"Yeah, it is. Never thought you'd fall. Hell, I

never thought any woman would want —"

"Drop it, Noah."

"Hey, I'm just here to do Theo a favor," he explained. "Don't take your frustrations out on me." The fact was, he liked John Paul, and he respected him. Maybe even admired him a little because he'd had the guts to walk away from a job that usually broke a man.

Avery had gone into the kitchen to get a cold soda for Noah. She stopped in the kitchen doorway. The men had returned to the porch, and she couldn't hear what they were saying. She put the bottle back in the refrigerator and decided to pack her bag.

She heard a couple of crude and colorful expletives; then she heard laughter. They're nuts, she thought as she went into the bedroom and shut the door. The bed looked as though acrobats had practiced their act on it. She quickly stripped the sheets, put on fresh ones, and dropped the soiled linens in the hamper.

There wasn't much to pack. She changed into her khaki pants and searched through her bag for her pink blouse. The clothes the woman at the police station had taken home to wash for her were folded neatly on the side of the duffel bag.

It was such a sweet thing to do, washing her clothes. When this was over, she would have so many people to thank for their kindness. She'd have to do something especially nice for the police chief. Letting them use his cabin was above and beyond his duty.

She went into the bathroom to collect her toiletries. Glancing in the mirror, she was startled at how tired and pale she looked. She put on a little makeup to cover the dark circles under her eyes, added some blush and tinted pink lip gloss. Then she brushed her hair, gathered up her toothbrush and toothpaste, and put them in her makeup bag. She tossed John Paul's toothbrush on top.

She was ready to go when John Paul walked into the bedroom. He shut the door, leaned against it, and looked at her.

After she'd finished zipping her bag, she stood, then nervously brushed her hands against her slacks, as though she were trying to iron any wrinkles out.

"Is something wrong?"

"I don't want to leave." He was looking at the bed when he made the comment.

"I don't either," she admitted.

"Come here." His voice was low and urgent.

She didn't hesitate. She ran to him, threw her arms around his neck, and kissed him.

When at last they drew apart, there were tears in her eyes. She had never felt this kind of desperation before, and it was wrenching, so heartbreaking she was afraid she would break down and sob.

How had she allowed herself to become so vulnerable? Love wasn't supposed to happen this quickly, was it? Why hadn't she protected herself? Love sucks, she decided then. All those stupid songs about how wonderful it was. All she felt was pain and fear, fear that something would happen to him. Damn it, she would not love him.

"You should go home," she said. She stepped back, nodded, and then repeated her decision, but this time she was more forceful. "I mean it. I want you to go home."

"Why?"

He had asked an obvious question, but she gave him an obscure answer. "You just should. I can drive myself to Florida. I don't need you or Noah to baby-sit me."

The more she explained, the more forceful her voice became. John Paul reacted to her outburst by simply grabbing his bag, dropping it on the bed, and then beginning to shove his clothes inside.

Noah was standing at the kitchen counter, drinking from a milk carton. He'd made himself a huge sandwich and was polishing it off as she carried her backpack to the door. John Paul was right behind her with her duffel bag and his.

"Let's go," he called to Noah.

"I'm right behind you."

She followed John Paul to the car. He opened the driver's door, popped the lid on the trunk; then, pausing to glare at her, he tossed their bags inside and slammed the trunk down.

"John Paul, I meant . . ."

He shook his head. "Don't."

"Don't what?" she asked.

"Don't insult me again. I told you at least three times I was in this for the long haul. Weren't you listening?"

She glanced at the door to make sure Noah wasn't there, then said, "I don't want you to get hurt. Okay? I couldn't stand it if anything happened to you . . . I don't think I could . . ."

"I love you too, Avery."

"It's too soon . . . you can't . . ."

"I do."

"How can you love me?" she whispered.

His left hand cupped the back of her neck, and as he slowly drew her toward him, he whispered, "Want me to count the ways?"

Tears stung her eyes. He wasn't going to be reasonable. "You're stubborn."

"So arc you."

"It won't work."

"We'll make it work."

"I'm a liberal," she whispered in desperation.

He kissed her and then said, "I can live with that, but I can't live without you. Simple as that, sugar."

His wonderful mouth covered hers in a long, hot, thoroughly arousing kiss. He didn't overpower her with his strength, didn't have her chained to him. No, he was being extremely gentle as his mouth slanted over hers. She could have pulled back, but she didn't want to. She greedily kissed him back.

He growled low in his throat, which only encouraged her to be bolder. And when at last he lifted his head, she sagged against him.

She pushed away from him when the screen door opened.

Noah walked out onto the porch, pulled the door closed, and then tossed the keys to John Paul. "You drive while I catch up on some sleep."

He caught the keys without taking his gaze off Avery. "You're gonna marry me."

"No, I can't marry you."

"Did I ask?"

"You just said . . ."

"Did I ask?" he patiently repeated.

Noah glanced at both of them, shook his head, and then dove into the backseat. "Lover's spat?" he asked.

"No." They both snapped the word at the same time.

She grabbed the keys out of John Paul's hand. "I'm driving."

He didn't argue with her. The dynamics between the two fascinated Noah. Who would have thought the bear would ever fall? He guessed the old saying was true. There really was someone out there for everyone. A soul mate. Wait until he told Theo about this. He wouldn't believe it either. The bear was in love.

He couldn't suppress his laughter. "What the hell's so funny?" John Paul grumbled.

"You. You're funny. Hey, Avery. Ever hear the one about the Marine . . ."

John Paul tilted his seat back and closed his eyes. It was going to be a long, long trip.

# CHAPTER 33

The plans kept changing. Carrie didn't like change, any kind of change, unless, of course, she was the one in charge of making those changes. Agent Hillman was point man, and Agent Bean was his gofer. Hillman's first command when he was placed in charge of Carrie was to order Bean to tell her the decision had been made to keep her in Colorado.

After Bean informed Mrs. Salvetti of the Bureau's decision and suffered her reaction, he returned to Agent Hillman and threatened to hand in his resignation if Hillman ever made him do that again.

"I'm putting in for combat pay," Bean announced.

They could both hear Carrie screaming from the waiting room. "Doesn't she realize there are sick people in this hospital?" Hillman muttered, clearly appalled by the woman's conduct.

"She doesn't care," Bean countered. "She's demanding to go to Florida and stay in the safe house with her niece."

"I take it, then, you didn't tell her we can't find her niece?"

"No, sir. I thought I'd let you explain that to her."

"For God's sake, man. You're an agent with the FBI. Surely you can handle a cranky woman."

"With all due respect, sir, she isn't just a cranky woman. She's a . . ."

"A what?" Hillman snapped.

A she-devil, Bean wanted to say but didn't dare. Hillman wouldn't believe him. Besides, he would find out soon enough what the Salvetti woman was capable of when she wasn't happy. "Sir, she isn't what I would call a normal woman. Normal women don't have fire shooting out of their eyes."

Hillman was disgusted. "She'll do whatever we tell her to do."

Wanna bet? The ringing in his ears, he noticed, had subsided into a dull echo. "Yes, sir, I'm sure she'll listen to you." He said the last without breaking into a smile and was quite proud of his achievement.

"We have the woman's best interests at heart. Surely you explained our motives to her, didn't you, Bean?"

"She didn't give me the opportunity to explain our position."

"When she calms down —"

They both heard another shout. Bean grimaced as Hillman demanded, "Who's in there with her?"

"Gorman," he answered. "He must have told her we haven't been able to locate her niece."

The door to the waiting room opened and Gorman stepped out. Hillman and Bean stood at the end of the hallway and watched as Gorman hastily pulled the door closed. His face was as red as hot peppers.

Gorman spotted Hillman, drew himself up to his full six foot two height, and walked down the hall to join them.

"Is she giving you trouble too?" Hillman asked.

Bean tried not to snicker. Of course she'd given him trouble. Just look at his face.

"She's a . . . difficult woman," Gorman said, trying to be diplomatic. "She refuses to cooperate. Told me she's going to Florida with or without Hill of Beans."

"Hill of Beans?" Hillman asked.

Gorman cleared his throat. "That's what she's calling you and Agent Bean. Hill of Beans. She's also demanding a beach house."

"A beach house? She wants a beach house?" Hillman asked incredulously.

Bean cast him a smug I-told-you-so look. Now, perhaps, his superior would agree that the Salvetti woman was as difficult as he'd told him she was.

"And what did you say to her demands?"

"I told her that wasn't possible, that since her testimony isn't mandatory, she'll be staying in Colorado. I explained the defense attorney has

495

the transcripts of Skarrett's first trial and he hasn't asked to depose Mrs. Salvetti again and that, for that reason, there wasn't any need for her to go to Florida."

"And her response?" Bean asked.

"She tried to grab my gun."

"I'm sure she was bluffing," Hillman said. "Let's give her a few minutes to cool off," he suggested.

It was going to take Carrie more than a few minutes to calm her temper. Blowing up was her response to the fear gnawing at her stomach. What the hell was Avery going to do? Did she think she could stroll into that courthouse and testify against Skarrett? Carrie kept picturing her niece being gunned down on the courthouse steps.

If Monk . . . or Jilly . . . got hold of her . . . Carrie rushed to the phone, got an outside line, and called Tony collect. She prayed he hadn't already left for the airport.

He must have been sitting by the phone, because he picked up on the first ring.

Carrie didn't waste time on preliminaries. "They're going to put me in a house and keep me here, in Colorado," she blurted.

"Where in Colorado?" he asked.

"They wouldn't tell me, but I heard one of them talking on his cell phone. He didn't know I was listening, and he mentioned a place called Wedgewood. It must be some kind of suburb."

"Aspen's too small to have suburbs," he countered.

"I don't know where the hell it is. Look it up on the Internet, for God's sake. Use your head. There can't be more than one Wedgewood suburb in Colorado." She burst into tears. "If I have to be in a safe house for a long time, what will happen to my company? I can't be away too long. I can't . . ."

"Honey, I can handle things here. I've run a company before."

"But I need you with me, Tony. You have to come."

"All right, I will," he promised. "I won't let you go through this alone. Do you want me to come to the hospital? Can they wait to move you until I get there?"

"I'll make them wait," she said. "Sara has already been moved into the new physical therapy wing. It hasn't even been opened yet, so security's easy. I'll stay there with her until they move both of us. I won't let them take me anywhere until you get here."

"Yes, okay," he said, sounding relieved.

"Do you know they can't find Avery? When she called me, she told me she wouldn't be joining me in protective custody. Have you talked to her?"

"No, not yet. I've been pacing by the phone, waiting. It's not like Avery to make me worry. I don't understand why she hasn't called."

"She knows you'll give her hell for upsetting

me," Carrie said. "She doesn't like to disappoint either one of us."

"I know, honey, but I'm worried sick about her."

"Me too. She'll call, and when she does, you tell her not to go to Sheldon Beach. Make her realize how dangerous it will be for her."

"Yes, I will," he promised. "I'm not going to let anything happen to her."

"What if Avery calls after you've left for the airport?"

"Honey, she knows my cell phone number."

Of course Avery did. Carrie was so rattled she couldn't think. "I'll see you soon."

Carrie hung up the phone and decided to call Avery's office to find out if her friends had heard from her, but she was prevented from making any more calls when Agent Hillman walked into the room and told her that Judge Collins wanted to talk to her.

"We'll be moving you into the new wing in a few minutes."

"Yes, all right. Whatever you say."

Hillman was surprised and pleased by her cooperation. He was feeling a bit smug too, for he'd been right. He'd told Bean and Gorman that once Mrs. Salvetti calmed down, she would cooperate, and she was doing exactly that now.

Maybe this wasn't going to be such a bad assignment after all.

# CHAPTER 34

Jilly had just had a full body massage and was now wrapped in a four-hundred-count Egyptian cotton sheet with the logo of Utopia stamped on the hem. She lay on her back, her eyes closed, while the female technician applied an avocado facial mask. The stupid woman wouldn't stop talking. She gave Jilly one compliment after another about her flawless complexion and her oh, so perfect body.

Jilly never tired of hearing compliments from men, but she didn't care what women thought about her, and just when she was about to tell the technician to shut up, she finished applying the goo and said, "We'll just let this set for fifteen minutes."

She was finally alone. Loosening the sheet, she let the cool air caress her body. It felt good to relax, especially after she'd become so distraught over the news that Carrie and the judge had survived the explosion. Fortunately, Monk hadn't been in the bungalow when that horrid news came on the television, so she didn't have to try to behave. He had never seen her throw a full-blown tantrum, and she didn't know how he would react. She certainly didn't want to scare him, not yet anyway, because he was so terribly useful. There was still too much to be done, and it was imperative that Monk stay the loyal lapdog.

Carrie used to call her fits rages, but Jilly had learned control over the years. Not much, but some, she qualified. Admittedly, if one of the housekeeping staff had happened to walk into the bungalow just after Jilly had heard the news about Carrie, Jilly probably would have attacked her. And enjoyed every moment of it.

Jilly had never killed a person. She'd let her men take care of her problems. Wasn't that what they were for? She had often wondered, though, what it would feel like to kill someone with a gun or maybe even with her bare hands. If someone caused her to be unhappy, then watching her die did seem fitting. Why should she deny herself that joy and satisfaction? She realized now that Monk had been right all along. He had wanted to kill each woman separately and make the deaths look like accidents, but Jilly had pleaded and cajoled until he'd given in and done things her way. How could such a brilliant plan not work? It was so perfect, so simple, so . . . brilliant.

Carrie. Carrie was the reason the plan hadn't worked. That selfish bitch had ruined everything.

Jilly threw herself on the bed and pounded her

fists into the pillows. She stopped suddenly. She heard the newscaster on CNN with the lead-in for the footage that was coming on the screen again. She bolted upright, impatiently wiping the tears from her eyes, and stared at the screen. The film was focusing on the judge, but Jilly wasn't interested in her, no matter how famous she was supposed to be. She waited, whimpering, until finally the camera turned to her bitch of a sister as she was being carried on a stretcher into the ambulance. Men, paramedics, no doubt, but still men, were actually fawning over her. How dare they give her any attention? How dare they? Jilly was more enraged by the men's behavior than by the fact that her sister was still very much alive.

The camera zoomed in on Carrie's face. Jilly thought she saw her smiling, and that proved to be the last straw. Screaming obscenities, she picked up a lamp and hurled it into the wall.

Carrie was ruining everything.

It took an hour for her to calm down. Then she called the spa and had a masseur come to the bungalow. The massage helped, and she was now able to think about a new plan. This one wouldn't be as complicated, she decided.

Why hadn't she given in to the urge and killed Carrie with her scissors? Because that wouldn't have been as much fun. After everything her sister had done to her, she deserved to suffer a long while before she died. It wasn't fair. Men worrying about her, taking care of her. Couldn't they see how ugly she was?

Jilly could feel herself getting worked up again. The mask on her face was beginning to itch. Her cell phone rang just as the technician came back into the suite.

"Go away," she said. "I'll wash this off. Shut the door behind you."

Jilly knocked over a stack of towels as she reached for the phone. "Yes?"

"I thought you would want to hear some good news. I found out where Carrie and the judge are."

She immediately perked up. "You know? Where, darling? Was I right?" she asked before he could answer. "Are they going to Sheldon Beach? Is that where they're going to hide Carrie until the trial?"

"Your sister isn't going to Florida because she isn't going to testify at the trial."

Jilly laughed with delight. "She's afraid."

"Yes."

The mask on her face cracked when she smiled. "That's wonderful news. Now tell me everything."

She listened carefully, and when he was finished, she told him not to worry, that she would come up with a new, even better plan. "But something less complicated this time," she promised. Then in a voice that sounded like a dove cooing, she said, "I miss you, darling."

"I'll see you soon?"

"Of course."

"I love you."

She smiled again. "Yes. I know."

She disconnected the call, dropped her towel, and went into the bathroom to shower. Wrapping herself in a terry-cloth robe, she called housekeeping to come and clean up the mess she'd made. The cost of the damage would be put on her credit card.

Two hours later, when Monk walked into the room, she was ready for him. She wore a black chiffon dress and high heels, but had decided against undergarments. When she stood in the doorway with the light spilling out from the bedroom, she knew he could see through the filmy material. She'd checked to make sure.

Monk was weary by the time he got there, but as soon as he saw the love of his life, he was rejuvenated. He knew the trouble she'd gone to just to please him. She had instinctively known he would need to make love to her and had prepared the bedroom. There were candles burning to set the mood, and she was wearing his favorite dress. It was identical to the red one she used to have, until he'd torn it. As he strode toward her, he told himself not to ruin this one.

He watched her mouth. She was slowly rubbing her upper lip with the tip of her tongue. She knew he liked that too.

Their lovemaking was wild and crude. Like animals in heat, they tore at each other. Her dress fell to the floor in tatters. And when he was finally satisfied, he rolled off her, threw his arm back, and closed his eyes.

She had pleased him, and now it was his turn to please her. "I think we should wait a couple of days," Jilly said, "and then, after you're rested, you can take care of Carrie and the judge. They'll be all settled in and feeling safe by then. Don't you agree? It shouldn't be too difficult for you to get in and do what needs to be done."

"I need at least two weeks to organize and plan."

"Did I just make you happy, Monk?"

"You know you did, darling."

"Then make me happy. I could wait maybe a week, but I'd go crazy if I had to wait any longer. Carrie was smiling when they lifted her into the ambulance. I didn't like seeing her smile."

"I understand."

"She told the police about me. Now they know I'm alive, and they'll be looking for me. You were right," she whispered. "I shouldn't have insisted on the letters, and I shouldn't have let her see me. But I thought she would die in the explosion, and I wanted her to know . . ."

"Don't cry, Jilly," he said as he took her in his arms. "It's going to be all right."

"Yes," she said, cuddling up against him. "As soon as she's dead, everything will be all right. She's made me so unhappy for such a long time. Promise me you'll kill her soon."

"I promise," he answered. "You know I'll do anything for you."

She smiled against his neck. Her hands

moved skillfully over his body. "Then we'll go to Sheldon Beach."

Monk's desperation to please her was making him frantic, but at the same time he felt he could do anything and succeed because of her faith in him. She often told him how brilliant she thought he was and how he underestimated and undervalued himself. He realized now that she was right. He could pull it off. He could get in and out without being noticed, no matter how many FBI agents were there.

He could even become invisible.

# CHAPTER 35

The drive to Florida took three days. They could have pushed it, but because they had the time, they took the more scenic back roads through Georgia.

They spent two nights in clean but no-frills motels tucked away in small towns. The first night they each had their own room. Avery hadn't invited John Paul to share her bed, and he hadn't asked or assumed. She was desperately trying to distance herself from him because she believed it would make their final parting less painful, but it wasn't working. She was only fooling herself. She loved him and didn't know what to do about it. She didn't sleep at all that first night, tossed and turned until she made herself dizzy, and by morning, her disposition was as charming as a rhino's. The second night, John Paul didn't ask. He simply paid for two rooms while Noah talked to one of his superiors on his cell phone.

John Paul followed Avery into her room and dropped his bag next to hers. She didn't argue but said, "We're just going to sleep. No sex."

Smiling, he stripped out of his clothes and headed for the shower. "Did I ask?" he said before shutting the door in her face.

The air conditioner in the window was cranked up, the room was freezing, and around two in the morning she woke up in his arms, feeling toasty warm and amorous. He was simply irresistible. They made love, and it was even better than the last time because now each knew what the other liked, and within minutes they were perfectly attuned to each other's needs.

The wall separating their room from Noah's was paper thin. She tried to be quiet, but when she felt those first tremors of exquisite pleasure coursing through her body, the feeling was so intense she bit his shoulder to keep the shout of ecstasy from escaping.

It was so wonderful that when she awakened at six, she rolled into his arms and, as Margo would say, she jumped his bones again.

He went back to sleep. She went into the bathroom, and after she'd showered, she stood in front of the mirror looking at her face. Her cheeks were red from rubbing against his whiskers, and her lips were swollen from his kisses.

Sighing, she shook her head and whispered, "Hi. My name's Avery, and I'm a sexaholic."

She couldn't blame anyone but herself. Vowing to leave him the hell alone, she picked up her toothbrush and tried not to think about him as she got ready for the day.

John Paul was in a much better mood as they started out. He was almost pleasant to Noah. Not quite, but almost. Avery thought the two men acted like adversaries in some kind of contest, but it didn't take her long to realize they both got a kick out of trading insults.

After they had stopped for lunch, she got into the backseat, put on her baseball cap to block the sun from her eyes, and decided to take a nap.

The men lowered their voices so they wouldn't disturb her. Noah knew about Jilly. He'd read Avery's file, and he'd come prepared.

They speculated about how she had connected with Monk and what their relationship might be. Noah, of course, knew all about Skarrett too, and thought that maybe he was calling all the shots. John Paul disagreed, pointing out that, once Monk had taken the contract, he did things his way.

One topic led to another. "Are you going to lose your job because you're helping us?" John Paul asked. "The FBI's looking for Avery."

"I don't work for the FBI. I'm what you might call an independent contractor."

John Paul was exasperated. "No, you work for the FBI. What the hell do you think that badge is for?"

"Better parking spots. It's the only reason I carry it."

"Get serious."

"Do you ever miss it?"

"Miss what?"

"The action."

"Hell, no."

"You still living in the swamp?"

"I live in Bowen."

"In the swamp."

"Yeah, I guess so."

"You think she'll want to live there?"

He pretended not to understand. "Who?"

He had forgotten how blunt Noah could be. "The woman you're sleeping with. The woman you can't take your eyes off even when you're driving. You've been looking in the rearview mirror every ten seconds since you got behind the wheel. You're gonna get us killed if you don't pay attention to the road."

John Paul was determined not to discuss Avery. "How far is it to that little town you picked out on the map for us to stay tonight? What was it called? Walden Point?"

"Now me, I don't think I'm ever gonna settle down. Too many fish in the sea," Noah said.

"And Walden Point is what? Twenty or thirty miles from Sheldon Beach?"

"I didn't think you'd ever find a woman who would put up with you, but I guess I was wrong."

John Paul couldn't pretend he wasn't listening any longer. "You don't even know me, Noah."

"Sure I do. I know all about you."

"Did you read my file?" He didn't give him

time to respond but muttered, "Doesn't 'classified' mean anything anymore?"

"Guess not," Noah drawled. He hadn't had access to John Paul's file, but he had talked to Theo about his reclusive brother-in-law. Since it obviously upset John Paul to think that his file had been opened, Noah didn't tell him the truth. He liked annoying him.

"So, do you think she'll like living in Bowen?"

They had just come full circle. John Paul gripped the steering wheel as he tried to control his temper.

"We won't need to stop for gas."

Noah grinned. "Man, you've got it bad. Your face is getting red."

John Paul thought about punching him. "It's not like that."

"Oh? You two don't have any kind of arrangement?"

He wasn't about to discuss his and Avery's relationship.

"No."

"No future plans?"

He glared at Noah. "No," he snapped. Turning back to the road, he said, "Are you ready to talk about something else?"

"Sure," he said. "What do you want to talk about?"

"Stop hitting on Avery."

He was sorry the second the words were out of his mouth. Noah laughed. "Why would I want to stop doing that? You just said —"

"I know what the hell I said."

"And she is a beautiful woman."

Maybe he could reach over real quick, open Noah's door, and shove him out. That ought to shut him up.

"She's sexy as hell too."

"Yeah, well, you leave her the hell alone. Now, how far is it to Walden Point?"

"Beats me." Noah tilted the seat back, adjusted his sunglasses on the bridge of his nose, and closed his eyes.

"You're the damn navigator. Look at the map."

"Sure thing."

He was sound asleep seconds later.

The rest of the afternoon was blissfully quiet. They arrived in Walden Point around six that evening. The sleepy little town was exactly thirty-two miles to the bridge leading into Sheldon Beach.

If Avery had been in Walden Point as a child, she didn't remember it. The streets were lined with palm trees, the grass was brown from salt water and sun, and the houses along the side streets were ill kept and weather-beaten. It was a dismal, forgotten-looking place until they reached the older, more populated section of town. The houses along those avenues had been spruced up. The grass was lush and green, and flowers brimmed over terra-cotta pots on freshly painted porches. It was apparent there was a renovation in progress.

There were several pretty bed-and-breakfast

homes along the main street to the waterfront, but Noah wasn't interested in stopping there. He found a motel about twelve blocks away from the beach and told John Paul to pull into the lot.

Avery thought Noah was joking. Milt's Flamingo Motel had flaming pink concrete block walls and a red-tile roof in desperate need of repair. There were hand-painted flamingos in different colors on each lime green door. The U-shaped structure with twelve units had a gravel parking lot. Whoever had chosen the color scheme had to have been color-blind.

There weren't any other cars around. Avery thought Milt must have flown the coop, abandoning the dump.

"Are you sure this is open?"

"I saw a guy watching as we pulled in," Noah answered. "It's easy in and out. We park behind, and the car's out of sight from the street. What do you think?"

Since he was asking John Paul and not her, Avery kept her opinion of their lodgings to herself. After having passed the lovely bed-and-breakfast a couple of blocks away with the charming white picket fence and rockers on the wraparound porch, she thought Noah's choice was awful. She waited for John Paul to protest.

"I like it," he said, dashing her hopes. "It kind of reminds me of my dad's bar. He's got a big flamingo on his roof."

"Yeah, I remember seeing it. I thought it was a pelican. I'll check us in."

"There's a bed-and-breakfast just down the road," she interjected. "It looked nice and clean. I noticed a vacancy sign in the yard."

"This is okay, isn't it?" John Paul asked.

If Noah hadn't been with them, she would have told him no, it wasn't okay, but she didn't want to complain in front of an agent.

"Yes, it's fine."

He smiled because she sounded so disheartened. "Not as nice as Tyler's cabin?"

"It's fine," she repeated.

Noah had just gotten out of the car when his cell phone rang. John Paul walked ahead to the office, but Avery stayed with Noah. She stretched her arms and legs, stiff from the long ride.

Noah, his head down, walked away, obviously so that the conversation would be private. She saw his expression, knew something was wrong, and anxiously waited.

The conversation lasted a long time. John Paul came back with two keys, took one look at Avery, and said, "What's wrong?"

"Something," she said, leaning into his side.

Noah ended the call and walked back to the car. His gaze was on Avery. "Your aunt and the judge are fine."

"What happened?" John Paul asked.

"There was a delivery; some tanks to be installed behind the physical therapy wing."

"Ah, hell," John Paul whispered. He already knew what was coming. "They blew, didn't they?"

513

Noah nodded. "The fire took out most of the wing."

"How did Monk get past security?" Avery asked.

"He didn't," Noah said. "The delivery man was killed as he was unloading them. Monk got to those tanks before they were set."

"How many down?" John Paul asked.

"Two dead. An agent named Gorman was injured, but he's gonna make it. That's all I know."

"How the hell did this happen?" John Paul demanded.

"I'll tell you how it happened. Monk was there on the hospital grounds all that time watching and waiting. He had to have known they couldn't move the judge so soon after her surgery. When the agents put those decoys in the car and drove off, he probably spotted something and knew the women weren't Carrie and the judge."

Noah led the way to their rooms. They were at the far end of the units and had a connecting door between them.

Their room was surprisingly clean. There was a double bed with a floral bedspread, two chairs by the window facing the gravel lot, with a small table and lamp in between. There wasn't a closet. On the far wall was a rack with hangers and built-in shelves next to it.

The second Noah stepped into their room, Avery asked, "Carrie and the judge weren't injured? You're telling me everything?"

"Yes," he said. "Your aunt had just wheeled the judge into the bathroom when it happened. The walls caved in on them and protected them from being incinerated."

Avery felt sick to her stomach. Noah's phone rang again, and he walked into his room. She waited until his back was turned and then went to John Paul, put her arms around his waist, and held him tight.

He could feel her trembling. "This nightmare will be over soon," he promised. Then, when she didn't answer, he asked, "Do you want to get out of here?"

"Yes."

"Where do you want to go?"

"I don't know," she whispered. "I can't think . . . I need to be able . . ."

He kissed her brow. "You need a porch swing, don't you?"

She nodded.

"With lilacs," he added.

She smiled because he remembered her happy place.

"I can't give you lilacs, and I can't drum up a porch swing for you, sugar, but water . . . I can give you lots of that."

Twenty minutes later she and John Paul walked hand in hand along the beach. Both of them had changed into shorts and had left their shoes on the steps where Noah sat.

Dark clouds were moving in, obscuring the sun. The beach was virtually deserted, and when Avery sat down and assumed the lotus position, John Paul didn't intrude. He walked back to the steps and sat down next to Noah.

"What the hell is she doing?" Noah asked when Avery hadn't moved for several minutes.

"Thinking," he answered.

"Okay."

When the sun was dropping, taking the light of the day, John Paul got up and went to Avery. Her eyes were closed. He squatted down in front of her and waited, knew she sensed he was there.

A moment passed before she acknowledged him. She opened her eyes and looked into his. A single tear slid down her cheek. She took a deep cleansing breath.

"I need to make a call."

# CHAPTER 36

Monk was ready to make his move.

There was a "no vacancy" sign in the window of the manager's office, and nailed to the door was another sign. "Closed until further notice."

Monk knew the targets were inside. He had already canvassed the area, knew it like the back of his hand. Three cars were parked behind the motel. He was certain two of them belonged to federal agents assigned to protect Avery. The third vehicle was Renard's.

Monk drove Jilly past the motel so she could see where it was going to happen, and she could barely contain her excitement when she saw the light shimmering along the edge of the tightly drawn drapes in the unit Monk had pointed out to her.

"She's in there," she whispered, her excitement brimming in her voice.

Monk pulled into the parking lot up the street from Milt's Motel. The lot did double duty for patrons of the old Spanish-style movie theater, complete with bell tower, and the spillover from the Church of the Risen. He parked the car so that it faced the street, then handed Jilly his binoculars and took a drink of his iced tea.

"You're now officially on a stakeout."

She giggled. "This is wonderful."

Her excitement thrilled him. "You're having a good time, aren't you?"

"Oh, yes," she gushed. "It's better than I could ever have imagined. Much better."

A car pulled into the parking lot, and she quickly lowered the binoculars. "Are you sure we're safe here?"

"Of course we are. I'll always make it safe for you."

They shared a smile, and then Jilly lifted the binoculars again. She could just see the light framing the window, and she was trying to imagine what was happening inside the room.

Another car pulled in and parked three rows behind them. There was a revival going on inside the church, and it was also dollar night at the movie theater. The lot was nearly full now.

Jilly offered him the binoculars, but he didn't need to look. He had already spent one full night and day doing reconnaissance. It wasn't enough, but it would have to do. Normally, he would have spent at least two weeks following his subject, learning his routine, but this wasn't a normal situation. Time was running out, and Jilly was too impatient to wait much longer. Like a child, she wanted instant gratification.

"How many policemen are inside with them?" she asked.

"Agents," he corrected. "Not policemen. There are four."

"And you'll get them all?"

"Yes."

They were sitting ducks. His for the taking.

The night before, Monk had watched Renard sneak out the back door, get into his car, and drive away. Monk hadn't had a clear shot at him, but he wouldn't have taken it even if he had because he didn't want his primary targets moved once again. He had something special planned for them. Pity, they wouldn't know what hit them.

Renard had returned to the motel thirty minutes later carrying four big pizzas and a plastic bag Monk guessed was filled with beer or soft drinks.

He was disgusted with Renard's carelessness. He was certain the man didn't have any idea he was being observed. Smug complacency. That's what it was. He was disappointed in Renard. He'd expected better from his adversary and had made the mistake of believing that Renard was a professional. An equal. He realized now how foolish that hope had been. No one could ever equal or measure up to his standards. Jilly had been right all along. He was a legend.

"I think it might be a good idea to do it tonight," Jilly said.

"You're eager."

"Yes."

"Tomorrow," he promised.

"I don't want to wait too much longer."

"I know."

"I wonder if Carrie is feeling safe again. Can you imagine how claustrophobic she and Avery must be feeling now? Being cooped up in that flea-infested room night and day? They must be going crazy."

"I've deliberately waited," he explained, "so that the agents would be bored and . . . lethargic. Yes, that's the word. Lethargic."

"Hour upon hour of sitting in that tiny room, waiting and worrying. They haven't let them out at all, have they?"

"Not while I was watching."

"I'm glad she didn't die in that hospital," she said. "This will be better because I'll get to watch."

Monk nodded. "Carrie demanded to come to Florida."

"She wants to die with Avery."

"She doesn't know she's going to die tomorrow," he said. "She thinks she's going to sit in that courtroom with Avery when the trial starts."

Jilly picked up the binoculars once again. Smiling, she said, "Third time's a charm."

Monk suppressed a yawn. He was exhausted, but he didn't dare complain. Jilly thought he was invincible, superhuman, and he was determined to maintain his knight-in-shining-armor image.

He knew he was taking risks he never would have considered before, but it was difficult to be cautious with Jilly constantly pushing him to his limits. She believed he could do anything, made him believe in himself.

Every once in a while a nagging doubt would surface in his mind. He had never walked away from a contract before. His word meant everything. If he wasn't reliable, his future would be in jeopardy, his reputation in tatters. The thought didn't repulse him, though. He had more than enough money to keep Jilly in the style she deserved. Maybe he could let this one go and walk away.

"You know, darling, we don't need the money," he said hesitantly.

Jilly knew where he was leading. "Do you know what I think?"

"What?"

"When we're finished here, let's sneak away to Mexico and get married. The trial will go for at least a week. Dale isn't going anywhere. Shall we?"

She knew how much he wanted a wedding. His fatigue vanished, and he was suddenly smiling in anticipation. "Yes, yes," he said. He was embarrassed because he'd sounded so eager, but he added, "I know a perfect place . . . you'll love it, I promise."

"As long as I'm marrying you, nothing else matters."

She put her hand on his thigh, leaned across

the console, and kissed him. Her hand moved upward to fondle him intimately.

He became aroused quickly. Satisfied with his reaction, she pulled away. "Why not put them out of their misery tonight?" she asked again, pouting now.

It took several seconds for Monk to understand what she was asking. He cleared his head and said, "You'll see it all tomorrow. Daylight's better. Besides, I have a few alterations to make, a few details before I'll be ready. You want it to be perfect, don't you, love?"

"Yes, of course. But why is daylight better?"

"No one expects to be hit with the sun shining, and in the past I've always tried to go in and get out during the night. Those agents believe they know my pattern."

"You think they've studied you?"

"Yes. When it's dark, their guard will be up."

She sighed then. "All right, I'll have to wait until tomorrow. Remember, you promised I could watch. You won't change your mind, will you?"

"No, I won't," he assured her. "You'll be safe, but in a wonderful spot where you can see everything. And I have a surprise for you. I was going to wait until tomorrow, but . . ."

"Tell me now," she pleaded. "Please."

"All right. I know how disappointed you were when you saw the house in Colorado blow. But this time will be different. I'm going to let you push the button."

She laughed with delight. "Are you going to dazzle me?"

He nodded. "Oh, yes. I'm a legend, remember? I'm going to dazzle everyone."

# CHAPTER 37

After Monk drove Jilly back to their hotel on the opposite side of Walden Point, he got back into the car and drove to a residential area a mile away from Milt's Motel.

He jogged a mile back to his hiding place and quietly climbed the stairs. He still had to put the finishing touches on the wiring. The job took much longer than he had anticipated, no doubt because he was weary, but when he was finally finished, he was content with his handiwork. Nothing was going to go wrong this time.

It was after three in the morning by the time he got ready for bed. Careful not to disturb Jilly, he eased down on the bed and sat next to her, watching her sleep. Oh, how he loved her. She was so beautiful, so exquisite . . . so perfect. He lay beside her thinking once again that he was the luckiest man in the world. He fell asleep with his arms around her, the scent of her perfume surrounding him, and dreamed of their honeymoon.

Fairy tales could come true. He and Jilly would live happily ever after.

Jilly dressed with care the following morning. She was going to church, after all, and so she wore a white skirt, white eyelet blouse, and strappy high-heel sandals. While she brushed her hair and curled it, Monk put their luggage in the car.

"Don't forget my tape," she reminded him.

"I would never forget that," he assured her, though, in fact, he had forgotten. She would have been beside herself if she'd lost it. She was so obsessed with what she called the evidence, that she insisted on always carrying it with her. A peculiarity he put up with just as she put up with his odd little traits. That's what a solid relationship was all about, wasn't it? Give and take.

He removed the tape from the VCR, slipped it into the carrying case, and put it on the bed next to her straw purse.

She was primping in front of the mirror. He watched her put on her red lipstick and smiled because he knew she only wore that color to please him. She'd told him so.

Jilly put the lipstick in her purse with the tape, picked up her straw hat with the white ribbon, and then walked into the center of the room. Whirling around in a circle, she asked, "Do I look ready for church?"

Her face flushed with excitement. "You look beautiful," he whispered. "You always look beautiful."

She went to him, adjusted the knot in his tie

just like an adoring wife would, and said, "You look wonderful in a suit. You should wear them more often."

"If it pleases you, I will."

She took hold of his hand and walked by his side to the car. He liked little things like that, he thought. Taking his hand. It was a sign of trust, wasn't it? The way she looked up at him with such admiration. He liked that too.

"I've already parked the other car down the street from the church," he said. "Just as a precaution. The key's behind the visor."

"We won't need to use it," she said. "You've covered every possibility."

He was certain that he had, and so he agreed, yet there was still that nagging little worry about the wires. He'd been so tired, he hadn't done more than one test, but that was enough.

The wind had picked up as they drove. Monk glanced up at the tower above the theater as he turned the corner. He pulled into the lot, parked on the end in front so Jilly could see everything. No one could block the front of his car, and if he had to drive over the curb to get to the street, he could do so without getting trapped.

He turned the motor off. "Are you ready?"

"Oh, yes."

"The remote's in the glove compartment."

She carefully lifted it out. "It looks like a garage door opener."

"That's what it is," he said. "Modified, of course."

"When do I push the button?"

"I thought it would be nice to wait until the church bells start."

Jilly turned in her seat to watch the men and women and children hurry toward the church. They didn't want to be late, she thought.

The show's outside. Too bad they wouldn't see it. "What time is it now?"

"Five more minutes."

"I don't want to wait. I want to do it now."

Monk reached under the seat and handed her the binoculars. "Whenever you're ready."

Jilly wet her lips as she lifted the binoculars. She adjusted the lens until she was looking at the room that had had the light on the night before.

"I'm taking my dream back," she whispered.

She pushed the button. Nothing happened, and so she pushed it again. Then again, harder, holding it down.

"Damn," Monk muttered. "The wind must have knocked loose one of the wires. Stop pushing that button, darling. I'll have to go up there and fix it. You sit tight. All right?"

He gently removed the remote from her hand. "If anything goes wrong . . ."

"You worry too much. Fix the wire," she said, a bit more sharply than she'd intended. "I'm sorry. I shouldn't be so anxious. I can wait another few minutes."

"That's my girl," he said. "Just in case, you remember what to do?"

"I go into the church, then out the side door, and get in the other car."

"And drive away on the side street I showed you. Don't drive in front of the motel."

"I won't leave without you."

Her loyalty was heartwarming. He patted her hand, put the remote on the floor by his seat, and then got out of the car. Slipping one hand into his pocket, he casually strolled across the parking lot and up the stairs to the church.

The bells rang as he walked inside. Thirty seconds later, he came out the side door, crossed the street, and walked three blocks to the north before he was convinced he wasn't being followed. He crossed the street and headed toward the movie theater.

The back door was locked, of course. He used his tools to undo the dead bolt, went inside, and quickly locked the door behind him.

He was in the back hallway. The door leading upstairs to the tower and the marquee was across the lobby. He stayed low and quiet.

He stood in the shadow behind the snack bar for several minutes, listening for any sounds, and when he was convinced he was all alone, he crept to the door. That, too, was locked, just as he had left it. He quickly unlocked it, opened the door, and looked up. The brown string he'd left on the third step hadn't been disturbed. No one had found his little hiding place. He stepped over the string and slowly, cautiously went up, aware that there was a squeak on the fifth step. He knew he was alone — the theater wouldn't open until the matinee at two — but he still avoided the step.

There was a trip wire at the top, much thinner than dental floss and all but invisible to the naked eye. Monk released the lever so that when he opened the door, he wouldn't be blown to kingdom come.

Good thing the owner didn't want to change the marquee today, he thought with a smile. He only changed the movies on Wednesdays, but Monk had set a trap anyway. Can't be too cautious, no matter what his darling Jilly believed.

He opened the door a crack and looked in. The rifle with the scope attached was still there in the corner, propped against the pillar.

His gaze went to the trigger mechanism below his homemade missile. Just as he had suspected, one of the wires had slipped down. It wasn't dangling free. The wind had loosened it just enough to break the connection.

He'd have it fixed in two seconds. He pushed the door open, stepped forward, and bent down on one knee. Then he froze. The voice came from his left on the other side of the bell. "Nice Roman candle you've got there."

Monk was too stunned to move. His mind was screaming, *No, no, no. The wire . . . the string . . . nothing had been disturbed. How did . . .*

Another voice came from his right. "I think he's having trouble getting it to work."

Monk lunged for his rifle. Neither man tried

to stop him. He rolled, firing as he moved.

Nothing happened. The rifle was empty. Noah stepped into the sunlight. Monk saw him and coiled back. "You," he whispered. "I know you."

John Paul moved forward from the shadows.

"How did you know?" Monk's face twisted with fury, and his voice shook.

"Easy. I'm smarter than you."

Noah's gun was pointed at Monk's forehead. John Paul saw the look in Noah's eyes and knew exactly what he was thinking.

"Cuff him," he said. "Then read him his rights."

Noah shook his head. "I'm gonna kill him first. Then I'll cuff him and read him his rights."

"Yeah, well, you can't."

"Son of a bitch." Noah released the trigger and put the gun back into his holster. He had the cuffs out and was moving toward Monk when they heard an agent shouting.

Monk lashed out with his foot, knocking Noah off balance. He stumbled in front of the killer, making it impossible for John Paul to get a clear shot.

Agents were racing up the stairs as Monk tried to get his gun from his ankle holster, but John Paul anticipated that response. He slammed his foot down on Monk's leg, pinning him to the floor.

"Quit messing around," he shouted. "Get the hell off him so I can shoot him."

"I'm gonna shoot him," Noah shouted back.

He hit Monk in the face, grunting from the sheer pleasure of hearing cartilage snap. He punched him again, trying to strike the exact spot so that it would hurt him more.

The door slammed into the pillar when the first agent came flying across the threshold. Monk seized the opportunity. With every ounce of strength he possessed, he shoved Noah off him and dove headfirst off the tower.

The killer landed on the slanted tin roof. He rolled to his hands and knees and crawled like a gorilla down to the marquee. When his right foot hit a bracket, he braced himself and went for his gun. He was swinging it up when John Paul and Noah, dropping down to the roof, fired simultaneously. Their bullets riddled Monk's body, sending him dancing backward like a marionette they were manipulating. He swung around and fell forward, his body draped across the marquee.

Panting, Noah put his gun away and then said, "You have the right to remain silent . . ."

"Damn right," John Paul muttered.

An agent leaning from a bell tower window called down to them. "Subject is on the move."

Noah pulled his walkie-talkie from his belt. He repeated what the agent had just told him.

"Roger."

"Was that Avery's voice? That was, wasn't it?" John Paul asked.

Noah spoke into the handset. "Avery? Is that you, sweetheart?"

He used the endearment just to piss off John Paul, and he grinned when he saw his reaction. If looks could kill, he'd be hanging over the marquee with Monk now.

John Paul snatched the handset. "What the hell are you doing, Avery? You were supposed to —"

"Are you all right?"

"Yeah, we're both fine. Where are you?"

"Roger. Over and out."

"Son of a bitch. She's in one of the tail cars."

They were both sprawled out on the roof. Noah laughed. "You could tell that from 'Roger, over and out'?"

John Paul ignored him and hit the button again. "Kelly?"

The agent in charge of the operation was quick to respond.

"Kelly here."

"Is Avery in one of the tail cars?" John Paul demanded. "Son of a bitch, I know she is. I told her to stay on that damn boat."

"Roger. Over and out."

Noah laughed. "Guess Avery's got a mind of her own." He leaned over the side of the building to judge the distance to the ground. "How the hell are we gonna get —"

John Paul shoved him off the roof. He followed him down and landed in a clump of dead shrubs beside the agent.

Kelly was on the handset again. "Do you have Monk in custody?"

"No, sir," John Paul answered.

"Where is he?"

He looked up at the marquee. "He's at the movies."

# CHAPTER 38

Jilly had grown impatient waiting for Monk to return to the car. What was taking him so long? She picked up the binoculars from the floor and watched the tower. Where was he? He knew how much she hated waiting. "Fix the damn thing," she muttered. "Hurry up."

Monk suddenly came into view. Jilly gasped in disbelief as she watched him somersault onto the roof. She thought he was going to break his neck. He came flying down from the tower, but while he was still in the air, he twisted around and landed like a cat on his feet. He lost his balance, skated down the roof on his hands and knees. She thought he was going to flip down over the building, but he caught himself in time.

Two men leapt onto the roof above Monk. They were moving so fast their faces were a blur.

"Kill them," she whispered to Monk. "Kill them now. Do it."

Gunshots reverberated around her. She thought she heard Monk scream her name, and she watched with detached curiosity. He fell so ungracefully and draped over the marquee, blood pouring down over the lights. He died with his ass sticking up in the air. She cursed his incompetent soul.

How dare he do this to her? Her disappointment overwhelmed her, and her eyes stung with tears. The remote. She frantically grabbed it and pushed the button. Once, then again and again. Nothing happened.

Damn. How could Monk be so thoughtless? He knew how important her dreams were.

Stomping her feet on the floor, she cursed him because he had ruined everything. Worse, he had made her unhappy.

"Damn you to hell," she muttered.

He'd left the keys in the ignition. Ignoring his order to take the other car if there was trouble, she hiked her skirt up over her thighs, climbed over the console, and got behind the wheel. Men, FBI men, she knew, were running to the theater, and there were people flooding out of the church to see what all the commotion was about. No one would notice her leaving. She pulled out onto the street, and so that she wouldn't draw any undue attention to herself, she stayed below the speed limit as she cruised through town.

The second she reached the on-ramp to the highway, she slammed her foot on the gas pedal. Muttering curses, she slapped the steering wheel, trying to vent some of her rage.

She had someone else ready to help, of

course. No one was going to steal her dreams again. No one. She knew Monk had weapons packed in his suitcases, and by God, if she had to kill Carrie and Avery herself to get her dreams back, then that's what she would do.

"Stupid Monk," she hissed. "Stupid, stupid man."

The tail car stayed well behind Jilly. There were three agents riding with Avery in the sedan. Kelly was driving, and she sat behind him. She tried not to let her anxiety show, but it was extremely difficult.

Her heart felt like it had stopped when she heard the gunshots, and she didn't take a breath until she heard John Paul's voice over the radio. She went weak with relief and then immediately started worrying again.

"Do you think she's spotted us?" she asked Kelly.

"I'm sure she doesn't know she's being followed," he replied.

Jilly was now so far ahead of them on the highway, Avery could barely see the back of her head.

"She's speeding, isn't she?"

"Yes," he answered. "She's going at least eighty."

"If there's a speed trap —"

"There isn't," he assured her.

"How do you know?"

"I know."

She moved on to another worry. "Shouldn't you get closer?"

"I'm not going to lose her, Delaney. Now sit back and relax."

"She's turning."

"I see her."

Avery forced herself to stop telling the agent in charge what to do. It would all be over in just a few minutes. If she could just stay calm that long, she could spend a month falling apart if that was her inclination. Stay cool, she told herself.

Jilly had almost missed the entrance to the Windjammer motel. Avery watched her slow her car, make the turn, and drive across the parking lot. She lost sight of her then as Kelly sped on. He pulled into the exit, circled around the motel, and parked next to the restaurant adjacent to the parking lot.

"She's parked in front of the steps," Kelly said.

Avery was looking up at the units. All the doors faced the street. Then she looked at Jilly. She wished they were closer so she could get a good look at her face.

"What's she doing?" she asked as she leaned forward.

"Brushing her hair," Kelly said.

Avery squinted against the sunlight. She saw Jilly pull down the vanity mirror.

"Is she putting lipstick on?"

"She sure is," Kelly said.

She sat back when the agent turned off the

motor and rolled the windows down. "You get out of this car, Delaney, and I swear —"

She didn't let him finish his threat. "I won't move."

Avery looked at Jilly again. She must have been satisfied with her appearance because she finally opened the car door and got out.

"Showtime," Kelly whispered.

Jilly ran up the first flight of stairs, raced along the outside corridor until she found the number she was looking for, and then stopped. Avery watched her spread the collar on her blouse so that cleavage would show. She smoothed her tight skirt, and then rapped on the door.

Avery's stomach lurched. She heard her voice calling out, "Darling, it's me, Jilly."

Tony Salvetti opened the door.

# CHAPTER 39

The trial in Sheldon Beach didn't drag on long. The attorney prosecuting the case was competent and effective, and with the evidence at hand, he was able to convince a second jury that Dale Skarrett had broken into Lola Delaney's home with the intent of kidnapping Avery Delaney. In the process of committing the felony, he had caused the premature death of Lola Delaney.

Skarrett insisted on testifying, which was a big mistake. He mumbled and squirmed, and by the time the prosecuting attorney got finished with him, the felon was screaming obscenities at him for twisting everything he said.

Skarrett insisted that he hadn't used Avery as a shield and that he was really only trying to assist the child to her feet when her grandmother fired the gun. He couldn't explain why he'd taken his belt off and beaten her nearly to death except to say that he was simply trying to coax her into going with him to see her mother.

The photos of Avery in the hospital proved

beyond a reasonable doubt that Skarrett had left her in that hallway to die. Within an hour, the jury rendered its verdict, and Skarrett was led back to prison, where he belonged.

John Paul stayed in Sheldon Beach with Avery through the entire trial, and Carrie flew in the day before Avery was scheduled to testify. The aunt had been to hell and back, and he expected to meet a shattered woman. She wasn't, though. If she was devastated by her husband's betrayal, she didn't let it show.

In between her calls to her staff in Bel Air, John Paul told Carrie he was going to marry Avery. She didn't want to hear that. If her niece was going to marry, she should find a man with potential . . . and money. What kind of life would she have married to a carpenter?

Oh, yes, Carrie was one tough cookie . . . and meaner than a crocodile when she didn't get her way.

He really liked her.

# CHAPTER 40

"Mr. Carter will see you now."

"Thank you." Avery straightened her skirt and smiled at the receptionist as she walked to the door.

"You want me to go in with you?" John Paul asked.

She shook her head. "You'll wait here?"

"For as long as it takes."

She opened the door and stepped into the freezer. She'd come prepared this morning and was wearing a long-sleeved jacket.

"Good morning, sir."

"Have a seat, Delaney."

He didn't look happy, but then, she'd never seen Carter smile before, so she wasn't certain if he was still angry with her or not.

She sat in the chair facing his desk, folded her hands in her lap, and said, "Sir, if you're going to fire me, I'd like the opportunity to preempt and resign first."

"Why?" he asked.

He'd stood when she entered the room but

now took his seat behind the massive desk.

"Resigning would look better on my résumé."

"No, I'm asking you why you think I'm going to fire you?"

"Because I didn't follow procedure," she said.

Her hands were trembling. She wasn't certain if it was due to the frigid air in the office or the fact that she was so nervous. He had the ability to turn her into an insecure twit simply by looking at her.

"I should have figured it all out much, much sooner, but in my defense, sir, I was busy jumping in and out of fivers and dodging bullets. I didn't have time to analyze the data, but I should have made the time," she hastily added so that he would know she was taking full responsibility for her mistakes. "I also used your name to force Agent Kelly to let me ride in the tail car, and you were very specific with your order that I should never do that again. I broke the chain of command. I didn't let the agents assigned to protect me do their job. Sir, I ran from them. I did. Oh, and I also bothered you during your monthly poker game when I called you that night from Walden Point, and everyone at the Bureau knows how sacred your poker games are to you."

She thought she noticed the corner of his mouth turn up just a little. Was he about to smile or sneer?

He leaned forward and stacked his hands on the desk. "Just so you know, I had a full house,

Delaney, but you used the priority code, so I had to fold. Why did you call me instead of going through channels?"

She might as well tell him the truth. She didn't have anything to lose. "I knew you'd listen to me and tell me if I was right or wrong. I also knew you'd help me, and we had to move fast. Because you gave the okay we could do that."

"Go on," he urged.

"While the agents were getting things set up in Florida, I called Aunt Carrie and told her that John Paul and I were staying at Milt's Motel in Walden Point and that she would be brought there to stay with us until Skarrett's trial. I knew she would call her husband, Tony, and tell him to come there. And, by the time she did that, agents were monitoring Tony's phone calls and e-mail."

"And if she hadn't called him?" Carter asked.

"Then I would have," she said. "But she did tell him, and just as I suspected, Tony contacted Jilly and gave her the news that Carrie and I would be together in Florida. Then he booked a flight there for himself."

She took a breath and continued. "By the time the agents pinpointed Jilly's location, she and Monk had vanished, but of course we knew where they were headed."

"Walden Point."

"Yes," she agreed. "I really hated using my aunt that way, blatantly lying to her, but it was the only thing I could do. After everything was in motion, thanks to the agent you put in charge, Tom Kelly, I called Carrie back and told her she'd be staying in Colorado for a while longer, and I told her why."

"How did she take the news about her husband?"

I broke her heart, Avery thought. "It was . . . difficult for her to accept. She's a strong woman," she added. "She'll survive."

"It was John Paul Renard who figured out how Monk would strike, wasn't it?"

"Yes. We moved to a houseboat while the trap was being set at the motel. The agents made it look like we were still there. It was John Paul who found the trip wire on the stairs leading to the tower, and he and Agent Clayborne got ready."

"Okay, I want to know. How did you put it together?"

"The Politicians, sir."

He raised an eyebrow. She nodded. "I was sitting on the beach . . . thinking about the situation, and that case came to mind. They had their own agenda, remember? They wanted everyone to think they were politically motivated, but it was really all about money. That got me thinking about agendas, I guess you could say. I realized I wasn't seeing the forest because of the trees. So I did the same thing I had done when I was working on the Politician case. I took it all apart and looked at each piece. Everyone had his own agenda," she added. "Monk and Jilly and Skarrett and Tony Salvetti." She couldn't bear to call the bastard her uncle now, not after what he had done. "They each wanted something desperately.

"It was what Jilly wanted that made everything fall into place. Carrie told me about the letter that Jilly had left for her. She said Jilly accused her of stealing her dream and giving it away. That kept nagging at me. I had read all of Carrie's diaries, and I knew what Jilly was capable of. I also knew how patient she was. She'd wait years to get even. I asked myself what she wanted most. Money? Revenge? Then it clicked. Jilly wanted to be a star. She craved adulation and attention. Carrie took her dream away from her. Carrie went to Hollywood and became successful and powerful. She made people stars. In Jilly's mind, Carrie had taken her dream. She blamed Carrie for all her failures. We found proof of her obsession when the agents confiscated her belongings."

Carter nodded. "Agent Kelly told me they found a tape in Jilly's purse. It was a copy of a commercial you starred in when you were a teenager."

"Yes," she said. "I think the commercial started it all. Jilly saw it on television, and I imagine became quite enraged. She began plotting and planning way back then. She knew who I was. Evidently Jilly felt Carrie had given her dream to me, and she was going to get even."

"She held on to that dream for over twenty years?" Carter asked.

"Oh, yes. She has a twisted, inflated opinion of herself," she said. "I asked myself, who did Jilly think could get her dream back? Who could make her a star?"

"Tony Salvetti."

"Yes," she said. "He was still co-owner of Star Catcher. I didn't want to believe Tony was involved with any of this. John Paul said that, on some level, I must have known all along because I never called to tell Tony where I was." She glanced down at her engagement ring and lovingly adjusted it on her finger.

"It was so easy for Jilly. When she met Tony, she found an angry, bitter man. Carrie and he had merged two companies. When they got married, they were supposed to run the business as equal partners, but Carrie started bringing in the accounts. She slowly squeezed Tony out of the operation until he didn't have any power at all. He told Agent Kelly that Carrie was trying to emasculate him. He knew he would lose everything when she divorced him, and that was inevitable because she was becoming more and more distrustful, especially after she discovered over a hundred thousand dollars was missing from their accounts. Tony told Carrie that the money was in the bank and that it was an accounting error, but she certainly would have had the company books audited.

"Jilly told Tony she had a connection that

would solve the problem for them both. She knew a man serving a sentence in a Florida prison who could help them get a hit man."

"Dale Skarrett?"

"Yes. She went to Skarrett and promised to help him get out of prison. If he would give her the name of a killer for hire, she would get rid of Carrie and me, and there would be no one to testify against him. She told him that Tony Salvetti was willing to put up the money to get rid of his wife. Jilly also promised Skarrett that she would be waiting for him when he got out. He was still obsessed with her. I'm sure she would have found a way to keep him believing she loved him long enough to get the stolen diamonds. She also promised him she would get rid of the judge who had sentenced him.

"And that brings us to Monk. When Jilly met him, she found a killer for hire, but she also found a lonely man. It took nothing for her to win him over. As it turns out, she didn't even have to offer him the money that Tony had given her. He fell madly in love and was willing to do anything she asked. So, nobody was the wiser. She could keep the money for herself."

"Who came up with the idea of putting all those women in the Colorado house?"

"Jilly," she answered. "She does like to complicate things. The drama appealed to her, and making Carrie suffer was an added bonus. Monk had already taken the contract to kill Anne Trapp, and he'd also taken money from

Dennis Parnell to blow up the mountain house. Parnell was convinced the judge would award the estate to his ex-wife," she explained. "And I can only imagine what he must have felt when he found out the judge had awarded the house to him."

"Monk was a busy boy."

"Oh, yes," she said.

"Did you see it on the news?" he asked. "Eric Trapp finally broke down and confessed. He's going to go away for a very long time. If your aunt hadn't given us that letter from Anne, we wouldn't have had the evidence we needed. Trapp told the interrogator his wife was taking too long to die."

"Just like the Politicians," Avery said, "greed motivated all of them."

"Amazing," he said then, "the way Jilly manipulated Salvetti and Monk and Skarrett. She was the piper and they were dancing to her tune, none of them knowing what she was up to. I talked to Agent Kelly a little while ago," he said. "Skarrett still isn't admitting much, but Salvetti's talking. The odd thing is . . ."

"Yes?"

"Neither one of them will say a bad word about Jilly. They're still singing her praises."

That didn't surprise her. "I'll bet she's not talking, though."

"No, she's still stonewalling. You're going to make a great field agent, Delaney."

"Perhaps, with the proper training, I could be

good, but sir, I don't want to, not anymore. If I've learned anything during the past weeks, it's that life is too short, and I don't want to waste another minute going after men and women who are beyond hope. I want to make a difference before it's too late."

She stood and waited until he walked around the desk. She shook his hand. "Thank you, sir."

"You're really going to resign? I can't talk you into staying?"

"I've made up my mind, sir. I need to leave."

"Have you decided what you're going to do?"

"Now that the trial and the parole hearing are over and Skarrett is back where he belongs, I'm going to spend a couple of weeks with my aunt, and then I'm moving to Louisiana and going back to school to get my teacher's certificate."

"I'm going to miss you," he said. "Good luck."

"Thank you, sir."

He opened the door for her, and as she walked past, he said, "One more thing, Delaney."

"Yes?"

"Good work."

# CHAPTER 41

The detective led Avery and John Paul down a long hallway to what he called their screening room.

"You'll be able to see her through the glass, but she won't be able to see you," he explained before he opened the door and stepped back.

Avery didn't move.

"She's in the interrogation room now with two detectives," he explained.

And still she didn't budge.

The detective glanced at John Paul. "I'll just let you take your time," he said before he turned and walked away.

"You don't have to do this," John Paul said.

"Yes, I do."

She stood on the threshold another long minute, and then she straightened her shoulders and walked in. The room was the size of a closet. She turned to the mirrored window, her hands fisted at her sides, and looked at the woman who had given her life and then had so desperately tried to take it away.

John Paul slipped his hand in hers and asked, "Do you remember her?"

"No. I was only five when she came to the house," she whispered. "So long ago."

Jilly sat on one side of the square metal table facing two detectives. Her back was straight, one leg crossed over the other, her hands folded on the table. The top three buttons of her eyelet blouse were undone, and the neckline opened a little wider each time she moved ever so slightly. She suddenly turned and looked directly at the mirror. Avery inhaled sharply and drew back as she felt the bile rising in her throat.

"Look," Avery whispered.

"I see her," John Paul said.

Avery shook her head. "Not her. Look at the detectives. Look how they're reacting to her."

Both detectives were leaning forward, as though they were unconsciously trying to get closer to her. One said something and then reached out and touched her hand.

"She's working them," Avery said.

A policeman opened the door to the interrogation room. Jilly looked up at him, then, like a languorous Persian cat, she stretched her lithe body and stood. As she followed him out the door, she paused to glance back over her shoulder and smile at the two men. Both detectives eagerly returned the smile. They watched her every movement until the door closed behind her.

Avery looked into John Paul's eyes. "I'm ready to move on now."

She led the way out of the police station. She didn't look back.

# EPILOGUE

Sunset was Avery's favorite time of day. She'd go outside and sit on the porch swing John Paul had built for her. She could hear the water lapping against the dock behind the house, and if she closed her eyes, she could almost smell the lilacs John Paul had planted.

The screen door opened and closed, and her husband sat down next to her. He put his arm around her, leaned back, and gave the swing a push.

"You ready for school tomorrow, sugar?"

"Yes."

"What were you thinking about?" he asked. "Were you going to your happy place?"

She put her head on his shoulder and smiled. "I'm already there."

# ABOUT THE AUTHOR

Julie Garwood is the author of seventeen *New York Times* bestsellers, including *Mercy, Heartbreaker, Ransom,* and *Come the Spring.* There are more than thirty million copies of her books in print.

The employees of Thorndike Press hope you have enjoyed this Large Print book. All our Thorndike and Wheeler Large Print titles are designed for easy reading, and all our books are made to last. Other Thorndike Press Large Print books are available at your library, through selected bookstores, or directly from us.

For information about titles, please call:

(800) 223-1244

or visit our Web site at:

www.gale.com/thorndike
www.gale.com/wheeler

To share your comments, please write:

Publisher
Thorndike Press
295 Kennedy Memorial Drive
Waterville, ME   04901